KEEP RIGHT O[N]

BY

STEPHEN BURROWS & MICHAEL LAYTON

DEDICATIONS

Stephen Burrows

To my wife Sue, for putting up with it all again, and to the 99.9% of Police Officers who are nothing like Rob Docker and put themselves at risk every day.

Michael Layton

To Andry for her continuing support, and to my mother Gladys, born and bred in Birmingham.

First Published: March 2017, by Bostin Books

Other books by Michael Layton and Stephen Burrows

Joint:Fiction:

Black Over Bill's Mother's

Non-Fiction:

The Noble Cause.

Walsall's Front Line. (Spring 2017)

By Michael LaytonNon-Fiction:

Hunting the Hooligans

Tracking the Hooligans

Police Dog HeroesBirmingham's Front Line

Violence in the Sun

The Hooligans Are Still Among Us

Authors' Note

Keep Right On is a complete story in its own right. It is however, the sequel to, and set within the timeline of, 'Black Over Bill's Mother's'. A number of characters appear in both books, and for those reading 'Keep Right On' first, previous events relating to joint characters are only alluded to, so as not to spoil the enjoyment of 'Black Over Bill's Mother's' by revealing the plot.

'Keep Right On' contains a large amount of genuine historical events, including football match reports, incidents of football hooliganism and the rise of the right-wing and overt racism in 1975 and 1976. A number of real persons are mentioned and every effort has been made to relate events and their part in them impartially and with accuracy. All of the plot characters are fictional.

CHAPTER LIST

Chapter One

'No-one likes us, we don't care'

1975

He stared out of his office window at the busy world below him, lost in thought. It was stifling, *'flaming bloody June',* he thought. He felt imprisoned in his office. If there was any justice in the world he should be in a proper cell, but Rob Docker was supposed to be a weapon of justice and he knew for a fact that there was no such thing. Good people died, the bad ones prospered. Over twenty years in the job and he had seen no evidence of God or justice, in fact quite the contrary.

If a deity or a set of divine scales existed, he would surely be on the wrong side, that of the guilty, but here he was, Detective Inspector Robert Docker, Special Branch, still alive, and with a proven track record of results, although colleagues knew better than to enquire too deeply as to his methods.

Docker had lied, cheated, bent and broken the rules, and none of that troubled him. It had been necessary and to some extent expected in the world of the CID in the Sixties and Seventies, but he was a troubled man now, and all that paled into insignificance. Much darker thoughts constantly crept to the fore from the inner recesses of his mind, and he fought constantly to keep self-control.

He could not stop the memories coming back, especially in the night, as he lay awake listening to Lilian's breathing and hoping it would one day stop and free him from the hell of living with her. There was no comfort there, he knew, and never would be. They kept up appearances, shackled together in wedded misery. They had an unwritten contract, forged in loss and mutual hatred.

During the last few weeks the memories had started to intrude more and more into his waking hours. He had expected the pain to fade with time, but it was getting worse, and he sometimes caught the staff, and even more concerning, the boss, looking at him, the unasked question in their eyes.

They weren't actually bothered about his welfare, he had no illusions about that, but a few were bonded to him in the shadows by past transgressions against morals and law, and the rest knew what he was capable of. No, they weren't worried about *his* health; it was their own that prompted that look. *'Could he be relied on? Was he cracking up? Would he break ranks if he did?* ' He didn't know the answer himself, but he was the ultimate survivor, and knew he needed to sort himself out and soon.

'Perhaps there is a sort of justice?' he reflected. This office *was* a cell. His current role was focused on the IRA and their bombing campaigns, and that daily contact with terrorism would never let him forget what he had done just a few weeks ago, how far he had crossed the line between good and evil.

'That bastard biker would laugh, wouldn't he? If he could see into my mind he would crack some joke about me having the blackest soul of all of them, and he would be right.'

Docker came to a decision and stood up. It was time for a

move.

***

It took three weeks to engineer the transfer he wanted. It had been relatively easy, as the boss not only owed him a couple of favours, but also knew that Rob had 'the black' on him. In reality the detective superintendent was only too pleased to get shot of him.

So here he was, back on his old turf – back home. He stood opposite the familiar building. It glowed in the morning sun, the terracotta burnished red, mimicking the heat.

'The Lane' – ' *time to get stuck into some real criminals again.'* He allowed himself a smile as he walked up the white-stoned steps and heard the familiar drone of activity inside. It was a comforting sound that reassured him that he had made the right decision.

It was July 1975. Rob Docker walked with a determined gait as he strode towards the CID office on the ground floor - the returning detective inspector entered the Victorian edifice of Steelhouse Lane, the hub of policing in Birmingham City Centre.

***

A month later, and his feet were well and truly under the table. He had resurrected some old relationships, both inside and outside the nick, re-established some 'business' arrangements and had a good look at his new crew. The bad dreams still came, but they were confined to the night. The daily reminders of Irish plots and bombings were gone - along with his old job, and could kindle no daytime memories.

He had left the 'A' Division – 'The Lane', two years previously. Docker had only been promoted to detective inspector for a few months before he had been whisked off to Special Branch on a secondment, following two years as a detective sergeant. Special Branch had wanted him because he had contacts, and that made him useful at a time when the IRA was bombing the crap out of England.

At the time it had seemed like a good move, but in the end it had all gone to rat-shit. In hindsight he wished he had stayed at Steelhouse Lane and cemented his place there. The DI had real power and the officers knew it - he could make or break them. Rob had a boss himself of course, the Detective Chief Inspector, but he was remote, more interested in climbing the greasy pole of promotion than getting his hands dirty. He was happy to leave Rob to get on with it.

They had worked together previously and had an understanding. Rob got results and the DCI didn't bother too much how they were obtained, as long as he could bask in the glory and rely on Rob to cover both their backs.

Rob's gaze scanned the CID office through the half-glass partition wall - nineteen men and a token 'split-arse'. One female officer per CID office and no more – that was the rule. It was 'dead women's' shoes for any female aspiring detectives, unless of course you found a sponsor, and that often meant sleeping with someone with power.

It was ten o clock in the morning and they were all still in the office, case papers scattered across various desks. A haze of smoke from numerous burning cigarettes hung in the air across the room, the stink of stale tobacco mixed with the exhaled remnants of alcohol from the night before.

The young 'attached-man' had returned from the canteen in the bowels of The Lane, his daily errand done, and most were stuffing their faces with bacon sandwiches that many could have done without, judging by their waistlines. Docker stared with disgust at one of the office fixtures, *'I swear that fat wanker Malcolm Reid is getting bigger by the day,'* he mused.

A number had their feet on desks, and there was a lot more banter than work going on. They must have known he could see them and clearly weren't bothered. There were a few who had potential - that wide-boy Cockney, Detective Sergeant Francis, for example. Rob could sniff out a like mind at a hundred yards, but it was time for a general kick up the arse and he had a lot of pent up anger to vent.

He walked to the door of the office. His Brummie accent always came to the fore as he was about to explode. Other ambitious colleagues had been to elocution lessons to soften the nasal tones but Docker was proud of his birthplace and felt no need to dress up his thoughts with fine words. He launched into a veritable tirade,

"Shut the fuck up and pin your ears back you lazy bastards." His voice silenced them and twenty faces turned towards him. He noted with some satisfaction that a few feet were moved from desks to the floor. A couple even made an effort at sitting up straight and subconsciously a number of ties were straightened. They waited.

"I don't know if those of you what know me think I've gone soft on Special Branch, and those of you that don't have assumed likewise. Time to put the record straight. Things are gonna change round here from today. I've had a few weeks to look at you, and your work, and frankly it's piss poor. The fucking about stops now. I want prisoners, I want snouts, I want the criminal scum out there to know who's boss, and that's me and this CID office, which is you lot, God help me."

A couple of them actually visibly gulped and the split looked like she was about to cry. *'Fucking hell I've got me work cut out here',* he thought.

"No-one goes out of here today before seeing me. You four are first", he indicated Reid and the other detective sergeants, "I don't give a fuck what order the rest of you come in, but I want all of you in here with all the work you've got on in your donnies for inspection. We're gonna have a bit of a career chat today, and anyone who doesn't wanna start working can fuck off right now and get a woolly jumper and big hat on." He waited a moment and let the oppression of silence build.

"And if any of you think I'm bullshitting, I suggest you have a chat with DS Reid about what happened to Alan. In fact Malcolm, you can get your arse in here first".

***

The leaves had begun to turn early, as autumn took hold after a hot summer. His team were on notice, treading very softly around him, and Rob was confident that he would be firmly in command in his old domain by Christmas. That was the only present he wanted. He hated Christmas. He hated all the tinsel and false bonhomie. It was all bollocks, and by January everybody would be back to stabbing each other in the back, hitting the wife, shagging the neighbours and stealing everything that wasn't bolted down. They were all just a lot poorer and in debt up to their eyeballs after buying a load of crap that nobody wanted or needed.

However, Christmas was a distant thought; it was late September and Rob was in the office as usual. It was a Sunday, but that meant nothing to a man who did everything to avoid being at home with his wife. Work was always a good excuse to get away. Besides, it kept the troops on their toes, no fucking about when the inspector might drop in unannounced at any time.

There was also the added bonus that none of the other senior officers would show their faces until Monday morning, at which time they would hold the ritual 'nine o clock post-mortem' into the weekend's events, all of which of course would be with the benefit of hindsight. Even better, most of the wankers, with the exception of the DCI who knew better, left their offices unlocked and Rob regularly scanned their paperwork on a Sunday for information that would prove of use.

Being in the office didn't mean he had to actually work of course, and Rob settled down in his office chair, mug of tea on the desk, a bacon sandwich in hand and picked up the *'Birmingham Sunday Observer'*, dated 21 September 1975, for his usual canter through the week's news and sport.

The first story that caught his eye awoke painful memories and did nothing for his humour. There was an announcement from Mitchells and Butler's brewery that the two pubs devastated in the November 1974 bombings were to be renamed.

'The Tavern in the Town' would become 'Teddies', *'stupid name for a place of death and carnage,'* he thought, and the 'Mulberry Bush' would henceforth be known as 'The Roundabout'. The sandwich stayed where it was – he had suddenly lost his appetite.

Rob shook himself back to reality and realised that he had been lost in reverie for several minutes and his tea was going cold. He could never forget that night. It had set in motion events that had changed his life for ever, and condemned him to Hell – if there was one, which he very much doubted, but he lived in a personal Hades in his mind for what he had done.

Another headline caught his eye,

'13 arrests in another black episode for football. Shrewsbury Town's ground was the scene of yet more football hooliganism yesterday. It took place as Town lost 4-2 to Crystal Palace. There were 13 arrests and a dozen ejections. Police officers were spat on as they tried to contain the trouble by moving onto the terraces to root out the troublemakers.

One supporter said, 'There were pitched battles on the terraces'. Police bought in dogs to keep the two sides apart and were assaulted and spat on by fans behind the Shrewsbury goal. A Crystal Palace supporter ran onto the pitch in his pants and shirt

*whilst a home fan 'streaked' across the pitch, sporting only his shoes
and a football scarf. Three of the arrested were from London, the
rest local. Police said they had all been charged and would be
appearing in court tomorrow for assaulting police, breach of the
peace and carrying offensive weapons. At Coventry v Stoke there
were 8 arrests, 5 at WBA v Charlton and one at Birmingham City v
Burnley'.*

'These bastard supporters are becoming a real problem', he
thought. He suspected that the Shrewsbury trouble may have had
something to do with Birmingham-based hooligans, but as yet he
hadn't had time to look deeper into what was going on. It was a
growing irritation though, and one that he was already getting some
heat from above about.

Neanderthal football fans running amok in the city-centre
were a very public issue, and the high-ups didn't like having to
answer difficult questions from the media, or more importantly a
very active Birmingham Retailers Association who wanted to see
some positive policing for the rates they paid. It was headed up by a
retired police officer who knew the score, and wasn't prepared to
listen to any bullshit promises that meant nothing.

Rob put the problem aside for the moment; he had too many
other things to sort out inside the nick, and his head, at the moment.

Deciding a little light relief was in order, he picked up the
phone and ordered two tickets to see 'The Foundations' at The Dolce
Vita the next day. He would take that new policewoman who had
been seconded into the Children and Families Unit. He had done the
preliminaries and thought he stood a good chance of a quick leg-over

if he pushed the boat out a bit.

Putting off a burgeoning issue was an uncharacteristic lapse of attention to detail for Rob, who usually wanted to be ahead of the game, and the following week football hooliganism slapped him hard in the face.

***

He was preoccupied the following Saturday with of all things, the weather.

Birmingham was lashed by storms accompanied by seventy mph winds, bringing down seventy trees and numerous power lines, cutting power to ten thousand homes, including his shiny new one in Solihull. Not only had Lilian been moaning at him all day about it – it had taken all night to get the power back on, and he had fled into work yet again on the Sunday morning to escape the misery.

Deja-vu, here he was again with the same newspaper.

He did follow the football a bit, and as a young kid his Uncle Charlie used to take him and Joe to the Villa, but when they were older they had switched their allegiances to the Blues, it was easier to get to on the bus, and they had both felt more at home there. The 'Bluenoses' had seemed less stuck up than the Villa lot.

The memory of his childhood with Joe lingered and then Rob deliberately pushed it away.

Docker started at the sports pages with the match report,

'The battle of Brum: it was the first meeting for a decade in

the League, and the fans of newly promoted Aston Villa had a joyous end to their long wait. Today they are the Kings of Brum once again whilst City were left with the 'blues' after a 2-1 defeat at Villa Park.

The Blues of St Andrews started best, Trevor Francis scored after only 12 minutes and their fans were singing in the rainstorms. A Kenny Burns free kick, a header by Peter Withe and a shot from Bob Hatton saw new £100,000 keeper John Burridge make a brave and brilliant save. But though he stopped it he couldn't hold the ball and there was Francis lurking and ready to slide the ball over the line.

Chico Hamilton stemmed the Blues' songs with a 51st minute equalizer. John Robson crossed from the right. For a split second Hamilton was unmarked and his right footed half-volley smashed past Dave Latchford into the roof of the net. 19 minutes later the claret and blues were in heaven. The 70th minute decider by Brian Little was a delight of individual opportunism when Burns uncharacteristically let the ball roll away from him as he tried to trap it. That was enough for the sharp and alert England contender Little, who swept it away from the defender, almost taunted the Blues- occupied Witton End, and rolled the ball into the corner of the net with incredible calm.

For a week Birmingham has been divided. Blues were without a manager since the sacking of Freddie Goodwin, but caretaker boss Willie Bell had lifted their fan's hopes of escaping the drop as his side hit seven goals in two games with wins over Burnley and Newcastle. Villa, after a bad run, got a mid-week boost with the signing of £100,000 goalkeeper John Burridge and then a match day lift with the announcement that key defender Chris Nicholl was fit to *play after all.*

They also signed £110,000 striker Andy Gray only hours before the kick off, and it will be interesting to see if he is as good South of the border as he was in Scotland. He could not play, but Villa did not need him, thoroughly deserving their victory in the first Division One clash between the two sides since April 1965. As for Blues-they can always look forward to April 3 next year, and the return fixture at St Andrews. Until then, Brum belongs to Villa'.

The crowds at the match may have kept just to singing, but later on, in the city, on Rob's patch, all hell had been let loose. Two pubs smashed up, three kids in hospital and a running battle along New Street. The Observer had an editorial backed up by a lurid article with photographs of drunk and bleeding youths in front of smashed shop windows.

Rob knew that a Monday morning bollocking all-round was going to be dished out by the powers that be and he didn't like the feeling. He had wasted a week when he could have got into these bastards, perhaps found a snout, but for once he was playing catch-up. Time to pay football and its so-called fans some attention; it was becoming a pain in the backside.

He turned to the front page and another episode of violence caught his eye, reinforcing the decision,

'100 hurt as fans halt match: West Ham's game with Manchester United was stopped for 19 minutes yesterday by fighting fans. 400 spectators spilled onto the Upton Park pitch as fighting broke out on the terraces. Screaming was heard, as a number of

spectators were crushed by fans surging-due to the fighting. There were 38 arrests and 132 ejections. 102 fans were injured and 9 needed hospital treatment.

It started in the second half, and the referee firstly stopped play for seven minutes, then led the players from the pitch. 200 police were deployed trying to stop the fighting and cleared the pitch after 18 minutes. Police later blamed West Ham fans for the trouble, not the visiting supporters.'

***

Early October 1975, and with liberal use of the 'carrot and stick', Docker had the office in the palm of his hand. Two detectives had left after clearly displaying loyalty elsewhere. Rob knew a grass when he saw one and he wanted no 'gaffer's narks' on his team.

He had head-hunted a couple of suitable replacements from uniform, older and experienced faces from the past who knew the patch and all the villains in it. They both had the added appeal of a history of bending the rules, sometimes beyond breaking point, and as a bonus they knew that Rob knew their secrets. There would be plenty of opportunity for 'scratchy back time' over the next couple of years.

He had kept the female, Sally, and to his surprise he had liked her. Not fancied her, she was a bit stocky for his tastes, but he had recognised that she had ability, an inner-strength and a 'pragmatic' outlook on life that got results. He liked the way she stood up to the banter and gave as good as she got, better in fact.

Rob could see that the lads liked her, and it was always good these days to be seen to support a spot of 'women's lib' - the bosses liked it. Anyway she had a bostin pair of 'top bollocks' that were a lot better to look at in the office than Reid's fat arse.

Rob had also researched the past of the Londoner, Francis. His original instinct had been correct, the bloke was classic 'Met' CID, bent as fuck, and had clearly engineered a transfer to Birmingham to escape one, or all, of three problems; anti-corruption department on his back, bent gaffers owed favours and increasing their demands, or a 'fall out' with some nasty villains who were too close for comfort. Whichever it was, the man was receptive to Rob's not so subtle overtures and had quickly thrown his lot in with his new boss.

Rob had ensured that Francis had been involved in a couple of 'fit-ups' as a test and the man had passed with flying colours. In fact he had shown a level of flair and assurance in bending the rules that could only have come from years of experience in London. Rob had him now though, Francis had already done enough to get the sack, maybe worse, and had accepted a few 'sweeteners' to cement his loyalty. Rob was so sure of him that he had put that cocky and ambitious cunt, Detective Constable John Burrell, on Francis' team.

That one was incorruptible. Rob had tested him and knew the signs, but Burrell was clever, clever enough to know the game being played and how to use it. He was also very handy with his fists having boxed as a teenager. He wouldn't rock the boat and was damn good for a five-year service man. He was clearly going places and Rob knew the value of investing in men of the future.

Francis would keep an eye on him though, and ensure that

Rob knew everything he did, said or thought. Rob kept a few 'personal' files in his locked informant's cabinet that were nothing to do with snouts, and Burrell already had several pages of notes in one of them.

The rest of the office had quickly toed the line after he had sorted the sergeants out, shown his bite was worse than his bark, and celebrated some good results with decent piss-ups in the bar in the basement at Steelhouse Lane.

They were becoming a team of sorts.

***

Things hadn't gone so well outside the nick though. There had been changes in the criminal status quo and the new order were causing problems that Rob was still trying to get his claws into. Of course, that didn't necessarily mean locking everyone up, after all a bit of crime made the world go round, and guaranteed both police employment and opportunities for advancement and earnings.

But his attempts to get into the football problem had been roundly repulsed. Two failures had really pissed him off, and one had made him feel at personal risk - and a pissed off and vulnerable Rob Docker was a dangerous enemy to have.

His 'business model' required that criminal scumbags showed him respect, took his advice and rewarded that counsel with a few 'favours'. That was the way it worked, and the reception he had received from some of the football scum was a threat to the established order-Rob Docker's order.

He had started with some research. He knew the Collator, compiler of information on criminals, really well. Bill Donovan kept an immaculate set of records on index cards and they were always bang up to date.

A couple of hours with Bill had swiftly revealed what Rob had missed during his absence from The Lane, although one aspect had been under his nose in Special Branch. He had been too preoccupied with the Irish to notice.

Far-right politics had mushroomed in Britain during the first half of the Seventies, and was particularly infectious in the big cities, where the largest immigrant populations had put down roots. The Midlands was a hot bed of activity: after all, local MP Enoch Powell's, *'Rivers of Blood'* speech had been the spark, and that speech had been delivered in Birmingham in 1968.

The National Front, The British Movement, Combat 18, (the one and eight representing the letters A and H for Adolf Hitler), had gained many adherents during the early and mid-seventies, particularly amongst the young and violent - and in football hooligans they had discovered a wellspring of recruits.

That was the other change he had missed of course. There had always been trouble at matches, football appealed to the worst tribal instincts in man, but it had developed, particularly in the previous couple of years, and his time in the intelligence office had revealed that a couple of local families had exploited the opportunities that a hooligan army presented, for criminal, violent and political purposes.

Of course, the Villa and Blues fans had always hated each other when football was the topic of conversation or being played. It was strange really, Brummies' could be school-friends, related, drinking buddies; but it made little difference once the blue and white and claret and blue were worn, they became different tribes, and blood could be shed at the drop of a hat. It was bad enough amongst the 'normal' fans, but the hooligan 'firms' were on a different level altogether.

Rivalry and reputation, establishing supremacy, occupying opposition territory on the streets, or at the football grounds, in pubs or localities, these were the gang's goals. A mutual interest in violence had resulted in the football becoming secondary to the fighting, which often took place by arrangement.

Disturbingly, the only time they came together peacefully was under a truce between the right-wing elements of both groups, who would combine without colours in pursuit of trouble under the National Front banner. On those days they were in the same tribe.

It seemed that from this mixture of rivalry and aggression had grown hatred between two local families, the heads of which led the respective football 'firms'.

Michael Carter had been at the helm of the Blues hooligans for as long as anyone could remember, and his arch-rival, Colin Murphy, had wrestled control of the Villa group into his own hands with extreme brutality some four years previously. It was common knowledge that he had put the previous 'main man' in hospital after a one-on-one showdown one night outside the boozer. The man had not showed his face again and no complaint had ever been made to the coppers. No report – no police action. Job done.

No-one really knew why Carter and Murphy despised each other so much, rumour had it that it was something to do with a row over a bird, but hatred had festered, grown and infected the loyal firm members.

Whether it was one incident, the football rivalry, or a clash of criminal interest, there was no doubt that there was bad blood and individual feuding between the rival groups, enough to warrant serious injuries, whenever and wherever they encountered each other. The boundaries around those levels of violence were becoming ever narrower as time went on, and there seemed to be an inevitability that at some stage someone would be paying the ultimate price.

Before he left Steelhouse Lane for Special Branch, Rob had known of Murphy, but never met him. He had history with Carter, and had expected to secure some sort of working arrangement easily. What was clear was that their influence had grown alongside the hooliganism, and they now exercised an impressive level of control in their respective criminal arenas, using football violence as a cover and a pool of 'manpower'.

They were not of the calibre of the 'businessmen' who quietly ran things in Birmingham, but they were affiliated to them, and tolerated because they were useful. Rob knew that there was no point in appealing above their heads to the 'puppet masters'. He had nothing to bargain with. Besides which, such supplication would undermine Rob's reputation, and reputation was a foundation stone of Rob's methods.

Those older, long-standing, organised crime groups were no problem to Rob. They were almost an institution. They played by certain 'rules' and that included keeping certain law enforcement contacts 'sweet'. Rob was one of the favoured few, but he was a cop and his credit had a limit of usefulness, once that was reached Rob was on his own - like now.

Murphy and Carter were big fish in a little pool, but it was Rob Docker's pool now, and he was used to being the biggest shark swimming in it. Things would have to change – and change dramatically.

Murphy's main interest was cars - selling them, stealing them, 'ringing' them. He also had a sideline in providing muscle for hire. He had two second-hand car pitches, in Summer Row and Hockley, both on Rob's patch, and a 'breakers yard' in Nechells.

Rob knew a profitable enterprise when he saw one, and was keen to either grab a piece of the action, or nip it in the bud before it became too much of a problem. It was obvious that Murphy's 'hooligans', were fully engaged in screwing as many cars parked in town as they could, especially on the huge Masshouse Car Park, and it was playing havoc with his crime figures, a third of which related to vehicle crime.

On top of that was the football violence, which was getting loads of newspaper coverage and making the gaffers unhappy. If the bosses got shit from the papers and local politicians, they were experts at ensuring it rolled down the pecking order and made sure that it stuck to those below them.

***

Rob had decided that a visit to Murphy in his portakabin office at *'Second City Car Sales'* was in order. He had known it was a waste of time almost from the moment he had arrived.

Rob had told a half-caste goon on the sales forecourt to get Murphy, but had been left cooling his heels for ten minutes, which hadn't done anything for his temper. Rob had eventually been ushered inside the portakabin and been made to stand like a naughty schoolboy whilst the goon and another twat had stood behind him making 'oink, oink' noises and sniggering. Mel Price and Benny Doherty were enjoying the moment. Murphy was a class act and they were happy to follow in his footsteps.

Murphy was sat behind a desk. He was a short-arse, but built like a bull, and Rob knew he could handle himself, his unopposed position as leader of the Villa hooligans was proof of that. He had peered up at Rob, and his opening comment had indicated the direction of travel of the conversation to come,

"Fuck off filth. Got nothing to say to you."

Rob had been taken aback by the vitriol in the man's voice before he had even opened his own mouth. He had been angered at the lack of respect shown and had made a mistake, trying the hard man approach, "We need to talk about your business, this is my patch and you're causing me a fucking problem. Let's have a natter man-to- man and sort out a way of working."

Rob indicated the two men behind him, "Tell these sniggering twats to sling their hooks and we can have an honest chat."

Murphy hadn't replied for a moment, but then had leapt to his feet and blown a fuse, the hint of an Irish accent surfacing,

"Don't you come onto my turf telling me what to do! Fucking honest chat my arse! I've heard of you Mr Detective Inspector Docker, I reckon you're dodgier than that five year old Mini with 10,000 miles on the pissing clock that's parked outside. So I'll tell you what's going to happen, you're going to leave, and if you don't my lads here will throw you out. And don't think you can threaten me with the law either. My business is legit, but yours isn't, and if you start giving me trouble I've got a couple of mates in the right place to dish the dirt on you and put you away for a good stretch, and I don't think that would be very nice for you. So back off and fuck off."

Murphy had sat down again and started counting to ten. Rob had been taken by surprise and his usual survival instinct kicked in - regroup and plan. No point fighting battles on the enemy's ground and terms. He had left in a hurry, his mind a whirl of thoughts. *'What does that bastard know? He's Irish, has he got connections? I need to think this through.'* The comment had struck to his core, because Rob Docker did indeed have a very big secret that could put him away for life.

***

That was the first knock-back. The second hadn't been quite as bad, but was still a dent to Rob's ego and reputation. He had only visited the intelligence office to fill in the gaps regarding Mike Carter, he knew the man well and they went back a long way, but the relationship had soured. Carter had moved up the pecking order and now controlled a good percentage of the door-staff in the city-centre, with the drugs connections that went with it.

Rob had the nasty idea that Mike Carter thought that he didn't need Docker any more, and Rob was struggling to find a reason to change that point of view.

Going off to Special Branch hadn't helped and he had found himself frozen out of Carter's world upon his return. The man just refused to return calls or meet.

Carter was based in a massive council house on a rough estate in Acocks Green. The house, with reinforced doors and windows, was on the turning circle of a cul de sac, protected by local supporters and a lot of frightened neighbours who permanently looked the other way.

Rob had been spotted and turned away before he had even reached the driveway of the house – it was made clear that no-one was at home. He had felt like a right wanker.

***

Rob was sat in his office gazing through the window. Carter was on his mind, *'the bastard's out of control and I need to get some sort of handle on him or break him.'*

Rob reached a conclusion, nodded to himself, and picked up the phone.

***

Mike Carter ran a tight ship. He picked and moulded likely lads from the terraces, tested them out in battle, and gave them a bit of training at a local boxing club he was involved in. Once they were up to scratch he supplied them as bouncers around Birmingham, particularly at the 'Blues pubs' in town and in Small Heath, Sparkhill, and the other suburbs that Birmingham City and Carter drew allegiance from.

Sam Wild, one of three trusted lieutenants, fronted the door business, keeping Mike's hands clean.

Carter had fought his way up from poverty in the back-to-backs of Hockley, and he was streetwise. He had sorted out 'territory' with the 'coloured's' from Handsworth who did doors, although that was as far as the co-operation went. He would have been pushing his grip on the firm if he had put white and black together, especially as his top 'football lieutenant' and nephew, Tony Carter, was an unbridled blade wielding 'nutter' with psychopathic tendencies and a strong allegiance to the National Front.

Mike Carter disapproved of street politics because it didn't pay, and he hated the Irish – and particularly the Murphy's, more than the coloured's, especially since the bombings in 74, but he put up with Tony's regular excursions to demonstrations and political meetings as long as they didn't disrupt business. There were some bonuses. For instance, it opened up a market for some of the weed and resin he pushed via the doors. It always amused Mike that the racist NF crews loved 'ganga' as much as the Rasta's did. Tony Carter was building a bad reputation; people were shit-scared of him because they knew he lost control when angry and always carried a flick-knife.

The drugs were another reason to keep his boys away from the spooks, he had a nice supply line going from the bikers and 'The Turk', and there was no love lost between them and the Handsworth lot.

Everyone knew there had been a big face-off a few years before, between the Handsworth lot and the Angels, but an uneasy truce now held.

He also knew that some of the bikers went on the NF marches, sporting their Swastikas and SS 'Death's Head' badges. Yet another reason for indulging Tony and any others who favoured a spot of right-wing orientated 'bovver'. It helped cement links with the bikers, and Mike knew that they were the meanest bunch of bastards around and he wanted them on his side.

He had heard that their main-man was Irish, but also that the man kept his distance from the Paddys locally. Mike wanted to keep it that way if he could; in particular he wanted to keep the biker leader away from Murphy by bonding his own lads with the Angels.

Carter's other line of business was acquiring handling stolen goods. He had grown a good network of distributors in the murky depths of the football fan swamp.

The likely lads on the terraces loved designer clothes at bargain prices, they were the uniform of the hooligans, and in Greg, 'Roly', Lyall, his third, and by far fattest, lieutenant, he had found a veritable superstar of shoplifting.

Lyall knew every technique for stealing in bulk, and to order, and had plenty of willing volunteers, particularly from the 'up and comers', eager to prove themselves. In return they would be rewarded with kudos and the clothes that they could never afford.

It was a good business model. The terraces supplied the raw material, the tribalism and violence bonded them, and the door and shoplifting enterprises employed them. The numbers, the reputation, the aggro, provided protection and respect and also focused attention on the hooliganism, rather than the lucrative criminality lurking below the surface.

Mike still loved the football most though, and the thrill of leading an ambush, winning a battle, putting the boot in. It was where he had started. It defined him, the unheralded 'King of the Bluenoses'.

***

For Rob Docker a frustrating week seemed to crawl past, the only bonus it brought was that he had got shot of another piece of deadwood. The old detective had been on the 'wind down' for about three years, the fact that he hadn't given a toss exemplified by the calendar counting down to 'freedom day', prominently displayed on his desk.

He had made it clear that he wouldn't cause Rob a problem and they had ignored each other until he retired with good grace, allowing Rob the enjoyment of extolling his virtues over the previous thirty years at his leaving do, followed by the much more enjoyable experience of free drinks for Rob, and plenty of 'arsehole licking' from his subordinates.

Docker had some plans in mind now, and as always they were risky and at the margins of the rules, but that was the way he liked to roll the dice. So far his luck had held – as far as the job was concerned at least.

During his 'vacation' in Special Branch, he had maintained his close contacts with the Regional Crime Squad and still regularly turned jobs over to them. He wanted to keep all of his options open, and a spell on the RCS might be welcome in the future.

Today, as he briefed the RCS team in his office on the details of the latest job, he felt mildly excited about the prospect of another good result.

***

Pete Stevens was twenty-four years old, and if he were to have a nickname, at this moment in time it would be 'Billy-no-Mates'. A bit of a 'ladies' man', the gold ear stud and blonde highlights in his hair added to his smooth appearance, but at 5'10" tall, with a rugby prop-forward build, he was also someone who could handle himself. The self-administered 'BCFC' tattoo on his right forearm gave his chosen team away.

As he stood sipping from a bottle of beer at the bar in the pub in Edgbaston Street, he reflected on his current circumstances. The bored barman had already heard the story of how Pete had made the decision to leave his job in Weston-Super-Mare to return to his city of birth, Birmingham, and that he was trying to get a job at British Leyland, Longbridge, the 'Eldorado' of the lazy.

Everyone knew that the pay was good there, and the workers spent half their time on strike or sleeping on the nightshift, safe from any sanction because the bosses were frightened of that convener, 'Red Robbo'.

Pete moaned to anyone within earshot in the bar that he felt he was a stranger in his own place of birth and didn't like it - or the fact that he had a UB40 unemployment card in his pocket, instead of a fat assembly line pay packet.

He flicked idly through the jobs section in the paper and watched the doorman at work.

Sam Wild, Mike Carter's chief doorman, was alone that night. There were normally two of them on the door. His regular partner was Chris, who was also in the Blues firm, but Wild had received a late call from Chris's mother to say that he had been picked up on an outstanding fines commitment warrant, for a public order offence, and was currently languishing in a cell at the Central Lock-Up. She didn't have the money to get him out so he would be off to 'The Green' in the morning to serve thirty days if his luck didn't change.

Her Majesty's Prison Winson Green wasn't a place for the faint-hearted, and Sam knew that Mike Carter would pay up to get Chris out the soonest, but not tonight.

It was far too late now to pay the fine or find someone else, but normally on a Friday night it wasn't too bad and he would just have to manage – just then four drunks turned up at the door demanding to be let in.

One of the four had a loud 'scouse' accent and was giving it large in the inner doorway to the pub, with the other three filling the small passageway leading to the outer door.

Sam Wild barred the way and politely tried to reason with them, "Not tonight lads. Try the place down the road. They get loads of birds in there."

The four were having none of it, particularly the scouser, who started to puff out his chest ready to force his way past Wild.

Wild put the open palms of both hands out to keep some distance between himself and the drunks, but knew that battle was about to commence. After all he had been in enough rucks of his own making.

"Back off or I'll call the coppers," he shouted.

The man from Liverpool promptly spat in his face, and a scuffle started. The narrowness of the corridor helped, but Sam struggled to keep the four of them at bay.

Behind the bar the licensee reached for the phone on the wall.

Sam had reconciled himself to getting a good kicking when he suddenly became aware of another man behind him. Pete Stevens was wielding a snooker cue and jabbed the scouser in the stomach, winding him slightly. It was enough to gain the initiative as Sam and Pete started to bundle them towards the outer door.

The licensee entered the fray, brandishing something that looked very much like a police truncheon. It was in fact a trophy from his former days as a copper.

"You'd better fuck off quick – the police are on their way," he shouted.

The four men got the message, turned on their heels but couldn't resist a parting shot, "You cunts, we'll be back to put your fucking windows in."

Sam Wild turned to Pete and shook his hand, "Thanks mate. I owe you one."

The licensee waved them to the bar and a free beer. As Pete drank from his dimple mug, Sam drew his life story from him, and more importantly his love of Birmingham City FC.

Sam was impressed, the guy was clearly a fanatic; he knew all the players, the scores, both home and away, and was a club member. In fact once Sam got him going he couldn't shut him up, such was his love of the game and his beloved team.

Sam made an easy decision that was music to Pete's ears – cover the door with him for the rest of the evening and he would cover his drinks. Better still there was a home game against the Leeds bastards next day and Pete was invited to meet up and make some new friends. Sam knew that a ruck with the Leeds had been arranged and wanted to see how Pete handled himself.

***

The Villa were playing out in the sticks, at Ipswich, and the Murphys had gone to have some fun with the 'carrot crunchers'. Villa had got stuffed away from home yet again, and a bad-tempered gloom had settled over the visiting supporters, rapidly channeling itself into pent up rage.

Nothing much could be done inside the ground, bar a spot of threatening chanting, some coin throwing and giving the back of the stand a good kicking, but afterwards the Villa firm found few police and lots of targets.

In one moment of 'glory' that was added to their unholy history, and grew in the recounting, the Villa mob surrounded a police van containing a lone County Police dog handler. An unhappy and sore Mel Price, one of Murphy's closest henchmen, and school friend of his son, Ryan, and another regular, Gary Docker, was sat in the front seat, balanced on one arse-cheek and handcuffed, waiting for transport.

Mel had made the mistake of punching hell out of a local fan whilst his back was to the approaching dog handler. Having been bitten on the backside by the dog he had then been arrested. Ryan had been leading a mob 'running' some Ipswich hard- men and Mel had been momentarily alone - in the wrong place at the wrong time.

The officer's dog was barking furiously in the back of the van as the hooligans began to rock it violently.

With the doors locked, the officer screamed for assistance as the mob began to chant, "Let him go, let him go," in a rising crescendo.

Suddenly a brick smashed into the windscreen, courtesy of Gary Docker, trying to help his friend - showering both of the occupants with shards of glass as a large hole appeared, "Urgent assistance required...urgent assistance...!" The officer had had enough and launched himself from the vehicle, truncheon in hand, lashing out wildly as he attempted to create a space to get to the rear doors.

He knew that he could hold them off with his dog but he didn't make it and was punched and kicked to the ground with a flurry of blows.

Colin Murphy leant through the driver's door, flicked the catch open on the front passenger door, and pushed Price, who was bleeding from cuts to the face, out into the street, "Come on cunty bollocks get your fuckin finger out and leg it. We can get the cuffs off later."

Mel Price did not need telling twice and staggered off supported by Gary and Benny Doherty, Ryan's other usual accomplice. Mel and Benny were like a comedy double act – but without the comedy.

Murphy smiled at the sight, then turned and kicked the motionless officer lying on the ground in the head.

"Give us a hand lads!" he ordered, and put his shoulder to the vehicle. A line of Villa fans put their muscles to good use and moments later the van was on its side, the sound of the yammering dog blending in with the bedlam outside.

Job done, they legged it to the sound of sirens – this one would make the front page of the local paper and get the Villa more kudos.

By the time Mel and Benny and Gary had got back to where their car had been left there were coppers everywhere, searching for a man wearing handcuffs. The trio turned on their heels and headed a short distance out of town, in the opposite direction to Birmingham, and waited for darkness to aid their return home.

The cuffs were killing Mel but they would have to wait. Benny thought it was hilarious and kept making bondage jokes. Gary, who was closest to Mel, was more anxious, suggesting that a hospital visit for a jab in respect of the dog bite was going to be needed. Mel responded morosely, "I suppose they'll stick that in my arse too, I won't be able to park my bum for a week at this rate," provoking more laughter from Benny.

About fifty officers, all of whom were looking for a chance to avenge their fallen colleague, corralled the mass of main Villa firm members, including Ryan and Colin Murphy, back to the railway station. One Villa fan that didn't take to walking in a line was dragged unceremoniously out of the column and off to a waiting van. The mob chanted non-stop until they reached the station.

An escort of five British Transport Police officers were waiting to take them on the 'football special' back to Birmingham – a grey-haired sergeant, a couple of 'old sweats' and two youngsters.

The fans were boarded and the local police withdrew – fifty law enforcers were now five.

To make things worse, the train didn't have connecting carriages and the officers were faced with an impossible choice. In light of the earlier attack on their police colleague they chose wisdom over bravery and split into two groups, covering the two coaches containing the most vocal supporters. Unfortunately that left three carriages without a police presence.

Before the train left the platform, the communication cord was pulled twice, and the tension was palpable as the train guard struggled to reset it before they finally set off.

The fans in the un-policed carriages then proceeded to demolish anything they could liberate from its fitting, and light bulbs, cushion seats, luggage racks and even the toilet rolls were launched from the windows. If it moved it went, and even parts of the ceilings were pulled down.

With every new expulsion of railway property onto the track, the fans in the policed carriages cheered and goaded their escorts, who could do nothing but hold their nerve with their backs to the locked vestibule doors.

Colin Murphy sat watching the police quietly. He had enjoyed his sport for the day but wasn't about to put his head above the parapet in a scenario where there was no immediate escape. He had also studied police tactics on trains closely and knew what the likely outcome was going to be when they got back to Birmingham New Street.

Sure enough, upon arrival there was a line of officers waiting on the platform. The escorting officers honed in on their chosen targets and three of the most 'gobby ones' on the train found themselves being wrestled to the floor and dragged away.

Symbolic arrests they might be, but at least three hooligans would be spending the night in a cell, some satisfaction for the police and the disgusted newspaper readers the next day.

Colin Murphy walked quietly away as two of the younger numpties tried to remonstrate with the officers on the platform and were themselves arrested.

Time to find a pair of bolt cutters and then off to the pub for battle stories and beer!

As Murphy made his way through the city-centre the newspaper billboards told stories of another battle – this time with the weather. After fifteen days without rain a deluge had struck whilst they were away, flooding streets and homes, causing car crashes, stopping a football match and causing two major Bonfire Night displays to be cancelled' leaving thousands disappointed. The flooding was blamed on drains blocked by fallen leaves. *'Only in England'* thought Murphy

Firework displays at Pype Hayes Park, Erdington and Senneleys Park, Weoley Castle, which had been expected to draw crowds of fifty thousand people, were called off. West Bromwich Albion supporter's cars were stranded with water up to their doors in Middlemore Rd, Smethwick, and the Walsall v Sheffield Wednesday game halted after twenty-seven minutes when torrential rain turned the pitch into a quagmire.

***

Birmingham Sunday Observer – *2 November 1975*:

'Ipswich 3 v Villa 0: Villa crash away yet again: Last

season's promotion push and Cup glory have faded and that Villa seemed content to try for a point seemed apparent from the way they set up. They packed the midfield but the defence looked off- key right from the kick off. They held out until nearly half time but then it all started to go wrong.

Woods put a low corner in and Peddelty ran in unmarked and struck the ball first time into the net. Villa started the second half with some purpose but couldn't get the ball to Andy Gray or debut boy John Deehan. Ipswich began to find space and punished Villa in the 56th minute. Bryan Hamilton got past Charlie Aitken and crossed for Trevor Whymark to power a header into the net. A few minutes later, Mills was fouled by Nicholl just outside the box. Mills took the free kick, putting the ball to Whymark. He drove the ball through a crowd of Villa defenders to Hamilton who put it in off the post. The only bright note was Deehan, who showed promise, but Villa's squad looked thin with Little and Leonard out injured and Leighton Phillips picking up a thigh strain in the first half.

Footnote: Police in Ipswich are investigating a savage attack on a lone police dog handler that occurred after the match, when he was surrounded by a group of Aston Villa supporters, described as a 'pack of animals', by local police. One man escaped wearing handcuffs and a number of arrests were made.'

Whilst many of the Villa firm celebrated their 'victory' the previous day, in their regular Sunday lunch-time haunts, Ryan Murphy gave himself a few hours off from football violence to view another form of violence from the safety of a seat in the Odeon Queensway Cinema. He had been excited about seeing his hero in

'The Legend of Bruce Lee' and wasn't disappointed.

***

On the 23 November 1975, the Blues celebrated their centenary with a party at St Andrews and a friendly game with Celtic. It was a non-event for Mike Carter's firm but gave Colin Murphy the opportunity to entertain some good friends from Scotland for a couple of days at his home. Murphy had kept his Glasgow connections sweet, there was a 'good Catholic' bond, and a useful criminal conduit he could tap into when the need arose.

***

Birmingham Sunday Observer - *7 December 1975*:

'Another day of shame for football: - Hundreds of fans invaded the pitch at Norwich's home game with West Ham yesterday. There were thirty arrests and charges. Innocent members of the crowd including children were injured and taken away on stretchers. There were also 25 arrests at the Stoke v Villa match at the Victoria Ground for scuffles and pick pocketing near the ground. Another youth was arrested at the Blues v Derby game at St Andrews.'

***

Rob Docker was in a foul mood and it showed. He was getting nowhere with the football hooligans. It had been bloody hard work getting the office into shape - all down to the moron who had succeeded him during his time at Special Branch who had spent more time on the golf course than in the office. Just to make matters worse the man's cronies at headquarters had made sure that his next move would be on promotion – wankers! Docker fumed.

Detective Sergeant Nigel Francis sat across the desk facing him, and said nothing. The ex-Met officer knew enough by now about the man facing him. When Docker was in this kind of mood it was better to practice your listening skills and keep your mouth shut. He had been up in Birmingham for two years now and was pleased with the move. Some of the villains south of the river had marked his cards and were well pissed-off with some of the questionable convictions he had obtained, and it had been time to get out, or risk seeing the inside of a coffin.

He had ditched his troublesome wife and transferred his somewhat dubious skills to Birmingham, and although it had taken him a little while to stop calling the bosses 'Guvnor', he had adjusted well.

Sat nervously next to him was DC John Burrell - the man driven by the need to go places. Thin but wiry, a typical lightweight boxer physique, over 6' tall, and gaunt faced, he looked like he hadn't eaten for a fortnight, but the steely eyes hid an inner strength and determination. His appetite was for results and Rob had recognised the welcome trait – the man was a natural 'thief-taker'.

Finally Docker looked up from his papers, "Fuck knows why I came back here. It's like a kid's nursery." He paused for effect, "I want you to do a special job for me for a few months. Drop all your other work and farm it out to the tossers out there. This is more important."

Docker briefed them carefully – they weren't volunteers and they weren't being given an option, but they were 'chosen men', which meant that they had some worth – it was enough.

For Burrell's part, as a true Brummie, he didn't particularly like the 'cockney spiv' he was going to be partnered up with for a while, but for the moment he would ride on his coat tails, keep his own nose clean, and see how it went. He was clever, and knew how to extract as much as he needed from another person's experience and re-cycle it as his own. He was a type of vampire, but with a thirst for knowledge rather than blood. He would drop Francis like a stone as soon as he had outlived his usefulness.

Docker concluded, "I want some bodies out of this. I don't care how you do it, what they're arrested for – just make sure that you hit Carter and Murphy's bunch of muppets in equal measure, and lay some false trails. By the time we're finished I want to see them on their knees. There's a bottle of whisky in it for the first body that you manage to turn."

**

So far it had been a Yuletide fun day, and Greg Lyall aka 'Roly' was determined to end it on a high.It was the 20 December 1975, and Birmingham City were playing Leicester City at St Andrews.Mike Carter, ever the tactician, had laid on the perfect ambush outside New Street Station, and it had worked a treat. 'Roly' had made sure that he was in the part that did not involve any running. The only physical exercise involved was that which he channeled through his fists.

At midday, as a group of some fifty of Leicester's main firm exited the station and headed towards the Bull Ring, they had been confronted by a dozen Blues fans led by Sam Wild, with Pete Stevens at his side. The new man had passed his test with the Leeds crew and was now 'on trial'.

Just one hundred yards stood between them as the Blues fans goaded the Leicester boys and gave them the 'come on'.

Red mist manifested itself in seconds, and the front of the Leicester group charged at their tormentors, the rest following, scattering members of the public, including children and the elderly, before them. The chase was on.

Sam Wild's group turned and ran towards Manzoni Gardens, the gap between them and the pursuing mob closing. However, as they reached the section of open grass near to the public toilets, a second group of a dozen Blues fans waited, led by Roly. The odds were still 2-1 against Blues as Leicester closed in for the kill.

"Get the bastards," a Leicester main boy roared, as fists and boots began to fly.

At that moment another fifty Blues soldiers, led by Mike Carter, with Tony Carter alongside him, emerged from a nearby subway and attacked Leicester from the rear.

It was all over in seconds as the Leicester firm were subjected to a brutal beating before they finally broke and ran, leaving two of their number unconscious on the ground, a fine aperitif for the football.

At the game, Roly continued to have fun. During the first-half, his trick was to make use of several clear plastic bags that he had carried innocently into the ground. In the gents he found no shortage of volunteers at the urinals and in due course discovered a nice little vantage point near to one of the dividing fences. Some of the 'up and comers' were encouraged to goad the away fans and as they came close to the divide to exchange torrents of abuse, Roly and a couple of his mates launched the urine filled plastic bags over the fence, before retreating back into the crowds.

The Leicester fans were furious as they retreated stinking of ammonia, invoking gales of laughter from Roly and friends, by now back in the middle of the Blues fans.

In the second half, Roly changed his tactics. Having consumed two meat pies by himself he used a couple more of his plastic bags to collect scraps of meat pies and beef burgers and gave it all a good dose of tomato sauce, with copious amounts of spit from willing volunteers.

In a re-run of the first half fun, the detritus was moulded into balls like snowballs and hurled in handfuls, over the fence. As police officers started to penetrate the terraces looking for the perpetrators, Roly decided to make an early exit – he just needed to find somewhere to wash his hands......

***

Birmingham Sunday Observer – *21 December 1975*:

'Birmingham 2 v 1 Leicester - Blues needed a disputed penalty, but it was a reward for a revival that has now seen three

home wins on the trot. The penalty came just before the break and it seemed to spur Blues onto victory. The performance wasn't top notch, but it was a good indication that Blues have the grit and resolve to save themselves from the drop, especially in front of the faithful at St Andrews.

Leicester will feel hard done by with justification. A driven Trevor Francis cross hit the hand of Denis Rofe. It was clearly accidental handball but the linesman flagged and a penalty was awarded. The Leicester players were so incensed that Steve Kember kicked the ball off the penalty spot before the kick was taken and got himself booked. It didn't put Francis off, and he thumped the ball into the net after it was put back on the spot. Before the penalty, Leicester had plenty of possession but never threatened.

After the break, a different Blues appeared. The decisive goal came unusually from a cross by Joe Gallagher who briefly found himself on the wing. The ball reached Peter Withe at the far post and despite being under pressure he headed in to make it 2-0. Jeff Blockley got himself booked for disputing the goal. Leicester pulled one back in the 81st minute when Bob Lee struck in a Frank Worthington cross but it never looked like they would get a second and in the end it was the disputed penalty that made the difference.'

***

After the final whistle, a victorious Roly met up with Sam Wild at the bottom end of Digbeth, and they made their way together into the city-centre.

They did a couple of circuits of the indoor Bus Station and

then waited in Station Street to do their last bit of Christmas 'shopping'.

Sure enough, within a couple of minutes two smart-looking young lads wearing Leicester scarves turned up at the bottom of the stairs leading up to New Street Station. Disappointed, and anxious to get a train home, they hurried up the steps, which were routinely used as an open-air toilet on Friday and Saturday nights and stank of stale urine.

Roly and Sam Wild followed immediately behind, and as they reached the first landing they hustled the two Leicester lads into a corner.

Roly took the lead, "Boys you're gonna have to pay some tax for the privilege of wearing them scarves in Brum."

The two Leicester youths knew that they were well outmatched and shook visibly.

Roly indicated Sam, "Me mate here is called Stanley – that's a big fuckin clue."

Sam Wild produced his Stanley-knife from a pocket, "You - jacket off – you shoes off," he ordered.

One of the two victims started to protest but was silenced by his friend – they did as they were told and Roly relieved them of the items, a broad grin on his face.

"Now fuck off quick to your mommies." Sam instructed. They didn't need telling twice and ran.

Roly took the shoes, and Sam Wild the jacket. They had spotted that both were good bits of designer gear that they would sell for a few quid in the pub later.

For Roly it had been a great day. Definitely one for the scrapbook, it was the best of times to be a football hooligan, it made life worth living.

***

It was the Post-Christmas away day, and the plan was for the Villa firm to set up early doors at a pub near to the ground to have an impromptu party.

Mel and Benny had done their usual trick and gone up by road in a 'ringer' - an estate car on false plates. They managed to squeeze three of the youngsters into the back seat and one more in the rear load area.

Another two cars followed behind in convoy, with ten more of the Villa firm inside. It gave them enough bodies, in case they came across any opposition, to hold their own, while they decided on fight or flight.

They parked some distance away from the Baseball Ground, and walked to the pre-arranged meet to await the arrival of the main group. Colin Murphy, Ryan, and Gary Docker were bringing them up by train, a group that also included most of the 'piss heads' who excelled in consuming as many cans as they could en route.

Colin had deliberately kept Gary close to him for the day. Whilst the boy might be keen, Colin wasn't so sure that he had the bottle for serious fighting, and wanted to see what he was like under pressure.

Once settled into the bar, one of the youngsters was dispatched to the railway station to await the arrival of Murphy and to guide them in.

No-one was wearing colours, and although the caution was sensible, it was not required as most of the opposition were still in bed. Likewise the local police had been caught off-guard and hadn't anticipated such an early arrival. They hadn't even briefed their officers let alone got them out on the streets, or deployed to the railway station.

The BTP were also in fact experiencing their own problems. The designated spotter had been having his bacon buttie, missed the forward train and had not been able to count out the Villa fans at New Street to provide the local police with an update on numbers. They were as good as blind to the threat on its way.

It was all about timing, and Colin Murphy had got it just right. With more than two hundred travelling by train and still more making their own way to the fixture by car, things were already shaping up nicely.

**

As Colin Murphy stepped onto the platform at Derby he smiled to himself – no police, no escort, no opposition, and no problems reported by the anxious to please 'up and comer' - perfect.

Murphy took his rightful place at the front of the assembled column and led the entire group towards the Baseball Ground. No chanting, no preening, he strode out with a purpose with over two hundred supporters - Villa scarves waving proudly from their wrists.

Behind them a worried station manager rang the police – he was a local man and didn't like the look of what he had just seen.

Murphy smiled to himself as they arrived at the pub to join the others without incident. It had been worth rousting the whole firm out of bed before the local police had got their act together. Any opportunity to divert, corral and escort them had been missed.

Colin Murphy posted some of the older boys to keep an eye on the doors and spoke to the licensee, who was by now feeling in need of an urgent visit to the toilet. Murphy reassured him that there would be no violence in the pub and plenty of money would be spent over the bar.

A sergeant from the local constabulary turned up ten minutes later and the licensee pointed him towards Murphy, who very politely declined to leave the premises to discuss arrangements. He spoke softly and reasonably, telling the nervous officer that they would leave when they were ready, which would be fifteen minutes before the game started, and a police escort would be welcome at that time but not before. Any effort to remove them by force would be resisted.

The sergeant was not used to being spoken to by a rough-looking Brummie in this manner, but thought better of a confrontation. He knew that they were being made to look like proper 'County Wankers' and he didn't like it, but he hoped that there would be the chance of a reckoning before the day was out.

Colin Murphy sought out one of the older men amongst the group and put a wad of money in his hands, "Get the drinks in for the boys. Everyone plays today. Make yours a double." The man didn't need asking twice.

Half an hour before the match, a public order transit van drew up on the pub car park with its front protective grill still fixed above the windscreen. Ten officers got out and flexed their muscles. They lined up legs planted wide, black gloves on hands that had already checked that truncheons were in place, they meant business – or so they thought.

A large group of the pissed Villa fans shot from the front door at the instigation of their leader, and subjected the officers to a barrage of bottles and glasses, then withdrew back inside leaving the transit van with a big hole in the windscreen. The officers piled back into the van and it reversed with tyres screeching, the general consensus being that this was a moment for discretion, not valour.

Police reinforcements gathered further down the road waiting for a decision from the match commander who was hurriedly revising his tactics, such as they were.

Bang on quarter to three, the Villa group emerged from the pub and lined up ready to march off, with Colin Murphy, Gary Docker, Ryan, Mel and Benny at the head. They waited passively, giving the police no choice but to line up alongside them, and off they went.

The wrong-footed local hooligans were by now trying to get

their act together but stood no chance as the police leap-frogged various junctions and side streets, making sure that the two sides were unable to meet.

***

Birmingham Sunday Observer – *28 December 1975*:

'Derby County 2 v 0 Aston Villa: League Champions, Derby County, put First Division new boys Villa in their place. Villa were fired up from a great victory over West Ham and were followed by an army of fans, but in the end it was not enough. County were missing several key players, but were still far too good for the visitors. Derby keeper Colin Boulton didn't have a difficult save to make, but Derby, though below their best, gave John Burridge, who was in fine form, a torrid time.

Honours were pretty even though until the 46th minute when Leighton James put in a cross from the right to the far post and Steve Powell headed in. Burridge was then forced into four fine saves. Villa nearly grabbed an equalizer when Andy Gray hit the post with a header from a Ray Graydon cross, but the ball bounced away to safety. The decider came from a penalty after Archie Gemmill was brought down by Mortimer. The decision was harsh but Charlie George made no mistake from the spot and the game was over, with Derby deserving winners.

On an unsavoury note, drunken Villa fans caused problems for the local police both before and after the game and there were injuries and damage.'

***

After the match, the Villa supporters were held back on the terraces to allow the police to disperse local fans, before being marshaled together for the return trip to the railway station. Whether you had a car, a train ticket, or neither, they were all going to the station – no arguments. With reinforcements drafted in, the police were finally intent on regaining lost ground by putting their stamp of authority on the proceedings.

They all marched off in an approximation of order but this time the journey was very different with the situation deteriorating quickly as the opposition launched 'hit and run' missile attacks on the column. Just outside the railway station, a group of fifty locals emerged from a side street and attacked the lead Villa fans, Colin and Ryan Murphy amongst them.

Mayhem broke out, and in the midst of the hand-to-hand fighting, Ryan Murphy spotted a lone policewoman isolated and struggling violently with one of the locals. Around her, other Derby members were pulling at her clothing and at her flapping ponytail, revealed because one clown had knocked her hat off and run off with his trophy.

Ryan responded instinctively, Gary Docker at his side. They ran to the struggling group and with one well-aimed kick he laid the main protagonist out on the floor whilst Docker laid into the others, who fled as the odds evened up.

"Have that one on me love," Ryan said to the shaken officer. For a moment their eyes met before Ryan and Gary ran back to the

—

Villa main group and reformed.

Some of the up and comers decided to do a run through the off-licence next to the station, and a number of bottles of good quality vodka either finished up underneath coats, or smashed on the aisles as furious staff chased them outside. One of the drunker fans failed to hide his ill-gotten gains well enough and was detained.

The locals had made a couple of other arrests, but otherwise the Villa team was untouched as Mel and Benny seized the opportunity in the confusion to melt away and get back to their vehicle. With all the police and Derby fans focused on the main group there was plenty of scope for a few car radios to be liberated on the way back.

The BTP had put a scratch return escort together and everyone was loaded within ten minutes, tickets or no tickets. The locals just wanted to get shut of their unwanted visitors. Protests were ignored as everyone was shoved unceremoniously onto the train. Some of them would need to come back again to retrieve their cars. The alternative was arrest and possibly a beating in the back of a police van by some very upset coppers, so it was a no brainer.

It was strangely quiet on the way back as the alcohol was shared out and many drank themselves into a stupor. The BTP sergeant persuaded the guard to turn the heating up on the train and it wasn't long before many of them were sleeping noisily.

Colin Murphy sat with Ryan and Gary, chatting as the train chattered away through the dark countryside. At one stage Colin slapped Gary on the back – "You did okay today mate." An endorsement indeed, from one who did not normally waste words.

Miles away, Mel and Benny had just deployed their bent coat hanger for the third time to flick the door catch of a likely vehicle. The fourth would require the services of a screwdriver to pierce the skin just below the key mechanism in order to liberate its car radio.

Four nice stereos would be available as extras to purchasers at one of Colin Murphy's car-lots by midday next day.

***

Rob Docker didn't usually celebrate the New Year, but he was so glad to see the back of this one that he bought tickets for the big New Year's Eve bash at the Grand Hotel on Colmore Row. Not for Lilian of course, she was getting pissed at home watching some Scottish bilge on the TV. He had treated Jane Smith, local reporter and occasional mistress. She was fun to be with, knew the score with the relationship, and they had a mutually beneficial working relationship to boot.

For a moment or two he could submerge the nagging of his conscience in fake comradeship as the balloons fell from the dancehall ceiling, and later, there would be a semblance of love.

He resolved that 1976 was going to be a good year for Rob Docker.

Chapter Two

'Hi Ho Silver Lining'

January 1976

Mike Carter rallied his troops – it was going to be a long day, but he had been looking forward to this Saturday for some time. A local derby was always a good excuse for a ruck and he was feeling lucky. He made a mental note to give 'Place the Ball' a go next day - with a £12,000 prize plus a nice Vauxhall Chevette on offer, it might just be the perfect end to a memorable weekend.

They had met in the Crown pub in Station Street as usual, and numbers were looking good. He had put the word out – absences would be noted and there would be consequences. Out of loyalty or fear, or both, they were there, in all their guises. The truly violent, like his nephew Tony, the 'scufflers', after excitement in their dull lives, the 'up and comers', who fancied themselves as the next generation, and those for whom being part of the gang with its collective kudos was the most important thing in their limited existence.

They all had one thing in common though, they followed Mike Carter, and he had somehow managed to draw all of the different elements of the tribe together and to instil discipline. He was their leader, and when he spoke others followed.

Mike had studied all of their strengths, and weaknesses, and had a core of 'storm-troopers' who would stand next to him and show no retreat.

His main boys, Tony Carter, Sam Wild and Greg Lyall, occupied one corner of the pub, one eye on the front door, relishing the battle to come. Pete Stevens was not yet a full member of this exclusive group – he had shown willing but that was simply not enough. For now he stood to one side, waiting for instructions with his fellow 'up and comers'. Desperate for acknowledgement, he nevertheless knew his place.

One of the foot soldiers stood at the door scanning the streets for any sign of the opposition, whilst others were already out spotting on New Street Station.

As the pub gradually filled up with the resident 'piss-heads' who claimed allegiance to the Blues, they were surveyed by Mike and his lieutenants with some disdain but they were needed – an extra layer of cannon-fodder that would add to the intimidation of the opposition. With each pint thrown down their necks this group got braver. Some would drink themselves into a stupor, and one or two might not even make the game, but for a few hours they could be 'special' in their own minds before returning on Monday morning to their mundane existence in some dreary office or being bossed around on a factory floor.

Suddenly a breathless teenage wannabe returned and reported to Mike, as a messenger does to his General – no salute but almost standing to attention.

Mike smiled and gathered the inner-circle around him – they were on and someone was going to get a 'right basting'..........

***

Birmingham Sunday Observer - *11 January 1976*:

'Football mob runs wild: Yesterday, a seventy-strong Birmingham City mob ran amok on New Street Station, attacking fans who had just arrived on a train from Wolverhampton before the local derby at St Andrews. Women dragged screaming children to safety as fans battled with broken pint glasses, sticks, and billiard cues, on the concourse, in a rampage that lasted for ten minutes before the railway police were able to restore order.

As the home fans eventually withdrew through the glass doors, onto the short- stay car park at the front of the station, the windscreens of three cars were smashed.

Two of the vehicles were unattended, but in the third, a man with a disabled child had to duck down to avoid being showered with fragments of glass. He said later, 'It was terrifying, I had to lie over my son to protect him from flying glass, and he was frightened to death.' In the aftermath, a number of people were treated for minor injuries by first-aid staff on the station.

The violent clashes continued as Blues supporters ambushed visiting fans in Manzoni Gardens. The grassed areas finished up looking like a building site with rocks, bricks, bottles and rubbish strewn around. Skips filled with bricks and rubble outside a pub being renovated near to the Rotunda provided plenty of ammunition, and scaffolding poles were launched like spears at the opposition.

In Digbeth, the 'hit and run' tactics continued as West Midlands Police officers desperately fought to gain control. Two arrests were made and an unnamed police source later indicated that the violence had clearly been carefully planned in advance and orchestrated by an organised hooligan group.

After the match, away fans broke away from a police escort as they were being taunted by home fans emerging from side roads near Curzon Street. Football chants, threats of violence and the sounds of police dogs barking filled the air.

Police struggled to contain the fighting, and two shop windows were smashed in the High Street, following which electrical items and clothing were stolen. Several thunder flashes were set off and Birmingham City Centre began to resemble a war- zone, filled with the sound of sirens.

At one point, a queue of people waiting outside the Futurist Cinema in John Bright St to see the film 'Shivers' were scattered, as rampaging fans fought running battles, and police motorcyclists attempted to break up the marauding groups.

As Birmingham City hooligans circled New Street Station, riot police in vans arrived and drew truncheons to call time on the frenzy of violence, making a number of arrests for public order offences.

West Midlands Police confirmed that a post-incident investigation would take place, with two visiting Wolves fans still receiving treatment at the Birmingham Accident Hospital for knife injuries – one classed as serious.

EDITORIAL COMMENT. Something has to be done to halt this tide of violence, this sickness blighting football in the guise of

*so-called 'fans'. They are nothing of the sort, they are criminals, and
we call on the police to get a grip of the situation. Innocent men,
women and children should never have to witness these sorts of
scenes ever again.'*

***

Mike Carter sat in the kitchen, half a full-English breakfast still to be
consumed, as he thumbed through the newspaper. He hovered over
the report of the match itself on the back pages but in truth it wasn't
his priority. He was a Blues fan whether they won or lost. It had not
been a good day for Blues though, and he re-lived the frustration as
he read,

*__Birmingham Sunday Observer__ - 11 January 1976: 'Wolves
pile on misery for Blues: After a bad week, the Blues find themselves
out of the FA Cup and back in the thick of the relegation fight. The
home defeat was not so much due to a special display by Wolves as a
tame surrender in which Blues didn't look like a First Division outfit
without Howard Kendall to guide them from midfield.*

*Wolves got the two points which look worth four, via a 54th
minute penalty, scored by Willie Carr after a mistake by out of form
Blues skipper Kenny Burns in his second 'horror' game of the week.
Burns got tangled up with keeper Dave Latchford before tripping
Bobby Gould to concede the spot kick.*

*For new manager Willie Bell there seems to be problem after
problem, with injuries and key players losing form at a vital stage of
the season with relegation looming. There were also
uncharacteristic misses by Trevor Francis and Bob Hatton. Malcolm*

Page hit the bar for Blues, but they played very badly overall.

After the Pompey FA Cup shock the St Andrews supporters were extremely tolerant although some could not contain their disappointment, and chants of 'what a load of rubbish' were heard ten minutes from the end. Archie Styles failed to overcome the absence of Kendall in midfield and with Terry Hibbitt in an emergency midfield role Birmingham's attack came in fits and starts. On this evidence Wolves have a better chance of survival than Blues, but it will be close.'

Carter returned to his breakfast and his thoughts. He ran through the action in his mind and reviewed the performance of *his* team.

Sam, Greg and Tony had done well, but Tony needed watching. He was beginning to get out of hand. Mike had seen it before. The lad was enjoying it too much, beginning to get reckless with that knife, and Mike suspected that Tony harboured ambitions to be number one. He might need reminding who was boss. The new man, Pete had done well again. He was brighter than the norm, thought on his feet and showed 'bottle' when up against it.

As for the police, Mike had a feeling that his old mate DI Docker wasn't going to be enjoying Monday morning very much. *'He's a crafty fucker though, and I need to keep an eye out for any of his tricks,'* he thought.

Mike pondered on the decision to break all links with Docker but decided it was still correct, *'I just don't trust the bastard, and I don't see why I should cut him in on anything now things are looking good. I'm above that now, don't need him and his favours.'*

He finished the last mouthful, belched loudly and contemplated his Sunday lunchtime drink. It was time to plan for next week.

From the kitchen-sink, Carol surveyed her husband with resignation and wondered when he would truly ever grow up. She had offered to bandage his bruised knuckles but had been brushed away with a cursory glance. The black-eye would take a few days to blossom as the bruising came out, but the badge of honour would be worth a couple of pints later in the day.

He turned to Carol, "I'm off to the pub. I need to see some of the lads. Just leave me dinner in the oven. Remember what I said about Joy. She's starting to spread her wings and some of the boys are sniffing round. She's got her schoolwork to do not buggering about with boys. I'll decide when she starts having a boyfriend and who it is. Do your job and keep her in line, or I will, and you know I can do it."

Just as swiftly as he had finished playing the hard-man, Mike Carter showed his sensitive side, as he slipped an envelope from his pocket and placed it on the table before scraping the chair back loudly to leave. Despite his harsh words he loved Carol and would have been lost without her. He just couldn't find a way to tell her but gave her a squeeze and said, "Two tickets for Mungo Jerry at Dolce Vita, Smallbrook Queensway next week. Get your hair done and your 'glad-rags' sorted out. We're going for a boogie missus."

***

63

Charlie Docker had been a life-long Aston Villa fan - it was his third love, behind his wife Vivian and his son Gary. His market trading and his other role, 'fronting' the licence of 'The Hole In The Wall' Club on Soho Road, trailed further behind. He went to as many home and away games as he could – a real martyr to the cause despite the pain every time they lost.

Charlie also made a decent living from the market stall he had taken over last year, together with one or two 'under the counter' enterprises stemming from his links in Handsworth. He had also added football scarves and memorabilia to the stall and was doing well.

Charlie could spot which 'tribe' fans belonged to from a mile away, and mentally filed away the various sub-sets that existed on the terraces.

Some would buy a scarf from him and wrap it around one of their wrists looking to play out the ritual of appearing tough and demonstrating visible loyalty.

The 'straights' would wrap it around the neck in a neat knot at the front, intensely loyal but anxious to retain their individuality.

The real fans hung them loosely around the neck, occupied the same spots on the terraces every week, and were proud of their team.

Charlie was a 'loyalist', totally devoted to the club, and usually enjoyed standing with the 'experts', those who knew every detail of the previous matches and the players, and were always wise after the event. He loved listening to the banter. Some of the people who stood around him at Villa Park had become good friends and they often travelled to the away games together.

He had no time for the heavy drinkers, who launched themselves with little encouragement into chorus after chorus of moronic chants and laughed at their own stupid jokes. He had seen enough of these people in the pubs in town and steered clear, although taking their money was fair game in the licensing trade.

Neither did he favour the company of the 'barrackers' – who would gather up enormous amounts of anger and vent their spleens at home and away teams alike, plus the referee, in equal measure.

Charlie just loved his football and would never dream of inflicting either verbal or physical abuse on another human being. He had lived his life around those who did, seen the tragic results, and wanted nothing to do with it.

Gary Docker, on the other hand, was not following in his 'old man's' footsteps.

Gary was a self-styled 'hard man' of the terraces, although in truth he fell short of the mark and was neither feared nor dominant amongst the real 'toughs' who did dominate the hooligan element.

He was one of the Villa firm, but sat outside the inner-core of the group with no sign of Colin Murphy allowing him in. His friendship with Mel Price and his classmate Ryan Murphy had, since school days, given him his entry ticket to the group, but he had failed to cash it in and make it into the elite of the Murphys and their trusted double act, Mel and Benny. He could handle himself in a fight, sure, and won most of them, but he lacked the steel inside to grit through the pain and win at all costs.

Ryan had that killer instinct, and Gary was scared of what Ryan was capable of when riled. Colin Murphy was simply in another league, with an inner ferocity only the streets of Belfast could bestow. Gary and Mel had often discussed where the Murphys would end up and both had concluded that life in a cell was a distinct probability. Mel was a true hard-man, but Gary thought that even he wouldn't cross that particular line and take a life.

Gary was respected by the 'up and comers', ignored by the 'nutters' and feared only by the 'creeps' and 'hangers on'. He had found himself in a sort of 'no- man's land' when it came to the pecking order of the Villa firm. As he grew into his twenties, Gary had realised that he was at the summit of his own little hill and going no further. The delights of the hooligan life were paling, and he had begun to wonder where he was going and what he was to do with the rest of his life.

Onto this fertile ground had unexpectedly dropped the seed of love. He was a good-looking lad and the ladies liked him, especially when he was able to muster up some half-true war stories', so he had plenty of experience.

This time however it was different – there had been nothing like this before. He was smitten and the fruit of his obsession was forbidden – he was playing with fire but couldn't stop himself.

Gary helped his dad out on the stall on occasions, when Charlie had other things to attend to, and when he did he had his own little side-line in Stanley-knives, flick–knives and knuckledusters imported from France – for Villa fans only of course.

Gary's life had reached a Rubicon, although he didn't know what that meant. His time as a member of the Villa crew had defined him and bought meaning to his dull life, and Mel and Ryan had been his entry ticket, but he was on the verge of betraying everything for love.

***

Ryan stared at Roseanne across the kitchen table. It seemed that they had nothing much to say to each other these days, and Ryan was trying to work out why.

Roseanne could feel his eyes on her but kept her head down, pretending to concentrate on her breakfast. She hoped he couldn't see her thoughts, and did not dare let him look into her eyes in case he could read the message they would not hide. She hated him. How had she ever loved him and ended up marrying him?

She gazed into the bowl containing cereal, but saw her younger self, the envy of all her friends, the girl who had Ryan Murphy as her boyfriend.

She sneaked a look at him; trying to remember the teenager she had fallen for. The reason was obvious; he was good-looking, tall, well built and unusually golden– haired for someone with Irish ancestry. The 'cock of the roost', a leader.

Back then he had been charming, funny, attentive, and protective of her. She had known immediately that he was the one, that they would marry, and she had wanted that so much, so much in fact that she had ignored the warning signs, the 'other' Ryan that lurked beneath the sparkling veneer.

They were the same age, twenty-two now, and had met at seventeen at a large pub on the Hagley Road. Under-eighteens could get in there easily so it was very popular. In those days a lot of the clubs and pubs in the city were really strict and many clubs didn't allow you in unless you were twenty-one, but this one seemed to court the younger set and was lively and full most nights. .

She had been sat with two friends when an older man had come over, sat himself down without being invited, and started trying to chat her up. He was drunk, and had begun pawing at her, causing her to tell him to 'piss off' in a louder voice than she intended. The pub had been crowded, and the drinkers sat at other tables and stood around nearby had looked over when they heard her voice raised, but no-one had said anything and the pesterer had continued. It was when he tried to force a kiss on her that she had stood up and poured her drink over him.

He hadn't liked that one bit, and had leapt, spluttering, to his feet, calling her 'bitch' and 'slag'. She had really thought the man was about to slap her or something, when Ryan had appeared and tapped her tormentor on the shoulder.

"Why don't you take a hint and leave her alone," he had said, very softly.

The man was in his thirties and looked like a rugby player. He had looked Ryan up and down and clearly was not impressed, even though Ryan had been big for a teenager.

———

"Why don't *you* fuck off and mind your own business, this is between me and the slag here," he had replied.

"I think it is me business though." That soft voice again. She knew now what that low tone meant, more deadly than soft.

The drunk had squared up. If he had been sober he might have noticed Ryan's sideways stance, minimising the target area. He might have picked up that the teenager was cool and confident, but he missed all the signs.

It took about thirty seconds. The drunk swung a telegraphed punch that was blocked easily. Lightning fast, Ryan had delivered a jab and a kick that floored the man, sending the table and drinks crashing.

She had heard voices from the onlookers and noticed two other youths wearing designer gear shout, "Nice one Ryan, Up the Villa!"

Then the bouncers were there, three of them. She caught a speculative look in her saviour's eye and realised that just for a moment he had been considering taking on the doormen, then he raised his hands in a submissive gesture,

"No trouble, he started it, I just finished it."

At this moment the drunk on the floor spurted a mouth-full of vomit, some of it splashing onto the bouncers shoes. Roseanne had felt obliged to intervene,

"This drunken twat was trying ta kiss me, had his hands all

over me, I thought he was gonna slap me but this lad stopped him." She gestured to the man on the floor who was on all fours now, still coughing and spluttering, "It was him what started it, threw the first punch"

The leader of the doormen indicated to his two companions,"Get him out, and get summat to clean this up." He turned to Ryan."You are on your final warning, anything else and you're barred."He turned to the onlookers, "And no more football chants in here, specially not fucking Villa ones, right nothing more to see." That was the beginning.

Roseanne shook herself from her reverie and dared another glance across the table. It was safe; he was reading the match programme from the weekend. Andy Gray was on the cover, just above the date, '*January 17th 1976, price 15p*'. He looked a bit like Ryan; the same tousled blonde hair and chiselled features. Ryan hadn't been too happy on Saturday after the match.

He had picked up The Birmingham Sunday Observer now and was reading the match report. She could see his knuckles whitening as he gripped the paper harder as he read. He slammed the paper down and began shovelling breakfast into his mouth.

The paper had landed at an angle whereby she could read the article.

'Birmingham Sunday Observer - *18 January 1976.*

Villa miss Mortimer after injury: It started well. Newcastle goalkeeper Mahoney fumbled the ball into his own net when being pressured by Andy Gray in the sixth minute, but Dennis Mortimer picked up an injury in the sixteenth minute and went off. After that

Villa lost all their sparkle and went to pieces. Alan Gowling powered home a headed equaliser on seventeen minutes – within forty seconds of Mortimer going off.

Villa showed grit and determination but very little else and although they got the ball into the net in the sixtieth minute when Deehan knocked the ball to Gray to sweep past Mahoney, the striker was obviously offside. After Mortimer's exit, Villa's best men were Gidman, who also received an injury in the second half, and Deehan. Two home points lost, and a mediocre season looks in prospect.'

Roseanne briefly considered showing an interest by making a comment, but thought better of it; she had been on the wrong end of his football frustrations before.

Her thoughts returned to the past, trying to make sense of how her life had descended into misery, forcing her to a decision to leave.

After the fight at the pub they had started seeing each other. Her friends were envious; Ryan was good-looking, entertaining, clever and witty. At first he had kept the football stuff away from the relationship. She quickly realised that he was obsessed with 'The Villa' but most of the local lads were into football and were either a *'Bluenose'* or a *'Villain'* and no love was lost between them. Scuffles and a spot of hooliganism was the norm, just bravado and teenage hormones working their way through.

As the months passed and she plunged head over heels in love, Ryan had opened up his life to her, and she had gradually begun to realise that there was another side to her boyfriend.

Now, sat at this breakfast table in 1976, with the benefit of hindsight, she marvelled at how she had persistently and wilfully ignored the other Ryan. Even her parents had tried to point it out, liking him at first, but eventually becoming disapproving, to the point of not attending the marriage. Another mistake, she had cut them out of her life, the rebellious teenager who knew best, and she had been alone throughout the trials of the past few years - until now.

The other side of her husband was all she saw now. She called it 'The Dark Half'. This was Ryan the Villa 'firm' hooligan, son of the leader, Colin Murphy. It was the wild and violent Ryan, with a cold temper made all the more lethal by the proficiency in Kung Fu that she had seen exhibited that first night in the Dirty Duck.

Like many others, Ryan had been transfixed by Bruce Lee in *'Enter the Dragon',* and had sought to emulate his feats of strength and fighting skill. For most teenagers it had been a craze, encapsulated by the Carl Douglas hit song and they soon moved onto easier pursuits. Not Ryan. He had persevered and become a champion, and a person to be feared.

He had used his fighting skills to good effect, accompanying his father in his hooligan exploits, and no-one doubted that he was the true heir to Colin Murphy. His reputation had grown, and he had formed his own 'firm within a firm' with the sanction of his father.

Murphy senior trusted his son, and knew that one day he

would hand him the mantle of leader. He considered it to be a good tactic for Ryan to draw support from, and lead, the 'up and coming' hooligans who respected Murphy senior, but had less affinity with him due him being forty-three years of age.

This had suited Colin Murphy, maintaining his family's grip on the next generation of potential rivals for 'king' of the Villa firm. A dynasty was crucial because he had seen the potential for using the hooligan network for criminal purposes – hence his brutal excising of the last 'king' and the maintenance of an iron grip via Ryan, Mel and Benny.

He had plans to create an empire to eventually oust the old criminal guard, the 'businessmen' to whom for now, he had pledged affiliation. He would brook no deviation from those plans. He had a small army of claret and blue in the palm of his hand, and the wit to use them.

Roseanne had also realised that Colin Murphy had passed another legacy onto his son. It took a while for her to find out what had happened to Ryan's mother. One evening, when they had both had a few drinks and were alone in a pub, he had finally opened up, revealing the scars that she suspected lay at the root of 'dark' Ryan.

He had been only eight, an only child, and close to his mother. Colin Murphy had been serving time, two years, for a crime he insisted was a 'fit up' by the police. Whilst he was inside, Michelle, his wife, had been diagnosed with a rare but aggressive form of cancer that had taken her within weeks. It was hereditary, an unlucky throw of the DNA 'dice', but Colin Murphy turned his hatred of the disease onto the police and the establishment that had incarcerated him during his wife and son's time of need, only grudgingly allowing him to attend the funeral, in handcuffs and with two prison officers by his side, before whisking him back to his cell before the wake.

That was the fury against the forces of law and order that lay at the core of Colin Murphy and had so taken aback the unwitting Rob Docker. This had been bequeathed to Ryan during his developing years.

As Colin served his sentence, Ryan had been cared for by Mel's mother for over a year after Michelle's death, forging a close bond with his mixed-race school friend that had generated a genuine dislike of racism which would later manifest itself in respect of a particular individual, with tragic consequences.

The two boys had a lot in common, both were now missing a parent, as Mel's Jamaican father had decamped years before and had never been see again. Mel thought he had gone back to the Caribbean, but had no interest in finding the father who had abandoned him.

Mel had a hard time growing up, with a single parent and bearing the tag of 'half-caste'. He had toughened up fast, and Ryan had stood by him, so it had been natural for Mel to follow him into the Villa 'firm'.

Mel's difficult schooldays and youth had led him into an even deeper friendship with Gary Docker, who as son of Charlie, the licensee, had privileged access to the Hole in the Wall club on Soho Road, Handsworth and thereby into black culture.

Mel's mixed race background had put him in an increasingly difficult position as he grew up. He went to all-white schools, but he looked more black than white. He had tried to 'be white', but had been rejected, bullied, abused by most, apart from Gary and Ryan at school, and later Benny with whom he had formed his infamous 'double act' as main men in the Villa firm. Via Gary, he had been drawn to the mainly black district of Handsworth, and found acceptance there, and now that was where his loyalties truly lay, with his 'own' people, with Gary Docker, and his father Charlie.

But Roseanne, at that time viewing her world through the prism of teenage optimism and hope, had ignored the signs of Ryan's 'bad' half and had been swept on a flood of emotion into marriage at eighteen. Thankfully, the union had not been 'blessed' with the complication of children, due to a combination of luck in the first two years and the pill thereafter, which Roseanne had begun to take secretly in contravention of the Catholicism that Colin Murphy hypocritically espoused.

That hidden trip to the Family Planning Clinic had been initiated by her sickening realisation of the truth about her flawed husband and the family 'business' to which he belonged.

The 'other' Ryan had come to the fore after the gloss of married life wore off. The darker alter ego welded the fighting skills to an inner ruthlessness, and manifested itself in a manic jealousy towards Roseanne that had made her married life a misery.

He sought to control her, and woe betides her if he thought another man was looking at her. That would be her fault for 'encouraging' the attention, and punishment would come later, when they got home. It got to the stage where she would not go out, and if she did, she wore clothing designed to make herself look dowdy and blend into a crowd. To add to her desperation, Ryan was no hypocrite sexually and she knew never looked at other women. She was his possession and obsession and there could be no escape from Ryan by his finding of a new love.

But now she had a plan, and a shoulder to cry on.

She knew that Gary Docker was no match for Ryan, but he was kind and they had secretly built a relationship that promised her an escape and a better life. The alternative was an existence of drudgery, pain and perhaps something more serious if Ryan's temper got the better of him. He knew the techniques for killing, and at times Roseanne knew that he had restrained himself with difficulty. It could only get worse as years passed, and love was replaced with hatred. She could only see a future of misery and death if she stayed.

She had reached the same crossroads as Gary, and their meeting of minds seemed more than chance.

Gary was slightly younger; in fact they had first met at Gary's twenty-first party at Rebecca's nightclub in Severn Street. Gary had clearly had aspirations to be a 'main man', but anyone could see that he didn't have the base 'mettle'. It was what drew her to him, he was kind and gentle beneath the scarf-waving yob act he portrayed in public, sensitive enough to recognise her plight.

The relationship had remained hidden so far for a very simple reason. Gary had been brought up with the Villa crowd, his father, Charlie, was a lifelong fan, but also had business connections with

Colin Murphy going back years. Gary and Ryan were at the same school, in the same street-gang as kids, so he had naturally been integrated as one of Ryan's 'men' as he grew up.

Because he was an insider, a friend and follower of Ryan's since school, he was not regarded as a potential lover for Roseanne: in fact she knew that Ryan had long ago written him off as a potential 'mover and shaker', consigning him to the dustbin of childhood remnant who would never quite cut the mustard, although Mel Price clearly did not share that view and had remained close to his childhood friend.

Gary had thus become invisible to Ryan, just a piece of the furniture. As such, he was beneath the jealousy 'radar', and they had been able to cultivate a relationship without Ryan guessing a thing so far.

It had started as sympathy, she knew, Ryan had been particularly evil at Gary's party, bruising her arm because a man had asked her to dance, but Gary's concern had turned to love. Now the point had been reached where something had to be done about it because Ryan was beginning to suspect she had someone else. He had begun asking questions, appearing unexpectedly, and she felt his eyes upon her whenever they were out, searching for a clue. It was inevitable that he would find out, and when he did Gary Docker was a dead man, and she would probably receive the same treatment.

So they had devised a plan. It was dangerous, but worth the risk to be together, neither of them would countenance going back to their old lives.

They were oblivious of the effects of their love on the fates.

For the hundredth time she reviewed the decision, the ending of her marriage, but the result was still the same. It was now or never, and Gary was the one.

Roseanne got up, collected Ryan's plate and went to the sink. He would be going out soon, and she could risk a conversation with Gary. Villa were playing a midweek match at home to Wolves in a few weeks, and she had overheard Ryan talking about giving the Wolves fans a battering, then going into town later.

He usually didn't get home until midnight on a home match night if he went out drinking. She had reasoned that the chances of escaping on a weekday were much greater than late Saturday to Sunday, when just about everything shut. With luck, and she felt that she deserved some, there would be the window of opportunity for their escape.

***

Birmingham Sunday Observer - *18 January 1976*:

'*Ten man Blues held by Parkes: The relegation shadows lengthened a little bit longer over St Andrews as Blues, fighting pluckily with ten men for the last thirty-seven minutes, went down to their eleventh away defeat of the season.*

They had used their substitute Jim Calderwood to replace Kenny Burns for the second half, and Tony Want limped off injured in the fifty-third minute. By the closing minutes they had pulled a goal back on their 2-0 half time deficit and had the Rangers defence looking decidedly shaky. Trevor Francis scored in the sixty-third minute and with Calderwood working like a young Trojan, Phil Parkes in the Ranger's goal had to pull out saves from Howard Kendall and Francis in the dying minutes. But it was all too late.

Despite their bright start, when they matched Rangers in every department, Blues handed the London club a gift goal in the twentieth minute. It was all Rangers needed to lift them on their way and check the poor recent run which has put a dent in their Championship challenge. Rangers went from strength to strength. Blues were constantly out thought and out run in midfield and Don Masson helped himself to another goal in the thirty-third minute. Rangers kept looking for more goals and their efforts brought Dave Latchford into action in the first four minutes of the second half.

Blues had resumed with Calderwood substituting for Burns who had been booked for a foul on Beck in the 9th minute. But the game took its most dramatic twist in the fifty- third minute when Want limped off with a pulled hamstring and did not reappear. Masson took his first goal from a cross by Beck who replaced injured England captain Gerry Francis. Latchford and Page got into a terrible mix up as the ball reached the near post and it spun away for Masson to grab the easiest of goals. The second was a firm header when, left unmarked, he met a right wing centre from John Hollins.

Blues' late revival was sparked off only a minute after Want had to retire. Kendall put in one of their best scoring efforts as he met a Francis cross with a header only inches over the bar. Page was the second Blues player to be booked in the sixty-first minute for a foul on Stan Bowles, but a minute later Blues broke and scored.

Peter Withe found Francis with a good cross and the young star turned smartly to hit a cross – shot wide of Parkes. But it wasn't enough and relegation still beckons.'

***

Malcolm pretended to be busy with a file at his desk whilst a few of his cronies, who had been let into the secret of his latest 'blag', looked around feigning disinterest and pre-occupation. There was nothing that Malcolm liked more than a bit of fun at someone else's expense – especially if it was a woman, and even more so if it was one that was not prepared to open her legs for him.

Sally was the perfect candidate and ticked all the boxes.

As she entered the office she caught one unguarded smirk and immediately noticed a brown A4 sized envelope, and a small package wrapped in brown paper sitting on top of her desk.

She sat down and settled back into her chair before opening the envelope.

It was a report, ostensibly from the Head of CID, Headquarters based, and addressed to all female detectives. She had already worked out that this was going to be a morning wind-up, but decided to play the fool for the moment,

(February 1976) 'I draw your attention to the Sex Discrimination Act, and the fact that from now on policewomen will have to do exactly the same job as male officers. This means working night shifts, dealing with drunks, arresting violent criminals and dealing with fights and hooligans. The Chief Constable has

guaranteed that female officers will be given the same level of protection as male officers, but realises that there are problems with the uniform as there is no pocket in which to put a full-size truncheon.

The only possible solution available so far for officers in uniform is that the truncheon for the women will only be about ten inches long. It is hoped they will fit in a woman police officer's handbag. We realise however that for female CID officers, who carry smaller handbags, this will not be possible and therefore you will be receiving a personal issue truncheon which will be about six inches long only. Training will be provided in due course and you must carry it with you at all times and not hesitate to use it if you feel the need to.'

Sally placed the 'report' on her desk and reached for the brown package – anticipation grew.

As she unwrapped it a few were unable to stifle giggles – it was a six-inch long vibrator that Malcolm had borrowed from one of his contacts at the sex-shop near the railway station.

Sally turned to Reid, looked him square in the face as he burst out laughing and said, "Do you know what Malcolm. That's just what I need. You won't be getting it back so I suggest that you buy yourself a bigger one so that you can shove it up your arse."

Reid laughed, "Well I knew that you wasn't getting any so I thought to help you out."

Sally finished him off in a literal sense, "That's for me to know Sarge and you to never find out. I doubt you've seen your little 'willy' for years anyway without a mirror, with the size of your gut. Does it look like a walnut whip – bet it does?"

Reid was losing the battle and his mouth started opening and closing like a goldfish as he searched for a suitable riposte.

They both clocked Rob Docker starting to stir in his office – it was time for the banter to end.

In the background John Burrell smiled to himself quietly. He was due to take Sally to see the film Earthquake at the ABC Bristol Road later, and was looking forward to a lot more than the earth moving and 'Surroundsound'. Their relationship was a secret to the rest of the office and that's how it would remain, especially from prats like Malcolm Reid.

***

The next Villa home game was against QPR, who had happily stuffed Blues two weeks earlier, plunging them deeper into a relegation crisis. It would be the best season ever if Villa's first one back in the First Division was marked by the hated enemy's relegation, assisted by a couple of Villa victories over the Blues, one of which had already taken place and was still being celebrated.

Ryan was due to meet some of the boys at midday in Aston but had decided on a whim to have a look around the City Centre to see what was going on.

He was a risk taker and got a thrill from being out on his own. He had supreme self-confidence in his ability to be able to fight his way out of any situation.

More importantly, today it gave him the chance to get out of the house early, and away from Roseanne who had woken up with a 'face like four pence'. It was a football day, not the moment to spend precious time trying to work out what was wrong with her today.

He was curious to see whether any QPR firm were arriving early, whether Blues were traveling in numbers to their away game at Old Trafford, and more importantly what approach the coppers were going to take.

Ryan was looking forward to some sport after the match, and knowing what sort of numbers the police were going to field, and where, was all part of the tactics of the day.

It was bitterly cold, and Ryan had his bomber-jacket zipped up to the collar. Even now as he stood on the concourse at New Street Railway Station, facing the ticket barriers, he felt a blast of cold air every time someone came through the glass doors to his left, from the short stay car park.

There was a smattering of BTP officers on the station but they were 'old- school', many of them brought in from the sticks for the day. It was a chore being on football duties and they wanted to get back to their home stations the soonest. Many of them had joined up after the war and had done their fair share of real fighting. They were looking forward to retirement.

The different styles of police raincoats, which they were wearing, paid testimony to their reputation of being a 'force of a thousand macs'.

They paid no attention to Ryan, and he watched as small

knots of bobble- hatted Blues fans brought their tickets from the Booking Office and made their way through the barrier to catch trains to Manchester.

There was no sign of any of the main Blues boys, and no Londoners.

Ryan went over to the circular bank of phone boxes to his left and made a phone call to Colin Murphy. Not much to tell but he was always anxious to please his father, to show him that he was worthy of his place, not as a son but as a valued member of the firm.

He went back to his position next to one of the tiled columns that rose from the grimy floor of the station, which were always good for providing a bit of cover. His attention was drawn to a young woman on his right, who was struggling with a young child in one hand, and a pushchair containing a baby in the other, at the foot of the escalators leading up to Birmingham Shopping Centre.

He watched the woman as she struggled to make a decision. Either side of the escalators there were stairs, but she couldn't possibly carry the pushchair and the child up them. At the same time the child seemed to be frightened to step onto the moving escalators, and the woman was clearly anxious.

Ryan strode over, "It's alright luv I'll give you a hand. Give me the pushchair and you take the little un."

He didn't wait for a response but the relief on the woman's face was enough - and a part of him felt an inner-warmth at doing someone a good deed.

As they reached the top, Ryan reached into his pocket, took out some copper coins and presented them to the child, "Get yourself some sweets to chobble," and turned to the woman, smiled broadly and said, "See you luv. Take it steady."

He didn't wait for a response – 'knights in shining armour' did not look for rewards, and he swept back down the escalators and onto the concourse, without the schizophrenic nature of his chivalrous act, compared with the way he treated his wife, occurring to him.

Another ten minutes, and Ryan was starting to get bored with the lack of activity – just time for a piss and then he would make a move.

Ryan brought a platform ticket from the little red machine next to the ticket barrier and presented it to a disinterested black-capped ticket inspector who sat in a little box like a sentry.

He went through, turned left on the overbridge to the gent's toilets, and once inside turned right up a couple of steps to where the urinals were situated.

He'd been bostin for a piss and as he stood there relieving himself, thinking about his brief encounter, his sense of peace was broken by a young lad, no more than seventeen years of age, who came in and stood at the next urinal.

'That's fuckin weird. The place is empty and this cunt has come and stood next to me,' Ryan thought.

The young lad smiled at him weakly. Thin build and scruffy,

he looked like he could do with a good wash and a proper meal.

His eyes lowered towards Ryan's penis, which was just in the process of being shaken a few times.

"Do you want to do a bit of business?" the young lad said softly, "We could go into one of the toilets. I could give you a wank for a couple of quid or a bit more if you want. I've got a condom?"

The sheer cheek of this kid thinking he was a bender! Ryan zipped himself up and took one step towards him, "I hate queers and rent-boys you little twat. This is all you're gonna get from me." His anger was immediate and relentless.

He nutted the lad, who let out a short scream.

As he reeled back against the urinal, the rent-boy received a chop to the neck and went down in a heap on the tiled floor. Ryan grabbed his head by the hair, pulled him up, and forced it into the urinal, then for good measure kicked him in the balls, and spat on him.

Ryan pronounced perversely, "Up the Villa" as if somehow this attack had been done in the name of the 'beautiful game', and his team, and strode off.

As Ryan left the toilets, he saw the attendant in his glass-walled office reach for the phone. The man had heard the scream but knew better than to poke his nose into some of the things that went on. He was there to use a mop and bucket, not to get involved.

It was time for Ryan to make an exit and he was already

striding across the concourse towards the Manzoni Gardens entrance as two of the 'mac brigade' passed him walking slowly towards the barriers.

Just a slight change of plan – for some reason he decided to go home first to see Roseanne before his meet. He couldn't explain it to himself but he just wanted to see what she was doing.

He also wanted to change his clothes just in case the 'queer boy' decided to make a complaint.

***

'Birmingham Sunday Observer - *1 February 1976*:

Nicholl injury blow for Villa: The conditions were miserable, the risk of a broken leg in the icy conditions was high, the players were brave, but couldn't stop Villa falling to their first home defeat in thirteen League games. In the final analysis, Queens Park Rangers had more skill, and that made the difference. Villa do have an excuse, they lost key man Nicholl in the thirty-fourth minute after he fell heavily and dislocated his shoulder. Even worse, it looks like he could be out for a month.

Leighton Phillips acted as a makeshift defender and John Deehan replaced Nicholl. Villa stood firm until the seventy-sixth minute when John Hollins scored his first for QPR after Dave Thomas beat two defenders to set him up with a simple goal. England winger Thomas then repeated the feat in the ninetieth minute for Gerry Francis to make it 2-0.'

***

'Birmingham Sunday Observer - 1 February 1976:

A cruel ending for Blues: In a body blow to Birmingham City, referee John Homewood gave Archie Styles his marching orders near to the end of the match for a foul on Steve Coppell. Styles appeared reluctant to leave the pitch and upon being eventually persuaded to do so by his team-mates he gestured to the Manchester United fans, eliciting a barrage of booing. There was more confusion, as it appeared that the referee had also sent off Withe in the melee, but it appears not so, although the referee refused to clarify what had happened following the match, stating ' No comment, I shall fill in the relevant forms and that is all'.

It was a poor ending to a game that Blues gave away in the first half before mounting a fight back in the second - then crashing again just before the final whistle. The conditions were difficult, with a frozen pitch making any control of the ball almost impossible.

United's first strike came in the thirty-sixth minute when a corner from Daly was not cleared by Gallagher. Forsyth pounced and smashed the ball into the roof of the net. They went two up in the forty-fifth minute when Hill dispossessed Calderwood and swung the ball into the area. Macari and Latchford both went for the ball but Macari got there first, rounded the keeper and scored, despite strenuous appeals for offside from the Blues players.

Blues were a different team after the break. Francis, Withe and Burns began to link well, with Burns hitting the post from a Kendall corner. Blues were back in the match in the sixtieth minute when a pinpoint Francis corner found Withe, who netted with a glancing header.

Blues put the United defence under siege, but a point remained beyond their grasp as a Gallagher mistake in the eighty-eighth minute let United in. Under pressure, he played a ball across the area that found Mcilroy rather than a team-mate and the United striker struck it home. The game's unruly end involving Styles' sending off and reaction left the Blues fans furious for their journey home.'

***

Tony Carter sat in one of the carriages on the train heading south from Manchester, accompanied by three of the main boys, and pondered whether he had gone too far.

Full of anger after the scuffling and sending off of Styles at the end of the game, he had deliberately headed into the city after the match with Manchester United. He hadn't been totally sure what he wanted to do, but he was burning inside and wanted to leave some sort of mark before he left the city. He knew it was dangerous, isolated as they were, so he stopped at a pub that looked reasonably safe, whilst he considered his options.

He had also wanted to calm down and avoid being herded like cattle back to Manchester Piccadilly Railway Station by some over-aggressive young coppers itching to get their pegs out. The mood Tony was in, he would end up in a cell for the night with a few bruises from those truncheons and the odd police boot.

He had sailed a bit close to the wind at the last couple of matches and nearly got nicked. He resolved to adopt a lower profile if only for a few weeks.

The four of them had sat in the pub chatting about the game, about tarts and shagging and cracking silly jokes, with one eye trained on the door just in case any of the opposition appeared. It had been drilled into them by Mike Carter – back to the wall, always in sight of the front door, always a planned exit, and never ever leave a mate.

They were soldiers. It felt more like being in Northern Ireland than Manchester – different types of war – same tactics, except that these were being played out to the tune of the latest number one, 'Mamma Mia', on the jukebox in the background.

They were just finishing their second pint, and ordered a third, when a young lad came into the lounge in a wheelchair. Maybe no more than seventeen years old, he managed the wheels expertly and with confidence. He was clearly well known by the bar staff and chatted away oblivious to the four strangers. The Manchester United scarf wrapped around his neck, to stave off some of the cold, made it clear where his allegiance lay.

Tony Carter watched him with interest, not much of a challenge but the bastards deserved what they got after booing Styles like that. The irresistible urge for some sport rose to the surface and the resolution to keep his head down evaporated.

The lad left after half an hour, and as he did so Carter motioned for the other three to follow him.

The lad wheeled himself down the street and as he went to pass an alleyway Carter timed it nicely, "Scuse me mate have you got the time?"

The lad spun round and immediately realised that he had made a mistake as Carter took hold of the handles on the wheelchair and pushed him down the alley, the other three covering him from behind.

The lad was petrified and the small dark patch in the groin of his jeans indicated the depths of his fear.

Carter grinned as he played with the infamous flick-knife that now appeared before the lad's face, passing it from hand to hand.

The other three managed fixed grins – there would be no help forthcoming from that quarter. They knew better than to be on the receiving end of Tony Carter's mindless violence. It was good to have him next to you in a fight, but bad to have him facing you with that knife, which had drawn blood more than once.

Tony Carter was enjoying the fun, "We just want the scarf as a present, something to remember this shithole by. Nothing else – just hand it over."

The young lad struggled with the knotted scarf then passed it to him.

Without warning Carter tipped the wheelchair sideways and left the lad sprawled on the floor, "You picked the wrong team to support today you Spastic. Don't get rushing off anywhere will you! If I hear so much as a peep from you in the next five minutes I'll come back and stick this blade in. Comprende?"

The lad, unable to move and in pain from the fall, nodded sullenly. They left him in the gutter.

Carter jumped into the wheelchair and motioned to one of the other three, "Come on then, me old legs are feeling a touch knackered. Give us a bit of a push."

As they careered off, tears welled up in the young lads face – he had been humiliated and would suffer the pain again in his mind for many months to come. They abandoned the wheelchair half a mile from Piccadilly but not before Carter had pierced both tyres with his knife.

It was a quiet journey home – not much glory to talk about - just hidden shame to push to one side of the mind – but warped justification would soon prevail – after all the cripple was the enemy.

By the time they reached Birmingham, sub-zero temperatures and arctic winds had started to set in. Car radiators froze whilst the vehicles were being driven. House pipes and water mains burst. The unusually strong winds, combined with forty-eight hours of below freezing temperatures, served to freeze everything solid.

Tony Carter didn't feel the cold on his way home – there was nothing inside him that wasn't already frozen

Chapter Three

'Birmingham, are ya listening?'

February 1976

Greg Lyall aka 'Roly' farted in bed and lay bathed in the stench, which just added to the stale air in his disaster of a bedroom. His wardrobe was the floor and that's where his clothes lived when he wasn't wearing them.

His mother, a true Brummie from Bordesley Green, had long since given up on him and never crossed the threshold into the room, the focal point of which was a large union jack flag with *'BCFC Rule'* in black letters in the middle, nailed to the wall behind his bed.

Roly heaved his legs over the side of the bed and his belly followed. He had some business to do in town, and then tomorrow a home match to watch at St Andrews, with the chance of running a few 'Mancs'.

It was going to be a good weekend, although Roly didn't actually celebrate weekends, not having a job. His monthly Giro, coupled with shoplifting, provided his income and the football his life interest. He wasn't a superstitious man, so the fact that it was Friday the thirteenth did not dissuade him from today's enterprise.

Roly met 'Spike' and 'JC' on the ramp that led from Birmingham Shopping Centre to New Street at the junction with Corporation Street. They were a seasoned and practiced team so there wasn't much need for planning – just some small talk and banter and off they went.

The curious onlooker might have noticed that all three were carrying identical holdalls, but this was Birmingham City Centre and people had places to go and people to see – they minded their own business.

Greg and Spike headed straight for the back of Rackhams Store in Corporation Street, and up the side entrance steps to the gents clothing section.

'JC' remained outside near to the Cathedral with the three bags. It was open ground but it also meant he had a good view of the store and could see any coppers approaching from a distance.

It was a quick process as Spike held the black bin liner bag open to its full width. All of the coat-hangers were facing the same way and Greg simply placed his arms either side of ten nice striped jumpers, lifted them in one go and dropped them, hangers and all, into the bin bag. They were out of the store within two minutes and hurried back to 'JC' where the bag was dropped into one of the holdalls.

'JC' headed off towards Broad Street with the full bag, and Greg and Spike picked up the empty holdalls and split up, one towards New Street and the other towards Union Street.

***

Spike sat on the small bench fixed to the wall in the holding area, waiting to be checked into the custody block. Some smart-arsed store detective had given his description out over the shop-theft early warning radio system and he had been detained and picked up in minutes. He was already a repeat offender and he could feel Borstal looming. *'Keep calm'* he kept telling himself, they haven't found any gear, the bag's empty.

Five minutes later he was still sat on the bench feeling the walls starting to close in around him when the outer wooden door was flung open and Roly appeared - dragged into the holding area by two hot and flustered officers. Roly was protesting his innocence loudly. He only got the message to keep quiet when a swift dig in his capacious belly winded him, and he was forced onto the bench next to Spike.

"Sit down next to your mate," one of the officers ordered, as the other holdall was dumped onto the floor next to him.

"I've never met this twat before in me life!" Roly protested, through coughs and splutters.

"Yea, thats why the pair of you have identical bags you dick-head." the officer retorted.

Greg looked at Spike and couldn't control himself any longer – he burst out laughing and continued smiling all the way through the booking-in process that followed.

***

Francis and Burrell both felt that they were too good to be dealing with poxy shoplifters, but it was a means to an end.

Greg Lyall frustrated the hell out of them and got a couple more jabs for his insolence, but for some perverse reason they both agreed afterwards that he was a likable rogue.

Greg and Spike were both bailed from the station pending further enquiries and managed to get to the Manchester City game the next day game where 'JC' gave them their cut from the sale of the jumpers.

***

Birmingham Sunday Observer - *15 February 1976*:

'Super Kendall inspires Blues victory: The Blues, the perennial escape artists who make Houdini look like an amateur, have set themselves up for another First Division great escape. After this victory, a second successive home win, they are three points clear of their fellow strugglers. They made a terrible start, showing that the pressure was getting to them, and falling behind in the twelfth minute. But they did not go to pieces after Asa Hartford's magnificent goal, showing that they possess the grit and determination to survive.

Howard Kendall, their ex-skipper, stepped up to the mark in their time of need, providing the motivation they needed to mount the fight back. Kendall, was absolutely brilliant in midfield and led the recovery. He also scored his eighth goal of the season, the match winner, in the fifty-eighth minute. Before that, the equalizer was netted by centre-back Joe Gallagher in the forty-first minute. Beginning with a left wing corner curled dangerously into the area by Trevor Francis, England defender Dave Watson made failed to clear, and big Joe was there to strike the ball cleanly into the net.

The goal was crucial as it came just before the interval, pumping confidence back into Blues for the second half. The winner was a fine goal. Kendall surged down the right and his pass found Francis deep inside the Manchester penalty area. Francis returned the ball and Kendall slotted it into the corner. After that, Blues always looked like winners and City keeper Joe Corrigan denied Blues more goals.

There is still work to do before Blues can book another season in Division One, but now they have established a points cushion from the bottom teams they should be able to maintain that vital confidence for their final matches.'

***

Francis and Burrell sat in Rob Docker's office with the opened whisky bottle on the desk.Docker raised his glass – "Cheers lads."

***

On Saturday 21 February 1976, Aston Villa played Manchester United at home.

The 'Red Army' had a huge fan base and Colin Murphy knew well in advance that the match would attract hordes of away fans from all parts of the country to Villa Park.

He had made a general 'call to arms' for the day but given the numbers he knew they would face he decided to mass the firm for one determined action after the match had concluded. The venue was to be Yew Tree Road near to the ground, on one of the main routes to Witton Railway Station.

During the course of the game some of the Villa 'piss-heads' got involved in minor skirmishes on the terraces, and were picked off by the police – they made easy targets.

Murphy chose to keep his powder dry until afterwards.

The all-ticket game resulted in a 2-1 defeat for United and the stalwarts of the firm were buoyed by the team's success, and ready for action, as they made their way in small groups to the residential street. Word passed from 'mouth to mouth'. Soon more than one hundred waited for their prey.

Fifteen minutes after the match had ended some of United's main boys walked up the road towards them, and as Murphy shouted a rallying cry, each side surged forward. Terror erupted as the enemy factions rampaged between moving cars in the roadway, and tore through resident's front gardens.

A stone was thrown through the window of one house where a heart-attack victim lived. He was unable to get upstairs due to his condition, so normally slept on a bed in the living room. He should have been in his makeshift bed when a piece of tarmacadam was thrown through the window. Luckily he was in the back room at the time, but had to receive oxygen afterwards because of shock brought on by the attack.

At another house, fans put their elbows through the windows of the front living room where two small children were playing, showering them with pieces of glass, and reducing them to hysterics.

At yet another address in the road, a middle-aged woman braved the fury of the mob as she grabbed her snarling mongrel dog 'Tex', and stood guard for an hour in the street to protect her new £1,500 car from the baying crowds.

Nearby, another woman was hit on the shoulder, in her own garden, by a fan who ripped off a car wing-mirror and threw it at her, stopping just for a moment to hurl racist abuse at her Asian husband who ran outside upon hearing her screams.

Murphy finally signaled job done and his boys melted back into the crowds leaving the ground. The damage trail consisted of forty windows smashed, several cars damaged, and a fair few United fans nursing sore heads. Granted they had given as good as they had got, but Murphy was satisfied that the message had gone out – this was Villa territory.

The *'Battle of Yew Tree Road'*, as it came to be known, earned the Villa crew a lot of respect for standing up the 'Red Army'. *'A good afternoon's work,'* reflected Murphy.

Police later revealed that the cost of damage to forty-nine houses, seven cars and a bus in the Yew Tree Road area after the game was £1,000.

It cost £6,000 to police the match, with two hundred and fifteen officers on duty – Villa had to foot just one fifth of the bill.

***

Birmingham Observer – *Monday 23 February 1976*:

'Fans fined after Villa clash: Fourteen people were fined by Magistrates in Birmingham today after admitting offences in connection with Saturday's Aston Villa – Manchester United game. Fines ranged from £10 to £80. Seven other youths, including three juveniles, were remanded. The magistrates heard of youths fighting, throwing stones, jumping on other people's backs on the terraces and shouting and swearing.

Six of the youths were from Birmingham; six were from Manchester, and the remainder from various parts of the country including Coventry, Leamington, Folkestone and Lincolnshire. All pleaded guilty to using threatening words or behaviour. Two youths admitted disorderly conduct – urinating against a wall near a toilet in the Holte End at Villa Park.

At the City's juvenile court, four more youths appeared on charges in connection with Saturday's game. A fourteen year old from Gloucestershire admitted using threatening words and behaviour in the Witton End of the ground, and was ordered to pay £10. The youth was pushing the crowd and had been threatened by other fans as a result. Two others denied the charges and their cases were adjourned. The fourth youth, aged fifteen years, admitted using threatening words and behaviour in Queens Rd, Aston, after the match, and was remanded on bail for three weeks for reports.

The 'Battle of Yew Tree Road' could end in a recommendation to the FA banning Manchester United fans from visiting away games. A group of City Councillor's have been studying a dossier on the damage and fear caused. The group will meet the Chief Constable on Wednesday to try and find a solution.'

The press coverage suited Murphy fine, as the Manchester United fans took the brunt of the negative media. Residents called for police officers with dogs to barricade the residential streets during games, and threatened to set up vigilante groups to protect themselves.

After the violence, First Division soccer clubs in the Midlands were being asked by police to stage all-ticket games for future visits by Manchester United.

A letter was sent to Sports Minister, and Birmingham Small Heath MP, Dennis Howell, highlighting the problem of football violence in the City, and elsewhere Rob Docker pondered on the progress of his operation. He had already fielded a number of telephone calls from senior officers looking for some reassurance and in some cases a quick result.

Suddenly everyone was once again interested in football hooligans. *'Fucking typical,'* Docker reflected.

Rob Docker was used to handling pressure and would not knee-jerk. Reassurance yes, but his bosses would have to be patient. He didn't object to cutting some of the branches off the rotten trees that the two firms represented, but he also wanted to pull out the roots and rip them from the ground. His bosses would have to wait, and as he was in the driver's seat they had no option.

*****

Birmingham Observer - *Wednesday 25 February 1976:*

> *'Fighting Wolves team and the referee get to the right result*

in the end: Wolves had their backs to the wall, fighting for First Division survival, and in front of a 47,693 crowd at Villa Park last night they displayed a mean streak which earned them a 1-1 draw amid controversy.

Referee John Goggins allowed crunching tackles to go unpunished right from the start. Amazingly, a clutch of questionable decisions conspired to produce the right result. Why was a Chris Nicholl header disallowed in the first half? Should it have been a penalty for the tackle by John McAlle on Andy Gray? In the final analysis only the referee's decisions counted so that was it.

In the end Ray Graydon equalized from the spot, levelling John Richards' fifty-fourth minute strike, and Wolves supporters went home the more satisfied with a point from a scrappy affair.'

***

Ryan Murphy had actually thought twice about going to the game. He was torn between his desire to tackle the visitors from Wolverhampton, with the definite possibility of some 'afters' with the Blues fans in town later, versus not wanting to leave Roseanne alone for too long.

He had an increasingly nagging feeling that something was going on, but in the end he chose the more familiar ground of his friends and football – the 'beautiful game' always won.

After the match he got a train from Witton, making the short trip into Birmingham to get a couple of pints with Mel Price and Benny Doherty.

He didn't register Gary's absence, he was just a piece of the furniture now, not a main player at all. School was a long time ago, and whilst he knew that Mel had preserved a strong bond with Gary, and understood why, he now had little time for his former friend, whose weakness he saw clearly, and despised.

Ryan felt strangely passive. It had been a contentious match but he had been distracted because of Roseanne. His mood had changed. Besides, the main Wolves firm had been a no-show, despite efforts to arrange a 'meeting'. The alternative of fighting with a bunch of anoraks was no challenge, and would not result in any medals being awarded.

He knew some Blues might be about in town but he hoped that there would be no confrontation tonight. He wanted a quiet drink and chat with his best mates, and he intended to subtly question them about Roseanne and whether they had noticed anything strange going on. Then he would make tracks home early and see what she was doing.

The deviation into town was a decision he would come to regret.

Benny was in a playful mood and suggested going to the late showing at the 'Jacey' Cinema to watch *'Diary of a half virgin'*.

Ryan's response was direct, "Why would I want to sit with a load of old pervs jerking themselves off in the dark under their dirty macs when I've got a piece of warm arse at home." That was the end of the conversation.

Within ten minutes they were back in Birmingham, the pub

beckoned for a swift couple, then home early to 'surprise' Roseanne.

***

Tony Carter walked out of the ABC Cinema in New Street after his first evening in the back row with Naomi Green, best friend of his cousin, Joy. He had fancied her for ages but this was the first time she had agreed to a date. Tony liked to think that his growing reputation had something to do with it. Encouragingly, she was hanging onto his arm and the closeness of their bodies in the cinema had given him a right boner.

They had just seen *'Jaws'* which had been running for nine straight weeks to packed audiences. Naomi had seemed genuinely scared by some of the scenes and hung onto him in the seats – that suited Tony fine, he appreciated the warm feel of her body next to him, the physical proximity a step in the right direction. He had even managed to stray a hand a couple of times and cop a feel which she hadn't repelled too fast. Mind you, even he had jumped and the whole audience screamed when the man's head had floated out of the hole in the sunken boat – a great film!

He had already convinced himself that he was onto a good thing and at minimum was looking forward to a bit of 'sticky finger' on the back seat of the bus on the way home.

Straight from the jaws of the mechanical shark, he walked into the teeth of a real one, as he virtually bumped into Ryan in the street on the way out.

Carter's hackles rose immediately, and on his first real date with Naomi there was no way that he was going to lose face.

With Mel and Benny either side of him, Ryan looked mildly amused at Carter's obvious discomfort, although he was cursing his luck at bumping into the one person he didn't want to see tonight. They had a long history, and plenty of unfinished business.

With both palms held open towards Carter, Ryan attempted to avert a confrontation, much to the surprise of his two companions, "Before you start let's call this a night off, Carter. I'm in no mood for a scrap tonight. Let's pretend we didn't see each other and you can take your bird home and give her a good seeing to with no harm done."

Naomi reacted, "You cheeky bastard. I'm not some slag you know."

Benny, emboldened by the presence of Ryan, and slightly confused by his leader's apparent reluctance to fight, intervened, "Shut up bitch and take this piece of scum with you. He looks like he's ready to piss his pants."

Carter lashed out and caught Benny off-balance with a good punch to the side of the head, sending him reeling backwards.

Ryan wanted this like a hole in the head, but decided to try and finish it quickly. He squared up to Carter as Naomi tugged at Tony's sleeve, trying to pull him away.

Carter half-turned towards her, trying to shrug her annoying, clawing hands off him, but in that moment of distraction Ryan caught him with a hard blow to the stomach, and then dead-legged him in the right upper leg. Carter went down.

Mel scooped Benny up from the floor as Ryan straightened himself and walked off towards High Street, without looking back.

As Carter struggled to his feet winded, Naomi continued to fuss around him, "Leave me alone you stupid cow. If you hadn't of pulled my arm I'd have had him. I've been after a showdown with that cocky bastard for ages." Carter had lost face and laid the blame completely at her door.

As Ryan disappeared into High Street Carter screamed, "I'll have you, you bastard – anytime!"

Ryan deliberately ignored the bait and turned to Mel, "Change of plan. Let's go to the Cedar Club for a few bevvies. It looks like Benny could do with a 'pick me up' – he laughed at his own joke.

**

Naomi sat in silence next to Carter on the bus home. The prospects of any romantic encounter were long since gone as he nursed a heavily bruised ego. She was silently asking herself what on earth was she doing with this strutting popinjay, who had fallen on his backside at the first blow.

She had heard of his reputation in the disapproving comments of her best friend Joy, who was his cousin, but he hadn't lived up to it. Joy Carter hated the violence, and wished her cousin Tony, who she was close to, was not such an arch- proponent of it. She had told Naomi many times that Tony would end badly if he carried on, but of course that had been some of the allure that had led to this date. It was true that the girls often fancied a rogue, but

Naomi had decided that this was her first and only night out with Tony Carter.

***

The Cedar Club had lived up to its reputation for a good night out, and Ryan alighted from the taxi at 2 am. He sensed that something was wrong as he approached the house, which was in complete darkness. He should have been home hours ago, but it wasn't the first time he had come home pissed, and she always left a light on downstairs if she took herself off to bed.

He keyed the door and shouted up the stairs, "Roseanne I'm back."

The chill of the empty house hit him as he bounded upstairs to check their bedroom before making his way to the kitchen.

On the table lay a plain white envelope with his name on.

He tore it open, an inner-panic starting to rise from his stomach. It quickly turned to anger.

It read simply, *'Ryan, I am sorry but I cannot take any more. I have left you and won't be coming back. Please do not try to find me.'*

He screwed the note up and swept the washing up she had left off the drainer and across the kitchen. Cups and plates smashed as they struck the wall. He already knew that she would not do this on her own - somebody had got into her knickers and head, and there would be a reckoning for that person and his errant wife. She would be coming back alright, and staying and paying for the rest of her life, however long that lasted, and his intentions towards the lover were murderous.

***

Pete Stevens had taken some persuading to spend his Saturday with Tony Carter at the National Front march, but Tony had finally convinced him that it was going to be a good ruck, and hopefully they would be able to crack the heads of a few 'Pakis' or 'WOGs' in the process.

Saturday 28 February 1976 was going to be a quiet day for the Blues firm with a game at home with Norwich, who had next to no firm themselves. There would not be much sport with the few country yokels who might turn up. Mike Carter had declared it to be a day of rest and Tony had seized his chance to drum up support for the short train trip to Coventry.

In truth, many of the boys had no trouble at all with the colour of people's skin, but Tony would have no truck with any suggestion of bringing non-whites into the firm.

Today, as Tony sat with Pete in a carriage for the thirty minute journey, together with half a dozen of the up and comers, he felt a sense of excitement. Today, Tony Carter was the main man and calling the shots. One day he would have the job full-time.

None of them had noticed the scruffily dressed Special Branch officer monitoring their movements on the platform prior to departure.

On arrival at Coventry Railway Station they made their way through the barrier, and onto the small glass enclosed concourse where a couple of British Transport Police officers were monitoring passengers, then out into the cold February air.

The group made their way to the National Front's party headquarters in London Road, in Coventry City Centre. Tony Carter was keen to be seen by the local NF head man, who was standing in the local by-election, and rubbed his hands enthusiastically to ward off the cold. He exchanged pleasantries with a small knot of other like-minded men, none of whom would have won a beauty competition, and felt good.

They waited outside the building for the main-man to emerge with some other national figures, but as they stepped out into the street it all started to go wrong.

From nowhere, a seventy-strong group of left-wing socialist supporters, who had managed to avoid a major police blockade, launched themselves at the NF party members and Tony Carter's group, who found themselves under attack from all sides.

One lone policeman on duty at the scene was caught up in the attack. Beaten to the ground and bloodied, he eventually managed to get to his feet and grappled with one of his attackers. He hung on to his prisoner for dear life as he screamed for assistance on his radio.

As the one-sided attack continued, several of the up and comers were hit by stones and sticks. They had bottle though, and stood their ground, with Pete keeping them in a tightly-knit defensive group, whilst Tony lost control completely and ran headlong into the middle of their attackers.

Pete needed to act, ordering the youngsters to stand firm with their backs against the building wall, and then he hurled himself after Tony, *'Fuck this for a game of soldiers,'* he thought, as he found the collar of Tony's shirt and yanked him from the melee and back towards the building.

Pete took control, "Tony we need to get out of this – some of these kids have had a good battering. They won't stand up to much more. I vote we go home."

Tony Carter was seething, but as he looked at the battered crew, the red mist went from him.

Meanwhile, Socialists swarmed jubilantly away from the building and headed to Coventry Cathedral Square, where they joined up with some seven hundred comrades to spread the good news – the NF had been given a bloody nose and that would be today's headline.

Half a mile away, hundreds of police officers, including twelve mounted officers, guarded a park where some nine hundred NF supporters were gathering to greet their leaders.

Their mood hardened as news of the attack on their leaders spread.

This had been the biggest deployment of police resources in Coventry since the funeral of James McDade, the IRA bomber, as they feared a repeat of scenes in London in which a Coventry student had been killed.

As police officers later fought to keep the warring parties apart, two further arrests were made for offences under the Public Order Act, but overall the police operation had been a great success.

Carter had been mute and glowering on the way back to the station, but he finally came out of his shell on the train back to Birmingham, "We gave as good as we got didn't we?"

Pete looked at him soothingly; this was not a moment for fighting amongst themselves, "We did Tony, and the lads here did well. Fuck knows what the coppers were thinking leaving just one copper there. The dozy fuckers couldn't plan a piss up in a brewery."

Tony laughed through his split lip and grimaced – now everyone was laughing, as the tension lifted. Pete cuffed one of the youngsters who was sporting a decent black eye, "You did the firm proud son – well done."

***

Mike Carter was not best pleased when he heard that some of his boys had been hurt.

He wasn't into this NF crap, and if it wasn't for the fact that Tony was the son of his brother he would have dished out some 'words of advice' – the kid was getting to be a problem.

***

Elsewhere that day, three men joined together by an unholy alliance sat in the bar at Steelhouse Lane Police Station watching the news on the BBC,

'Ex Yard chiefs accused. Former Sweeney Chief Kenneth Drury was among twelve top Scotland Yard detectives charged today with conspiring to accept bribes from porn merchants. They were all arrested in an early morning swoop and were bailed to appear at London's Bow Street Court on Monday.

The twelve, all retired or suspended from duty, include ex Flying Squad chief Drury, former Obscene Publications Squad Head, Detective Chief Superintendent Bill Moody, and Commander Wallace Virgo, former head of the Yard's Murder Squad and holder of the Queen's police medal and twenty-five commendations. The investigations stem from claims by Soho porn and strip king James Humphreys and his wife June 'Rusty' Humphreys....'

As the commentator droned on Rob Docker, Malcom Reid, and Nigel Francis sat in silence until the report had finished, "Your round I think Malcolm," Docker directed him to the bar.

Francis looked at Docker – it was not necessary to repeat the obvious but nevertheless he did, "Silly bastards got greedy," he said.

Docker nodded. He had done far worse and got away with it, but the anti-corruption bastards seemed to be on a mission, including in his own force. His tactic of working through third parties who were ignorant of each other had worked so far though. He reminded himself to take extra care on any 'visits' to criminals that he made himself in the future.

Upstairs, John Burrell was just booking off-duty after a long day and had deliberately avoided the session in the bar. He had other plans with Sally – the Gay Tower Ballroom in Reservoir Road, in

Edgbaston.

It was Leap Year's Eve, and there was dancing on from 8pm until 2am. He had made it clear to Sally that the emphasis would be on fun and that he would not be expecting her to go down on one knee or to make any surprise announcements from the revolving stage!

Chapter Four

'You'll Never Walk Alone'

March 1976

Ryan was hunting. He had woken up the morning after Roseanne left with a hangover and a different kind of anger. The fiery rage had been suppressed beneath an icy and deadly intent during the night he had spent alone.

The reality of Roseanne's betrayal had hit him hard as he lay in the marital bed - the only sound in the house, the blood pounding in his temples. The familiar sounds of her clattering around, cooking his breakfast, were absent; as was the cup of coffee she usually served him in bed.

He switched on the transistor radio at the side of his bed and *'Save your kisses for me'* by the Brotherhood of Man came on. He was sick of hearing it, bloody rubbish. In a sudden eruption of rage he hurled the radio across the bedroom, smashing it against the wall.

He had genuinely loved Roseanne, at least thought he did, although his love had manifested itself as obsession and control, but he couldn't see that. His emotional blindness was part of the legacy that his father had carved into his upbringing, a replay of Colin Murphy's own relationships. And now Roseanne had dared to challenge him, to humiliate him.

He felt the shame keenly. No-one had dared to say anything

to his face, but he fancied that he could hear the sniggering behind his back, the jokes, and the whispers. The great leader and fighter Ryan Murphy, fucked over by a woman, and almost as bad, made to look a fool by that treacherous wanker Gary Docker.

It was in his mind constantly, and as the days passed, the fire fought with the ice trying to break free, the two elements combining into an obsessive determination for revenge on them both, and anyone who had helped them. Ryan knew that he was already out of control, and in a lethal mood, but any boundaries within him disappeared when he thought about confronting Gary Docker. He lay awake at night planning what he would do when he found him, relishing the thought of the pain he would inflict.

He had started the hunt with those closest to him, but it was clear that Benny and Mel knew nothing and were as surprised as he was. They were intensely loyal - had always been, and he trusted them with his life. They were 'deputised' into the hunt, and demonstrated a determination to avenge their leader's hurt almost as intense as Ryan's own. Their stars were tied to his and he was able to 'vent' to them, explaining his intentions in graphic detail.

Mel had tried to advise Ryan to not ruin his own life with a lengthy prison sentence but Ryan had brushed him away, reiterating his determination to 'finish' Docker once and for all, whatever the consequences.

His father had reacted predictably. Colin Murphy saw everything through a prism of physical and emotional control, respect and reputation, overlain with a shell of hypocritical Catholicism. He espoused the type of religious devotion that manifested itself in the slavish following of traditions, whilst violence and dishonesty could be absolved in the confessional.

Colin saw the elopement of Roseanne and Gary Docker as a problem for himself and his organisation. His son had been disrespected, and so had the family name and reputation. His religion had been besmirched. A visible reckoning was demanded, and his son needed to deliver it, but Colin would help, his reputation was at risk as well. People had to know that he couldn't be crossed like this, or things would begin to fall apart.

It had taken a couple of weeks to confirm that Gary Docker was the other party. Ryan had to admit that the missing couple had been very good at hiding the relationship. He gave himself a mental kicking every day, and resolved never to ignore his instincts again. *'I knew, didn't I, knew something was up. I could have stopped it before it went too far.'* Now it was too late. There was no way back for Gary, and Ryan had plans for the rest of Roseanne's life when he retrieved her.

Gary had become chief suspect after he failed to appear at any gathering or football match over the week following Roseanne's flight. Ryan, Mel and Benny had interrogated everyone, and finally two of the youngsters had independently recounted small nuggets of information that seemed to confirm Ryan's suspicions.

One had seen Docker in deep conversation with Roseanne on a street corner, and thought it odd, another had witnessed a seemingly casual physical contact, just a non-accidental brushing of hands at a party, and had filed it away, resolving to watch for something more, then curry favour with Ryan by reporting his suspicions. The disappearance had occurred before he had done so. Mel had been shocked and disbelieving at this evidence of his best friend's treachery.

The two sightings were enough. Ryan knew that Roseanne couldn't have vanished without help, and Docker had family connections to some tasty people. And they *had* both vanished as if the earth had swallowed them up. They were not in Birmingham, or nearby, or they would have been trapped by now, Colin Murphy's local contacts were good. No, some careful planning had gone into this, and he doubted that Gary had the wit to do it all himself either.

Ryan was correct to a point in his assumptions, but he had continually underestimated Roseanne, and he did so now by assuming that Gary had been assisted by his father and his Handsworth connections, when his wife had in fact been the organiser of her own flight. She, after all, knew the stakes involved better than anyone.

As the weeks passed without any trace, Ryan bent his enquiries towards the Docker family, and now he was focused upon the father, Charlie Docker, and had struck more frustration.

Confirming Ryan's suspicions, Docker senior was proving very difficult to locate. Rumour had it that he was ill, but Ryan discounted that. His market stall was empty and attempts to infiltrate the 'Hole In The Wall' club that Charlie 'fronted' as licensee had been repulsed out of hand by Docker's spook mates. The home address was empty and locked.

Ryan's frustration and venom built. He had noticed that his

normal 'cool', his long fuse, so useful in a fight or planning, had been replaced with a reckless violence that he was trying to control. At recent football skirmishes he had fought his rage down on more than one occasion before he went too far. At night, alone in their bed, he laid awake, imagining pain and death.

***

The truth that Ryan could never comprehend was that Charlie was totally innocent.

Roseanne had planned everything, and Gary had been her agent. Roseanne had good fortune in her choice of lover because Gary, despite his limitations on the violence front, was popular and connected. He was at heart a decent man, and it was only his friendship with Mel and the coincidence of being classmate of Ryan, and the rebelliousness of teenage years, that had drawn him into the football hooligan scene.

Gary also had an asset in his father Charlie who was liked and respected by everyone, especially the Handsworth blacks who also revered Gary's cousin, Joe Docker, and would never forget that Charlie was the first white man to help them in Birmingham.

Charlie's credit within the black community extended to Gary, who had been brought up amongst them, had many of them as friends, and could count on them in a time of need. They had also seen him help Mel through the bullying and persecution of schooldays, and that honest friendship had won Gary much credit.

When Roseanne wanted new identities for them both, Gary knew someone who could get the necessary documentation forged.

They did it all the time to get 'associates' from the Caribbean into the country.

When Roseanne identified a safe place to run to for their new life together, a town with no local football groups, Gary was able to locate rooms to rent.

Whatever she wanted, he sorted, whilst she stayed at home like a good little wife and kept Ryan's attention elsewhere.

Charlie Docker knew nothing until the day after the disappearance, when he found a note from his son on the kitchen table. In it, his son explained his love for Roseanne and the decision they had made. Gary had known that the spotlight would fall onto his father, and this was his warning. The letter didn't say where his son had gone, but Charlie knew that no-one would believe that, especially not the Murphys.

Charlie had lived amongst criminals and gangsters all his life, and had no illusion about the pain that could come the way of his family. He was a great believer in the healing power of time, had called in a couple of favours and taken his wife on a holiday in Jamaica for a few weeks, hosted by friends. He was now in the sun, hoping that the heat back home would die down. Charlie actually couldn't imagine that his son was capable of remaining hidden for long, but a few weeks head-start without worrying about his dad would help.

Charlie knew that he couldn't stay away forever, but his experience told him that these sorts of problems tended to quickly resolve or evaporate, albeit occasionally via the evaporation of those causing the problem.

In this case he was wrong, and it would cost him dearly.

***

Pete Stevens reached for his diary,

'6 March – played West Ham away. Another long day but at least we won 1-0. Up to a hundred fans with some of the firm went by train. Not enough for a good ruck. Mike decided to stay in Brum and left Greg, and Sam to run the ship. Train pretty full. A bit of damage on the way down. Greg liberated a few light bulbs out of the window and Sam ripped some of the seats to shreds with his knife. Loads of police on platform at Euston. Tried pushing us about but we got into Eversholt Street and then went down to St Pancras. Stayed together. We tried to break away from the police in Euston Road but the Met were having none of it. A lot of mean-looking faces. Some police dogs at the barriers but walked through and got the Northern Line to Moorgate. Sam and Greg kept the boys tight. At Moorgate pushed our way out of station into Fore Street looking for a pub to base ourselves in. Too early for Upton Park. Got pushed back by the police to Moorgate and tried to make us pay for tickets. Dogs and Vans everywhere. Back on Tube to Upton Park with police escort. Off the tube and passed the Queens Pub some West Ham tried to have a ruck but were pushed back inside. Greg was doing his usual worst impressions of a cockney. Escorted to the ground. Us one side of the road and West Ham the other. Police in the middle. Plenty of 'wanker' signs. One of the boys got nicked just for doing this. Green Street packed with shoppers and souvenir sellers. In Castle Street a load of horses and we were searched on the way in.

Sam had to ditch 'Stanley' but he's got plenty more. After the match they bussed us back to Euston. No sport except watching Greg nick all the toilet rolls on the train on the way back. He says he's gonna sell them to his mum. Can't help but like the wanker. A couple of bored railway coppers on the train. The firm bunched together. The usual reception committee waiting for us back at New Street Station.'

***

On Saturday 13 March 1976, Birmingham City were playing at St Andrews against Liverpool, and Aston Villa were tackling Spurs at White Hart Lane.

Two days before the matches, Titch and Spike were summoned to Mike Carter's council house fortress.

Carter did not make a practice of inviting every 'Tom, Dick and Harry' into his home, but he needed to get this right, and wanted to make sure that the youngsters were well-briefed, motivated and focused. At sixteen years of age, the two 'up and comers' were desperate to impress their leader and sat in awed silence drinking in the privilege of actually being invited into his home.

They had been ushered into the kitchen, sneaking glances into the living room where Joy lay on a settee reading *'Catcher in the Rye'* for her English A Level studies. In the background the radio, on low, was playing *'I Love to Love -but my baby just loves to dance'* by Tina Charles.

Joy was yet to experience the first emotion but was well up for the second and although tightly supervised by her parents she loved the idea of immersing herself in music. She had heard about a new disco at the Chalet Country Club, in Rednal, with half price drinks, called *'Deano's Disco'* and was currently working on her father to see if she could go. It was proving to be an uphill battle.

Titch and Spike had both heard rumours about the daughter of Mike Carter and would be able to claim some status amongst their peers by confirming that she was as beautiful as reported.

Now they were facing Carter, eyeing some rather curious items displayed before them on the kitchen table– four Aston Villa scarves!

Mike Carter was a good tactician. The skill separated him from the herd and was one of the reasons that he had risen to be leader. He had read lots of books about famous battles and knew that the skill was not in how many soldiers you had but what you did with them, supported by information regarding the enemy and combined with as much of the element of surprise as could be arranged. His latest plan was audacious and could yield a large dividend in kudos. He couldn't wait to see what would happen. Now he locked eyes with the eager young faces on the other side of the table,

"I've got a really big job for you two lads if you're up for it. If you pull it off, *'Shit on the Villa'*, will take on a whole new meaning, and you two will be getting a shitload of praise. What do you say?" Carter paused.

Two vigorous nods were enough, as Carter continued,

"On Saturday I want you to travel down to Euston with some

of the Villa boys. Wear one of these scarves each and carry the other one. Just mingle and keep your heads down, you're not that well-known yet, so as long as you don't start singing *'Keep Right On'* like a pair of wankers you should be okay."

Carter laughed at his own joke then paused again for effect before passing some cash for train tickets, and a piece of paper with a phone number on, to Titch, before going into yet further detail,

"When you get there get yourself a bite to eat, no alcohol and just wait for the Villa shit to come back to Euston. When you know which train they're traveling on, you phone that number, it's The Crown in Station Street, and then ask for me. On the way back tie the scarves on the outside of four of the coach door-handles, on the right-hand side, and then find a seat close to the engine at the front and stay there, to the left-hand side."

Carter rehearsed things with his two excited secret agents twice more before he was satisfied with the arrangements.

***

On Saturday morning, Titch and Spike duly met on the concourse at New Street Station. In truth they were shitting themselves, but the chance to be a 'somebody' and move up the ranks was just too good to miss.

They had the money from Carter to purchase two adult return tickets, but had decided that they could 'liberate' some cash for booze without Carter ever knowing. After all, why pay full price when all they had to do was get some kid wandering around the station to get them two child's tickets for under-fourteens? That was mistake number one.

Tickets purchased, they passed through the barrier and hovered around the station overbridge awaiting the traveling Villa hordes that didn't take too long to appear. The two excited undercover operatives merged with the claret and blue clad chanting masses, and the human tide swept them down the metal-rimmed steps onto the grimy characterless platform. Within minutes they were on their way to London Euston.

Carter had given them specific instructions not to drink, but Titch and Spike had just started to acquire the taste of lager. With a couple of hours to waste on arrival in the big city, and cash in their pockets from their ticket 'scam', they went in search of a sympathetic 'off-licence' and some courage in a bottle.

The Villa group, numbering some two hundred, noisily entered the underground and disappeared without anyone noticing the two abscondees.

A couple of cans wouldn't do any harm would it? Mistake number two.

***

At around about 2pm, as Titch and Spike were dispensing with their third can each, sat on a bench in the gardens outside the front of Euston, Mike Carter was briefing his lieutenants back in Birmingham.

Tony Carter would remain in Birmingham City Centre with the main crew and keep 'JC' close to him, affectionately nicknamed because he couldn't stop shouting 'Jesus Fucking Christ' every time that they got into a ruck.

Greg Lyall aka Roly would make his way to Coventry with four of the youth element, who looked up to him with awe and fear.

Sam Wild was given orders to be at Curzon Street by 6.30pm with some more of the 'up and comers'. He wasn't called 'Stanley' because of some witty reference to Oliver Hardy, but rather because of his dexterity with the vicious craft knife of hooligan choice.

They had plenty of time on their hands but if all went well this would be worth waiting for.

***

Mike Carter had just one more thing to do, and made his way with Pete Stevens to a pub in the City Centre, where his spotters had told him the main Liverpool firm was holding court prior to making their way to St. Andrews.

He knew he was taking a calculated risk, but these were the moments that gave him the highest adrenalin rush, so in he strode. Pete was there purely for effect, and to test his bottle. He had been told to keep his mouth shut.

As they entered the bar area all eyes turned on them as Carter went straight for the main man and stuck his hand out.

He might as well have been holding manure in his hand as the man facing him looked on with complete contempt and ranks closed around them.

"I'm Mike Carter." He announced.

"I know who you are you fuckin cunt. You've got some brass neck coming in here," his foe countered.

"This is my patch and I'll go where I like you Scouser twat," Carter countered, then continued, "Just to let you know we have other business today so it's a no-show from us."

The Liverpudlian sneered, "Fucking wimps – I ought to take your head off here and now."

Carter kept his cool, "Call it an adjournment – this is me number. Phone me after today and we can fix a firm meet. Anywhere suits me fine." he slapped a piece of paper onto the bar and turned to leave.

His opposition judged the moment – beating the fuck out of two outnumbered Bluenoses would give them no credibility, and in truth he admired Carter's 'brass neck', "Fuck off cunt – I'll be in touch," he called after their backs as they left.

Plan in place, Mike still had time to make St Andrews before kick-off.

***

Birmingham Sunday Observer - *14th March 1976*:

'Blues fans seethe as luck runs out: Blues 0-1 Liverpool. Blues fans were left seething with a deep sense of injustice by events that resulted in them being dragged back to within one point of the

relegation places. The feeling was made even worse by the news that Wolves had won away at Sheffield United to close the gap in the relegation battle.

Kenny Burns and Archie Styles were out suspended, and goalkeeper Dave Latchford was a late injury due to a groin strain. To compound the problems, Howard Kendall was stretchered off in the second half. Then there was the disputed penalty in the last few minutes that cost them the match. A Jimmy Case shot was going wide; there was a jostle at the far post and horror around St Andrews when referee Alan Robinson pointed to the spot. Phil Neal converted to the left of nineteen-year-old Steve Smith, a late debutant due to the injury to Latchford. Due to the injured absentees, Blues adopted a defensive stance and Malcolm Page succeeded in keeping Keegan quiet all afternoon. They rode their luck but it ran out right at the end.'

***

At 6pm, Titch made the phone call from a box on the concourse at Euston. The main Villa crew would be leaving by train within fifteen minutes. Message passed, both he and Spike got in the queue with their new and very unhappy Villa 'friends'. They soon picked up the gist of what had gone wrong at the game.

***

Birmingham Sunday Observer – *14th March 1976*:

'It's a nightmare for Villa as Spurs cut them apart: Spurs 5-2 Villa. A dismal show left Villa on the wrong end of a hammering at White Hart Lane, and still looking for their first away win of the

127

season. They lost their way after one or two bright moments. Cut to ribbons at the back, lacking initiative and composure in midfield, and with only the ever -alert Andy Gray posing any sort of threat up front

. Villa's plans, whatever they were, got upset by a freak 23rd minute goal when Coates cut inside and shot. Burridge appeared to have it covered but the ball hit Chris Nicholl and cannoned into the net. Villa equalised six minutes later, when Little crossed under intense pressure and Graydon converted, but Spurs were back in front 60 seconds later through Perryman. Pat Jennings made a great save from Andy Gray's header but Spurs scored a third 4 minutes before half time and looked out of sight. Perryman robbed Little, passed to Duncan, whose shot beat Burridge.

Villa started the second half well, and Andy Gray headed their second and for a while they looked the better side. But it was Spurs who provided the barnstorming finish. In the 65th minute McAllister forced the ball in from a Coates corner and eighteen year old Martin Robertson provided the final indignity after Coates tore through the Villa defence and crossed, leaving the youngster a simple task of netting. Villa nearly scored again, but Jennings was in fine form to deny Graydon and Hamilton.

After the whistle teenage girls tried to mob pop idol David Cassidy who watched the game, Villa might have been better off if he had played!'

***

Three cans had become four – mistake number three was about to become mistake number four, as someone in the queue stepped back unexpectedly and stood on Spike's foot. The alcohol took control of his rash response.

"Fuck off you stupid cunt," Spike shouted as he pushed the man back. Unfortunately, his expletives drew the attention of an ultra-keen young British Transport Police officer, who was anxious for a 'body', and just happened to be passing at that moment.

Spike was bundled out of the queue and given a dressing-down. It was time to keep his mouth shut but the earlier errors were now compounding themselves.

"Let's see your ticket," the officer demanded, and as Spike fumbled in his pockets to produce the child's ticket the alcohol once more got the better of his common sense, "You ain't proper fucking coppers, just fucking ticket collectors," he spat out the words.

The man in blue wasn't about to take such cheek from a Brummie kid. He gripped Spike firmly by the back of his neck and frog-marched him off towards the BTP Police Office at the far end of the concourse. Titch's heart sank as he forlornly watched his friend disappear - he was on his own and he suddenly didn't feel so brave.

***

The train rattled through Watford, and the Villa firm couldn't believe their luck. With just five coppers on the packed train there was little they could do to control the language, the chants and the drinking.

Just past Rugby, Titch pulled the windows of two train doors down and tied the scarves onto the 'slam-lock' mechanism. The carriage was too rammed with Villa fans to allow him passage to the front so he took refuge in one of the toilets. Boredom combined with alcohol and a sudden surge of misplaced bravado and he busied himself covering the walls in graffiti with the marker pen he always carried in his sock – *'Shit on the Villa', 'Up The Blues' 'BCFC' 'The Kop Rules OK'* – Titch couldn't resist it, and imagined himself crowing about his valour in front of Mike Carter in the pub later.

As the football special slowed to go through Coventry Railway Station, target carriages marked by the Villa scarves flying from the door handles, Titch heard the sound of breaking glass and screams as Greg Lyall and his small group launched a volley of missiles at the train from the island platform. It was point-blank range and the Villa fans were showered in glass shards, bricks and lumps of rubble.

Titch rubbed his hands with excitement, flicked the 'occupied' catch open and burst out into the train corridor – straight into the arms of Ryan Murphy who was in no mood to be stepped on by some young runt who looked vaguely familiar.

As one of the firm's leaders he needed to assess the damage and rally the troops. This little twat was an unnecessary distraction.

"Watch the fuck out, where you going?" Murphy barked, but as he went to walk away, the train jolted and the door of the toilet swung open with the Blues graffiti on full display.

Ryan Murphy put the equation together fast - the attack had

been timed and focused to perfection, and that meant a spy in the camp. He gripped Titch firmly by the front of his ill-fitting T-Shirt, and then twisted his arm, provoking a squeal. "You're a fucking Blues scum ain't you, I thought I knew you, I've clocked you hanging around behind Carter and his mates ain't I?"

Fuelled by alcohol and fear, Titch decided his only chance was to fight back and swung a punch that Ryan easily blocked. Unfortunately for Titch, the attempt blew the lid off Ryan's suppressed rage at Roseanne and Gary.

Murphy dragged the struggling youth towards the train door like a rag doll and maintaining his grip with one hand he pulled the window down.

"Let's see how brave you are now you little cunt," he roared as he pushed Titch's upper body through the window, hanging him outside the speeding train.

Titch was screaming, terror gripped him as the blast of the wind exploded in his ears.

At that moment two things happened that would change both of their lives forever.

A volley of missiles from the bridges in Curzon Street, launched by Sam Wild's group, again spattered across the train, bouncing off carriage roofs, some finding their mark – more screams.

As Murphy instinctively ducked, he loosened his grip just as another train heading south passed them in the approach to New

Street. Titch was sucked into the vortex and as both trains passed each other, his broken, lifeless body was deposited across the tracks.

Murphy reeled back from the window in horror as he tried to process what had happened. Titch's despairing scream would be etched forever into his brain. The enormity of what he had done struck him, he was a murderer. He had been planning to kill Gary Docker, but not some kid. He vomited.

Within five minutes, the train was drawing to a halt on Platform Twelve of New Street Station. Five exhausted British Transport Police officers alighted to join a couple more anxiously waiting on the platform near to the parcels deck. The gates were already open, waiting to speed the exodus into Station Street.

The Villa fans looked like they had been in a battle with lots of walking wounded – sore heads, blood-stained clothing, venting anger and fury.

Mike Carter and Pete Stevens had re-joined Tony Carter and about thirty of the firm including 'Jim', a short man who was an 'out and out' pisshead, but in drink was like a wild man. Not really one of the firm, but he loved a good fight.

Mike led the charge as they swarmed through the open gates and crashed through the platform area, a wide-open space occupied by Royal Mail vans and little trucks pulling wire meshed wagons with parcels, called 'Brutes'.

It was mayhem for a few wonderful minutes as the Blues fans, refreshed from an afternoon of anticipation and relaxation, attacked in a welter of fists and boots. This was designed to be a rout of an already damaged army, and the demoralised Villa fans gave way and broke, their leader for the day, Ryan, nowhere to be seen.

With Colin Murphy up North at a car auction buying a couple of late model Hillman Avengers, Ryan's steely leadership was sorely missed.

Then it was all over.

As police sirens were heard in the background, the Blues team melted away with much hand-slapping and whooping. There would be plenty of war stories later as they celebrated a crushing victory over their rivals.

Titch had done his job – he was one of the boys now – Mike Carter would make sure of that.

From the shadows of the train Ryan Murphy emerged. Still in shock, he wiped the last trace of vomit from the stubble on his face and surveyed the carnage. Shoulders hunched, and with one eye out for the opposition, he made his way to safer territory, his mind in turmoil.

***

For the next few days, Ryan scanned the newspapers and the television news every day, and waited for the knock on the door. He had watched the dead kid's parents go through hell on camera and could not get their faces out of his mind. The story ran and ran and Ryan kept his own counsel. Everyone assumed that he was just pre-occupied with Roseanne and the debacle at the station.

The following Friday morning he caught sight of a headline on the board outside the newsagents. *'Football youth's death accidental'*. Ryan hurriedly bought the paper and scanned the front page.

Titch's body had been so badly disfigured that it was initially difficult to make a proper identification, and the findings of the post-mortem were consistent with him being hit by a train. On the face of it, Titch had fallen from the open carriage window, and very early on the British Transport Police had indicated that they were not treating his death as suspicious. He wasn't the first over-excited football fan to die in such a manner, and he wouldn't be the last.

No witnesses had emerged, and the injuries masked any evidence of a violent assault – Ryan was in the clear.

The only person he had told was his father. He had been in need of a confessor and despite the at times violent nature of their relationship, Ryan knew his father would never betray him, could help if necessary, and needed to know anything that could jeopardise the family business.

Colin Murphy had not been happy when he heard the revelation from his son's lips. He was not in the slightest bit bothered about the death of a Blues fan, nor the fact that his son was unburdening himself as a murderer. No, he was appalled at Ryan's agonising which he interpreted as softness, and any weakness in his son could put their criminal enterprises and Colin's dynastical 'succession plan' at risk.

The medicine he meted out was just the latest in a long line of violence that stretched back to Ryan's toddler days. Ryan could handle himself better than most, but whenever his father was violent towards him he just took it – fighting back would release a torrent of uncontrollable fury from his father and it was better to take what was coming. It was the cause of his fractured personality, but he hadn't realised it yet. That revelation was to come, and would change everything.

"Grow some balls you cretin", was the phrase that Ryan Murphy had tattooed on his mind, as his father fumed. Someone would have to pay for the ambush on the Villa fans and the target for revenge did not take long in coming.

***

Titch's body was released to his family and arrangements put in place for a proper 'Blues' send-off. Mike Carter had no inkling of how Titch had died but he had met his death taking risks for the firm and he would be recognised in a manner befitting 'fallen comrades'.

Mike paid for all of the funeral expenses, and arrangements were made for the cortege to start its journey from St Andrews itself.

Blues fans lined the roadway outside the ground on both sides, and scarves adorned the railings. The 'up and comers' formed their own tightly-knit group, some close to tears, whilst Mike Carter and the main boys stood for a few minutes either side of the hearse - the guard of honour sending a powerful message.

The irony of the Blues scarves tied to the hearse door handles was not lost on Mike Carter.

A large banner said simply *'Titch - RIP – one of the boys.'*

The blue and white flowers in the coffin spelt his name and everyone wore Blues shirts. They were adorned with the club's regalia in all its forms.

A minute's silence was held and some of the fans held up the traffic. No-one dared to pass, and the local police were conspicuous by their absence- leastways the uniform ones were, as Rob Docker had arranged for a watching brief from a couple of officers in plain clothes from outside the city. They were not looking for bravery awards and kept their distance.

As the cortege prepared to leave, hundreds of Blues fans launched into spontaneous applause, and then the Birmingham City anthem began – emotion filling the air,

'As you go through life it's a long, long road

There'll be joys and sorrows too

As we journey on we will sing this song

For the boys in royal blue

We are partisan

We will journey on

Keep right on to the end of the road

Keep right onto the end

Though the way be long let your heart beat strong

Keep right on to the end

Though you're tired and weary

Still journey on 'till you come to your happy abode

We'll be there. Where?

At the end of the road.

Birmingham! Birmingham!'

As the song finished, another huge round of applause broke out and the cortege left for a private family service.No place for football hooliganism there. It was a place where the family could mourn the loss of their loved one - a real person who had living flesh and bones, before they were shattered playing tribalistic games.

As they departed, the 'experts' within the crowd, the true Blues fans, reminded those around them that the song had been doing the rounds for more than a decade and came to the fore during the 1956 FA Cup matches when players and fans took up a version of *'Keep Right On'* by Sir Harry Lauder, and adopted the Scottish classic song as their own.

Lots of people hung around for a while, chatting and remembering better days whilst others drifted off towards the city centre. The Blues 'firm' wake was to be held in a pub with history too.

***

The Old Contemptibles pub in Edmund Street was just a short

distance from Colmore Row and Snow Hill Railway Station. The name of the pub honoured the First World War heroes, the British Expeditionary Force, led by General Sir John French, who suffered heavy casualties in holding up the German advance at Mons. Kaiser Wilhelm II ordered his men to exterminate French's 'contemptible' little army, which led to the nickname sticking and the creation of the 1914 Star Medal.

The main bar filled up quickly, friends amongst friends, whilst upstairs a private room was big enough for the inner sanctum to talk freely without prying ears. Mike Carter was in no mood for humour. He was there because he had to be, but in truth he felt a deep sense of guilt for placing Titch in danger.

Downstairs he could hear the room getting livelier as bursts of Blues anthems filled the pub every now and then.

By arrangement, Colin Murphy met up with his firm in St Phillips Churchyard. They arrived in threes and fours – a good turn out with fifty plus in all, and some tasty ones amongst them, pockets bulging with various weapons of war, billiard balls in socks, black rubber brake pads wrapped together with tape, lock- knives, iron bars – each to their own favourite.

He had spotters out, so a few brief words with Ryan, Mel and Benny and they were on their way – not quite the Kaiser's speech but the sentiments were the same.

Five minutes later every window on the ground floor of the 'Old Contemptibles' was shattered as volleys of missiles were launched by the Villa firm, showering the occupants of the bar with

138

glass, and shouts of 'Up the Villa' rose.

The female bar staff dived for cover as cries of pain filled the air and blood began to ooze from several of the fans with head wounds.

Once the barrage had subsided, Ryan charged through the left-hand door with twenty of the Villa firm and swept through the bar area, lashing out indiscriminately and creating further fear and pandemonium. A frenzy of blood and violence erupted.

Colin Murphy led twenty of the older guys towards the stairs, but their way was barred by Mike Carter who stood at the top, wielding the short wooden cosh that he always carried. Either side of him, Sam Wild and Greg Lyall wielded short iron rods. They barred the way.

They had the advantage of height and the narrow stairs funnelled the attackers into a manageable front. Over the top of their heads came a volley of stools that rained onto the heads of Murphy and his crew – the attack faltered.

For a moment Colin Murphy's eyes met Mike Carter's – pure hatred with no quarter given or expected, but Murphy was no fool. The attack had achieved its purpose and there would be another day for a reckoning.

Murphy and his group fell back as Carter advanced down the stairs with a baying mob of the 'inner circle' hard men behind him.

The Villa group massed again outside and launched one more volley into the pub before melting away into the streets.

***

Saturday 20 March, and Birmingham had earlier concluded a pretty mundane 1-1 draw at home to Coventry. Mike Carter had once again called for a full turnout. After Titch's death and the fight at the Old Contemptibles he had a point to make.

The city centre belonged to the Blues and it always would. The other firms and the police needed to know it. It was time to piss on all the boundary points to make sure that the other animals kept away.

***

Pete was physically drained – the adrenalin surge replaced by physical exhaustion. He sat down in his sparsely furnished flat with the sink full of unwashed dishes and pondered on life, *'Is this the best it gets?'*

He reached for a can of lager and his diary:

'After the game we walked with hundreds of fans towards the city. Mike Carter was leading the main firm but no opposition in sight. That fucker Spike is always hanging on his coat tail and trying to get up his arse. Where the fuck was he when Titch needed him on that train? One to watch for the future though. We got to St. Andrews Street and suddenly everyone started running for no reason, and next thing in Lower Dartmouth Street a few of the up and comers started bricking the police horses. They started charging at us clattering across the road swinging those great big sticks. Nearly got hit. Mike got everybody to calm down and we walked up Great Barr Street, into Fazeley Street and up Albert Street. We hung

around High Street for a couple of minutes and still no sign of the opposition. Mike led us on to Stephenson Street, Navigation Street and John Bright Street. Familiar territory. The police on foot were still trying to keep up with us. Went up Hill Street in the middle of the road, Mike leading the way and Sam next to him. It was a show of strength for the Blues. Stopped all the traffic and a bus driver was shouting at us through the windscreen. Silly fucker. Sam tried to pull the bus door open to get at him but Mike pulled him away. The police blocked the road in front and turned us back so we ran back down and turned left and went into the Bus Station. I got separated from Mike and finished up in the Indoor Market with a few of the lads. A couple of police officers tried to make an arrest inside but finished up on their arses after they got mobbed. I managed to make it out into the Outdoor Market but it was getting a bit hairy with more and more police. Went up the spiral staircase with about ten of the firm and into the Bull Ring but again got turned back. The police were well wound up looking for bodies. Out into St Martins and found Mike again with Sam and the main group. Again stopped the traffic in St Martins Circus Queensway and went down the subway at Moor Street. Big mistake. Police jumped over the wall to block one end and a police van blocked the other. Mike roared at the group and we charged towards the van as they piled out of it and got stuck in. Bodies and bricks everywhere. A couple of the slower lads were nicked. One got a truncheon down the middle of his head. Blood all down in nose and face. Spike bricked the copper from behind. Like a battleground. Managed to get out of the subway with Mike. Saw a police motorcyclist across the road. Sam and some of the lads bricked him and he thought better of it and fucked off towards the Fire Station at Lancaster Circus. Made our way to New Street Station but got thrown off by railway coppers. The old ones don't give a fuck but the youngsters are too keen. Mike said to call it a day and arranged to meet Sunday lunch at his house before going for a pint. A lot of running around but Mike Carter owns this place and today he showed it again.'

Writing the diary was cathartic for Pete. He was always calmer after. It put his thoughts in order but he couldn't get one thing straight. Tomorrow he might see Joy and despite every effort to push thoughts of her into the background, the idea of forbidden love would not go away.

He was smitten by a girl who didn't even know it.

He reached for a second can – this was getting to be a serious business – people were starting to die.

Chapter Five

'You're Not Singing Anymore'

April 1976

Francis put the phone down, leant back in his chair in the main CID office, and stared at the ceiling, whilst Burrell sat opposite him waiting for his cue.

Finally Francis announced, "We'll do the Birmingham Shopping Centre today and work short between the ramp and the escalators down onto the station. I want some of the security cameras fixed in that area and make sure that security know that we are going to be about in plain clothes. I don't want to finish up getting bitten by that scraggy mutt they drag around on a lead with them. It gives me the willies every time I see the fucking thing."

Burrell nodded and made some phone calls.

Francis spoke to the Duty Inspector and managed to persuade him to let Francis have three of his PCs. All youngsters, they would fit in well albeit they were all pretty 'wet behind the ears' and would need guiding.

Time for a full English breakfast in the canteen before knuckling down to some late paperwork, a short briefing and they would be on plot by midday.

***

It was the big day, the second local derby since Villa's promotion and Blues had lost the last one.

There were bragging rights at stake both on and off the pitch. Mike Carter's focus had been on keeping the main firm together so as to be able to engage Villa fans in Digbeth, and in the side-streets en route to St Andrews. There was something special about local derby games, especially Blues v Villa, and Saturday 3 April 1976 would be no exception. He was looking forward to the inevitable confrontations with his arch foes.

Tony Carter had been anxious to run with the 'up and comers' for the day and Mike had reluctantly agreed to his proposal that they set up some diversions in the city-centre so as to spread the police resources to the maximum.

***

Spike was out and about early, and doing what he did well – spotting for Villa fans.

Since the death of Titch he had kept himself to himself, and those close to him understood that he was suffering from a sense of guilt for not being there when Titch had died. He had finished up with a fine for shooting his mouth off at Euston and walked away from one shoplifting charge after the coppers messed the evidence up. His luck had held and he was respected in the group. Despite this he didn't feel very lucky.

Tony Carter was running things with the youngsters today. Spike didn't like the psychopathic bastard but he had a job to do, people were relying on him, and he wouldn't let them down.

Tony - the 'young pretender,' had already done a few circuits of the New Street, High Street and Corporation Street area together with some twenty Blues youngsters, and dished out obscenities to some 'grandads' wearing Villa scarves. They also managed to jostle a couple of young black kids who were carrying sports bags. Tony Carter managed to pull a 'bobble hat' from the head of one of them and dared them to challenge him, "Fuck off niggers unless you want some of this." His knife flashed in his hand for a moment before returning to his pocket.

The two boys ran as some of the group behind Carter jeered and made chicken noises - some of the group, but not all. A bit of fun was fine, but there were some of the Blues boys who had good friends from school who were black or Asian and they did not share Tony Carter's racist and right-wing views. For now they kept their counsel – they knew what that knife was capable of.

***

Spike came running up to Carter in Cannon Street, breathless and excited with his news,"There's a Villa crew just gone towards the shopping centre, maybe ten of them, with an Asian lad in front. They're on the ramp at the moment playing silly- fuckers, gobbing on shoppers walking underneath. If we're quick we can take them." He waited as Tony Carter weighed up the options.

"Let's take the cunts out," he shouted – the hunt was on.

By the time that they had reached the ramp the rear-guard of the Villa group were just entering the shopping-centre.

Carter and the rest quickened their pace and in moments were on them – a merciless attack from behind that left the Villa boys reeling.

Boots, fists, screams, shouts, a whirlpool of mad activity during which there was a flash of a knife and Carter found his victim.

"Fuck off out of our country, Paki bastard," he screamed at the prone figure clutching his chest, as blood oozed onto the marble floor. Carter kicked him once in the head and turned on his heels.

His group rallied around him and they started to strut like peacocks back towards New Street.

As they reached the ramp, Francis and his team struck and Tony Carter was taken violently to the floor where he left most of the skin on his chin for good measure.

"You're nicked for public order," Francis shouted as he handcuffed him and yanked him upright. "Get this piece of shit out of here," he instructed one of the probationers, and turned to make sure that their other prisoners had been secured.

Moments later, flushed with excitement, the young officer pushed Tony Carter into the back of the police vehicle in Stephenson Street. Closing the door on him he turned to one of his colleagues to check which custody block they were going to, before engaging in a few moments of mutual 'back-slapping' and self-congratulation. This CID work was good stuff.

It was Carter's only chance to avoid disaster and he took it as the knife was palmed from his pocket and then quickly pushed down behind the back seat of the car.

The door opened, "Move over you little cunt," the officer ordered as he sat down in the back seat alongside him, oblivious to the piece of damning evidence that was two inches behind his back.

In training the officer had been told several times about the need to check police vehicles thoroughly after prisoners had been in them, but this was one officer who didn't take too well to rules. He knew better.

***

The Asian youth was taken to Birmingham General Hospital with two stab wounds to the chest and two defensive wounds in his hands, incurred as he had tried in vain to shield himself from the knife blows. He would live, but he wasn't about to make life easy for the police and refused to make a complaint. No victim – no knife – no case to answer.

***

By the end of the day, fifty Blues fans had been arrested and Blues had won by three goals to Villa's two goals. A solid bank of Blue and White scarves waving triumphantly to the background of *'Keep Right on to the End of the Road'* brought St Andrews alive. At long last everything came good for the Blues as pride in the team was restored and their bitterest rivals were sent back home beaten – even if only just.

A local derby which never released the 46,251 crowd from its tense grip was settled in the last six minutes by the local hero,

Trevor Francis. A header, placed just inside the near post, as Howard Kendall crossed from the right. It was the signal for those few fans who could evade the police to race onto the pitch and to mob 'their Trevor'. For Blues and their fans it was a moment to savour.

Inevitably there was some ankle-kicking, and lots of bruises during the match, but considering all that was at stake it was a sporting occasion which was thoroughly appreciated by genuine fans. The return of controversial Blues skipper Kenny Burns made news for the best reasons. Although he wore the number 6 shirt, he played as a third striker alongside Francis and Andy Needham. His presence up front provided more skill and penetration through the middle, and, gloriously for the recently criticized Scot, a second goal.

Terry Hibbitt had given his side an 18th minute lead with his first goal for Blues – a superb left foot volley from an angle out on the left of the box. That was the start of a scoring see-saw which ended as it began, with Blues in front. Villa were always working well, and five minutes before the break they were rewarded with a splendid equalizer as Gray thundered in to sweep the ball over the line. The feeling began to grow that Villa, attacking rather more than Blues, would rub in the home side's relegation problems.

That feeling never spread to the players in blue and white shirts. There were close calls at both ends before Burns drove the ball between John Burridge and the left hand upright. Villa reacted as before-by pushing up again, and when Graydon went down under a challenge from Joe Gallagher a penalty was awarded, which Graydon converted to equalise. But Francis and the Blues fans had the last word, and bragging rights, courtesy of that wonderful header.

Off the pitch it was a different story.

***

The twenty cells at Digbeth were full, as some of Mike Carter's group had been picked off by some very determined officers with chin straps down and black gloves donned. Jim, pissed-up to the eyeballs as usual, had been amongst them. Arrested for being drunk and disorderly he decided to hold an impromptu 'sing-song' and by the time he had finished, both corridors in the cell block were reverberating to the sound of *'Save your kisses for me'* by the Brotherhood of Man.

"Let me out Sarge, I need to get out to watch the Eurovision Song Contest!" he repeatedly bellowed through the open metal trap in the door in between renditions, until the custody sergeant got bored and slammed it shut. As the hot humid air of the cell took hold, Jim slept it off for a few hours.

Elsewhere, seventeen persons were in custody at Bromford Lane Police Station following disturbances in and around the ground. Mike Carter's luck had run out as he was caught fighting hand-to-hand with Benny from the Villa main boys at the Watery Lane traffic roundabout after the match.

Tony Carter sat in his cell at Steelhouse Lane Lock-Up, with three others languishing in the Juvenile Detention Rooms, Spike amongst them. He had fronted the plain-clothes coppers, refused to leave as Carter was put to the floor, and paid the price by getting nicked as well for obstruction.

Tony Carter was shitting a brick but so far so good. If he

walked out with a charge sheet just for fighting it would be a result. He was thinking that God and luck favoured the white man after all.

***

As usual, Pete made his assiduous notes in his diary. He had only seen part of the action and fortunately hadn't been arrested. Still, his diary was building into a veritable history of the glory days of the firm.

'Home Game St Andrews against the Villa: The away fans were coming down Garrison Lane as we walked down Lower Dartmouth Street. At the island police on horses in the middle to keep us apart. We went up Great Barr Street and Fazeley Street into town. Under the bridge at Fazeley Street Sam set up a big Blues chant. It was echoing everywhere. Well scary. There was a stand-off with police in Corporation Street and not long afterwards got thrown off New Street Station. Stood looking over the parapet at the short stay car park outside the station, looking down into Station Street. There were some mounted police below. Spike and a couple of the youngsters dropped some stones and empty cans onto them. One of the horses and a rider got hit and he fell off. Pandemonium with a fucking horse rearing up and kicking anyone who got near it. Some woman actually grabbed it. Fair play. The other police horses turned around and rode towards the ramp leading up to the station to get to us. We fucked off pretty sharp.'

***

A week later they were back together, away this time to Burnley at Turf Moor -another crap town, matched by another crap game for the

Blues. Mike Carter sometimes wondered why he spent his hard-earned money traveling to the 'back of beyond' to watch something that was loosely called sport.

The answer was of course that he was after a different sort of sport.

Due to the distance he had decided to travel by road for this fixture. He didn't want to sit on a train with a load of 'bobble-hats' and be scrutinized every ten minutes by the railway police. He also knew that the local police would be waiting in strength at the railway station, and whilst he was always up for a bit of 'promenading' from the station to the away ground, the downside was being corralled together by a mixture of over-enthusiastic men in blue, police vans with flashing lights, horses and dogs straining at leashes. It was like going to war rather than walking the streets on a Saturday afternoon.

Carter had decided on three mini-vans in convoy. They stopped off on the way for a quick 'pint and a piss' in a small village, and frightened the shit out of the local community who looked as if they had never seen a man in anger, and definitely not an intimidating group wearing 'bovver boots'. Carter was careful on timings as usual though, and they were back on their way before the local police turned up.

He had twenty-eight of his best boys out for the day, plus himself, and whilst they were not great in numbers he was completely relaxed. They would go anywhere with him, were fearless, and reveled in violence. Despite a few minor charges and fines from the week before they were cock a hoop at beating the Villa on the pitch and off it.

Before the match they parked up on an industrial estate about twenty minutes from the ground – nice and quiet with no attention from the locals. None of them were tooled up as it was inevitable that they would be targeted for a good frisking on arrival at the turnstiles. Today it was going to be steel toe-capped boots and fists if necessary – plus a bit of cunning.

They walked the short distance to Turf Moor as a solid group, ranks three abreast, with Mike Carter in front. No smiles, no chat, just fixed determined looks, the faces of hard men willing the opposition to find them.

They were individually searched and entered the ground without incident, where they were ushered into the away end, occupying an area adjacent to home supporters. Between them was a line of 'cardboard cut-out' coppers all stood with their arms folded staring vacantly into space. Seeing everything but actually seeing nothing. Behind them a high fence with spikes on top, and the other side the 'come on' signs and 'V-finger' signs from the opposition. Carter reflected, *'Pretty brave behind that great big fucking fence'*. He had seen it all before so many times.

As the 'bobble-hats' got into full voice on both sides, Carter assessed the situation.

The locals had a nice little firm on the other side of that fence but he saw nothing that his mob couldn't handle. They had the numbers but he had the tactics and the spirit.

***

The game itself proved a damp squib after the heroics of seven days previously.

Blues were now at serious risk of losing their First Division status with a poor display, following a 4 – 0 loss away to Newcastle in midweek. They barely had a shot until the last few minutes when Peter Withe and Steve Bryant had attempts. The only chance before that fell to Trevor Francis in the 32nd minute following a great back-heel from Withe. Francis tried to get the angle of his shot precise, but got it wrong. It proved an expensive miss.

Burnley, who had come close to scoring twice in the first eight minutes, punished Blues late in the second half. A short clearance from ex-Villa goalkeeper Gerry Peyton to newcomer Terry Pashley began the move. His pass found Ray Hankin who controlled it, evaded a crude tackle by Joe Gallagher, lost Kenny Burns and planted a shot past Dave Latchford from just inside the area moments before full time.

The absence of injured Howard Kendall was sorely felt in midfield. Page, Bryant and Emmanuel put some good passes together and there were a couple of trademark runs from Francis on the right wing but apart from that Francis miss they never looked like winning it. Blues boss Willie Bell later told the newspapers that he blamed injuries for his team's growing relegation crisis.

'I had Hatton sat in the stand unfit, Kendall never had a chance of making it, and but for our situation I would not have played either Francis or Gallagher. Gallagher played with his back strapped up and was in such discomfort at the end he had to get another player to take his boots off. Francis ought to rest his thigh injury, and in the circumstances did very well. Kendall will be

doubtful for Tuesday but I will try and get the others fit. We are not worried about goals, its points that count, and with four matches left there is a still a long way to go.'

For Burnley, manager Joe Brown said that Blues had come for a draw, *'with twenty-one players in one half of the pitch on many occasions it was difficult to play.'*

***

Mike Carter's worst fears were realized, as in front of a crowd of 13,679 a dull game for eighty-nine minutes was lit up with that one tremendous individual effort from Ray Hankin, which gave the home supporters lucky enough to have stayed to see it their one minute of pleasure, and none at all for the Blues fans.

Fifteen minutes before the end of the game, Mike Carter was somewhat taken aback when he was approached by an Inspector, accompanied by a rugged-looking sergeant, and a couple of PCs.

The conversation was brief and to the point. The Inspector wanted to know where their vehicles were parked and gave the sergeant instructions that he, and five PCs, would escort them back to their vehicles at the end of the match. Mike didn't argue – he knew better, but he watched with interest as the sergeant briefed some of the officers in the line facing them. He watched with even more interest as he clocked one of those officers turn to the home side and engage in a brief conversation through the fence with a particularly ugly looking individual, with a bald head, who swaggered off back into the crowd.

At the end of the game all of the away supporters were kept

back until the home stands were deserted.

The 'bobble-hats' reverted to being sheep as they were herded together to be shepherded back to the railway station.

Carters group remained – he had used the time to brief his boys. His instinct told him that they were going to get some attention. Would it be the 'boys in blue', the opposition, or both?

They set off in a small column, the sergeant walked with Carter, whilst three PCs spaced themselves along the sides, and two brought up the rear.

Sergeant Rees-Morgan was not a man to waste words. He had five years left to do in the job and when he was done he would go home to the Welsh Valleys where he was born, and where his heart, which was now somewhat harder, remained.

As they got closer to their destination the atmosphere changed dramatically as the odd missile was thrown at the column from narrow side streets, and Rees-Morgan quickened the pace.

Unseen figures launched random volleys before disappearing back into the shadows. Most of the missiles bounced harmlessly off the road or struck parked vehicles, which forlorn owners would inspect later once the interlopers had gone. One or two found targets but the group was lucky and no-one suffered any head injuries.

Relatively unscathed, they reached the car park on the industrial estate to find that the windows of all three vehicles had been smashed. Glass and house-bricks littered the floor.

As they stood surveying the damage a loud roar suddenly erupted behind them in the roadway as more than one hundred opposition hooligans spread out across the car park entrance, effectively blocking them in.

Time froze – at the other end of the car park was a brick wall - there was no escape.

As the massed ranks closed, the ugly man at the front extolled his troops to do their worst.

Twenty-nine hooligans, and six police officers, one of whom was clearly a bent bastard, facing up to odds of three to one. Carter allowed himself to smile – he was in heaven!

Rees-Morgan took stock of the situation and made a decision.

He turned to Carter, "I'm not taking any more of this bollocks. Are you up for this?"

Carter nodded – it was enough.

His boys already knew what to do and formed one solid line with Tony Carter in the middle urging them on. Mike Carter positioned himself slightly in front with Sam Wild and Greg Lyall either side of him. Pete Stevens stood slightly to one side – he had been briefed separately.

Rees-Morgan stood behind with his officers, "Hats off boys, they're only going to fall off anyway. Gloves on, pegs out and give this bunch of shit some wellie.

They won't be fucking about with us for the rest of the

season. I want no prisoners – just crack some heads."

Mike Carter turned momentarily, "Hold the line boys – we're Brummies – don't forget. They're just a bunch of titty babbies you'll see!"

Another roar and the away fans charged forward.

Whilst Carter's boys had no weapons they did all curiously have a set of car keys on them which had now been placed strategically between the fingers of fighting hands. A good punch with a sharp key to gouge out skin and produce blood would create panic – it always did. A few had also removed their leather belts and were now ready to use them as whips as well as their opponents advanced. Those with larger waistlines decided not to take the risk!

As they closed on each other, Mike Carter, Sam Wild, and Greg Lyall made straight for the 'ugly man'. There was no finesse in the move – the aim was to win.

Amidst the screams, shouts, and sounds of bones crunching Carter's boys stood firm whilst the ugly man was pummeled to the floor and knocked unconscious with boots and fists, before the three withdrew back into the line.

The charge faltered as the small group of police officers waded in with truncheons wielded fiercely and effectively – this was not community policing at its finest.

One of the officers was felled by a half-brick during the skirmishing as an unseen hand targeted him. He went down and stayed down. Pete Stevens had found his mark.

Carter barked, "Hold the line boys, nearly there." Without their leader, who lay prone on the floor, optimism turned to doubt.

A half-hearted rally had no impact on the Blues gang and as Carter shouted "Get the bastards," the Burnley firm broke, as twenty-nine battle-hardened hooligans charged as one with a huge roar. Rees-Morgan looked on with detached curiosity as some of his officers applied first aid to their fallen colleague.

Half of the opposition had been running around aimlessly at the back and as the fighting got closer they fled.

Suddenly the car park was empty.

Sergeant Rees-Morgan turned to Mike Carter, "Best you fuck off then" and turned on his heels. There were no handshakes – nothing had changed.

Carter did not need telling twice.

Rees-Morgan gave instructions for the 'ugly man' to be scooped up. He would be good for affray and the assault on the wounded officer.

It was a draughty ride home to Birmingham, and the three drivers wore sunglasses, that made them look like the 'Blues Brothers' in order to avoid the bits of flying glass that kept dislodging themselves from the shattered windscreens, but morale was high.

In the end the score-line off the pitch had been a good one again.

***

The following day Pete Stevens had something different to think about, as he contemplated a three-day shutdown at Longbridge where he had finally secured a job on the track. The plant could be silent by Thursday. Allegro production would stop on Monday, and the Mini by Wednesday. Component shortage would hit Cowley production of the Princess and the Marina soon, and thirty-five thousand workers would be laid off. One thousand Longbridge tool room workers would go on strike.

They were going to ignore their own Union, the AEUW, after a vote the previous Friday had been 2 to 1 in favour of a strike. Also, seventy Maxi workers were on strike in Birmingham, six thousand Triumph workers in Coventry, restricting output, plus eighteen Lucas workers on strike threatening battery production.

Pete had not voted for the strike but knew that he would have to toe the line. Ironically he had got a couple of tickets for the Birmingham Motor Show at Bingley Hall between 10 - 20 April. At just fifty pence for entry it looked like he was going to have time on his hands to go and have a butchers.

***

Charlie had been back from Barbados for two weeks, and had out of caution missed three Villa matches since returning, including the one at St Andrews, whilst he worked out how the land lay. It had been quiet, and his strong belief of expecting time to sort things out was telling him it was all going to be fine. The need to see his team was building and he had missed a lot of matches.

Gary was still missing, but Charlie had heard nothing about Ryan Murphy still looking for him, so assumed that the cuckolded husband had accepted the facts of life.

Unfortunately for Charlie, his assumption was wrong. Ryan's mind had been elsewhere, focused upon Titch and a possible life behind bars, causing Ryan to 'duck his head' for a while, even missing the Villa versus Blues game as well.

Charlie had still been in two minds about going to the match on Good Friday, 17 April, but finally a call from a pal in London, who lived within walking distance of the ground, persuaded him to make the trip down the day before.

He spent the evening in London putting the world to rights over a few pints and a couple of snifters to help him sleep. He had even managed some light banter about his one passion – the current fortunes of the Villa.

He thought it would be safe enough to go, he was going to stand with his mate in a home area, away from the travelling Villa fans, and he fully intended to stay in London a second night.

A good fry-up in the morning, and a couple of lunchtime pints in a back-street local, and he was almost looking forward to the game. He certainly needed something to take his mind off things.

Gary's disappearance with Roseanne had been a great shock to him and he felt helpless. He cast his mind back to his sister Mary, and how despite all the obstacles she had managed somehow to protect her children. She was a woman in a man's world but she had been like a tigress and kept the darkness away from them. He saw some of that grit in his wife, Vivian, one of the reasons he loved her.

He also loved his son, and despite the fact that Gary had refused to stop fucking about trying to be a hooligan, he was Charlie's flesh and blood and he wanted him to make something of himself. He still thought that pissing about with a married woman and hiding away from the likes of the Murphy family would end in tears, and was waiting for contact from his son so he could try and talk some sense into him.

He had considered speaking to Colin Murphy 'man to man', but in truth he was out of his league with a man who he knew was capable of extreme violence. Charlie decided to try to get on with his life and keep his head down hoping that it would just all go away.

In the 'home-end', Charlie practiced keeping quiet during the game. A Brummie accent just wasn't going to go down well amongst this lot, but thankfully their venom was reserved for a noisy group of Villa fans who were trying to make their presence felt at the away-end.

***

With a score-line of 2-2, Villa nearly achieved their first win of the season at Upton Park but wasted their last chance. They rushed into a two -goal lead after only ten minutes but before half-time the Londoners had snatched one back and in the second- half Villa surrendered the initiative.

West Ham could have been affected by their Cup Winners Cup Semi Final against Eintracht in midweek but after half-time they seemed to find fresh energy. Villa seemed content to hang back and defend their single goal lead, but England's Trevor Brooking struck the equalizer.

Villa steamed into the lead after five minutes when John Deehan, returning after ten games, headed in an overhead kick from Andy Gray that dropped beautifully for him. Five minutes later, John Gidman crossed to the far post and Steve Hunt scored with an angled header. In the 15th minute, Brooking's corner was converted by Keith Robson with a tidy header. West Ham nearly equalized in the 32nd minute when a low cross by Frank Lampard bounced off Billy Jenning's shins and away.

After the interval West Ham were in complete charge, and Findlay, in for Burridge, made some fine saves. Villa rallied towards the end of the match, and the West Ham keeper, Ferguson, in for his first senior game in three seasons, made good saves from Gray and Hunt. Villa manager Ron Saunders showed his frustration after the match, commenting, *'This match was the story of our life this season. It is always disappointing when you have done enough to win as we did today.'*

***

After the match, Charlie made a quick exit and soon found a place in the snug of a local pub with his mate. Halfway down his first pint he was assailed by guilt for leaving Vivian alone and phoned her from the payphone on the wall.

He could tell she was missing him, feeling vulnerable, so he made a quick decision and decided to go home. It took a few minutes to finish his pint, collect his overnight bag, and make his way to the station, Vivian and Gary on his mind.

After purchasing a ticket, he went straight down the long ramp onto the platform and boarded the train, which rested just short of the buffers, waiting to depart.

There were half a dozen BTP officers hovering about on the platform, mostly practicing being bored, and a couple of Metropolitan Police officers who seemed to be engaged in some form of animated radio conversation.

Charlie Docker was not uncomfortable about being around police officers. He had operated 'wide of the mark' for many years but he didn't class himself as a villain and after all they had a job to do – one that his nephew Rob seemed to be pretty good at.

Charlie took a seat in one of the front coaches and nestled into his overcoat, his thoughts drifting back to Gary again. He checked his watch – they should have left by now. The reason for the delay never occurred to him

Minutes later, he heard the sound of chanting coming from the concourse as a group of a hundred plus Villa fans were led in a long snake onto the platform. The platform was curved and from his seat Charlie could see them approaching – so much for a quiet trip back. What he hadn't expected was that they had been held back in the ground for half an hour until the home fans had departed, and he had forgotten that this was the station used by the police for visiting fans - there had been none of course the day before when he had arrived there. Charlie's luck was about to run out.

Amongst the Villa fans were a group of twenty hooligans led

by Ryan. The trip across London had clearly not been uneventful, and some of them wore their badges of violence with pride; bloodstained shirts, black eyes, the remnants of spittle on their backs. The Villa boys had clearly not had it all their own way and were boiling.

To cap it all, the Met officers had been very forthcoming with their pegs if anyone stepped out from the confines of the column – this was the 'Big City' and they were used to dealing with rubbish – no 'County Wankers' here.

Charlie sank lower in the seat and breathed a sigh of relief as the group was boarded into the rear two coaches and five BTP officers followed them on.

As the train headed back to the Midlands, with the heating turned up, most of the Villa fans fell asleep, Charlie deep in his own disturbed thoughts at the front in a virtually empty carriage, and the rest huddled in groups at the rear, grown men sleeping on each other's shoulders like babies.

Just past Coventry Railway Station people stirred, ready for the arrival home in about twenty minutes - the night was not yet done.

Ryan yawned, and stretched, then decided to go for a walk to see if there was any sport to be had. He wandered off up the carriages and initially attracted no response from the BTP officers who in truth just wanted to get home themselves. They had been given no trouble and were not looking to create any. That said, the sergeant in charge was curious when Ryan Murphy did not return and sent one of his more experienced officers to go and find him whilst the rest kept their 'flock' in check.

The officer found him minutes later with both hands gripping Charlie Docker fiercely by the collar of his coat in one of the empty vestibules.

"What the fuck's going on," the officer demanded as he pushed Ryan away from Docker, who was already displaying reddening to his left cheek-bone.

Ryan's boiling rage told him to go into attack mode, but his brain ordered him to hold back. He would get six months for assault police and he was on a train with nowhere to go. This was not the moment to get locked up.

Docker interjected trying to calm the situation, "It's nothing. It's family business. It's fine."

The BTP officer wasn't particularly looking for a prisoner, a trip to the 'Lock- Up' and a five-hour delay before going home, and all these long hours were getting to him. He felt drained. He wasn't a spring chicken anymore and rolling around the floor with drunken piss-heads and football hooligans left him cold. He wanted out, but still had two years to go to get his pension.

That said, he still retained a personal sense of pride as a police officer and would do his job. Try as the officer might though, Charlie steadfastly refused to make any form of complaint.

By the time they had arrived into New Street Station, the officer had taken details from both of them, and put a flea in Ryan's ear before seeing him on his way a few minutes after Charlie.

Charlie went first, up the steps onto the bridge-link, and through the ticket barrier onto the concourse.

He walked with a purpose, anxious to leave the station, but his pursuer was young, fit, and gaining on him from behind.

Charlie went up the escalators onto the Birmingham Shopping Centre together with a fair number of Villa fans, and headed towards the ramp leading to the junction with New Street and Corporation Street.

Charlie slowed down as he saw groups of men gathered at the junction – *'shit, Blues fans'* he thought, and instinctively headed down the steps leading to Navigation Street to try to avoid them, forgetting that he wore no Villa scarf today.

As he reached the bottom of the steps he saw more Blues scarfs and instinctively ducked into the nearby toilet entrance. Above him, the ramp was packed with football fans, and the ancient enemies were already fighting, innocent Saturday evening revelers ducking quickly back into the Pallasades Shopping Centre to escape. Charlie had placed himself momentarily out of sight, in one of the most crowded places in Birmingham.

Ryan had ditched his scarf too, he didn't want to get diverted into a fight with the Blues fans when he still had his prey in sight. As Charlie peered around the corner of the toilet entrance to see whether the coast was clear, he was suddenly spun around from behind and came face to face with Ryan who once again gripped him by the collar with one hand, and punched him in the stomach with some force, with the other.

Charlie went down like a sack of spuds and Ryan kicked him once in the head before dragging the man to his feet again.

"I'll ask you once more you cunt. Where's your bastard son Gary and me missus?" Ryan spat the words.

A trickle of blood came from a corner of Charlie's battered mouth, together with a moment of rash defiance, "I don't know and if I did I wouldn't tell you." he gasped.

Ryan shook him violently like a rag doll; all sense of self-control gone, "Where is he. The little cunt's got me missus and he's going to pay."

Charlie suddenly felt angry on behalf of his son. He would never have the opportunity to reflect on the words he chose; they just tumbled out, "What's the matter Ryan, couldn't you get it up any more?"

Ryan was an inferno of suppressed rage. He took one step back and then 'Kung-Fu' kicked Charlie in the stomach sending him flying backwards and down the solid stone toilet stairs. Ryan vaulted down the steps, delivered two more kicks to the head, and ran back up.

Charlie Docker, head shattered by the fall, breathed his last in the fetid stink of the urinals on a grimy set of steps. Having survived the war and everything that the Germans could throw at Birmingham, he had succumbed to a fellow-countryman, born in the same City, and a follower of his beloved football club.

Ryan took a look at the motionless body and the face of Titch suddenly appeared in his mind's eye. He heard the screams again and a chill seized his heart, extinguishing the flames. Suddenly he was in full flight, back up the stairs, and as he reached the top of the ramp again he saw that some of his firm were engaged in hand- to-hand fighting at the bottom, with no police officers in sight. He ran down the ramp and launched himself into the melee, punching and kicking like a maniac.

Each side gave as good as they got until the sound of approaching sirens spelt 'time up' for the two factions, and they dispersed in different directions.

Ryan did not look back, and it would be some hours before his worst fears were realised. The early morning news confirmed that a man had been found dead following disturbances between football supporters.

Ryan went cold – what the fuck had he done? Twice now, how could that be? At home, he looked into the bathroom mirror, trying to see the face of a killer, but all he saw was his own staring back, unchanged.

***

The phone rang at 1am in the hallway downstairs.At this time of night it only meant work. Rob Docker climbed out of bed. He never slept well, and was already alert by the time he reached the phone, whereas Lilian slept on, oblivious to the world, and oblivious to him,

"The place could be on fire and the silly cow would sleep through it," he mused.

Rob listened intently to the voice at the other end – this was no time for questions and in any event this was just a messenger.

He put the phone down, and for a moment a wave of sadness consumed him – not enough for tears but enough to provoke memories of better times, family times, before 'the job' had consumed him. The death of Charlie Docker, his uncle, and the only person Rob cared about, shook him. It was one less link left with the past, and he was running out of those fast.

Docker went upstairs and got dressed in the dark in silence. He woke Lilian just before leaving and announced, "I've got to go to work." She just about roused herself from her drunken stupor.

***

Docker parked in his space in the small police car park at the top of 'The Lane', but instead of walking down to the nick he made his way to Newton Street and walked up to the Central Mortuary, briefcase in hand.

He pressed the buzzer, and waited until the white-coated mortician opened the door, corned-beef sandwich in one hand, "Hello Mr. Docker. Long-time-no-see, where have you been?" Ged proffered his free hand, *'God knows where that's been'* Docker mused.

Rob Docker had spent enough time in the place watching post-mortems to know Ged's little habits quite well.

Docker needed to get this small-talk over with, "I've been on another job for a while Ged – 'hush-hush', you know, that sort of thing. I want to see the body of the man that's just been brought in from the football violence."

Ged's break had been disturbed, but the quarter bottle of whisky that Rob pressed into his hand reminded him that this bloke was okay.

They went through to the main body storage area, and as they did so Rob was hit by the chill of the place – a deathly chill broken only by the low hum of electricity in the background.

Ged indicated a body under a white sheet on one of the trolleys, in the centre of the room, next to a table on which was piled clothing and a number of personal items.

"The guys have stripped him off, but they just got called down to the station. Some senior officer was shouting his mouth off demanding to have an update from them. They'll be back in half an hour to sort all the paperwork out and log everything." Ged felt the need to cover their backs, as in truth they had just broken the first rule about continuity of the body.

Docker responded soothingly, "That's no problem at all Ged. I completely understand. Just go and get on with your break and save me a snifter from the bottle. I'll just be a few minutes here."

Ged willingly left Docker to his own devices and went in search of two clean mugs.

Rob Docker pulled the sheet back and stared at the face of his uncle – he felt a huge well of anger inside. This was not how anyone should meet their end. Charlie had been a decent man, and had helped Rob when he needed it most.

'Football hooligans – scum of the earth, you're all going to pay for this, and the one who did it is going to suffer,' he vowed to himself.

The pale white face stared back at him as Docker reached into his suit pocket and retrieved a small plastic poly-bag. No resistance from Charlie as Rob pulled several strands of his hair from his head and slipped them inside the bag, which went back into his pocket.

Docker went through the items on top of the table and slipped a wristwatch into his pocket – it was an anniversary present with Charlie's name inscribed inside. Finally he reached for the Villa scarf that lay bloodstained amongst the jumble of clothing. He slipped it inside the briefcase.

Time was of the essence, and he wanted to avoid the returning uniformed officers, but Docker kept his nerve and had the one drink with Ged before leaving.

"Ged I've still got a few of these hush-hush things going on. I shouldn't be telling you but I know I can trust you – State secrets that sort of thing. I don't want anyone to know I've been here – life and death. Do you get me?" Docker piled it on.

"You can rely on me Mr. Docker. Me lips are sealed." Ged felt the warmth of the last drop of whisky go down and his thoughts turned elsewhere. What did it matter anyway; everyone in there was dead bar him. They wouldn't care and he liked Docker - his kind of policeman.

Rob returned to his car, deposited the briefcase and the two items from his pocket and went to the nick.Docker didn't want this to be complicated. His uncle had been murdered and clearly there was no way that he could be directly involved in the investigation. It would not have been ethical. Besides, he wanted to remain in the background to ensure that his own brand of justice was dealt out to the murderer.

On the other hand, Docker knew the area like the back of his hand and had an, 'ace card' – he had two 'experts' in football hooliganism under his control.

When Docker offered Francis and Burrell the job of investigating the murder they bit his hand off.

Docker made a private phone call to Francis and made it clear that notwithstanding that he would be on the murder enquiry for a while, their working relationship remained unchanged.

Job done for now, Docker made another phone call. He wasn't one to waste an opportunity and as he was out he thought to visit an, 'old friend'. She wasn't best pleased at being disturbed but no-one ever said 'no' to Rob Docker, leastways Jane Smith.

***

Mike Carter as usual surveyed the Sunday edition of the 'Observer' that morning for the match report:

'Easter Saturday 17/4/76. Blues 3 v 1 Spurs:

Fans are beginning to smile at St Andrews after a great win left Blues only needing one point from their last two games to be sure of avoiding relegation. This was a fantastic victory under pressure, a pressure that showed in a succession of first half misses. But that was all forgotten as three goals in the second half secured the vital two points. The first goal came in the 50th minute when Osgood gave away a free kick for handball. Page took it quickly to Emmanuel, who crossed for Joe Gallagher to head in. The second came in the 63rd minute from a Hibbitt cross which Francis took in his stride and planted the ball past Jennings to ease the tension.

Relief was short-lived though, and in the 77th minute Coates put the ball into the area and Pratt converted. Step forward Kenny Burns, who played his captain's part in full. Three minutes from the end Withe won the ball and passed to Hatton who shielded the ball, laying it off for Burns to smash Blues' third, and the blue and white faithful erupted in joy.

Manager Willie Bell commented, 'We still need one point to stay up, but this was a terrific tonic. Terry Hibbitt is doubtful as he caught his studs in the pitch and did his knee ligaments in his left leg.'

On one of the inside pages another article was of more interest to Mike:

'Rowdies out at Albion and elsewhere - West Brom had their second biggest crowd of the season for the first match of the Easter Holiday football programme, and with it came trouble. A crowd of 26,447 generated thirty-five arrests, the majority for disorderly conduct.

Almost as soon as they got inside, visiting Nottingham Forest fans charged onto the pitch and towards the Albion supporters on the terraces. Whilst the game was on, police had to enter the ground to stop fights and separate fans. One Albion supporter was carried off on a stretcher. In Smethwick, four more were arrested for breaking windows on their way to the ground.

The bottom of the table struggle between Coventry and Wolves at Highfield Road resulted in a further fifteen arrests for disorderly conduct. Another eight were detained at Walsall's goal-less game with Hereford. The Birmingham versus Spurs game was marred by seven arrests for rowdyism, and a further two in Birmingham City Centre after the match.'

Carter had not been at the fight in Birmingham the previous evening, it had been a spontaneous meeting on the ramp. Still, it was a nice little ruck out of nothing. He continued reading, and his brow furrowed as he learnt that beer was going up to twenty-five pence a pint.

Uncharacteristically, he failed to spot something in the 'stop-press' on the front page, which was probably more to do with Joy and Carol pestering him to get tickets for Barbarellas' *'Easter Jump Up'* in Cumberland St the next day, with the Matumbis and the Cimarons playing. He was more interested in the forthcoming game with Stoke himself.

'STOP PRESS - *Police are investigating the death of a Villa supporter found collapsed on toilet steps last night during disturbances with Blues fans in and around the Pallasades Shopping Centre ramp....'*

***

In the aftermath of Charlie's death, both Mike Carter and Colin Murphy had instinctively retreated into the background to preserve their business interests, whilst trusted lieutenants maintained hit-and-run tactics on behalf of the two groups. Carter felt a sense of injustice that his boys were being falsely accused, whilst Murphy needed to preserve the sense of outrage and thirst for revenge that a Villa fan had been murdered by the main opposition.

Only he and Ryan knew the truth.

Colin Murphy couldn't really get his head around Ryan being a double killer, but he was family, and family came first. Anyway, the thicko police were bound to blame a Birmingham fan. Colin smiled to himself, *'They'll be desperate for an arrest and conviction, some poor fucker is going to have it for sure, and it won't be Ryan.'*

***

Francis and Burrell had done a good job of making themselves useful, and had the ear of the Detective Chief Inspector leading the murder enquiry, who was looking for a quick result and wanted to move on. There were though, some who felt that football hooliganism was not proper CID work and that the yobbos all deserved the pain that they inflicted on each other.

Vivian had made an emotional press appeal for witnesses to come forward, but it had been met by a wall of silence. They might hate each other and fight on sight, but they had a deeper hatred of the police, no-one would 'grass'.

On the 24 April, a minute's silence was held at the ground for Charlie.

It was Villa's last match of the season and they won 2-1 against Middlesbrough. Charlie would have been pleased, Aston Villa's first season back in the top-flight ending in a victory.

Their third win since Boxing Day came against a poor Middlesbrough side. It was Frank Carrodus' day, a reward for his fine performances in midfield throughout the season. He scored the winner, his first goal of the campaign. It came in the 52nd minute after Villa came out after half-time full of purpose. McDonald played a low ball in and Deehan tried a flick that bounced off keeper Platt. The keeper did well to parry a shot from Gray but Carrodus struck it into the corner.

Villa started the match at pace, scoring after ninety seconds when teenagers Andy Gray and John Deehan combined. Nicholl found McDonald wide on the left. He crossed it high, Gray challenged Platt, causing him to punch rather than catch, and Deehan converted with a header. Middlesbrough showed determination and Terry Cooper was not only their best player, the former Leeds and England full–back, playing in midfield, was also best on the pitch. Middlesbrough had equalized in the 31st minute but Villa were too strong in the second half and ran out worthy winners.

To Charlie's friends and the press the ignominious and tragic death all seemed a bit pointless – a loved and blameless man murdered for the sake of a round ball. Vivian wasn't so sure, but reserved her opinions for Rob's ears only.

What the investigation fortunately did have was some black and white images from the security cameras at New Street Station. Charlie Docker was captured on the concourse and the escalators to the Birmingham Shopping Centre. Pictures of the returning Villa fans also identified Ryan Murphy plus Mel Price and Benny Doherty, with a number of the regular hangers on.

A number of rather grainy external Midland Bank cameras at the bottom end of New Street, near to the ramp, showed Sam Wild, Greg Lyall, 'JC' and Tony Carter, with a strong team of Blues fans at the junction with Corporation Street.

It was time to stir the pot.

***

Prior to the dawn raids, Francis sat in Rob Docker's office discussing the options.

Docker would have his moment, but he was also in it for the long haul. His aim was to avenge his uncle and destroy both gangs, and he knew that was unlikely to be achieved by a single knockout blow.

He discussed the likely 'players' with Francis, and after getting the latest update from one of their informants, a decision was made – he reached for his briefcase – his war was about to begin.

***

At 6am the next day, a number of doors were removed from their hinges at the same time, as sledge-hammers tore through wood and glass in Bordesley Green, Stechford, and Aston.

Members of both groups found themselves being scooped up and deposited in various police stations. Both Carter and Murphy had separately told them to expect it and to keep their mouths shut.

Francis led one team and quickly secured the prisoner who had been dragged from his bed, handcuffed and removed to a police van in short measure.

Left on his own in the bedroom for a few moments Francis reached inside his jacket.

Minutes later, the uniform officers returned and Francis delegated them to conduct a thorough search.

He left them to it, and got the target's long-suffering mother to make him a cup of tea downstairs whilst he waited.

Ten minutes later, he heard the buzz of conversation upstairs and it wasn't long before he was presented with some good news.

At another address Burrell was giving Ryan Murphy time to get dressed. Ryan had been uncharacteristically co-operative as the police burst in, but now he was starting to regain his composure after being told that he was being arrested on suspicion of being involved in an affray, he had feared something else.

A search of the house proved negative and he was soon on his way to the nick.

***

With the station buzzing with activity, Docker kept out of the way and waited for news. It wasn't long coming.

Most of the Blues boys had kept their mouths shut apart from a couple of the kids who had admitted being in a fight in Corporation Street – good enough for an affray charge.

Francis led one of the interview teams and worked his way through events methodically, drawing the prisoner in to the point where he admitted being in New Street but no more.

The coup de grace came with the placing of two items wrapped in clear evidence bags on the table in front of the prisoner and his solicitor.

The recovery of Charlie Docker's watch from the bedroom drawer, coupled with the Aston Villa scarf found hidden under some clothes in the wardrobe, was solid evidence, and forensics would later confirm that hair samples found in the scarf belonged to Charlie Docker.

It was enough – 'JC' would be charged with murder. He had to be physically dragged back to the cell, protesting his innocence, but it would be to no avail. In the wrong place at the wrong time, a young life ruined to match the old one taken. He heard Francis' parting shot as he was pulled along the corridor towards the Lock-Up, "If you want to play with the grown-ups you need to be able to take your medicine son. If you can't do the time, don't do the crime."

At another station, Burrell went to work on Ryan Murphy in a cell. The Villa hooligan was used to pain and easily withstood the selective beating that was administered. This was Burrell's trademark, and he was frustrated with the lack of progress. At the end, unbroken, Ryan had spat blood from his mouth into his assailants face and told Burrell, "Hope I meet you on the street one day you bastard, I'll break you in two." He got an extra couple of digs for his trouble, but Burrell left the cell, defeated.

For Ryan's part he couldn't believe his luck. They kept asking about the fight but nothing about Charlie Docker – they obviously didn't know his secret, and it stayed that way.

***

At the end of the day most of them walked, but as Rob Docker sat reflecting in his office, one charged with murder, a couple for affray, and a couple of witness statements from Villa fans who said that they had been attacked, it was not a bad start.

Downstairs, the head of the murder enquiry had put a round behind the bar. Docker would make sure that his own first drink of the day would be included, as people around him bemoaned the death of comedy actor and *'Carry On'* star Sid James who had just died on stage at the Sunderland Empire Theatre having suffered a fatal heart attack.

Docker still felt restless. He couldn't get the nagging feeling that he had missed something out of his mind. He knew that fitting up 'JC' was a good result, putting the case to bed publicly, and removing the spotlight from the murder. It allowed Docker space to do things his way, but he also knew that the real murderer was still out there, unpunished.

180

***

The phone in Rob Docker's office rang – as usual he was in a foul mood. Lilian was a fucking nightmare to live with and it took him a couple of hours each day to get her out of his system, but the news at the other end made him alert as he shifted in his seat.

He had not seen the Detective Inspector from the British Transport Police for a few months now, but he wasn't a bad sort and was always keen to help Docker if he could. He had thought to let him know that an officer who had been off sick with stress for a few weeks had provided him with something of interest.

On his last tour of duty, before going sick, the officer had worked a train with Aston Villa fans returning into Birmingham New Street.

On the train, just as they were arriving, the officer had come across a Villa fan trying to throttle an older Villa fan in the vestibule of a carriage.

The older man had insisted it was a family issue and refused to make a complaint so the officer took their details and sent them on their way – one with a flea in his ear.

The details had been diligently recorded in his pocket book – Charlie Docker and Ryan Murphy....

Docker arranged to get a copy of the pocket-book entry and told his friend to leave it with him – probably 'something and nothing'. He knew where to go now for some information, a source that only he could access.

***

In the aftermath of 'JCs' arrest and charge, Mike Carter had two matters to look at urgently. Whilst 'JC' was not one of his lieutenants, he was one of the main boys and had been ripe for the 'inner-circle', his charismatic approach to violence had been particularly attractive to the younger element who were eager to follow.

Carter had to fill the void, and the obvious choice was to look towards Pete Stevens who had passed all the tests and kept his cool. Better still, he was below the radar with the coppers, having only recently come up from Weston Super Mare.

Pete was hard but he wasn't 'gobby'. The guy had potential and knew his place with Tony, Sam, and Greg.

Anyway he would be a good influence on Tony, who had been up to his usual tricks, dragging some of the youngsters off to Bradford for a National Front march where twenty-six arrests had been made.

Carter's second task was to speak to some contacts he had with Millwall and Crystal Palace hooligans who operated south of the river in London.

This conversation wasn't about arranging to beat 'seven bells of shit out of each other'; it was a matter of the law and justice.

Mike knew that 'JC' had been fitted up by the coppers, and having watched Francis in the witness box at court on one of the remand hearings, when bail was refused, he wanted to know more about the man with the cockney accent who clearly thought a lot of himself.

It was time well spent...

Chapter Six

'We Are Bladesmen'

May 1976

It was the 4th May, and the last game of the season, with Blues playing Sheffield United away. They could have been relegated but drew 1-1. That one point was enough to survive and they finished nineteenth. Villa didn't do that much better and finished sixteenth in their first season back in the First Division.

***

Birmingham Observer – *Tuesday 5 May 1976*:

> *'Blues fans spur team to survival: The Blue army of 10,000 travelling fans, packed into trains, buses, cars and vans, spurred their team onto a skin of the teeth, last-gasp survival effort at Bramall Lane. They seemed to calm the first half jitters and stayed behind to applaud their heroes even if they had not actually won anything. The Sheffield pubs did a roaring trade.*

> *During the match it was clear that transistor radios were tuned into local radio relaying events at Molineux as the Bluenose's emotions went through a rollercoaster, one minute relegated, the next safe. The Blades went ahead midway through the first half when Alan Woodward scored a 20th minute, thirty yard scorcher, and hearts sunk as the score, Wolves 1 – Liverpool 0 came across the airwaves. Sheffield, already relegated, then played with a freedom*

the Blues could not match, racked with relegation jitters as they were, and the Blues fans were quiet. The scores remained the same at half-time and Birmingham looked down and out. They were playing badly, and Sheffield looked in control, but then the fans redoubled their efforts and their emotion seemed to fire up the team.

Terry Hibbitt snatched an equalizer out of nowhere 3 minutes into the second half with a jab into the net and the faithful got word that Liverpool had scored at Wolves. By the final whistle Blues had held on and were safe, by a single point.

The wonderful Blues fans, who always moan, but never give up, had given their team the sort of support that make other teams envious, one can only wonder what it would be like if they were in danger of actually winning something. One fan commented, 'That's the third time we've squeaked out of relegation; let's hope next season we've something better to cheer about, my nerves can't stand this much longer.' In fact the repeated slogan of the fans, echoed by manager Willie Bell after the match was 'Never again.' We shall see!'

***

Liverpool won the First Division title and the UEFA Cup in their second season under the management of Bob Paisley. They finished just one point ahead of QPR, who had emerged as serious title contenders under the management of Dave Sexton. Manchester United enjoyed a strong First Division comeback by finishing third, but then suffered a shock defeat to Southampton in the final of the FA Cup.

Derby County's defence of the league title ended with a fourth-place finish.

Leeds United continued to recover from the departure of Don Revie by moving up to fifth place, a year after finishing ninth.

Manchester City compensated for a failure to mount a title challenge by winning the League Cup.

***

Birmingham Observer – *Tuesday 5 May 1976*:

'*Forty in court after Molineux relegation drama: Forty fans, of which twenty-one were from Liverpool, will appear in court today following violent scenes during Wolves' unsuccessful attempt to stave off relegation. The supporters were charged with a variety of offences including threatening behavior, obstruction, assault police, and burglary.*

Police were forced to eject four hundred fans who broke down gates before the ground opened, but it is thought around three thousand people got in for free after smashing the same gate just before kick-off. Most of them were Liverpool fans that had been locked out, having made the journey from Merseyside. There were pitch invasions after all three of the Liverpool goals that secured the First Division title and fans had to be removed from the floodlight pylons and the stand roof.

Police were called to several Wolverhampton pubs when post-match Liverpool celebrations got out of hand, but there was only one arrest for burglary after a window was smashed.

Wolverhampton fans in contrast trailed glumly from the ground as they contemplated the reality of relegation to Division Two.'

***

Pete Stevens reflected on the day's events. Recording the history of the firm in a diary had been a good idea, but a chore to begin with, however by now it was second nature,

'Went up with a big firm by train to Sheffield for the game with United. Ninety minutes on the train which was rammed. There must have been five hundred on the one we were on. The railway coppers couldn't get through the coaches to see what was going on and at one stage the coach I was in was rocking as some fuckin idiots started running from side to side. Frightened me to death. There wasn't a light bulb or fire extinguisher left on the train by the time we arrived. Greg and Sam actually got some of the lads together to wrench half the ceiling down. There was more wires up there than in a telephone exchange. Mike Carter just sat there quiet but he's always got one eye to the front and one behind him. He's definitely a canny fucker. The message had gone out – this was wrecking day for the Blues. Up or down we would leave our mark on anything that could be smashed, unscrewed, sprayed, or pissed on. Jim even crapped in one of the toilet sinks and wiped his arse with a Villa programme. Spike was not far away again – the undisputed leader now of the up and comers, he's come up the order quick for a youngster. Tony's too busy with his skinhead mates to see what's going on. Just before we got into the platform at Sheffield someone pulled the communication cord and the train stopped short on the tracks. Every door flew open and the lads poured out as the reception committee ran down towards us. Absolute fuckin mayhem,

dogs barking, police shouting, and half the Blues fans climbing over the stone walls at the back. Most of them had only got platform tickets so there was no point queuing up was there. The cheeky fuckers went round to the front entrance to wave at us before the police had let us through the barriers. Jim was pissed as usual and waving his shitty Villa programme around. I don't think he knew that he was in Sheffield. He lives with a can in his hand. They tried to put us on some buses outside the station but most of us managed to push through the police. Mike had given the order. No cooperation today. Make the fuckers work. There wasn't enough police. Walked through the city-centre and did some noisy chanting. Plenty of locals scared witless. Jim shouted at some coppers and finally got himself nicked for drunk and disorderly. Still clutching that shitty Villa programme and waving it in the coppers face – hilarious. By Sheffield Cathedral Mike led the charge against a big group of 'The Bladesmen'. In the shadow of a church the Blues punched fuck out of them. In fact I think a couple of them ran inside to get away. Sanctuary! Not so tough, a couple of their main men were pummeled and Sam left his mark with a Z shape Stanley knife wound on the back of one. It was a bloodbath. One Sheffield got a flick-knife out and fronted Mike who smashed him over the head with his little cosh. It came out the bottom of his sleeve like a magic trick. The twat went down like a sack of spuds and stayed down. A couple of the youngsters had spray cans and sprayed the wall of the Cathedral in blue 'Blues One – Bladesmen Zero'. Vans turned up from everywhere. This was the bad boy coppers. Mike got everybody together again and did his usual and got us in some order. A real General. As the police tried to corner us Mike marched off walking quickly pushing the police so that they had to keep up. It was funny watching them. Greg tried to march in front like a fat drum-major – ever the joker. Loads of coppers at the turnstiles and after everyone had gone in, the ground outside was littered with all sorts of weapons. I actually watched the game for once instead of the numpties on the other side of the fences - leastways for a bit. Police everywhere and apart from a bit of goading just no chance for anything in the ground. Lots of 'Going Down, Going Down' at the Sheffield lot. We got forced onto a bus back to the railway station and a couple of buses got bricked on the way back. One Blues fan got a nasty head injury. At the station some of the Sheffield firm tried to mingle with normal passengers and then attacked Sam and a group on the platform. Someone had fingered him for the slashing. They bit off more than they could chew and Mike and Greg steamed in with the firm and five of the Sheffield lot finished up on the tracks. Sam and Greg always had each other's backs. That's the way it is. The railway police were going ballistic. They had to stop the trains and drag them back. The Sheffield lot got nicked but all they wanted to do with us was shuffle us back onto a train asap. A few more of us on the train on the way back, and plenty of singing and banter. Somehow Jim had been let off with a caution and on the train back he tried to start singing 'Fernando' but got mobbed. He's a fucker for his music and I reckon he likes Abba really. The railway coppers thought that they had got away with it. As the train got into the tunnel at New Street Station Sam pulled the cord. Mike's orders were again carried out to the letter and the train carriages were smashed to fuck. It limped into platform twelve and we fucked off. A good day for the firm.'

Sheffield United's terrible season saw them relegated in bottom place after five years back in the First Division. They went down with Burnley and Wolverhampton.

***

The destruction of criminal empires and tackling football violence were secondary concerns now. It hadn't taken Rob long to work out the links between the death of his uncle and the disappearance of his cousin, and he had inside information, being family and all.

The murder of Charlie had hit him harder than he had expected. He rationalised it to the fact that he still felt vulnerable and guilty over what had happened last year. The Dockers seemed to be under attack.

Charlie Docker and his wife, Vivian, had been the people who had stood by Rob in his times of need, when others had scorned and betrayed him. They had taken him in when he had fled the family home as a teenager. They had always been there for him, ready to listen, dispense advice, and help him as much as they could. They had accepted him for what he was. They were his true family and now one of them was gone before his time, and for what, some scumbag's anger and relationship failure.

Uncle Charlie had been one of the few people Rob respected. He had admired his uncle's self-integrity. Not exactly the type of integrity a philosopher would recognise. Rob knew that Charlie had close connections to serious criminals, that he knew things that were worth money and would have helped Rob climb through the ranks more quickly, but in all those years of meetings between them, his uncle had never 'ratted'.

Rob respected that stance; it gave him confidence that his own conversations were safer than in a confessional box, although

Rob Docker was not a man for religion.

In some ways Charlie could be described as a successful businessman, but men like him did not get honours. He was never going to make Harold Wilson's *'Lavender List'*.

They had met once a week, for a few pints and snooker at Charlie's working- man's club in Kings Heath, the *'Loyal Caledonian Corks'*. It was private there, and no-one ever looked twice at a younger man taking his older relative out for the evening. Charlie was the only person in whom Rob had confided everything, *'well all bar one thing',* the good and bad, and there was plenty of the latter, but Charlie had never judged him, just provided the catharsis of sharing, and good counsel.

And now he was dead, beaten and killed for nothing. Rob had visited his uncle's widow after the funeral. Auntie Vivian was the 'source' that only he could access, and he was not surprised that she had filled in the pieces. She was no fool, and had stood by her husband during, and since the war, through thick and thin and family tragedy. When he visited, Vivian still had a suntan from the Barbados trip, and she was under no illusion as to why her husband was dead.

Vivian was normally strong and steadfast but she let her feelings run-riot for a few moments, "It's our Gary's fault. Run off with some married tart, head over heels he was. Left a note the night he done a runner, warning Charlie to make himself scarce for a while. Seems that this woman was married to some sort of heavy criminal. Whoever it is must have been tasty, took a lot to worry Charlie with his connections as you know. That's why we went off like we did without warning.

I said to Charlie, *'lets stay longer'*, but he figured it was safe, the shit had died down, and he missed his home, you, the club and his mates, and the blessed football. First time he had been away with the Villa since we got back it was, the night he died."

Rob had asked if she knew the name of the 'tart' and where Gary had gone.

Vivian frowned,"Dunno where he is, it's like the earth has swallowed him up. We've had nothing but one postcard to say he was ok, I'll get it for you."

She disappeared upstairs and returned bearing the card. Rob examined it. It had a picture of Brighton Pier on the front, and just the single word, *'OK',* on the rear.

"Do you think that's where he's holed up?" Docker wasn't used to interrogating old ladies.

Vivian looked at the floor, her mind locked in memories, "Gawd knows. He's never been to the place in his life so I dunno why he would go there."

Rob steered the conversation back, "And the name of the woman?"

Vivian considered, "Only heard him on the phone to her a couple of times. Called her Rose. Don't know the last name but he made a couple of jokes about the Irish so I think she's a Mick."

The astute Vivian clearly knew that whoever had been

charged with the murder wasn't the culprit, after all, why would Rob have arrived to ask all these questions? She knew her nephew, and she approved of the fact that he wanted to exact retribution in the old way, with blood, which would also protect her son.

Before he left, Vivian had made Rob promise that he would do everything in his power to find and protect Gary. When Rob gave his vow, he meant it. He owed Charlie and Vivian, and anyway, Rob Docker was not about to let the perpetrator escape Rob's type of justice.

Rob left the house and went straight to the Collators office at The Lane. Bill Donovan had been his usual fount of knowledge and his card index was renowned for filling in the gaps.

Docker came straight to the point, "Bill, I'm after a Villa bad boy who has a girl called Rose, possibly Irish background."

Ten minutes later he heard the name Roseanne Murphy for the first time. The jigsaw pieces fell into place.

**

Rob had put the feelers out, and it hadn't taken long for a whisper that Ryan Murphy was looking for his missing bride to reach his ears. Rob felt a grim satisfaction; there was a reckoning to be had. He told no one about his suspicions, this was personal and he wasn't about to go through official channels. Anyway, 'JC' was in the frame, which left the way clear for Rob.

He had been reluctant to pursue the other obvious line of enquiry, but it was something only he could do, and he needed to try and remove a possible obstruction. Docker hadn't been close to Gary, thought him a bit of a dick-head, acting the hard-man when Rob could see he wasn't up to it. But Rob knew Gary had been close to his uncle's links and correctly suspected that being 'swallowed up by the earth' required professional help beyond Gary's abilities.

Rob had gone alone.

He had parked the car up in Thornhill Road Police Station car park and then walked down onto Soho Road, feeling conspicuous and vulnerable. It was like a different country, the shops sold saris and Caribbean chicken, and his was the only white face. He quelled the trepidation and donned the usual tough veneer as he approached the door staff at the 'Hole in The Wall'. They eyed him with open hostility.

One of them barred his way, "Stop right there, white boy, don't think this is the club for you."

Rob stared deep into the eyes of the bouncer, careful to show no fear, and produced his warrant card.

Rob maintained his gaze, "That's fuckin rich ain't it, operating a colour bar. I'm Charlie Docker's nephew. You go and tell Lloyd I wanna see him about Charlie and I ain't taking 'No' for an answer."

Ten minutes later he sat facing the head man. Lloyd had been a band member with Rob's brother Joe way back when. They had started the 'Hole In The Wall' together and Lloyd had worked for years as part of the doorman company that the friends ran from there. It was no surprise that he was in charge now.

There was no attempt at friendly conversation, even though they had both loved and respected the same man. The huge black man regarded Rob with undisguised hostility. *'That's my uncle all over,'* Rob thought, *'He's told them all about me, so they trusted him. Glad I never told him what I done in the end.'*

Lloyd was direct. "You aren't welcome here Mr Docker, so tell me real quick, what do you want?"

Docker tried to find a connection, "I know that I'm as welcome as a fart in a lift, but this ain't about cops and robbers, or white and black is it? It's about family and friends, my family, your friends. My uncle is gone. He did plenty for you lot. You owe him, dead or alive. My cousin is gone too, he ain't dead, but he fucking will be unless I get to him before those bastards what killed Charlie do.

I want to save his skin and get the fucker that topped my uncle. By get, I don't mean courts and that shit. I ain't your run of the mill cop; I do things my way, the way you'd approve of."

Lloyd regarded him silently for a while. "But surely the killer is behind bars and Gary Docker is safe?

Rob made it clear that Ryan Murphy had been involved in the murder of Charlie Docker and that in his 'professional' opinion he would not stop until Gary Docker was dead as well.

Lloyd made it clear that Docker could talk to him until the cows came home - he would not under any circumstances help the detective. They had reached an impasse.

Docker left.Rob knew that he would never find Gary without Lloyd's help; so there was only one way to protect him, remove the threat. And he needed more than small-time gangsters to do that.

*****

Gary went to the stone pier every morning. He sat on the granite benches, watching the fishermen and the boats busily ploughing their way in and out of Weymouth harbour, and he thought things through, but no resolution appeared.

He was a storm of conflicting emotions. His dad was dead, murdered, and it was his fault. He was a coward for running away and leaving the old man to take the heat. He wanted revenge but had no clue how to get it. He had searched his soul and found fear there too. He was afraid for himself and Roseanne, afraid that Ryan would find them, and fearful of what he would do when he did. Gary was certain that Ryan, Colin or one of the main-men had murdered Charlie, either as a message, or in an attempt to find him that had gone wrong. Either way, a line had been crossed that left both Gary and Roseanne expecting worse than a beating if they were found.

The whole thing was a disaster, and the irony was that it was borne of love. Their first few weeks together after fleeing Birmingham had been idyllic, the flat overlooking the harbour was far better than they had expected, they both had evening jobs in pubs, and neither of them wanted to give up the life they had bought with risk and sacrifice.

So he sat on the pier, brooding. Should they stay or run again? Could he live with himself if they did? Was Roseanne more important than revenge? Even if he knew who the murderer was, had he got the bottle to face him and extract retribution? Was he capable of murder? The seagulls whirled endlessly overhead, almost a manifestation of his thoughts.

A hand tapped him on the shoulder and he jumped and turned, expecting to see the face of Ryan Murphy, but it was an old friend,

"Hello Gary. I've got a message and a present for you. Park yourself back down there; we've got a bit of talking to do."

The visitor handed over a cup of coffee in a plastic cup. "Here, have a swig of that while we sort out what we gonna do about this mess."

After the unexpected meeting Gary sat on the bed in the apartment by the marina, and stared at a revolver wrapped in the package together with a number of bullets - self-protection was what he had been told. -*'Fuck me this is serious shit we are in,'* he mused, as he scratched his head wandering how to explain this to Roseanne. *'Probably better not to, until I've decided what to do, and maybe not then either.'*

He hid the gun away, but couldn't hide its presence from his thoughts as he debated with himself on the pier each day.

***

A week later Rob Docker shifted in his seat. Decision made, he shut the door to his office and picked up the phone. It was a short conversation – a bond formed of mutual hatred and necessity between the two ensured that pleasantries were excluded and Docker came straight to the point.

At the other end of the line silent curses and burning anger were only just kept under control. The one person that Docker never wanted to speak to again, the only one he feared, but needs must, and in this case there was only one man he trusted to succeed.

***

Greg 'Roly' Lyall sat in the Broadway pub in Bordesley Green feeling absolutely on top of the world.He loved his team and he loved the firm, he was proud to be a part of it.

He even loved his mum most of the time, and he loved his 'pit' where he could dream about girls and the sort of life that he would never be able to touch or feel.

'Fuck that shit anyway'. He had status in his chosen world and was respected by the 'up and comers' and main boys alike. He had stood 'toe-to-toe' against the best London firms and never flinched. He was there when Mike Carter had called them to hold the line up in Burnley and been part of the ambush of some of the Millwall firm at London Bridge. He fucking loved the violence and he was somebody.

Better still, he was one of the most prolific shoplifters in Birmingham City Centre with a good team who were prepared to travel and had some wheels to use. Stratford on Avon was next on the list for a visit, and he already had his eyes on some expensive designer shops.

As Greg supped his fourth pint at the bar he smiled broadly to himself – a nice little wedge from today's effort at *'Marks and Sparks'* was burning a hole in his pocket.

"How's things then Roly you fat bastard?" one of the regulars shouted across the room.

Amongst friends, Roly bore the size of his girth with good humour. The truth was that he *was* a fat bastard, and for the firm he wore it like a medal.

"I'm feeling better than you – you daft twat" he responded as he waved a wad of ten pound notes in the air in defiance.

Two more pints and Greg was ready for the off – his pit was calling, although at this rate he would more than likely be getting up for a piss all night.

He downed the last drop, belched loudly, and slammed his glass down on the bar. A round of 'Ta- ra's' to the licensee, the barmaid with the short skirt that drew Greg's gaze every time she bent down, and the two regulars sat fixed to their chairs, and he was off out of the door. Stale smoke filled the room.

Greg paused at the door, steadied himself and took in the cold rush of air – yes life was pretty good and he was looking forward to future rucks – it was a way of life.

Stepping out onto the car park, he passed a couple of clapped out motors waiting for some clapped out 'over the limit' drivers to drive them home and suddenly came face to face with some unusual visitors for the area – three bikers, none of them kids.

The three men in black leathers were stood next to three bikes and eyeing him with mild amusement, "What are you looking at you fat bastard?" the smallest of the three asked almost casually.

"I'm looking at fuck all," Greg responded – six pints had reduced his fear levels.

The small biker with the big mouth stood forward from his bike, "Mom always told me I was a bad boy if I swore," he said quietly as he placed himself directly in front of Greg, barring his way.

Greg instinctively went for a pre-emptive strike, 'nutting' his antagonist and pushing him violently backwards resulting in one of the bikes being knocked from its stand.

"Frank, you're slowing down," muttered the tall one.

"Come on then you cunts I'll take all three of you on!" Greg screamed as the red mist descended.

It was the wrong move.

The three bikers moved quickly, and the tall one was too fast and neatly tripped Greg, putting him down onto the tarmac surface. "Hold him down," he ordered – this man was a leader.

Try as he might, Greg's bulk worked against him on the floor and the alcohol weakened him as two of the bikers straddled his upper body.

Deftly, one of them forced a filthy rag into his mouth as the tall one, well- built, but so light on his feet, drew an iron bar from the sleeve of his leather jacket.

One stroke hit the bone of Roly's right lower leg – a hard blow – decisive and practiced, the bone cracked.

A second blow to the left lower leg – the same result.

Greg screamed in agony, but no sound except a muffled grunt left his lips as the rag was kept in place.

The process was repeated on the shattered limbs – they would take some time to heal, and it was doubtful that Roly would be walking in a straight line again in a hurry, or ever.

As the leader stood back to survey his work, the other two bikers released their grip and stood up, but Greg's torment was not yet over as steel-capped boots rocked his head from side to side. He went into a fit and lost consciousness.

Engines revved – the bikers left.

***

Greg was discovered a few minutes later, by the barmaid with the short skirt, on her fag break. From his position on the floor he had a birds eye view up the skirt, but his attention was currently elsewhere. He was taken by ambulance to East Birmingham Hospital, where he was immediately placed on the critical list and monitored in the Major Injuries Unit.

Mike Carter got the message within the hour and made his way there with Sam Wild. Greg's mother was at his bedside sobbing silently.

Greg's bones would mend but his brain would probably not – facing life in a wheelchair was his best hope. Greg was brain-damaged and his days of hooliganism and shoplifting were over – he would spend a lot of time dribbling in the future but not on the field of play.

***

Mike Carter went to the pub with Sam Wild and Pete Stevens to have a much needed drink. He would see Roly and his mom alright, but business had to go on. In every war there were casualties, and you didn't just give up the fight when things got difficult.

"Are you up for this Pete?" Carter posed the question.

"I won't let you down Mike", he responded. The firm had a new lieutenant.

***

On the 8 May 1976, placard-waving demonstrators, including Tony Carter and Pete Stevens, kept a noisy vigil outside Winson Green Prison as race campaigner Robert Relf began a hunger-strike in his cell.

Relf had been jailed for contempt of court for ignoring a court order to remove the 'For Sale' sign outside his house in Cowdray Close, Leamington Spa. The sign read, *'For sale to an English family only.'* The sign had initially read *'Viewing. To avoid animosity all round positively no coloureds,'* before Relf had amended it.

Relf, aged fifty-one, had been the first person jailed under the new Race Relations Act, sentenced to a year and a day for defying a court order to remove the offending sign. He had instantly become a 'cause celebre' that the burgeoning right- wing groups had seized upon to mobilize their supporters onto the streets.

The leaders, following their adored icon, Adolf Hitler, and his methods in Munich, hoped that seizing the streets would be the first steps in seizing power. They were happy to use any muscle available, and football supporters were proving a rich recruiting ground for their new 'Brownshirts'.

The demonstrators, around fourteen in number, chanted *'Free Robert Relf'*, whilst surrounded by a cordon of helmeted police. Tony Carter was clearly in his element, but Pete Stevens less so. Football violence was one thing, but politics something quite different, and standing with a group of obvious 'head-bangers', he wasn't feeling in the best frame of mind. He would, as quietly instructed by Mike Carter, watch Tony Carter's back as best he could, and hope that the twat might grow out of his fascist fixations.

Across the road from the noisy group, two elderly Jamaican women walked slowly past the prison gates, on the way to the local community centre run by the Winson Green Residents Association. They looked on curiously at the motley group opposite them, bemused by the placards and chants.

One skinhead amongst the group spotted them and shouted out, "What are you looking at you fuckin coons. Get back to your own country!"

A couple of officers wearing black gloves intervened immediately and wrestled him to the ground before dragging him off in handcuffs.

Instinctively Carter flexed his body to go to his assistance but Pete caught him by the arm, "Don't commit suicide Tony, there's too many of them. There will be another day to sort those fuckers out." Carter shrugged him off but the message had gone home.

Police officers then moved the group across the road, away from the prison gates, although some were allowed inside later to speak to Relf.

Afterwards, a man from Oldbury, a member of the National Front, addressed the group. Several members of the press also listened intently, "He will not give in while we are outside giving our support. He is not taking any food whatsoever. We will be here every day. There will be hundreds more joining us this week".

The media had their headline, and a rallying call for the left and right to confront each other would follow shortly.

Pete's heart sank as Carter applauded enthusiastically and punched the air.

***

Birmingham Observer - 16 May 1976:

'Fifty officers injured as race-hate battle erupts: Fifty policemen were injured, several seriously, when race riots erupted in Birmingham yesterday. Only a human barricade of police stopped

an outbreak of extreme violence sweeping through the city's immigrant areas.

The scenes of race-hate fury, the worst in the Midlands since the Black Country riots of 1962, came at the height of rival demonstrations outside Winson Green Prison over the jailing of race-law rebel Robert Relf. In the end the police charged and quelled the 'Battle of Winson Green' by throwing themselves between National Front demonstrators and left-wing protestors.

Twelve officers were taken to Dudley Road Hospital and several had stitches put in wounds. Many injured policemen refused hospital treatment. A girl was also taken to hospital. Police said last night that twenty-eight arrests had been made during the riot.

Prisoners were taken to Handsworth, Ladywood and Smethwick police stations and all were charged and later bailed. They are expected to appear in court later this week.

One of the people arrested was a leading member of the International Socialist Movement.

Police trying to prevent the Winson Green flare-up, first faced hundreds of National Front demonstrators demanding the release of Relf.

Left-wing protestors, more than one thousand strong, then weaved their way towards the prison from the opposite direction.

Police tried to divert the left-wingers onto a demolition site but were caught out when the marchers continued straight on. They were only halted when a police cordon five-deep trapped the demonstrators in a side street.

The frustrated left-wingers who had been screaming, 'Death to the National Front,' began throwing stones, bottles and bricks in a barrage against police ranks.

The main battle was in Franklin Street and Foundry Road, and police ranks bulged until a baton-charge by mounted police forced the mob back.

When the police horses failed to clear the street a number of police motorcyclists began a 'motorized cavalry charge' sweeping protesters before them along the pavements.

An ambulance trying to reach an injured policeman in Franklin Street came under attack and a window was smashed as policemen ran to the rear of houses to collect dustbin lids to use as shields.'

***

At the Dudley Road side of the prison, on another patch of waste land, the National Front demonstration proceeded with more than two hundred supporters present, Tony Carter, Pete Stevens and Spike amongst them.

As their ranks were swelled, Spike suddenly spotted some familiar faces amongst the crowd. "Fuckin hell Tony, there's some Villa scum ere." He pointed towards them.

Carter furiously strode off towards them followed by Spike and Pete, "What the fuck are you wankers doing here, got that fuckin half-caste Price with you then?" he demanded a response.

The Villa firm stood their ground, "We've got just as much right to be here as you Carter, so fuck-off unless you want your nose re-arranged."

Two NF stewards spotted the confrontation and steamed in. One of them got the measure of the situation immediately and got between them, "Not today my friends. None of this football shit. Today we are brothers fighting for the rights of white British people. Stand together or fuck-off. There will be enough chances to use your fists later."

An uneasy truce broke out as a huge balloon kite with the slogan, *'Free Relf '*, was hoisted into the air and reeled out enthusiastically over the crowd by a Wolverhampton NF member. He tried unsuccessfully to guide the device downwind over the prison walls and the crowd cheered as a national NF officer urged them to wave their Union Jack flags and banners.

In another corner of the demonstration, a small group of men in black leather jackets stood quietly surveying the scene. Both the police and the NF organisers gave them a wide berth as the bikers lent their silent support to the rights of white men to reign supremely over 'lesser' mortals. A contingent of the 'Black Souls' and 'Pagan Priests' were having a day out.

***

Rob Docker surveyed the scene in Franklin Road from his hidden observation point, which was manned by a number of scruffy individuals engaged in frantic radio messages, peering through binoculars, or busy scribbling away furiously on paper logs.

No-one questioned what he was doing there and he kept his own counsel as anarchy unfolded before their eyes.

It was like watching a violent movie, but this violence was real, and terror ruled the streets below as bricks flew everywhere.

He watched as one young couple fled their home carrying their four-month old daughter, as police launched a rescue operation to free those unfortunate Winson Green families trapped in their homes by the unfolding anarchy.

The father gripped his young daughter as police officers cleared a path for them, whilst his wife dragged their six–year old son behind her, as they fought their way out of their own home and ran to a car.

With windows being smashed everywhere, three police motorcyclists escorted the car from the street as the family made their break to safety.

Docker watched as more than fifty windows were smashed by house bricks and lumps of concrete. He saw three bricks smash through the front windows of one home as the owner ran to the front door pleading with the demonstrators to stop. The response was a further brick that just missed his head and went through the door.

It was some time before the lines of weary police managed to disperse the demonstrators and restore an uneasy peace to the street.

Finally, Rob Docker left his vantage point and caught up

with some of his ex- colleagues in Special Branch, before going to check on the situation at Birmingham's Dudley Road Hospital, which had become a police casualty unit as ambulances ferried in injured policemen. Several of the officers were having x-ray checks and many more had flesh wounds stitched. One waited with blood pouring from a gash in his face.

One uniform officer recognized him and said, "You wouldn't fuckin believe it sir. They just let us have it with everything they could get their hands on. We just had to stand there and take it." Rob slapped him gently on the shoulder before moving on – it was very important to keep the morale of the troops up.

One sergeant sat with a towel oozing blood from a head wound, courtesy of a direct hit with a house-brick on the forehead.

Yet another was lying on a treatment bed with a badly gashed leg, having been hit by a lump of concrete.

A lot of the injured were policemen from the Walsall area who had caught the brunt of the brick barrage. Several left the hospital heavily bandaged and with their arms in slings, *'The Yam Yams won't be keen on coming back to Brum for a while,'* Rob thought to himself, before checking the remainder of the casualty areas and leaving.

***

Pete Stevens once more sat down to write in his diary in the quiet and stillness of his dilapidated room. Empty and solitary, it held no warmth for him, and there were times when he truly questioned how he had got himself into this situation.

Having finally managed to get himself away from Carter and Spike he had been home for an hour, yet still had difficulty holding his pen as his right hand shook. It had been a pig of a day, and the tumbler of whisky on the table next to him went down quickly, followed swiftly by another,

'What a day! Tony Carter has lost the plot completely and his obsession with the National Front will end in blood being shed. He carries that fucking knife everywhere with him and was constantly threatening to get it out if any left-wingers got close to us. After the demo had finished we made our way up to Dudley Road Park next to the police station. He used the knife to scratch NF on the bonnets of several parked cars along the way. Things got worse as we got into the park. Tony spotted some Asian women with their kids having a picnic with a blanket laid out and food everywhere. He actually ran at them with the knife in his hand screaming 'Fuck off Pakis' and they scattered screaming. The kids were in tears and hysterical and Tony kicked the food all over the place. A police officer shouted from one of the upper windows of the station and we ran. It was crazy and when we stopped, Tony just kept laughing and started doing Nazi salutes. Spike and I exchanged a look but said nothing. I need to speak to Mike. This cunt is going to ruin the reputation of the Blues firm or worse.

I wish I could speak to Joy. I wish I could tell her how I feel about her. Every time I see her I find it difficult to hide my thoughts'

Pete paused, and put a pen several times through the last two lines.

A silly moment of distraction – he didn't want to mix words

---

of violence with feelings of love. He picked up the little black diary he had started – the one reserved for his innermost thoughts.

***

Birmingham Observer - *16 May 1976*:

'Black doctor treats hunger striker Relf: - As the battle of Winson Green raged yesterday, the man at the centre of the racial storm was receiving medical treatment from a black doctor. Mr. Robert Relf had been moved from Winson Green to Stafford Prison on the orders of Home Secretary Roy Jenkins only a few hours before the demonstrations began. His wife and daughter went to visit him and as she left Stafford Prison, Mrs. Relf said that her husband had complained to the Home Secretary about being moved to Stafford, where he is continuing his hunger strike.

She disclosed that Mr. Relf is going to speak to the prison Governor about his medical treatment at Stafford being provided by a Nigerian doctor. Mrs. Relf said her husband was in good spirits but annoyed at the way he had been transferred. She said, 'He was bundled into a taxi and handcuffed like a common murderer. He is a fifty-one year old man on hunger strike and I really cannot see that it was necessary to treat him in this way. I am asking for him to be moved back to Winson Green.'

Fifty National Front supporters demonstrated for three quarters of an hour outside Stafford Prison, on their way back to Manchester from Winson Green. They threatened 2,000 demonstrators would be brought in to protest unless Mr. Relf was released by May 29th. Fifty Staffordshire policemen, led by the Chief

Constable, Mr. Arthur Rees were at the scene. There was no trouble and no arrests.'

***

The day before the news article, Colin Murphy decided to mix business with pleasure and attended one of the Home Internationals with his Celtic mates. He wasn't much bothered who won but it was good to keep the relationship strong.

With a final score-line of Scotland 2 - England 1, a schoolboy error gifted Scotland the Home International Championship. A scuffed shot from Kenny Dalglish went into the net via Ray Clemence's arms and between his legs. That was the winner, as England never looked like equalising.

England Manager Don Revie said, *'If Clemence lives to be ninety he'll never make another mistake like that. There was no pace on the ball and it would have probably been better for him if Dalglish had hit it properly. Clemence is very upset.'*

England scored first after Channon converted a Roy McFarland cross in the tenth minute. The equalizer came from a corner by Eddie Gray in the 17th minute. Joe Jordan's leap distracted the English defence who didn't pick up Don Masson's run which culminated in a header into the back of the net. Ironically, on the day of Clemence's howler, Peter Shilton declared that he would not play for England again.

'Who gives a shit anyway', mused Murphy before making to the local pub. The trip had been worth it. He had made a few more friends amongst the Celtic firm, some of whom could be useful for

business. With inflation down to just 18.9% he had a few cars to shift and there was a market North of the border.

***

On May 22nd, the wife of Relf said that she was very worried her husband was going to die after being on hunger strike for eighteen days. His condition in Stafford Prison was said by the Home Office to be satisfactory, but his wife, Sadie said, *'We are very worried now that he is going to die.'*

She made her comment when, accompanied by her two married daughters, she stepped out of the prison after spending fifteen minutes with her husband. She added, *'He has deteriorated so much and has lost so much weight and yet he is as determined as ever. I have never been more proud of him.'*

Speaking while seventy demonstrators waved Union Jacks outside and chanted, *'Release Robert Relf,'* she said, *'I hope next Saturday everyone who sympathises with my husband will come here and stand up to be counted to make a really massive demonstration.'*

Plans were drawn up to avert violence and prevent injury at Saturday's demonstration. Recommendations were considered to close off a section of central Stafford and to divert traffic away from the area.

On the 29th May the most intensive police operation yet seen in the Midlands beat the troublemakers and ensured peace as hundreds of demonstrators descended on Stafford. More than 1,500 policemen, some carrying riot-shields, sealed off the whole of the town-centre in a successful effort to keep groups of right-wing and left-wing demonstrators apart. Two marches were organised at Stafford jail, supporting and opposing the stand being taken by Relf.

Special contingency plans were drawn up for the Stafford marches and police leave was cancelled. Hundreds of policemen were drafted into the town from the Leicestershire and West Midlands forces and special march routes drawn up.

The first march was that organised by students and other left-wing organisations. Turnout was not as good as the organisers had hoped, and only three hundred and fifty people took part, some carrying *'Women's Lib'* banners and others from the *'Right to Work'* movement. The marchers chanted, *'Smash the National Front'*, and *'let Relf rot'* but there were no incidents, and after marching round the prison they all dispersed.

The National Front march in support of Relf was much larger with more than 1,200 people taking part. In the absence of any football, Tony Carter had been able to drum up some good support with the promise of an 'out of season' ruck and a few pints afterwards.

They marched from the railway station to the prison under heavy police escort and were met by a human barricade. More than three hundred policemen on foot and others on horseback wearing crash helmets barred them from the prison entrance.

There, the organisers made speeches and the marchers chanted anti- immigration slogans. Mr. Relf's wife, Sadie, made a short speech to the crowd saying the prison warders were treating her husband well but that a Spanish psychiatrist was being employed by the authorities who was trying to convince him that he had no support.

After Stafford's Mayor, Councilor Rowley Tongue, thanked the protestors for their good behavior, the only incident of the afternoon occurred when one of Tony Carter's skinhead mates got arrested for gobbing off at the police. He was later bailed.

To prevent their property being damaged some shopkeepers had boarded up doors and windows. The town's slaughterhouse owners had even put grease on their front gate to prevent anyone climbing over. Two demolition sites near the prison had been fenced off and were guarded by police to stop demonstrators getting at the thousands of bricks lying on the ground.

After the marchers had all dispersed a police spokesman said, *'Everything went remarkably well. We actually expected a little more trouble than this despite all the precautions.'*

***

Tony Carter would not be persuaded from his right-wing views, but following Pete's quiet intervention, Mike Carter had a strong word in his nephew's ear. His priority was the Blues firm, and as far as he was concerned, whether they be black or white, as long as they were faithful to Birmingham they were welcome.

Tony was fast becoming a liability, but he was blood, and that was the kind of loyalty you didn't easily dismiss. Besides, Pete was still new, and Mike Carter was mindful that he might be ambitious to climb the pecking order at Tony's expense.

They both deserved watching – after all Pete had only been around for five minutes.

Chapter Seven

'Mr. Blue Sky'

June 1976

Mike Carter lay on the settee, newspapers strewn on the floor by his side. It was Sunday afternoon and as was his wont, he had spent lunchtime in the pub with his main men, followed by a large roast dinner.

It was very warm. He had read that the weathermen were forecasting a long hot summer, perhaps a record one, but they always did that, and they were always wrong, he was sure that the summer of 1976 would be no different.

The combination of beer, a full belly and warmth had induced sleep, but he had awoken after an hour and was now considering the dilemma that had been buzzing around in his mind when he regained consciousness.

Mike was not used to having a problem that could not be solved by tactics, muscle, money or sheer numbers, but this one was proving challenging.

He regarded the problem and she felt his eyes upon her, looked up from her book and smiled the smile that always softened him, "Welcome back to the land of the living dad, you were snoring like a pig with a cold."

He always marveled at her lack of accent, her correct speech,

'How had that happened?'

"Hope I didn't disturb your studies?" he joked.

Joy teased him, "Nah, I'm used to it."Her attention returned to the book in her lap. Mike surreptitiously checked her clothing, and was as usual horrified at how little she had on.

It was hot in the front room of the council house, but Mike was a father that at heart wanted his little girl to stay cute childish and malleable, and the tight T-shirt and shorts showed all too clearly that his girl was fast becoming a woman, and a very pretty one at that.

He often joked that she had got her looks from her mother Carol, who was still a fine-looking woman, and her stubborn determination from him. He said that it was a good job it hadn't been the other way around, but that was in fact the problem in a nutshell.

Joy was seventeen, beautiful, clever, and imbued with Mike's iron will and ornery nature. It was a combination that he truly loved but also feared. She was proving to be beyond his control and the sharks, in the form of men, were beginning to circle.

Take Pete Stevens for example. Mike had clocked him looking at Joy, 'mooning around her' would be a better description, and he didn't like it. He made a mental note to have a quiet word with his new lieutenant.

Mike had wanted a son, like a king of old, wanted an heir, but there had been one girl and that was that. There had been complications with the birth, and Carol had been given the news that she couldn't have any more children. He still remembered sitting next to her in the doctor's surgery, the new baby girl on her lap, when the devastating news had been delivered. He remembered Carol's questioning look at him, a look suffused with fear and vulnerability.

They had gone for a coffee afterwards, and Mike had made it clear that Carol was the only one for him. They had been childhood sweethearts and Mike wanted no other woman, so all his efforts and plans were altered to suit, and channeled into his daughter. His decision that day had ensured his wife's fierce loyalty and support, a trait he valued more as the years went by.

Sometimes he was a bit short with her, usually when the business side of things leached into the household relationships, but he prided himself on his efforts to keep the two halves of his life separate, and Carol was still here for him, Joy the cement that bound them together.

Mike often wondered what would happen when Joy eventually left home. Would there be any feelings left between him and Carol to build upon? He didn't know the answer and he felt some fear at the prospect of finding out; another reason to keep Joy at home for as long as possible.

Joy was a different matter altogether. The close attention and control had been fine throughout her childhood. She had worshipped her father and followed his wishes. But the warning signs began to manifest themselves as she entered her teenage years and her own personality came to the fore.

Early on, Mike had realised that Joy was clever. She was usually at the top of her class, the teacher's reports were glowing, and they all said that a bright future lay ahead. Mike had conceived of a different future for his daughter than he would have planned for a son, a future that he himself had been precluded from because of the poverty of his own origins.

Joy had been gifted with intellect, and Mike wanted her to maximise that gift. O levels, A Levels, University and a professional career was his intention for her. His own preference was the law. He knew from experience that the briefs were the usual winners from everyone else's crime. Investing in having a lawyer with family blood running in their veins was a different way of having an heir.

And so he had pushed her remorselessly, and she had responded by excelling. Oxford, or Cambridge, was even within her reach, according to the school, although Mike's plans envisioned an establishment much closer to home. She had breezed through her O-Levels with straight 'A's' and he had managed to get her into the Sixth Form at Moseley Grammar School, which had only recently accepted girls into what had been an all-male establishment. It was a good school and she was on course to pass A-Levels' next year with flying colours. But now he was worried.

Joy could almost sense what her father was thinking, and the resentment was growing. *'Hadn't she been the dutiful daughter?'*

She had worked hard, very hard. She too wanted to use her mind, to succeed. She wanted broadly the same things for herself as her father, but his way felt increasingly like imprisonment, punishment. She knew what he did, what he was like, and the unfairness of the comparison fed rebellion into her mind, *'what right does he have to decide my life?'*

She looked in the mirror several times day, as teenage girls do, and saw a beautiful woman appearing, but no boy had ever been allowed to get close. Her bedroom wall was decorated with pictures of pop stars ranging from David Cassidy, via David Essex, to David Bowie. Her teenage hormones were raging, and she chafed at the restrictions surrounding her. It seemed obvious to her young mind that her father intended a nun's life for her, all work and no play.

Naomi, her best friend, wasn't subject to such parental control and filled Joy's head with tales of boys, clubs, pubs, concerts and drinking. Joy wanted to taste that life and this straining at her father's, 'lines that weren't to be crossed', had become a significant issue between them, gnawing away at their hitherto close bond.

Iron will met stubborn stone and sparks flew, but Joy knew she possessed the cards to win in the end. She was constantly working away at her prison, gaining an inch of leeway here, a break in the fence there. Her mother silently supported the efforts. Time was her ally, the magic age of eighteen was in sight, and there would be a university in another town, even though her father had told her it was Birmingham University for her. Then she would spread her wings and fly. She had absolutely no intention of having anything to do with the football, the fights and the criminality.

She hated it, hated what her father had to do to maintain control, the type of man he had to be. She was repulsed by violence and her own plans envisioned freedom, a redrawing of her relationship with her father, and a life of her own.

Mike picked the paper up from the floor and cursorily read an article on the new Rover SD1, which he fancied.

He made a decision. He would try a new tactic. He would give Joy a spot of leeway, but chaperoning Joy would become a duty of Tony, Pete, Sam and Spike, once he had briefed them. Perhaps the 'little chat' shouldn't be reserved just for Pete; they would all be his daughter's platonic guardian angels when she was out of his sight, but she would still be under his control.

***

Birmingham Sunday Observer - *6 June 1976*:

'Race hate' killing disputed: London police are investigating the murder of an eighteen-year old Sikh, in the largely Asian area of Southall.

Despite claims from local people that the killing was racially motivated the police are saying that they did not think the killing was a 'race-war' incident. The part-time student at Southall Technical College was stabbed outside The Century Cinema, The Green, on Friday night and staggered, bleeding, into a nearby pub. Although locals rushed him to the West Middlesex Hospital, he died shortly after being admitted.

After a meeting with Asian leaders yesterday, The Police Community Liaison officer for Southall said, 'They expressed their desire that nobody should try to give this any racial overtones.' The Secretary of the Committee on UK Citizenship retorted, 'For the past three months Asians have been singled out for a hammering by Mr. Enoch Powell and the National Front. I hold him and them responsible for this situation. I just cannot understand what Asians have done to justify this antagonism.'

The Editor of the National Front Magazine, 'Spearhead', said yesterday, 'The charge that Mr. Powell or ourselves are responsible in any direct way for this murder is ludicrous. The multi-racial society is collapsing, and we are helping it collapse but we don't hate these people – only the politicians responsible for bringing them here.'

***

Birmingham Sunday Observer - *6 June 1976*:

'Race –row Relf back in court - Robert Relf, the fifty-one year old Leamington man who has spent a month in prison on hunger strike, will appear in court again tomorrow. It is now twenty-nine days since Relf was sentenced for contempt of court after refusing to obey an order to remove a 'For Sale to an English Family' sign from his house in Cowdray Close, Leamington.

After visiting her husband in Stafford Prison yesterday Mrs. Sadie Relf left with four National Front demonstrators who had been protesting outside the jail before her visit. It is thought that the Home Secretary is looking for a way to break the impasse that has caused such trouble locally. Relf has become a 'cause celebre' for right-wing groups who have repeatedly clashed with anti-fascist groups, notably in Winson Green and Stafford recently.'

***

Saturday, 12 June 1976, was a 'red letter day' for Tony Carter – his twenty-first birthday.His father, Brian Carter, was determined that they should try to celebrate the day as a normal family, and for once the subjects of football and 'immigration' were to be banned for a few hours.

Brian was a staunch Blues fan but was no longer close to his brother Mike. Brian prided himself on having built up a legitimate and successful engineering business from scratch and through graft and straight dealing.

There had been no big fallout with his younger brother Mike, but the paths they had followed had diverged, and Brian had politely kept his distance for years. He had attempted to keep his son out of Mike's circle of influence and bring him into the family business, but Tony was wild and rebellious, and could not resist the seduction of the football gangs as a teenager. Brian could not help but apportion Mike some blame for what his son had become.

Brian was no fool though, and he knew that Mike was not responsible for Tony's other main interest. He had watched, powerless to intervene, as his son lurched dangerously to the right politically, and when he wasn't in the company of the main Villa firm he was spending more and more time with a bunch of skinheads who espoused hatred for everything 'coloured'.

Still he loved his son, and had adopted a tactic of waiting and hope that Tony would grow up and out of his violent life. He had promised himself that he would be there for his son when that time arrived. Thus there had been no rupture in the father - son relationship, and he intended to give Tony the best 21st party he could afford.

224

Brian had booked the 'Bali Hai Suite', at The Locarno in Hurst Street, for an evening private party, and he had done his best to discourage Tony from inviting the more extreme elements within his circle of friends from attending. He had put his foot down when Tony had asked if Mike could come, but had compromised and invited Joy, knowing Tony was close to her.

He had told Mike it was a 'young person's' do, but that he would be there to police it. Mike, knowing the real reason, but indulging his brother, had accepted the explanation, checked that Naomi was going, and entrusted his daughter's safety and conduct to Brian, with a warning that he expected him to, 'keep the boys away'.

The Locarno, just next to the Hippodrome Theatre, also had a very strict code on under-age drinking, as well as a requirement for males to wear a shirt and tie. Brian was fairly confident that whilst some of the knob-heads that Tony knew might possess a shirt they certainly wouldn't have a tie.

There was also going to be a good mix of females at the party, and Joy, whilst suspecting that her uncle was her chaperone for the evening, had in turn promised Brian that she would keep an eye on her fractious cousin Tony.

Joy believed that she had some influence over Tony, and Brian had seized upon that belief like a drowning man – in reality they were both mistaken. Tony liked his cousin and humoured her, but that was all. He went his own way.

The start of the evening began well, as invited friends and family gathered in the private party-room, surrounded by false palm trees and tropical wall murals. They had a birthday cake with blue and white icing - the only dispensation to the Blues.

Brian thought that he had restricted football to that token until someone produced a blue and white scarf and draped it around Tony's neck as those gathered there sang *'Happy Birthday'* loudly. The lads present finished up by giving Tony the bumps, before dumping him unceremoniously on the floor. The ceremony concluded with a slightly drunken rendition of *'Keep Right On'*, until the manager had a quite word with Brian, who put a stop to it.

Things appeared to be back on track until Brian spotted a couple of skinheads who had joined the party late. Looking distinctively uncomfortable in their short black ties, they slapped Tony on the back and took it in turns to give him a bear hug.

The three of them sat down in a corner and started to make full use of the free bar, and Brian's mood changed for the worse as the occasional loud expletive reached his ears and drew looks from some of the older guests.

He made an effort to remain calm, he didn't want to spoil things for his son, but he didn't like the speed at which the rum and cokes were going down, and he had a quiet word with the bar staff to limit the measures.

The problem for Brian though, was that although he had hired the bar area, the club as a whole was open and heaving with the usual Saturday night crowd, and the birthday celebrants shared the dance floor with the public. As members of the party came and went from the room to the dance floor, Brian began to lose track of people.

For her part, Joy was certainly not intending on spending her first night in a real night-club in a corner with some drunks under the watchful eye of her uncle, and was dancing the night away on the main dance floor with Naomi, who had already fully recovered from her one and only date with Tony.

Upon arrival, Joy had entered through the front double-doors, down four steps and into the reception area, past the cloakroom, a hangover from the Locarno's ballroom dancing past, and the toilets. A short corridor and through double doors into the main dance hall, with its sprung floor, now occupied by disco dancing, not Salsas and Tangos.

The glitter balls were still there, casting a constellation of coloured lights as they span, and she suddenly realised that everything glowed white in the beams of a number of cleverly positioned UV lights.

She had felt as if she were entering another world. Tonight she felt like a princess, although, casting a hopeful eye across the dance floor all she had seen were the human equivalent of frogs, and she knew that no kiss would work its magic there at the moment.

She might still be a virgin, but it didn't mean that she wasn't looking, although she was only too aware of her father's views on the matter. Never mind though, she could cross that bridge when she came to it.

She had the confidence, endemic to pretty teenage daughters, that fathers, even ones like Mike Carter, could be swayed when required.

Joy was fussy though, and had no interest in the thugs and 'doom-brains' that surrounded her father, with the exception of Pete, in whom she had detected a spark of something different.

She was Mike Carter's daughter, and was not going to be dazzled by any old toe-rag who fancied his chances. She had no illusion that any liaisons would have to be hidden in the short term, or the suitor might find himself with a broken nose, or worse, and Joy would be 'grounded' forever.

As she had walked around the edge of the dance floor through the already crowded tables and chairs, and towards the entrance to the Bali Hai, the resident band, *'Red Sun'*, was on stage playing their cover versions. As she traversed the main room they had struck up the new and fast selling future number one, *'You To Me Are Everything'*, by *'The Real Thing'*, and the floor had filled with couples and groups showing off their disco moves.

The lightshow swept across the dance floor creating crazy shapes across the heaving mass as people were consumed by the music. Joy itched to join them, but she had to do her family duty at the party first, and then find a way to escape her uncle's watchful eye.

Joy had dutifully taken part in the official birthday celebrations and sneakily consumed a few vodka and oranges. She had noticed her uncle's preoccupation with Tony and the skinheads, and had used the diversion to sneak out of the Bali Hai with Naomi, shielded from sight by another group from the party.

Now they were in the middle of the dancing, and Joy loved every minute of her new-found freedom. Suddenly, one chancer pulled Naomi away from Joy's side for a dance and for a few minutes Joy found herself on her own.

In the middle of the mayhem, Ryan Murphy stepped back and bumped into Joy Carter. They both turned at the same moment and their eyes met.

For a few seconds neither of them could hear the sound of the music and were oblivious to the people around them.

For Joy it felt like her heart stopped for a whole beat. The instant attraction was palpable and swept away all thought of fathers, uncles and school examinations leading to university.

For Ryan there was a feeling of surprise. He had thought he loved Roseanne, and that he knew what love was, but this was a totally different emotion, a fierce attraction, and he was shocked by the revelation, his defences collapsing under the onslaught. Such was the intensity of the moment that they stood motionless and struck dumb in the middle of the dancers for what seemed like an hour but was probably less than thirty seconds.

Nearby on the dance floor, Mel Price gave Benny Doherty a nudge, as they did a disco-dance together, and pointed towards Ryan and Joy shouting above the music, "Considering we had to drag the cunt out for a drink he suddenly seems very happy. She's a fuckin boster!"

Privately, Mel also thought that the girl's companion looked a cracker, as some twat pulled her away for a dance.

Ryan had indeed been reluctant to come out for a night on the town. He was obsessed with thoughts of Roseanne and Gary Docker being together, and spent a lot of time brooding in the house, but finally he had relented. Mel was if nothing else a persuasive individual. Indeed he was genuinely concerned at Ryan's blood lust. Gary was Mel's friend and he was torn between the two.

The trio had spent an hour drinking in one of the bars in The Locarno, hidden from sight from the Bali Hai, and completely unaware of the fact that their arch- enemy was not only close at hand, but fired up with heady combination of party-spirit and liquor.

Mel and Benny had finally persuaded Ryan to come out into the main dance floor area where the view was much better, with plenty of skirt on show, in the hope that he would find something to take his mind off his errant wife. They had both seen the effect of her desertion on Ryan's mental balance and were now congratulating themselves upon their match-making, oblivious to the disaster about to unfold.

"I'm sorry love, I didn't mean to bump into you," Ryan yelled into Joy's ear over the din, whilst taking the opportunity to breathe in the scent of her that made his head whirl. It wasn't the best chat-up line, but it didn't seem to matter.

Her cultured voice surprised him, "That's okay as long as you don't do it again. But as you're facing me, you may as well have the next dance" Joy smiled and surprised herself with her self-confidence and veneer of calm as she surfed the raging emotions beneath.

Ryan thanked whatever gods he worshipped when the opening strains of *'Hey There Lonely Girl'* by Eddie Holman came over the speakers. It was *the* classic slow dance and he wasted no time in taking an enthusiastic Joy into the slow circular shuffle that necessitated full-body contact, and passed for dancing in 1976. The sight would have had the ghosts of the sequined dancers of the past twirling in their shrouds.

Ryan had already signalled to Mel and Benny to give him some space, and elsewhere on the dance floor Naomi was giving the chancer a bit of encouragement. Mel was waiting for his opportunity to move in.

In the Bali Hai Suite, Tony Carter had just downed his eighth rum and coke, and was thinking that a shag on his 21st would be a damn good idea.

His thoughts immediately turned to Naomi Green and the memory of the parts of her body left unexplored because of the debacle with Ryan Murphy. He scanned the Bali Hai for her, and when he couldn't see Naomi or Joy he knew where they would be.

His attention began to waver from his skinhead drinking companions and towards the entrance to the dance floor. He got up, "I'm off to see if I can pull, coming?" Tony led the way, thoughts of Ryan and the recent embarrassment he had inflicted on Tony on his only date with Naomi at the front of his mind.

As the tempo of the music increased again, Ryan and Joy were lost in their own world, but after twenty minutes both were flushed, hot and sweating. Ryan realised that they had not spoken after that initial exchange; in fact it was nigh impossible due to the volume of the music and the cacophony of clapping, foot- stomping and chatter from the other dancers.

He waited for a break in the music, "Do you fancy going into the reception for some fresh air?"

Joy nodded, grasped his left hand gently and led the way. She could not believe that this dreamboat had fallen her way on her first ever visit to a club.

They stood chatting in the reception area by the cloakroom, and the subject of football did not come up once, and neither did the fact that Ryan was married. In fact, all thoughts of Roseanne had fled his mind, for the first time in many years of control and jealousy. Something wonderful had happened, he didn't know quite what it was, but he liked the feeling.

Ryan couldn't remember the last time he had felt such an inner peace and sense of normality; it had been missing from his life. Not only was Joy beautiful, she had simplicity about her, an honesty that made her vulnerable, and she was someone that instinctively he wanted to protect.

The anteroom to the dance floor, where they stood, was the favourite place for chatting up and first kisses, and there were several other couples dotted around, leaning against the wall. Ryan couldn't help but lean forward and kiss Joy softly on the cheek, fearing rejection but unwilling to let the moment pass.

Joy pulled him gently towards her and kissed him on the lips. That first proper kiss bonded them and they both felt that their lives had changed in the moment it took. For Ryan a channel opened up to the long suppressed, 'decent' part of his character, which spilled out suffusing him with a sense of well-being and contentment.

The idyllic moment was shattered abruptly as all-hell broke loose.

Benny tumbled out of the doors leading to the main dance floor, closely followed by Mel who was bleeding heavily from the nose, with half of his shirt torn at the back. Behind them advanced Tony Carter and the two skinheads, three angry men full of alcohol and rage ready to inflict further punishment. Tony had forgotten any notion of sex, he knew what he wanted at this moment for his birthday present and it wasn't Naomi fucking Green, she could wait for later.

Upon leaving the Bali Hai suite, Carter had stood scanning the dance floor, looking for Naomi. Attuned to watching for dark faces, he had instantly registered the presence of a 'half-caste' dancing with a white girl, and then his jaw had dropped in disbelief when a shaft of spotlight illuminated the hated face of Mel Price together with his ex–girlfriend of one night –Naomi.

Seconds later he had spotted Benny playing the fool with a couple of girls from the party and the liquor-induced fire in his stomach had instantly consumed his brain. He had attacked before the element of surprise evaporated, his moronic pals in tow.

Mel and Benny had been overpowered in the initial onslaught and had opted for flight and regroup, straight towards the reception area.

As Carter burst through the doors from the dance floor, the incomprehensible and incredible sight of Joy standing close to Ryan turned his fury white-hot, and whilst the odds had now evened up, Carter was a mass of adrenalin, hatred and amazement, laced with alcohol. He plunged straight for the loving couple.

"Take your filthy hands off her, you piece of shit. I'll fuckin kill you this time," he screamed.

Ryan was taken completely by surprise at this apparition. He took a couple of steps backwards; the last thing he wanted was to get into a fight in front of Joy, or for her to get hurt by a stray blow.

Joy was rooted to the spot in shock and confusion, trying to make some sense out of a situation that seemed to have none.

Mel launched himself at Carter but was knocked to the floor by one of the skinheads. Carter kicked him viciously in the chest and screamed, "They don't allow fuckin monkeys in here you fuckin black bastard."

Ryan moved to protect Mel from further punishment as Joy looked on in appalled shock, but before he could do anything four burly doormen appeared from the door and separated the warring parties.

"They fuckin started it." Benny shouted, "We was just having a good time dancing until they barged in, fuckin racist twats."

Ryan backed further away as Brian Carter arrived and pushed his son roughly against the wall "Cut it out. For fuck's sake it's your birthday not some fucking wrestling match." Brian was a strong man and held Tony there until his eyes grew less wild, although he knew his son, and that the pent up rage still burnt brightly within.

"What do you want us to do Mr. Carter?" one of the doormen queried, anxious to restore normality. Fights were not good for business.

Brian tried to salvage the situation, "I'll keep me son under control. We've got a party to finish. I'd be grateful if you could get rid of those three," pointing at Ryan, Mel and Benny. He nodded towards his son. "He'll calm down if they make themselves scarce."

He looked at Ryan, recognising the leader, "Just take it easy kiddo, best to go without any more trouble and have a good time somewhere else."

He returned his attention to the lead bouncer, "And while you're at it, tell these two wankers to sling their hooks as well," indicating the two skinheads.

Tony Carter tried to protest but his father was powerful and fuelled by a desperation to diffuse the situation and get both Tony and Joy under control. He hadn't liked the look of what she was doing in the corridor one little bit, and had no wish to have to confess any abrogation of 'guard duty' to his brother.

He propelled the still struggling Tony out of the reception area, around the dance floor and back into the Bali Hai. He beckoned to Joy to follow him and with one glance at Ryan she did as she was told. She was still trying to comprehend what was going on, and had already decided that the blame lay with her cousin and his horrible Nazi mates for attacking the coloured kid.

_____

The doormen had their instructions, and carried them out. Each one of them was an experienced street-fighter and would tolerate no resistance. Some of those that had tried to come the hard-man with the door staff in the past had found themselves in hospital having been at the wrong end of the small rubber coshes that each of them carried in their suit pockets.

The two skinheads were sent on their way first, told to turn right and 'fuck off', in quick time.' Now that the odds had changed they did precisely that, running along Hurst Street and disappearing onto Smallbrook Queensway. They knew exactly who Ryan was, his reputation - and he looked mad as hell, shooting baleful glances in their direction.

Once the skinheads were out of sight, and Mel was back on his feet, they were all ushered out by the doormen.

Outside in Hurst Street, the three of them huddled in a doorway.

"What is it with you two? Every time we see Carter one of you finishes up on your arse. That's twice that he's decked someone now." Ryan chided them as he made a cursory effort at wiping some of the blood from Mel's cheek, "It's like having two babbies to look after." They all started laughing.

"Well thanks for nothing. You were so busy with that bit of skirt that me and Benny had to protect the good name of the firm on our own." Mel retorted, light- heartedly, not wishing to ignite Ryan's short fuse. "Mind you, she's worth it, what a cracker! I wouldn't climb over her mate to get to you either!" They all laughed and the tension evaporated.

Ryan had come to a decision. "You two get yourselves off home or go and have a drink. I've got a bit of business to do and I'll see you tomorrow. Try not to get into any more bloody trouble."

Mel and Benny knew that there was no point arguing and headed off into the night.

Ryan knew that what he was doing was crazy, but he felt driven. He was unable to get Joy from his mind. That first kiss had been a revelation, the whole encounter had, and he was raging at the bad fortune that had interrupted it.

He was also coming to terms with the fact that Joy was a Carter. '*Why is nothing to do with women straightforward for me?*' he mused, as he stood in the doorway alone.

He was desperately afraid that Joy would disappear for good, together with that tantalizing and addictive hint of possible happiness that had swept through him as they kissed. He had realised from her aghast face that another confrontation would be disastrous so he waited patiently by the Hippodrome doorway, scribbling down his name on the back of one of Colin Murphy's business cards.

He persevered for an hour and a half, and had almost given up hope, when Joy and Naomi stepped out into the street.

Joy had insisted on catching the bus home, despite Brian's protestations and offers of taxis. Joy wanted some time with Naomi, to think and to discuss the evening before returning to her home and parental cage. She had been rocked to the core by her encounter with

Ryan and then the shocking violence that had shattered the enchantment. But she was entranced by Ryan, couldn't forget his face and the feel of his lips on hers. She also wanted to see what Naomi had found out from the coloured lad that she had seemed to quite fancy.

It had been Joy's first meaningful kiss, and she was convinced as only a seventeen year old could be, that true love had found her. She hadn't yet worked out who Ryan was and why Tony hated him so, but she was no fool and sensed that he was taboo, which made him all the more alluring. He was a mystery to be solved.

She was also worried about Tony. They had been close as they grew up and she cared for him. He had become a main-player in the Blues group and its ancillary enterprises, and she accepted what that entailed in terms of violence, but hadn't liked it. She had no illusions about her father's activities, but respected his ability to control and plan. Tony now seemed to be careering along a path that ended who knew where, and this right-wing stuff had been the catalyst for a concerning leap in the type of violence that Tony seemed willing to perpetrate.

Football rucks were one thing, but the zealous glint she had seen in his eyes as he kicked Mel smacked of a growing fanaticism that would leap boundaries. He seemed to have gone insane, *'who in their right minds would pick a fight on their birthday just because someone was coloured?'*

Ryan followed the chattering girls from a distance, checking they were alone. They were both lookers, Joy blonde and Naomi raven-haired. Joy was tall and thinner, more model-shaped, whilst Naomi had a voluptuousness that implied happy times for the man who could charm her. The girls eventually reached Colmore Row, from where the late buses departed, fending off comments, and admiring glances from groups of drunken male revelers, that they passed.

It was now or never for Ryan as he strode over to Joy at the bus stop, "I couldn't leave it like that. I just had to say sorry about earlier. I hope you didn't get too scared." He pressed the card deftly into her hand.

Naomi Green looked at him and then the penny dropped, "I know you. You're that Villa fan that beat Tony up outside the cinema in New Street. Joy, you can't see him again, your dad and Tony would go spare. She turned to Ryan, "If you care anything for Joy then show it by leaving her alone – just walk away now!"

Ryan looked into Joy's eyes, "I'm sorry Joy, I didn't mean for you to get scared - honest."

He backed off, but as Naomi turned her back on him he could see Joy's eyes following him. He brought his little finger and thumb to his right ear in the universal sign for the telephone and noted the recognition of the gesture and the slight nod.

Joy grasped the card firmly in her closed hand then shuffled it into her coat pocket. She watched him until he was out of sight, her heart beating faster - *'Taboo indeed!'*

Naomi stood back, taking her friend by the shoulders, "Joy you're playing with fire. Take it from me I know a nutter when I see one. You should keep well away. This would only end badly."

"I bet you're going to see his mate again though aren't you, I know you, can always tell. You liked him. Did you get his number?" Joy retorted.

Naomi looked sheepish, then giggled, "That would be telling"

***

Joy spent the next few days alternating between periods of romantic fantasy, panic at the implications of her feelings, and determination to follow them anyway. She just couldn't get his face out of her mind, and re-lived that first kiss over and over.

But re-visiting that moment brought with it the memory of Tony's face contorted in anger, and the violence that had erupted at the club. Here was a dilemma indeed. She had of course quizzed Naomi on the way home and since, exhausting her friend's paltry knowledge.

She had then moved onto Pete Stevens, her new confidante. She liked Pete. He was different to the usual boneheads that surrounded her father. Yes, he could take care of himself, he wouldn't have risen through the 'ranks' otherwise, but there was something more underneath the 'jack the lad' hooligan he portrayed.

He was clever and had an emotional intelligence that surfaced every so often when they talked. He empathised, listened, and gave good counsel. She thought that he might be falling for her, she had seen her father watching them, and in different circumstances she might have responded, but those few devastating moments with her golden-haired prince had expunged all those kind of thoughts in respect of Pete from her mind.

He had proved to be a treasure trove of information, but none of it improved matters. She now knew who Ryan really was, and why her cousin had reacted as he had. She also knew that he was forbidden to her, which made contacting him again an irresistible challenge to her rebellious teenage mind.

She knew that she would see him again, had to see him again, but there was her father, the enmity between the clans, her plans to escape the very life of violence to which Ryan clearly belonged.

Belonged and didn't belong. He was all the more intriguing because of the obvious tension within him. One moment tender and caring, the next a man clearly used to violence, who had traded blow-for-blow with Tony, and apparently won the encounter. Joy wanted to resolve that tension and see if she would fit with what remained. She was already falling in love, or whatever passed for that emotion within the head and heart of a virgin teenager boiling with emotion and hormones.

Having resolved to pursue the relationship against the advice of Naomi and Pete – both had been sworn to secrecy from her father, Joy's mind turned to planning, without which she would never escape the watchful eye of her father, the arch- tactician.

She began an intensive campaign to recruit her lifelong friend Naomi to the cause. Luckily she already had a foot through the door because Naomi was in contact with Mel, in fact had seen him twice since the Locarno. That fact made Joy all the more jealous and eager and Naomi's resolve crumbled quickly. She was an honest friend, and could see the hypocrisy of her own position, forbidding Joy from seeing a white man just because he supported a different football team whilst she had crossed the forbidden divide, a white girl seeing a black man at a time of racial strife.

***

Pete sat in his room, the small black diary open, pen poised,

> *'What a mess! Of all the bastards she could fall for, it had to be Ryan fucking Murphy. Fate must be working here, what are the odds of them meeting like that and hitting it off? That's screwed any chances I had unless I can turn her off him, got to be careful though. She's clearly besotted and I'm in a dangerous position knowing about it and not reporting it. Daren't though, Mike would be bad enough but what would happen if that nutter Tony found out? And telling would raise questions about my feelings for her and why she told me, could look as if I was helping her, and that would fuck up my position here. Wasn't at all comfortable when Mike spoke to me the other day. He's no fool and has noticed I fancy her. Got a definite warning there. Still, at least she told me and is asking what I think. Don't want to be 'just good friends' and someone to talk to about other men! But it does put me in a place where I might be able to do something. It might all burn out, she might not be able to see him again, but I wouldn't put anything past her, she's too clever and stubborn. Need to be subtle and wait for the right moment.'*

Somehow writing the words down was cathartic, getting them out of his whirling mind and enabling him to maintain hope –

however slim.

***

Birmingham Sunday Observer - *13 June 1976*:

'More trouble in London – but Police deny it's racial - A seventeen year old white boy died in hospital from stab wounds yesterday after a clash between two Asians and a group of white youths. The stabbing occurred about an hour after a march through East Ham, London, by right-wingers chanting, 'Blacks Out'.

However, a Scotland Yard spokesman denied that the incident was in any way connected with the earlier march. 'Any suggestion that this incident was inspired by racial conflict would be purely speculative', he added. The youth was stabbed at a shopping centre in East Ham. Two Asians and a number of white youths were helping police enquiries last night.'

***

Birmingham Sunday Observer – *13 June 1976*:

'BBC apologises for race-hate graffiti - You couldn't make it up! The BBC had to hurriedly dispatch a team around Birmingham to scrub racialist slogans off buildings following angry complaints that a film crew had defaced walls in the city. 'Relf Rules OK' and 'Wogs Go Home' were among the offensive slogans scrawled on shop windows by the BBC film team during the making of a fiction series on factions in the city. But they forgot to remove them when they moved on. A BBC spokesman apologized and said the slogans were in the context of the story but should have been removed when

filming finished.'

***

Birmingham Sunday Observer – *20 June 1976*:

'100 arrests in Anti NF Demo - Police arrested around one hundred people at a sit- down demo in Bradford yesterday. The participants were demonstrating about the National Front. About three hundred people marched into the city centre from Lister Park and sat down in the busy Forster square.'

***

Birmingham Sunday Observer – *20 June 1976*:

'Relf's For Sale sign goes down – and up! - Race row rebel Robert Relf remained in prison last night after a day of turmoil tinged with humour after it appeared momentarily as if a gust of wind would cut through the legal stand-off and secure his release.

The debate started when the now infamous sign advertising his Leamington house for sale 'To an English family only', was blown down. Relf's stubborn refusal to remove the sign was the only reason for his imprisonment for contempt forty-three days ago. With the sign gone, solicitors argued that the whole complexion of the case had altered and it was possible he could be freed. It is rumoured that Government solicitors had been searching for a way out of the tangle that has seen Relf on hunger strike and that they would be only too happy to utilise this 'act of God.'

But last night the original sign was back in place. It was

244

apparently replaced by his wife, Mrs. Sadie Relf, upon her return from visiting her husband in Stafford prison. She said, 'It is his sign and he would want it to be there. The fact that the wind blew it down does not mean he took it down. It makes no difference at all.'

In a bizarre and humorous twist, for the few hours while the sign was missing another one appeared quoting, 'Normal prejudice will be resumed as soon as possible.' Mrs. Relf said she did not know who had put up the new sign but described whoever it was as a 'mindless illiterate', although this paper would contend it exhibited more wit than illiteracy.

Mrs. Relf also revealed that her husband, who is still on hunger-strike, was now, 'very weak indeed, no more than a bag of skin and bones. He is confined to his bed in the prison hospital and allowed up to sit in a chair only to meet visitors. I am hopeful of something coming of the Official Solicitor's meeting with the Judge on Monday,' said Mrs. Relf, 'But I am not allowing my hopes to get too high. The last time I thought something was going to happen it didn't and I suffered a shattering shock.' Mrs. Relf said she had given up trying to persuade her husband to end his hunger strike, 'I have decided that my attempts to make him give up are causing him such distress that it is making his health deteriorate quicker so now I'm just waiting and hoping.'

The Relf situation continues to polarise views and yesterday two rival demonstrations in Leamington organised by the British Movement and Leamington Trades Council took place. Police formed a cordon between the rival factions and reinforcements stood by in case of trouble but there were no serious incidents. An estimated five hundred people turned out for the Trades Council march. Their spokesman said last night that it had been a great success except for a minor incident when there was a scuffle with a dozen British Movement protestors.

He said, 'The march went well and the leaders of both the white and coloured communities made speeches pointing out that the troubles we face are not caused by any particular group but by government policies. We changed the march route to avoid the town centre because leaders of the Indian community felt that might be inviting trouble. We shall continue the campaign for racial harmony in many ways'.

***

Postscript - *Relf's plight was taken up by the tabloid press as an example of the supposedly draconian nature of race legislation and there was initially a public outcry that he had been put in prison for his beliefs.*

However support for Relf's cause soon died after articles about his background began to appear in the Sunday Times, revealing that he had been a member of the British Movement, and had served as a bodyguard to Colin Jordan, long time right-wing agitator and National Front leader, as well as attempting to organise a UK branch of the Ku Klux Klan.

Robert Relf was released from prison later in 1976, by which time much of the popular support that he had gathered had died away. Although courted by the National Party and the National Front, he went on to re-join the British Movement, although he left due to his dissatisfaction with the leadership of Michael McLaughlin and instead devoted much of his energies to the World Union of National Socialists. He moved away from the Midlands and memories faded as the National Front peaked and went into decline in subsequent years.

***

Mike Carter locked stares with Tony. It had not been a happy meeting. Tony was the first to break the impasse by looking away, but it had taken too long for the Blues' leader. *'Getting too big for his boots. Pete might just be right,'* thought Mike, who was fast losing patience,

"Tony, what's going on in your head son? I'm getting pissed off at the time you're spending with these Nazi fuckers instead of helping with business. It's getting that every time you see a black face you lose your mind and get that fucking knife out. I can't have that. We had a deal didn't we, from way back, when you was just a streak of piss. I turned you into a leader, gave you something worth doing, made it clear to everyone that you were second in command, and one day could take over, and this is how you repay me."

Mike shook his head, "It's got to stop. I don't want you going on any more of these demos and marches. I want you to focus on business, on the Blues' firm, OK?"

Tony was not OK, and moments passed before he responded, "Its just that I think it's important. Our country is going to the dogs, all these dirty Pakis and coons, look at the state of Handsworth and Sparkhill already, like fuckin Calcutta High Street. It's bigger than football, it's politics, and unless people like me stand up and do

247

something, fuck knows how it'll all end up. Enoch was right you know, it'll be rivers of blood, our blood."

Mike curbed a rising temptation to take his nephew by the scruff of the neck and shake him, "Can't you see they're just using you as muscle on the streets Tony? People like these National Front wankers look at what Hitler done with his henchmen and try to do the same thing here. And what happened to them people after Hitler took power? He butchered most of them. Don't be a fool, I'm as leery of some of these immigrants as anyone, but there are some good lads amongst them, and they can be good for business too. Look at the Turk, he's OK ain't he? And that lot from Handsworth, they done us a good deal on the doors, they're sound too."

Tony began to speak but caught the message in Mike's eyes. He knew his uncle, had felt the power of his fists, and had seen the punishment meted out to those who crossed him. This was not the moment to take him on. He thought, *'I'll play it cute. One day soon it'll be my turn to be boss, and then we can do some fucking business – on the immigrants, not with them. The lads follow me, not him, my day is coming.'* His words were very different,

"Perhaps you're right Mike, I'll have a good think about what you said, end of season, summer to plan stuff, and then we can make a big splash in the first few matches. There's going to be a nice bit of sun by the looks of the weather, while we sort out business." *'And by September you'll be out if I plan it right,'* the little voice inside added.

***

Back at Steelhouse Lane, Rob Docker also sat plotting in his office, oblivious of the undercurrents and changes. He still wasn't happy, still getting grief over the football stuff, although he had a few weeks in hand now the season had finished and everyone's thoughts were focused on holidays, heat and drought. He had some irons in the fire, but progress was slow, too slow. *'I need a break, a bit of luck, something that'll bust these bastards wide open and give me the chance I need to sort things out my way,'* he thought. You made your own luck though, by being ready to exploit opportunities.

His train of thought was broken by gales of laughter in the office outside. Reid was waving the newspaper about and all eyes were on Sally who appeared to be holding a large pair of tartan trousers. Docker grabbed the newspaper from Reid's sweaty paw, and as he did so Reid spluttered out between laughs, "Read this boss, just got her a special pair to go in her new kit."

Sally advanced towards Reid as Rob read, "Thanks, Malcolm, I can use these old strides of yours. They're just what I need to make a Rod Stewart scarf for my niece. I expect they're from your Bay City Roller days?"

She paused for effect making sure that she had everyone's attention, "I reckon they pulled the boys OK a few years ago, but I can see you've grown out of them. Anyway, nothing can work miracles, and when you've got a face like a welder's bench like you, and a belly like a zeppelin, it must be a lot harder to attract the blokes these days." Sally always enjoyed promoting the idea of that Reid was a closet homosexual, it always riled him, so it might be true.

Rob sighed, Reid would never learn, Sally always wiped the floor with him.

Docker slid the newspaper round to see what the source of merriment was all about.

Birmingham Observer: *'Policewomen to wear the trousers - The saga of where a policewoman can put her truncheon has finally been resolved, by the movement that created the original problem – 'women's lib'. The Sex Discrimination Act was the cause of the move to put the women on the front line, the streets, and for that they demanded a truncheon to protect themselves. The problem now is where do they put it? West Midlands County Council has come up with a proposal that represents another revolution – issue the women with trousers.*

The request originally came from the Police Federation that represents rank and file officers. At their Wednesday meeting the Police Committee will determine whether to cancel an order for six hundred skirts – replacing them with trousers. That will generate another issue, as the current jacket is too short to wear with trousers, but for this winter the ladies can wear an overcoat and next year a new style jacket will be provided to go with a skirt and trousers. And the trousers have a truncheon pocket – just like the men's.'

***

Perhaps it was because Mike's attention and thoughts were focused on Tony; perhaps Joy played it just right. Whatever the reason, once she had persuaded Naomi to help her, the relationship with Ryan prospered. Naomi proved to be a very effective go- between and as a bonus, had really hit it off with Mel, who Ryan used as an intermediary, after swearing him to secrecy.

Mel had been happy to help, hoping that Joy would take Ryan's mind off Gary and Roseanne. But whenever Joy wasn't around, and they were alone, Ryan still returned to the topic of revenge, in the most lurid terms.

To Mel there seemed to be two Ryan's now, the caring, humorous and gentle man with feelings and emotions he had known in younger days whenever he was with Joy, or talking about her, and the cold, violent and chilling would-be killer when the subject of his wife and lover arose.

It was clear to Mel that there was something significant going on in Ryan's head, but try as he might, he couldn't get inside it.

Joy was ecstatic when Naomi, who had a lot more freedom, reported that she had slept with Mel. It meant that her friend was in a more compromised position, and ensured her loyalty to the cause. It was as if Naomi was rebelling against Tony and all he stood for, by dating a 'coloured' man.

Truth was, Mel was a lovely guy, in temperament and looks, and Naomi had at first come to despise, and then hate Tony Carter, the final straw being the fracas he had caused at his own birthday party.

After Ryan had left, Tony had tried to rekindle his relationship with Naomi by means of some drunken pawing's with the result that she slapped his face in the Bali Hai bar, and only

Brian Carter's restraining arms, for the second time that night, prevented Tony from punching her.

Mel in contrast was caring and witty, and Naomi was already hatching plans to draw him away from the world of football and the Villa firm. She hoped for a life together somewhere where they could live without the constant looks of condemnation and racist comments whenever they were together in public.

Of course, Tony had reported back to Mike concerning Joy's passionate moment with Ryan Murphy. Mike had been incandescent, and if he could have locked Joy up twenty-four hours a day, would have done so. But he knew that he couldn't keep her caged anymore.

Mike was not a stupid man, and he reviewed his plan from earlier in the month and found it still viable.

Putting on his 'reasonable' persona, he sat down and had an adult chat to Joy. He hoped that she would respond well to this and was not disappointed. She seemed pleased that he was going to allow her some freedom, and happy with the concept of being accompanied. He suggested all of his lieutenants one-by-one, and not surprisingly she chose Pete, and also her best friend Naomi.

Mike could live with that, having already had his chat with Stevens, and Naomi was a known quantity. After they had finished talking, he sat back in his chair and congratulated himself on his subtle handling of the situation.

Carol watched him from the kitchen, and as a woman smiled at how easily Joy was running rings around her dad.

Meanwhile, Joy was in her bedroom, singing inside, a little victory achieved and her route to Ryan enhanced by her unwitting father.

As June faded into July, and the endless sunshine continued, Joy and Ryan had grown ever closer.

For her years, Joy had a keen sense of how far she could push people, and so she cleverly used Pete, behaving impeccably when out with him, laying a false trail. She sensed Pete was in her thrall, in fact enjoyed the power of playing his emotions for her own purposes, although sometimes little pangs of guilt intruded, reminding her that he was a decent guy, and should be treated as such.

For that reason she did not see Ryan when out with Pete. They, including Naomi, would go to all the expected places, with the expected people. That gave Pete some safety and cover. But there were other occasions when Naomi and Joy were supposed to be out with him, that he covered for them whilst they went far afield in Ryan's beloved Ford Capri, metallic green with a black vinyl roof and furry seat covers. Mel and Naomi would go off together and she would be able to snatch precious time alone with Ryan.

The final Saturday of the month was a scorcher, and Joy had been working on her father for days. Eventually he relented. He would allow them to go to Weston for a weekend, the first time he had allowed her to spend a night away from home. He checked the arrangements, even telephoned the hotel, to ensure that Naomi and Joy had a room together whilst Pete said he would keep an eye on them but stay with friends he had made whilst living and working down there.

Mike had thought about sending Sam or Tony secretly as well, but wanted to keep Tony close at the moment, and Sam had doors to sort out in town at the weekend. Spike was still being tested and Roly was gone. In the end he decided to trust Pete, who had done a good job so far.

Joy never knew just how close she had come to the disaster of Tony or Sam appearing as she congratulated herself on her planning.

Pete drove them down the M5. It was so hot that cars were strewn along the hard shoulder, overheated, and the inside of the car was like an oven, even with the windows wound down. *'Red-hot for a red-letter day,'* she thought, as the face of Ryan danced in her mind.

She dutifully phoned Mike upon arrival, the next morning and before departure. *'That's Ok then, panic over,'* he thought as he put the phone down after the final call. *'She's had her bit of freedom and no harm done.'* He congratulated himself on the success of his strategy.

Meanwhile, Pete drove gloomily back up the M5, thoughts in a whirl. A recall to work had been issued for Longbridge after another lengthy strike, so it was back to the day job for him, although they would no doubt be back out again in a few days.

For a few days there would be less time for action and more to brood on the assembly line.

In the back seat a different Joy was returning home, no longer a girl, no longer a virgin, but a woman with plans.

All she could think of was those precious moments with Ryan at the hotel, and how difficult it had been to part from him in Weston.

***

Birmingham Sunday Observer - *27 June 1976*:

'Midlands at melting point - British heat records were smashed yesterday as the temperature hit 95 degrees in London, the highest temperature ever recorded. Birmingham hit 88.7 degrees, the hottest since 1886.

As temperatures soared, thousands of Midlanders headed for the coast and countryside in search of cooler air. The sweltering heat is predicted to go on for days yet and bosses fear production will be hit as 'heatwave breaks', are required in factories. It is also a worry that high temperatures mean short tempers and the conditions could hit fragile industrial relations with minor issues leading to walkouts.

Those not at work formed jams on the motorways as cars overheated, and the RAC and AA struggled to cope with breakdowns. The M5 jammed solid and there were queues to leave at the Weston and Minehead junctions. Weston police reported every parking space in the town taken with hundreds of cars still looking for room. Hospitals struggled to cope with a flood of heat exhaustion victims but ice cream sales boomed.

Reservoirs are beginning to empty but officials are not proposing crisis measures just yet. Birmingham's Welsh reservoirs are coping at present but areas served by smaller ones may have to resort to supplies by water tanker soon.

Chapter Eight.

'He's Got The Whole World In His Hands'

July 1976

Just a week had passed; a mere seven days, but it had wrought changes in Ryan. His mind kept returning to the hotel room by the sea, to Joy. In a vain attempt to divert his thoughts he had taken in *'Enter the Dragon'* at the ABC Bristol Road, but much as he loved Bruce Lee, it hadn't helped. In fact the fight scenes had left him strangely cold, there was a struggle within him, between violence and love, and it was finely balanced.

Ryan could see now that he had never loved his wife, it had been a pale imitation of the real thing, and he truly understood now why she had left him. *'Must have been fate, clearing the way for me and Joy, it was meant to be,'* he thought.

But the other side still surfaced, chafing for revenge. He had been disrespected and humiliated and at these moments still felt that he should settle this outstanding business before moving on.

Thus he continued to issue dire threats about what he would do to Gary and Roseanne when in the company of Mel and Benny. It was becoming just macho bravado as Joy's benign influence took hold, but Mel and Benny did not know that, and Mel in particular fretted that at some stage he would end up between Ryan and Gary with a hard decision to make.

If love was a drug, as Brian Ferry had crooned last year, then Ryan was addicted and suffering withdrawal symptoms because there had been no contact at all from Joy since Weston. Likewise Mel hadn't seen or heard from Naomi, and they had been becoming increasingly worried, imagining all sorts of terrible scenarios.

Finally, on this steaming hot Friday, Naomi got a message through. Family holidays had been the cause of the silence. Naomi's parents were avid 'caravan draggers', and had finally cracked at the prospect of endless sun in Britain.

Naomi's dad worked for Rover at Lode Lane, and there was still trouble with plenty of workers failing to heed the return to work call. There was a rumour that there was going to be a big protest at the Leyland Motor Show at the National Exhibition Centre on the forthcoming weekend, so Mr. Green had decided that being elsewhere was the best option.

They had packed the van and headed off to Wales, literally decanting Naomi from Pete's car upon her return from Weston and into what was for Naomi, an excruciating few days of alternating stress and boredom, marooned in the Brecon Beacons, knowing that Mel and Ryan would be concerned.

Naomi had been terrified that Ryan and Mel would come looking for them, precipitating what to Naomi's fevered imagination seemed likely to be the end of the world. The caravan had been pitched in the middle of nowhere and it had taken her four days to find a working phone box and to grab the opportunity of making a call without her parents knowing.

By what was to prove an unlucky coincidence, *'or was it fate, this time conspiring against us?'* Ryan later wondered, Mike Carter had taken his family off to Benidorm on a package holiday. He had got a good last-minute deal from a travel agent he knew that owed him a 'favour'.

Joy had no alternative but to go, but had no chance of speaking to Naomi beforehand. She had trusted that Naomi would get a message to Ryan via Mel, not knowing that in fact her friend had also been whisked away.

As Mel recounted the tale, Ryan was puzzled over why anyone would need to go to Spain when the temperature was ninety degrees at home - perhaps it was cooler there?

The upshot of all this drama was that Ryan, Mel and Benny had a free weekend. The weather was unbelievable, records being broken everyday, and everyone wanted to get out of the boiling city.

It was Benny who suggested a second visit to Weston. He had missed out the week before and had a new girlfriend to impress. He spent the week wheedling at Ryan and Mel, and prevailed when they suddenly found that they had nothing better to do.

To Ryan it was a way of getting closer to the emotions awakened by Joy those few days before, and a chance to think, away from the world of his father. Things would be clearer there. It was an easy decision, but the coincidences were mounting up and the fate that Ryan had been praising was about to reveal another face.

***

Spike found Tony Carter stood outside The Crown in Station Street, downing the contents of a cold pint of lager. "Alright Tony it's fucking hot innit." Carter puffed his chest out – ever the rising star, "If it's like this in July what the fuck is it going to be like in August. They'll be calling this the Costa-fuckin-del- Brum soon!" He loved the hot weather; it meant he could wear a tight T-shirt to show off his muscles to the girls.

Spike chose his moment, making sure that he had Carter's full attention, "I've got some news you might be interested in. I know a bird that's going out with one of the Villa boys, that Benny Doherty, the one you put on his arse. He always hangs around with that bum-boy half-caste Mel Price..... Anyway they're off to Weston on Saturday for a day out."

Tony looked at him with slight interest at the mention of Mel, he had unfinished business with the black boy, "So fuckin what? Why should I be interested in that tadpole Doherty, he's fuck-all?"

Spike smiled, "I hear Price is going as well - and Ryan Murphy – just the four of them. I thought you might find that interesting, as you've got some scores to settle."

Tony slapped Spike on the back, a broad smile spread across his face "I think you might just be due an ice-cream on the pier Spike. Get a couple of the lads together for the weekend. We're off to the seaside!"

***

It was a slow trip for the second week running, as Ryan's Capri once more crawled down the M5. A three-hour drive saw Ryan, Mel, Benny and his new girl arrive at the Grand Pier Boulevard in Weston-Super-Mare.

They had made an effort and got up early though, beating the worst of the crowds, and at least there was some parking left.

Mel Price was in one of his irrepressible moods and was making everyone laugh, cracking jokes the whole way down. Even Ryan laughed, although he spent the whole drive down missing Joy and trying to work out how to cut the Gordian knot of enmity that prevented them being together normally. He didn't know that Gordian knots are only solved by thinking 'outside the box' and Ryan's good side hadn't yet re- emerged sufficiently to think beyond the world of the rival clans.

Benny's thoughts were more down to earth. He was out to impress his new girlfriend, and hoping that the combination of seaside, sunshine, and a couple of lagers would lead to some sex in the sand-dunes at Brean later.

***

Two hours behind them, another car containing Tony Carter, Spike, and two of the up and comers, arrived, wended its way past the railway station, and on through the 'bed and breakfast' streets of Weston.

***

The pier was the centre of Weston, everyone was drawn to it, and Ryan's group was no exception. There was no sign of the sea; it was 'out', a running joke amongst weekending Brummies' who called the place *'Weston-Super-Mud'*. And there were acres of mud showing, as far as the eye could see, a few lapping waves could just be glimpsed, glinting on the horizon.

The promenade was filling up with strolling groups and families, and the usual infestation of small children were occupying the thin section of sand before the expanses of quicksand and mud began, building castles, digging holes in a frenzy, building walls to keep the sea back and throwing sand around.

As Ryan and his group were leaving the Pier, having lost a few bob in the slot machines, they came face-to-face with Tony's crew.

A beaming smile spread across Carter's face, "Well, well, what have we here? Two bastards, a monkey, and a slut."

Benny's new girl shrank behind him, shocked at the aggression leaking from Carter's voice and demeanour. It jarred with the rest of the scene, the sun beating down on their heads, the promenade full of happy families brandishing candy floss, ice-cream, beef-burgers, and everything suffused with the smell of fried fish and chips.

Carter squared up to Ryan, ignoring Mel and Benny, "I've been looking for you, you fucking bastard. You won't get as lucky as you did the last two times, no daddy to rescue you here. What about it then, just you and me? Right here – right now!"

Ryan could not believe his ill-luck. The morning at the sea had resolved him to move on from his life of fighting and crime, he had better things to plan for, and he knew how much Joy abhorred violence. If she heard about him scrapping with her cousin again he was afraid of losing her, the relationship was after all in its infancy, and by the look on Carter's face, this would not be a quick scuffle. He wanted blood.

He suppressed the urge to wipe the triumphant smirk from his adversary's face and stepped back into a defensive posture. As Mel and Benny looked on in astonishment he raised his hands, palms showing, "I'm not here for trouble. I'm here for a quiet day out."

Carter was taken aback for a moment by this surprising manifestation of what seemed to him to be cowardice, and several moments passed as his acolytes looked to him for a lead. He seemed to reach a sudden decision and quick as a flash slapped Ryan across his face with the back of his hand, "Fuckin chicken bastard, I thought you was supposed to be fuckin hard, are you the best the Villa have got?"

The milling throng of holidaymakers around them started to create space, and parents with children hurried them along, sensing the tension in the air and that trouble would soon accompany the sound of raised voices.

Every nerve in Ryan's body screamed *'fight'*, and adrenalin pumped through him, but he suppressed the urge and took another step back. This was Joy's cousin, she had grown up with him and he had given Joy a promise to stop the fighting. He could not risk losing her for a petty scuffle on the street.

As he stood there, the face of Titch, and the sound of his final scream, appeared in his head, followed by a vision of the huddled form of Charlie at the bottom of the toilet steps. These were demons he had been fighting for months; demons that had helped infuse a pretty young girl with the power to stay his hands, "I won't fight you Carter. Just fuck off and leave us alone."

Carter could not believe his eyes and ears, and Mel and Benny were rendered mute at their leader's submission. It merely added credence to Carter's self-inflated views of his own reputation. Bolstered by the recent months of right-wing scuffles, football violence, and the incident at the Locarno that he had already turned in his own mind into Ryan running from him after being rescued by Brian Carter's intervention.

In reality, Carter had been careering further and further off the rails of sanity all year, his ego filling with self-delusion. He saw himself as the nascent leader of the Blues' firm, a rising star of the National Front. The flawed philosophy of Nazism dominated his thoughts and actions, and refused to be constrained. Pete Stevens had seen it, Mike Carter had tried to stop it, but that effort quickly evaporated on the promenade in the moment when Ryan Murphy had taken a step backwards.

They had all underestimated Tony Carter, underestimated his capacity for violence and hate. He was mean, small-minded and a bully and Ryan's retreat just egged him on. He had persuaded himself that Ryan had been lucky that one time he had put him down.

He was certain that he could get the better of Ryan and here was his golden opportunity. Here was his chance to beat and humiliate Ryan Murphy in front of witnesses, and to use the kudos to claim the crown he felt was his by right. He was not about to pass it up. This moment would be a game-changer.

Carter closed in, producing his beloved flick-knife. Behind him an attendant in one of the little boxes at the end of the pier anxiously reached for a phone.

Mel Price had been rooted to the spot by the scenario unfolding before his astonished gaze, *'This is what comes of getting all lovey-dovey with a girl,'* he thought, and the hypocrisy of that steeled his own resolve.

He squeezed himself between the two of them, the honour of the Villa crew at stake.

In war, Mel might have won a medal, overcoming his fear to storm a machine- gun emplacement, but he had to make do with putting himself on the line, knowing that he could not beat Carter one-on-one, but still intent on trying, "Not here, there's women and kids around as well as coppers."

Mel paused and stared into Carter's face. "I'll take you on, you twat, and your three tosspot mates, but not here. Take the Kewstoke Road toll road down to Sand Bay and we'll see you on the beach to the far side of Pontins on the Beach Road. One hour – be there."

Tony suddenly became aware of the fact that he was stood by Weston Pier, holding a knife, and surrounded by hundreds of people. Victory was within his grasp, but a stray copper spotting him could wreck it all.

It wasn't the fight Carter really wanted, it would be too easy - but any fight was better than none, especially with the bonus offering of the half-caste. He wanted to test Murphy's determination to stand by whilst his mate was carved up in front of him, "You fucking better be there Sambo, don't run away on me again."

Carter pocketed the knife, turned on his heels and was swallowed by the crowds, Spike and the up and comers hurrying after him.

Spike had a bad feeling about this, things were looking as if they could get out of hand, and now he found himself caught up in something he could not back out of without losing face.

Mel watched them leave then turned to Ryan, "What the fuck is up with you, letting that toe-rag talk to you like that, you can take him any day of the week?"

Ryan just stood, silently rooted to the spot. He sat on the promenade wall and stared at the ground, then spoke, almost a mumble instead of his usual confident voice, "I don't know if I want to do this anymore, what kind of life is it anyway? Under my father's cosh every day, fighting and nicking stuff, what's the point, we're all gonna finish up inside with a cell door slamming behind us?"

Mel sat by him. Since meeting Naomi he had begun to have similar thoughts but this wasn't the moment, "We can't just walk away."

"Can't we, why not? I think we should just fuck off home," said Ryan.

Benny interjected, aghast. "Fucking hell, have you both gone soft in the head? We can't back down or run, it'll be all round town before we even get home. We'll look like wankers, your dad will go off his rocker Ryan, and it won't stop Tony- fucking Carter finding us somewhere else and we'll be in the same spot. You'll never live it down ever, and neither will the Villa crew. I ain't standing for that."

Mel was abashed at his own little moment of weakness. "He's right, Ryan, it's got to be sorted today, and if you can't I will. What's the worst that can happen, a few bruises all round?"

Ryan looked up, misery written across his face, "It could be worse than that. He's a nutcase and he loves that blade too much. Don't do this Mel."

It was too little too late. Mel had reached a decision and was not to be persuaded otherwise, "Ryan, you don't really believe what you're saying do you, this is all Joy's fuckin doing, she's got inside your head. You won't fight a dog like Tony, but you still want to kill Gary, one of our own, how does that stack up? Well you can stay here and mope around if you want, we'll get a taxi and meet you later."

The mention of Joy and Gary in the same breath made Ryan angry with Mel; he was wrestling with a tornado of conflicting emotions that had been distilled into poison by Carter's taunts. Mel became the target, "Gary Docker is different He stole my wife, Carter isn't worth the effort. I'll fuckin drive you there, but don't expect me to help you out a third time when you lose. I'll drive away and leave you there rather than fight today."

"Let's get on with it then," said Benny and led the way back towards where the Capri was parked, pulling one very bewildered, frightened and strangely excited girlfriend behind. This wasn't quite the day that she had hoped for, but at least it was something a bit different.

If only Benny had known her thoughts that morning he might have supported Ryan - the girl had intended to lose her virginity to him that day.

***

Thousands of miles away, Mike Carter sat by a swimming pool, sipping a cold beer.

He cast a glance at Joy and Carol who were laid either side of him, cooking gently in their Ambre Solaire oil. He was a man at peace. Everything was going well, Joy was enjoying her little dose of freedom, Carol approved, and he had got Tony back on track. He lay back, satisfied.

In Wales, Naomi trailed her parents up the path to the summit of Snowden. It was another beautiful day, and the array of peaks soothed her. She had done well, getting the message to Mel, and when Joy returned they could work out what they were going to do. She had a feeling that everything was going to work out.

Back in Birmingham, Pete was on his way to the new National Exhibition Centre with a few of the guys from Leyland. There was a Leyland Cars Motor Show on, they had got free tickets and even better, a free coach had been put on by the union. It would take his mind off Joy and Ryan, a break from the violence. Anyway, nothing could go wrong whilst the girls were both away, the break might give them time to reflect, come to their senses, especially Joy. Maybe she would come back 'cured' of Ryan.

Amidst all these happy thoughts, fate was quietly 'slipping on the knuckledusters' in Somerset.

***

Mel Price knew the Weston area well, for years his mother had hired a static caravan on one of the small sites in the area for their only holiday. He knew that he had picked a good spot for the showdown, even on a busy day like today, there would be few onlookers and the police would be tied up in town dealing with drunken 'Brums' and lost children

As Ryan drove in silence, fuming at the vagaries of circumstance, his mind racing, and trying to work out what to do without losing face, Mel sat grim-faced, giving directions, full of determination and trying to work out how the fuck he was going to get the better of Carter, "Once this gets out back in Brum we'll be a fucking laughing-stock. You've got to take him out Ryan, and put an end to this."

Ryan turned to him, "I won't fight him today Mel and that's it. It's my choice and I don't answer to you. You put yourself on the line, you sort it out. I'll tell Carter the same thing again when we see him. If you wanna get yourself hurt, don't go thinking it'll make me change me mind."

Ryan could see the pain on his friend's face as the words were spat out, and he regretted them immediately. *'Could he really stand by and let Mel take a beating for him?'*

Mel Price was disgusted with himself and Ryan, frustrated, angry, and to be honest, a bit scared. *'How have I got myself into this mess?'* he thought ruefully.

But Ryan's angry retort and Benny's belief strengthened Mel's resolve and they travelled on in silence, both with jaws set.

***

They sat next to the windswept dunes separating the roadway from the beach, having parked in a small car park at the end of on an isolated stretch of the road. A shimmering heat-haze now obscured any chance of glimpsing the sea across the acres of mud. Even Benny was quiet, and the girl just looked from one face to another and huddled closer to him. She was frightened now; she could sense that this was turning into something more than a punch up.

Fifteen minutes later, the car containing Tony Carter and his crew pulled up alongside. During the journey, Carter had further convinced himself of his own invincibility and was already mapping out how today would be received back home. It would be legendary, and he would be the hero, it would be a war-story worthy of retelling many times in the pub. It would cement his position as leader of the young bucks, a status he could then use to oust his uncle.

Once in place he would mobilise them as his own 'Stormtroopers', assuring his position as a rising star of the National Front. Then there would be some punishment meted out to the filthy immigrants ruining the country. What a day! It was all coming together beautifully.

He jumped out of the vehicle first, followed less enthusiastically by the other three. Spike had at first tried to find a way to head the confrontation off, but Tony had slapped him down in seconds.

Spike, a rising star, had concluded that he would be a winner either way. If Tony won, some of the kudos would rub off on Spike, if he lost, then his standing would reduce and Spike could aspire to become second-in-command. He was going to let Tony have his head, for good or ill.

The two youngsters were in awe of Tony and obeyed his every whim, but they too had recognised something in his face when he pulled his blade on the promenade. They were up for a bit of a rumble with the Villa, but neither wanted to be part of murder, and that is what they had seen in Tony's eyes.

Carter marched across to the Capri. Mel and Benny were already out, the girl and Ryan hadn't moved, "Come on then fuck-face lets be having you." Carter rapped on the driver's window and did a bit of shadow boxing.

Ryan wound the window slowly down and shouted, "I told you, I won't fuckin fight you Carter!"

Tony Carter punched him hard in the right side of the head, through the open window, and stepped back waiting for a response – he got none from Ryan, but Mel shot around the front of the car and screamed, "You and me Carter on the beach – let's do it – now!"

Mel turned back to the car for a moment, the driver's window was still open and Ryan was sat, rubbing his jaw, "Benny you come with me, Ryan you stay with the girl if can't find your bollocks today, I can't fuckin believe it."

He turned to Spike and the two youngsters, "This is one-on-one, ok?"Spike nodded and the others followed.

It suited Spike to stand by, and the up and comers followed his lead.

Tony was already fifty yards away, storming towards the beach. The disparate group of enemies and the confused straggled along behind.

***

Mel Price was a much better car-thief than he was a prize-fighter, and whilst he had shown bravery in countless hooligan skirmishes he did not possess the cunning and thirst for blood that others did.

Tony Carter on the other hand was a strong man who had become ruthless and possessed with a certainty in the power of his beliefs, manifested through his fists and blade. He promised himself that he would see to Murphy afterwards, but first the aberration in front of him was going to suffer, *'Third time unlucky for you, half breed,'* he promised himself.

Carter's knife was his friend and after sinking it into that Asian Villa fan a few months previously he had started to really enjoy the feeling of hurting people. He wanted more, and worse.

The fight was one-sided and short.

Carter completely outmatched Mel, almost playing with him

to start with, as they danced around in the sand, before finally felling him with a series of quick-fire punches, and finishing him off with several full-on kicks to the head. It was over in less than two minutes.

The onlooker's attentions were fixed on the uneven struggle and no-one noticed that Ryan had got out of the car and was watching too, unable to just sit there any longer.

He knew that Mel would lose and that Carter was capable of anything today, so he too was drawn to the sands. He had told the girl to stay put and she obeyed, curled up on the back seat and watching, fixated and horrified in equal measures.

***

The violence was as savage as it was short.

Tony Carter stood towering over his fallen challenger, screaming at the unconscious Mel Price to get up. Carter was flapping his arms up and down like some prehistoric bird of prey – legs akimbo. He had well and truly lost it.

Blood oozed into the sand from a wound in Price's head – there was no time soon that Price would be standing up anywhere.

Carter kicked sand into Mel's eyes, "Come on you fucking bastard. I'll give you some more!"

Spike moved first and tried unsuccessfully to pull him away, "He's had enough Tony –leave it."

In answer Carter shook him off and pushed him back, a glint

of madness in his eyes. He produced the knife, crouched down and held Mel's head steady by the hair. He put the tip of the knife within half an inch of the bloodied face.

Everyone froze and Price became very still. "I'm just gonna leave you a memento or two. What'll it be, an eye or a few slashes?" Carter seemed to consider for a moment, "No, that's not enough; I think we need to put a few holes in you, stop you running with white women for good."

Carter was absolutely mesmerised by the sun flashing along the blade, and how it looked against the brown face. In his entranced state he took no notice of anything around him. All eyes were upon him and nobody saw Ryan start to run.

As Carter raised the knife Ryan kicked him off Mel's prone body.

Ryan stopped, placing himself between Carter and his prey.

Carter rolled, and sprang to his feet, spitting sand, knife brandished before him. He was wild-eyed, almost foaming at the mouth, "Found some balls have you, Murphy, I'm gonna finish you and then I'm still gonna do your coon friend."

He charged like a raging bull, giving Ryan no choice, he either defended himself or the madman hurtling towards him was going to kill someone.

Ryan's ice-cool fighting composure claimed him. He assessed Carter's trajectory, neatly side-stepped, rabbit punched him and danced away. Carter's face was blood-red, spittle shooting from his snarling mouth, a force of nature, all thoughts crushed beneath the overwhelming desire to stick the knife into Ryan.

He charged again and stabbed downwards but Ryan blocked him easily and swept his feet from underneath him with a left-footed blow to his opponent's right lower-leg. Carter fell heavily on his back but rolled away again. He paused on one knee and eyed Ryan balefully, "Them fancy Kung Fu tricks ain't gonna work anymore, this time it's the end for you."

He began to circle in a more circumspect fashion, and Ryan realised that this was a more dangerous moment - he needed the wild Carter to return.

Deliberately he goaded Carter, "I'm gonna take that knife off you and shove it up your arse you fuckin pansy. Them I'm gonna take it home and show everyone that I took it off you easy. I'm gonna finish you as a big man Carter, everyone'll know you for a fraud and a right wanker. And I'm gonna fuck the arse off your cousin too. Been seeing her you know, she already thinks you're a tosser but I'll make sure she tells all her mates about this."

At the mention of Joy, Carter flipped and ran at Ryan, slashing the blade backwards and forwards. This time Carter was waiting for the sidestep and the knife slashed across Ryan's chest, drawing blood.

Ryan leant back just enough to prevent more than a superficial cut and caught hold of the knife hand. In a practiced move, he bent the wrist inwards, spun behind Carter and scythed his legs away. Carter fell face first into the sand and Ryan dropped onto his back with all his weight. A whoosh of air exited Carter's lungs.

Ryan bent towards Carter's ear, "This is where you give up and we call it quits. I take the blade and we all go home. I'm willing to leave it at this, no-one gets told anything by me. What do you say Carter?"

There was no reply.

"Come on, stop playing silly buggers." Ryan was desperate to stop the madness. There was still a chance to recover the situation – it disappeared.

Still silence from the man beneath him. Suddenly Ryan realised with a sinking heart that Carter was not struggling. He stood up and backed away, fearing a trick, but Carter was still.

The silence was only broken by the sound of gulls above. In Ryan's mind they were vultures. He stepped forward and poked Carter with his toe, "Move, c'mon."

Wild panic took hold of him and all thoughts of trickery were forgotten.

Ryan took hold of Carter and rolled him onto his back, revealing the hilt of the switchblade protruding from Carter's chest. There was a huge bloodstain around the wound. Ryan knelt and felt for a pulse, listened for breath, but there was none.

Ryan's wrist twist had turned the knife inwards at the exact moment that Carter had fallen forward and his beloved switchblade had pierced his heart. A truly ironic piece of bad-luck that made

Ryan Murphy a triple killer, and this time there were witnesses.

He stood and noticed the blood on his hands. He needed time to think. For the first time since charging at Carter, Ryan noticed the onlookers. The group were still alone but there were bound to be others arriving at the beach as the minutes passed.

Mel was still on his knees, dazed and dumbstruck. All he could say was "Fucking hell Ryan," in a weak voice as the enormity of the situation hit him. Benny just stared.

The two Blues youngsters looked at each other for a moment, and then ran. They had no idea where to, but didn't care – they would walk back to Birmingham if that's what it took.

"Is he....?" asked Spike, all thoughts of rivalry gone for the moment.

"Think so, I'm no doctor but he ain't breathing and there's no pulse I can find. You saw what happened, it was an accident," pleaded Ryan.

"Yea but it was you that killed him, accident or not," retorted Spike.

Ryan turned to Benny, "Get Mel in the car and make sure that tart doesn't start screaming, for fuck's sake."

Ryan cast another look at Carter's body, expecting him to sit up and proclaim the whole thing a trick at any moment, but it was plain that the blood was no longer flowing, the heart no longer pumping, and Carter's skin was taking on a waxy pallor in spite of the sun.

He stepped towards Spike, who couldn't help himself from retreating a couple of steps.

Ryan tried to reassure him, "Don't be fuckin daft, I'm done with fighting, but he wouldn't have it would he? Find a phone and call the cops. We'll be gone by the time you get back. You tell them what happened straight, that it was self-defence and an accident. Do you hear me?"

Spike raised his hands, "I'll tell them the truth but you're still gonna do serious time for this."

Ryan nodded and turned away to the Capri.

He had now been responsible for the deaths of three people, a young boy, an old man, and a crazed right-wing fanatic. His thoughts were a mad whirl, he needed time to think, to plan. The good Ryan was appalled, and cursed the fates, and the violent half that had brought him to this dead-end. Then Joy's face appeared in his mind. He had killed her cousin after vowing to renounce the hooligan life. He could take prison, but not losing her; but how could she love him now? How could he tell her what had happened? How he felt about her, and how could they be together ever again?

Ryan drove the Capri up the motorway and across the bridge into Wales, after a brief detour to Clevedon where Benny bought some fresh clothes for him. The bloodstained ones were consigned to the sea. They stopped at a phone box and Ryan had a conversation with his father.

Mel was semi-conscious, shaking his head and muttering in a slurred voice, "What have I done?" The girl was sobbing quietly, Benny's arm around her.

At Cardiff, Ryan got out near to the main railway station. He told Mel not to blame himself, nothing would have persuaded Carter to stop, and then Ryan disappeared through the station doors. Mel and Benny both wondered whether they would ever see him again. The girl hoped she never did.

Benny drove the car back to Birmingham with Mel cradled in the young girl's arm on the back seat. Mel was conscious, but suffering from a bad case of concussion as some rather large lumps increased in size on his bloodstained head. He continued to rave and apologise about what he had done.

As they drove back into Birmingham violent thunderstorms hit the city, and sheets of rain lashed the parched streets, in what seemed a fittingly apocalyptic commentary upon the events of the day.

They reached the outskirts of the city and dropped Mel off at the Accident Hospital. Benny left Mel sat in casualty and by the time he returned to the car, the girl had disappeared. Benny was relieved, one less problem. Unless she went to the cops, and he doubted that very much, she could be left out of it. He had an urgent appointment with Colin Murphy, and then no doubt the coppers would be calling.

***

Ryan's brain raced through the permutations. It seemed that the only option was to disappear – for good. He was now a fugitive. But he knew that could not live without Joy.

He was on his way to Glasgow to stay with some friends of his father's. Colin Murphy had been furious but he would not give up on his son. He needed time to think too, were there strings he could pull, perhaps favours he could call in?

Ryan sat in silence as the train sped him away from his life and the one thing he cared for. He had no way of contacting Joy and even if he could have done he had no words to put things right. How could he expect her to ever forgive him for killing her cousin?

***

Rob Docker had been out to visit his current conquest, a young female officer who was young enough to be his daughter, but was desperate to make her way in a man's world – the CID. She had calculated that Docker could be useful to her and he didn't mind being used.

He had been back home for half an hour, and as usual Lilian was prone on the sofa snoring loudly, with a very empty bottle of white wine on the floor next to her – five o'clock in the afternoon on a Saturday - give her a couple of hours and she would be ready for the next one.

Rob decided to go for a bath to wash the smell of sex from him and no sooner had he got into the warm inviting water than the phone rang downstairs.

Easing himself out of the bath, and reaching a towel, he suddenly heard Lilian ranting down the phone, "Don't you fuckers ever give him a day off," she screamed at the poor unfortunate at the other end of the line, who was simply the messenger boy.

Docker hurried down the stairs, dripping wet, and in just a towel. He grabbed the phone from her hand and pushed her roughly to one side. Still unsteady, she slipped and fell to the floor, but the look that Docker gave her ensured that she dared not respond. She understood the consequences of further protest.

Rob Docker listened intently to the caller and then gave some very specific instructions – job done. He was well-known within the Force, and when he spoke people listened. Whilst he could be, and was, routinely abrasive, he was known for working his bollocks off to get results and got respect for it.

That said, Docker took nothing for granted and knew how quickly things could change.

Only recently, the West Mercia Chief Constable had given his Head of CID a vote of confidence as controversy over the Lesley Whittle murder enquiry raged on. The Chief had said that the truth would come out at the end of the trial of Nielson. This was after the force had been criticized by the judge for alleging that Staffs police had allowed a marked Panda car to enter the area where the ransom trail was being followed.

Police officers were like politicians, and sometimes a vote of confidence was merely a step away from being sidelined.

Docker could read the signs as clear as the *'Brew XI'* neon one on the Rotunda building.

Within a couple of hours the phone was ringing yet again.

This time he told Lilian to go into the kitchen and stay there – it was a longer conversation but Docker felt elated as he poured his first glass of whisky for the evening.

Lilian remained quietly in the kitchen, working deftly away with the corkscrew on the next bottle.

***

Birmingham Sunday Observer - *4th July 1976*:

'Hotter than the Sahara! - Heat records are falling every day. The 23rd June is now being talked about as the start of the 'Great Drought'. Heathrow has had eleven consecutive days over 30 °C (86 °F) with no end in sight. The same period has seen temperatures reaching 32.2 °C (90 °F) somewhere in England, every day. Furthermore, five days saw temperatures exceed 35 °C (95 °F). On 28 June, temperatures reached 35.6 °C (96.1 °F) in Southampton, the highest June temperature recorded in the UK.

The hottest day of all was yesterday, with temperatures reaching 35.9 °C (96.6 °F) in Cheltenham, one of the hottest July days on record in the UK. The great drought is thought to be due to a very long dry period. The summer and autumn of 1975 were very dry, and the winter of 1975–76 was exceptionally dry, as was the spring of 1976; indeed, some months during this period had no rain at all in some areas.

There is no end in sight, according to the weathermen. Birmingham and The Black Country are melting, every weekend sees an exodus of the hot and bothered seeking a sea breeze, and places like Weston-Super- Mare are under siege from these 'refugee's, although the ice cream sellers aren't complaining! Neither is 'iceman' Bjorn Borg, who yesterday kept his cool in over 90 degree of heat to claim his first Wimbledon title in three sets from Ile Nastase. At twenty, he is the youngest champion for forty-five years.'

***

Birmingham Sunday Observer – *4th July 1976*:

'Stop Press: Storms end the heatwave – but just for a day or two: After thirteen days without rain, the hottest heatwave on record ended momentarily in thunder and lightning and a few spots of a strange clear liquid that fell from the skies last night. Violent thunderstorms raged and some rain fell in Staffordshire. Lightning struck an electricity transformer at Cropredy near Banbury and three hundred people were left without power for an hour.

In Worcestershire and West Mercia the police reported that the power of the electric storms was 'playing havoc with radios'. In Chesterfield the West Indies v Derbyshire cricket match was delayed for ten minutes by a storm. The public address system at the ground announced, 'What is falling is called rain'.

Birmingham Observatory hailed the rain as, 'the end of the drought – but not the end of the heatwave.' A spokesman said more storms would hit the area during this afternoon and evening bringing some welcome cooler air. But 'sun lovers need not worry', he said. 'There will be storms but the temperatures will remain high for this time of the year. The weather should return fairly quickly to settled conditions, with temperatures around the 80 degree mark.'

***

Pete Stevens' day had been little better. He was sat in a cell with a black eye, waiting to be charged and bailed. All he had wanted was a day away from trouble, but it had started to go wrong the moment he got onto the coach to the Motor Show. Looking around, and listening to the conversation, he had realised with a sinking heart that he was riding along with a bunch of striking militants who intended to protest at the Leyland showpiece.

He had tried to give his colleagues a wide berth when he alighted at the National Exhibition Centre, and made a vain attempt to go and look at the new cars on show alone. He was spotted and encouraged back into the group, who had assumed that he was wholeheartedly on their side. He could hardly deny it, he had to work, or in reality, strike with these morons, and so he found himself swept along, into firstly a protest, and then a punch-up.

A grizzled police sergeant had given him a good dig in the eye and Pete's defensive actions had been misconstrued as resisting. Two other cops had piled into him, and here he was. It would only be a fine at worse, more likely a conditional discharge, but it was hardly how he had intended to spend Saturday night.

Birmingham Sunday Observer – *4th July 1976*:

'Track workers bring violence to Motor Show: As tempers frazzle everywhere in the heat, there was fisticuffs between Police and Rover car workers at the Leyland Motor Show in the National Exhibition Centre, near Birmingham. The uproar ended with thirteen

arrests – and hospitalized four injured policemen.

Four track workers have been bailed to appear in court tomorrow, charged with assaulting the police, and the other nine have been bailed under the Magistrate's Court Act to report to Chelmsley Wood Police Station where further charges will be considered.

The police were called to the NEC by concerned security officers, when employees at the Solihull plant attending the exhibition became disorderly. When police tried to eject them, a nasty scene occurred. A sergeant and three constables were later taken to East Birmingham Hospital for treatment to cuts and bruises. The sergeant received an eye injury and one constable is thought to have collapsed from heat exhaustion.'

***

From the outside, the mock Tudor exterior of *'The Doublet'* pub in Park Road, Glasgow, looked more like a working-man's club, and someone's idea of a bad joke in architectural taste. Built in the 1960s, the bar hadn't changed much, but the jukebox and the buzz created by Glaswegian's putting the world to rights made it a decent place to relax.

Andy McBride had taken Ryan into the bar a few times just to chill out and to try to stop him going on all the time about the fix he was in. Andy had taken the refugee with the funny accent under his wing and into his spare room. It was a favour for his boss in the Celtic firm who had close links to Colin Murphy and the Villa crew.

Both teams shared a broadly Catholic history, although the

Villa faithful had broadened in beliefs over the years, in contrast to the staunchly Papist Celtic crowd.

Andy wasn't entirely clear why Ryan was running, but whilst he had grown to like him, he thought that his guest was soft in the head, mooning around like a love- sick teenager, with long silences and repeated mentions of some girl that he couldn't live without.

Andy hadn't seen any evidence of the so-called 'hard man' from Birmingham and had decided that repeated submersion in the world of the Scottish male was the antidote. It would also give the Sassenach an opportunity to show his mettle.

It seemed to be working. Ryan had even got to know a couple of the pensioners that perennially occupied the same round wooden table in the same corner, stale cigarette smoke swirling around them, as fag ash was tapped into glass ashtrays, and more often, onto tables and laps.

Andy had introduced Ryan to his new friends, and with a name like that they had all assumed at first that he was Irish, that is until he opened his mouth, at which point he needed the services of an interpreter. They all thought he was a bit peculiar, preoccupied, but shrugged their shoulders and called for more beer whenever women were mentioned.

In Glasgow you were either a Rangers fan or a Celtic fan, but in here at least there were no flags, and music took precedence over football. The Old Firm was discussed but the gaffer of the pub had made it clear that this was a neutral place and that all-comers were welcome - even an Aston Villa fan.

In a city with a reputation for big drinkers and wild and windy weather, this little watering-hole was not a bad place to be, and for a couple of hours each day it allowed Ryan to free up his mind and to try to plan.

Andy was ordering a couple of Scotch pies at the bar whilst Ryan chatted to the pensioners.

Suddenly the amiable scene was shattered as Reggie McNab aka 'Slasher' walked into the bar with a group of five other Rangers fans.

McNab and his group went to the opposite end of the bar from McBride and stood there in a huddle. McBride's presence had not gone unnoticed – after all he was well up Celtic's hooligan pecking order, but Ryan was a stranger and therefore an unknown quantity.

"Six pints of heavy, landlord." McNab placed his money on the bar.

The licensee surveyed the scene in front of him and instinctively knew trouble when he saw it, "Alright boys. You're in here to enjoy yourselves I hope. Any problems you take them outside. Understood?'

McNab nodded "Of course. We're just here for a quiet bevy."

Some of the other drinkers at the bar moved down a little, leaving a clear space for the Rangers group to occupy. *'Here we go again,'* thought Ryan, *'wherever I go it seems to find me.'*

Ryan re-joined McBride who gave him a half-smile and said, "It's going to get a wee bit busy here but you're my guest. This isn't your fight so stay out of it."

Ryan had already decided that unless he went far away, the violence would seek him out. There was no point standing idly by, things would only get worse if he did. He put his arm around the shoulder of the man who had given him refuge and whispered in his ear, "Like fuck I will."

Before McBride could respond he strode over to McNab.

The eyes of everyone in the bar followed him and the babble of chatter stopped. The customers had a highly developed survival instinct borne of many a similar scenario.

Ryan got straight to the point, "I'm guessing you've come here for a reason, and won't take no for an answer so let's cut the crap, not upset the pensioners, and go outside to sort this one-on-one."

Ryan looked into McNab's eyes searching for signs of fear – he saw none. "Who the fuck are you?" McNab demanded. "Ryan Murphy, and me old man is top-gun in the Villa firm. The man behind me is me friend – we're both good Catholics, so if you want him you go through me first. You win and you get your man. I win and you walk away with your boys – agreed?"

McNab sneered. He hadn't understood every word but the gist was very clear. He had been offered a one-on-one fight in public and could not afford to lose face. He motioned to the door, "It's your funeral you English twat."

Ryan would brook no protests from McBride and the two groups left the bar, the jukebox incongruously blaring out the top twenty hit *'Dancing Queen'* by Abba.

The licensee surreptitiously returned the wooden cosh to its home below the till - blood on the pavement outside was allowed.

In the alleyway at the side of the pub McNab smashed the end of a pint glass that he had hidden under his coat, and held the remnants in front of him, beckoning Ryan to attack.

The others closed in around them.

"Come on you English bastard – make a move. I'm gonna spoil your pretty wee looks for you." McNab urged him on.

Ryan stood with his feet apart, elbows bent and close to his sides, both hands in a fist.

He moved swiftly, and with one kick knocked the glass from McNab's hand, then stood back, reassumed the position and waited.

McNab fumbled in his jacket pocket, removed the flick-knife, his trademark weapon, and flicked the blade open.

Ryan wasted no time – another flying kick to the chest sent McNab reeling back against a wall and as he bounced off it Ryan delivered a straight punch to the Adams-apple leaving McNab gasping for breath.

As the knife dropped to the floor Ryan kicked it away and finished McNab off with a sweep kick, followed by a hammer kick, which put him firmly on the floor writhing in agony.

Ryan bent down and gripped McNab by the throat, "Remember the name Ryan Murphy - my firm doesn't take shit from the likes of you," and pushed him roughly back to the floor.

He turned round to the minions behind him, who had made no effort to get involved, "If anyone else wants some I'll be in the bar with me friend." - there were no takers.

Ryan pushed McBride gently before him through the group and back into the pub, "Where's me Scotch pie Andy?" McBride clapped him on the back. "You can have two ye wee bastard that was some show."

Ryan settled down at a table. He had won, but the enjoyment hadn't been there. He wanted Joy and a new life.

He had made the decision to change his world and cut that Gordian knot – he had to escape from a world that was suffocating him.

Chapter Nine

'I'm Forever Blowing Bubbles'

August 1976

Tony Carter had been dispatched to meet his maker quietly. Neither his father, nor his uncle had wanted any fuss, for entirely different reasons.

Brian wanted no football firm or right-wing mourners, no ritual, and no ceremony.

Mike had lost one of his top men, and the leader of his young bloods. He had failed to divert Tony from careering along his course to eventual disaster and could well do without any further ritual to rub it in. Besides, it was a defeat, and a blow to the reputation of the firm. This despite the version of events that Mike had instructed Spike to put out, whereby Ryan was painted as having the knife on him, and using it when he started to lose.

In the end Mike Carter's view was that the quicker everyone moved on, the better.

That seemed to suit. After his death, many commented that Tony had been out of control and that they were concerned how extreme he had become. A surprising number disassociated themselves from his politics and the National Front.

Another shock to Mike and Carol had been how badly Joy had taken the news. Yes, she had liked her cousin, grown up with him, but she seemed disproportionately distraught, moping around with 'a face like four-pence', and randomly bursting into tears. She seemed to be far away, preoccupied with something that neither of her parents could touch nor console. In the end Mike shrugged his shoulders and put it down to the fact that she was a young girl facing the reality of death for the first time. Life went on - Tony was history.

Mike's first task had been to sort out his hierarchy.

With no heir apparent, and Roly out of the picture, he was left with Spike, Sam and Pete.

Sam was the longest serving and had proved reliable with the doors.

Spike was a good lad, showed promise, but was still young, and had been left shaken by the death on the beach.

Pete was still new and an unknown quantity. Clearly bright, he had proved himself on several occasions, and he had been right about Tony. Mike could see that the lad was still besotted with Joy, but perhaps that would be OK. The business with Ryan Murphy had been a warning, Pete would be a more acceptable and controllable suitor for Joy, and had conducted himself impeccably in his 'chaperoning' duties. Mike vowed to himself to try and encourage a relationship.

Mike, ever the tactician, decided not to decide as yet. He encouraged them all. Sam continued with doors, Spike took over the shoplifting and thieving; Pete was second in command for matches and fights, and given encouragement on the Joy front. One of them would prove worthy.

Joy was in a personal hell. Her agonies were covered by a genuine show of grief over Tony's death, but it was more than that. She exaggerated the extent to which Tony's death had affected her, but at least half of her grief and mental turmoil was focused upon Ryan.

She thought about him constantly. Her mind bounced between extremes. She loved and hated him in equal amounts. One moment worried where and how he was and a minute later thinking, *'good riddance'*. She wanted him caught and punished, she wanted him to escape so that she could imagine him living free somewhere in the sun. In short, she didn't know what she wanted.

She had a recurring fantasy of years passing, and then meeting him on a beach somewhere and being taken in his arms. But that fantasy always dissipated in the mental image of Ryan standing over a dead Tony, bloody knife in hand. She could not progress past the fact that Ryan was a cold-blooded killer, and the betrayal of their love that fact represented. She had fallen in love with a charade, and beneath the mask lurked a killer. The act of murder destroyed the purity she had imagined between them. It made him a liar and a cheat who had said anything to get her into bed.

Naomi and Pete held her together. They took her out, listened, and comforted. Naomi had tried to raise the subject of Ryan, the possibility of contact via Mel, but Joy blocked that conversation dead whenever it arose, surprised and a little appalled that Naomi was still in touch and thought that Joy would want to be.

Joy couldn't even think of Ryan without pain, let alone speak of him or hear about him. She became closer to Pete. He was kind and thoughtful, and occasionally she thought about him as more than friend, but each time the image of Ryan rose up in her mind and strangled those emotions in their infancy. She was so self-obsessed that she could not see the pain in Pete's eyes.

As the weeks passed and there was no announcement of his arrest, her life began to return to its pre-Ryan course, one more year at school, A-levels, then university, then a 'career'. The rebelliousness seemed to be extinguished, and with it any desire for relationships. She shut Pete out in that way, and vowed to herself never again to allow a man to get into her head and to hurt her like Ryan had.

***

It all changed one Saturday night in mid-August. The new football season was a couple of weeks away. The weather was unbelievable. The drought was at its most severe that month. Parts of the South West went forty-five days without any rain in July and August. As the hot and dry weather continued, devastating heath and forest fires broke out in parts of Southern England.

In Birmingham, standpipes and water tanks were on the streets. Hosepipes were banned, grass was brown and dead, lakes dried up and a Mediterranean atmosphere took hold. Everyone was thirsty, and at the end of each scorching day, cold beer, long iced-drinks and dancing cast a calypso style spell that could not be resisted.

Joy found herself at *'Barbarellas'*, in Cumberland Street, watching a local rock group on stage. Pete and Naomi, coupled with the holiday effect of another roasting day, had prevailed upon her to go out with a load of the boys and girls. She liked Barbarellas. It had a very relaxed dress-code, played rock music and attracted interesting people and stage acts.

It was one in the morning. The rockers had finished their set. Joy had been dancing, then decided to go outside with Naomi to cool down. They shared a cigarette, and Joy noticed a figure sat in the shadows when he struck a match and lit up. As his face was illuminated briefly by the flare of the match, she recognised Spike.

He was one of the party that night but had kept to himself inside the venue, staying with a group of the males who seemed more interested in drinking than dancing. It was the first time she had been this close to him since Tony's death, in fact, she realised that she had not passed a word with him since then, which was strange, almost as if he had been avoiding her, *'Perhaps he blames himself, can't face me,'* she thought.

Joy strode across and sat beside him.

If Pete had been there, he would have intervened, recognising the danger, as Spike had confided in Pete shortly after Tony's death.

He had to tell someone and he felt a trust for the new man, who seemed solid and controlled, unlike Tony.

Pete had been wrestling with the knowledge for weeks. His infatuation with Joy told him not to tell her, his inherently fair and honest nature said that he should, even if it meant the end of any chance he had with her. It could also put her in danger, dependent upon her reaction. He had dithered for weeks, precisely balanced between these opposite poles, but fate was once again about to intervene and render his agonies irrelevant.

Spike looked up from his reverie as she sat down. He seemed very drunk and his words were slurred, making the accent even more impenetrable than usual, "How you doing Joy."

Joy adopted a soothing tone, "I'm Ok, what about you Spike, you've been very quiet since Tony's death?"

Spike shook his head and looked away, "I should have stopped it. Tony was out of control; and it's my fault what happened."

Joy was curious, "How can it be your fault Spike? That Ryan was out of control, just like you said; he was a killer and a coward, using a knife like that."

Spike took her hand and bent his head over it. She could barely hear his mumbling, but then it tumbled out, a revelation that was to set off another turn of fate's wheel,

"I feel so guilty cause it wasn't like that at all. Your dad told me to tell it like that, so that the Villa got painted bad. It wasn't that Ryan; it was Tony who had the knife. He was like a madman, wanting to fight everyone.

We went to Weston that day because I told him that Murphy would be there, so it's my fault, twice over. I told Tony and I didn't stop it when it was getting out of hand. I tried, but not hard enough, and Tony shoved me away.

Murphy was trying to protect his mate, that's all. Tony was going to stab the half-caste kid. That Ryan didn't wanna fight, backed off, but the half-caste bloke said he would go one-on-one with Tony. You can imagine, can't you, Tony jumped at the chance to do him, a coloured."

Joy listened intently as Spike relived every painful moment.

When Joy heard that Ryan had refused to fight even after being slapped and punched, her heart leapt, knowing that Ryan would have been thinking of her and not wanting to fight her cousin. When Spike told her that Tony's death was an accident, and more self-defence than murder, the clouds of the last few weeks lifted a little.

Joy left Spike brooding, and returned to Naomi.

She suddenly needed to know what Naomi knew, and whether any lines of communication were still open.

***

Rob Docker was brimming with frustration.

Tony Carter's death was being handled by the local police in Somerset, and he had no influence there. He had tried to offer help with information but had been politely rebuffed with the implied suggestion that if he had sorted the hooligans in his own back yard, the locals in Weston might not have had to put up with the overflow of scum from Birmingham killing each other.

The death had also increased the pressure on him to get results with the Villa and Blues hooligans. Francis and Burrell had made some inroads, but he knew they were scratching the surface. Something more fundamental was required.

He was also aware that the 'carrot crunchers' by the seaside had spoken to three lads, two Villa, one Blues, and that a very different story had emerged to the one being put around by the Blues lot.

He knew that there was a very real chance that Ryan Murphy could get off at court with either a manslaughter charge, or even be found not guilty on the grounds of self-defence. He knew that it had been Carter's own knife that struck the fatal blow, that Carter had been holding it, and that he had been the aggressor throughout. That was not the sort of punishment he had in mind for Ryan Murphy. He didn't give a toss about Tony Carter, but Murphy had murdered his uncle Charlie, and there was a debt to be paid.

Rob had a feeling that the importance allotted to Carter's death was slipping quietly down the CID tree in yokel-land, and had seen no evidence of any energy being put into tracing Murphy.

Six weeks and no arrest - Ryan Murphy seemed to have disappeared.

The longer it went on, the more plans Docker tested and discarded to resolve the matter in his own way.

Rob had also made a promise to Vivian that he would try to protect Gary, and he knew better than most that once the boundary of taking a life had been crossed, it got easier to do it again.

As far as Docker was concerned Ryan Murphy was already a double killer.

***

Bill Donovan tapped on the half-open door gently – he had known Rob Docker long enough to know that he could be brittle at most times of the day and he wasn't looking to get on the wrong side of him.

Docker slipped his feet off the table and beckoned him in, "What can I do for you Bill?" he asked.

"I'm sorry to bother you sir, but the 'powers that be' at Headquarters have come up with this new 'tension indicators and community engagement' document and asked me to get some feedback. Personally I think it's a load of bollocks, but I'm just a lowly Collator so what do I know.

There's fuck-all in there about locking people up so you probably won't be interested, but I could do with your comments please?" Bill had done his bit for progress and his bacon sandwich was calling. He dropped the document on Docker's desk.

Docker smiled, "Leave it with me Bill, I'll think of something intellectually fucking challenging to say about it. I might start with half the trees in the world that they are chopping down to make the fucking paper for this."

As Bill did a sharp exit Docker thumbed through the document dated, *'August 1976'*. It was prefaced by a senior officer who Docker considered a total wanker that had never got his hands dirty, and this confirmed it. An 'ideas man' who had letters after his name, rather than only before them to denote rank like a 'proper' policeman should.

He was beginning to feel that the job was moving away from his particular brand of 'practical policing'.

He held the document gingerly, as if it could somehow poison him, and began to read,

*'**Electoral Scanning & Economy** - An MP has claimed that 'alarming' and hardly-noticed figures given in the Commons could mean about 500,000 new Commonwealth wives and children are entitled to come to Britain. The figures were given by the Treasury to a Tory MP after he had asked for the number of children and wives resident overseas for whom taxpayers resident in Britain were given allowances against income tax*

A written reply said the following, 'It is estimated that child tax allowances are given at present for about 500,000 children who are not resident in this country. I regret that information about the number of non-resident wives of taxpayers in the United Kingdom is insufficient to enable an estimate to be made. It is understood that about a third of the 500,000 are the children of Irish workers in Britain.'

The document noted the MP's response - *'That suggests there is a tax fraud of enormous proportions or that the number of potential immigrants is larger than has previously been thought.'*

Actions Required: Local beat officers to monitor any negative responses towards the resident Irish community and other

immigrant communities.

Government and Trades Union Congress agree a more severe Stage II one- year limit on pay rises. Latest figures show 1.5 million unemployed.

Actions Required: Special Branch to monitor any negative responses from left-wing activists.'

The next piece had also clearly been lifted wholesale from a newspaper, no cop that Docker knew would write like this,

'Environment - *The Midlands are now almost as arid as the Sahara. Cattle are panting, crops shriveling, boats are high and dry in closed canals, rivers are a trickle, ponds and brooks are drying up, hosepipes are banned, and a pall of smoke from unchecked grass fires hangs in grim epitaph to the summer the rain stayed away.*

Last year's grill-hot summer, an extra mild winter, and another heatwave this year, has left a scorched earth legacy which a mighty clap of thunder and a sudden downpour or two will not cure. The wells are dry, reservoirs retreating. The Severn Trent Water Authority with eight million parched throats to slake is waging a war on waste, for we use our water at an astonishing rate. Every pint of quenching beer we drink took fifteen pints of water in the making.

It is the worst drought for five hundred years. There are now only eighty-five days' worth of water left in Elan Valley and seventy-five in Derwent reservoirs. Government 'Drought Minister', Denis Howells, MP for Small Heath, is asking for industry to conserve water urgently. A hosepipe ban has been in place for weeks, bath water should be no more than 5"in depth, we should use showers instead etc.

Action Required: We need to review our Headquarters and local civil emergency contingency plans in the event of further restrictive measures being imposed. We can't have people in the streets fighting over water.'

'**Events -** *An umbrella organization drawing together nearly three hundred immigrant groups has met for the first time in Birmingham amid warnings to the National Front to expect united black opposition in the future. Delegates to the special two-day conference at Birmingham University gathered to work out ways of presenting a united case for all West Indian, African and Asian opinions.*

Actions Required: Special Branch to feedback to senior management the results of monitoring meeting. Local Divisional Chief Superintendents to liaise with ACC Operations regarding community impact issues.

The Notting Hill Carnival is scheduled to take place at the end of the month. Initial intelligence from the Metropolitan Police suggests potential for large-scale disorder to take place.

Action Required: Officers to feed any potential numbers of people travelling to London to this event to Headquarters Intelligence Department.

A number of high-risk football matches are due to take place in the West Midlands at the end of August as the new football season commences. The usual Aston Villa and Birmingham City rivalry is anticipated, with added potential stemming from West Bromwich

Albion's recent promotion to the First Division. Last season saw a significant escalation in hooliganism and all indicators suggest this will continue.

Action Required: Due to the increase in organized criminal activity in relation to football hooligans, all Divisions to review their capacity for additional public order support to City Centres and Divisions with football grounds.'

Docker closed the document; he had seen enough to convince him that the author would definitely be visiting the hallowed halls of Bramshill Police College in the future on promotion. There was nothing about 'enforcement' in the document, he noted.

For his part, the only bit that interested him was the last few lines.

Sometimes taking your mind off a problem suggested a way forward. A decision had crystallised in his mind whilst reading. He tested it, as he always did. It had risks, but it seemed the only way now. He sprang up and marched out of the office. Reid watched him go, *'I know that look, someone's in for it, but not me this time,"* he thought, and returned to reading the Playboy magazine that he had hurriedly pushed into his desk drawer as Docker had erupted from his office.

As for Docker, he had to meet the last person in the world he had intended to see again.

***

It was the first match of the season and Villa was at home to West

Ham, whilst Birmingham City was away to Manchester United.

Mike Carter had called for a three-line whip of both the main boys and the youth group. He wanted everyone up in Manchester to show a strong presence – Saturday 21 August 1976, was to be a red-letter day and one to be remembered.

Blues needed to re-assert themselves after the Tony Carter debacle, and the home of the *'Red Devils'* was perfect. But that wasn't the prime motive for him requiring their visibility in Manchester, Mike had another purpose.

He was determined that their voices would be heard on the streets, at the railway stations, and on the terraces, and he put himself right at the front of the action, pushing the buttons of as many local police as possible but being careful not to cross the line. The boys were there to be seen, but scuffling wasn't today's priority for him.

***

Back in Birmingham, preparations were underway for a few of the Villa boys to get some attention. It was inevitable that West Ham would come in numbers by train, and Detective Sergeant Francis had determined that there would be some sport to be had on New Street Station after the game.

To a degree Francis and Burrell had become creatures of habit, and keen to please Docker, they routinely made their presence felt at known hot-spots. Their boss was always pleased to see a couple of football related 'bodies' in the 'traps' from the weekend action, and the railway station was like fishing in a barrel.

Whilst New Street Station came within the jurisdiction of the British Transport Police, the railway police never turned their noses up at the prospects of receiving a few extra pairs of hands.

Francis had arranged, together with John Burrell and another couple of plain- clothes officers, to supplement the BTP CID who routinely positioned themselves on the concourse for the 5pm return from the local grounds of away fans, and those that would inevitably be hunting them.

As expected, many of the West Ham fans came in by train from Witton and Aston, hard men who gathered in clusters on the overbridge waiting for the next London train, a few deciding on a quick pint in the station bar, monitored by a return escort of London-based officers who had grown weary of their macho charges.

Ever alert, the London boys oozed violence.

Three of their number had already been hurriedly dragged through the barriers by BTP officers after being taken off one of the local Aston trains for causing damage. They were protesting loudly, and the officers wanted to get them up to their office sharpish-before any of the West Ham fans already on the station decided on a rescue mission.

It left the blue line painfully thin on the ground at the station.

One group of ten West Ham fans, headed by a bald man whose head fitted like a pin on top of a huge body, decided to head into the city-centre for a longer drinking session. They obviously believed that they were invincible, and chests were puffed out even further as they passed through the ticket barrier heading for the escalators leading up to the Birmingham Shopping Centre.

The Villa main boys closed in.

Colin Murphy had been around long enough to know that charging into the station as a group would lead to the unwanted attentions of snarling police dogs and glove-wearing police officers, who would tolerate no back-chat. In the absence of Ryan, he had assumed leadership from the front.

To avoid the undesirable attention of the law, they dribbled into the concourse from several directions in twos and threes. On a Saturday evening, the concourse could easily swallow up hundreds of genuine passengers, so fifty determined Villa hooligans did not present as a problem.

Thus far it had been a good day with Villa winning 4-0, but Colin was hoping that it was about to get better. He had left a good team outside in New Street to intercept any West Ham fans coming into the city by bus, and all they had to do now was close the net.

***

Birmingham Sunday Observer – *22 August 1976*:

'   *Classy Villa start the season with a bang! - Villa showed that they are no longer the new boys in the First Division in a fantastic opening performance. Gray and Graydon shared all the goals in the second half, but the goals were the icing on the cake of a superb performance. Villa were so superior that they could have netted double figures, whilst the Hammers were restricted to a couple of half chances.*

Villa served up a treat of passing and control in the first half without scoring, but the best was yet to come. They upped the pace considerably in the second half, making the West Ham players look stuck in second gear, and added clinical finishing that had the supporters on cloud nine.

It all bodes very well for this season's campaign. Andy Gray is fast establishing himself as new hero for the Holte End. He has flair, good looks and a swagger, coupled with an unerring sense of where the goal is. But in this match, Gray was not alone in excelling, with the likes of Leighton Phillips, Ray Graydon, Brian Little, Frank Carrodus and John Robson providing as good a show. Villa's new style looked fit for success in the First Division.'

***

As the West Ham group was halfway across the concourse, the shrill sound of a whistle was heard and they were attacked from every direction, boots and fists flailing.

On the overbridge, shouts went up as other West Ham fans ran towards the barriers, which were closed off as BTP officers struggled to prevent them from joining the fray.

Francis and Burrell were suddenly in the thick of it.

They had already spotted Colin Murphy standing next to one of the pillars with Mel Price, and Francis had a clear view as Murphy pursed his lips to emit the shrill noise that sent people into a panic.

Nearby, three BTP officers were grappling on the floor with 'pin-head' who had gone 'ballistic' at the first sign of violence. As the two officers struggled to get handcuffs on, other officers surrounded them, truncheons drawn, to stave off any rescue attempt.

One of the officers was a female CID officer who was kicked violently in the stomach as the struggle continued. Although clearly in pain she launched herself again at the 'honey-monster' and gave as good as good as she had got. She wasn't about to take any shit off this prat and there would be time to inspect bruises later.

A number of the vastly outnumbered West Ham group received a good hammering from the Villa firm who engaged in a feeding frenzy of violence, as blood was spilt and obscenities filled the air. The atmosphere was electric with ferocity as bodies swarmed backwards and forwards.

Murphy and Price were leading from the front and didn't see Francis, Burrell and the other members of his team until it was too late.

Both were bundled unceremoniously against a wall, faces first, as Francis screamed, "Police. You're both nicked for affray."

As Colin Murphy felt the steel of the handcuffs on his wrists he stood very still. His rage quickly controlled, he saw no sense in giving the coppers a chance to give him a dig for nothing.

Francis did a quick search of Murphy's pockets and as he did so expertly palmed a steel comb with a tail that had been filed down to a sharp point, into his jacket.

Mel Price's brain didn't quite work that quickly and as he went to react that's precisely what he got, the punishment that

Murphy had avoided, with a quick rabbit- punch in the lower ribs from Burrell.

As he was marched off in handcuffs, Mel's thoughts once again turned to Ryan's comments on the promenade wall at Weston.

They were frog-marched quickly towards the glass doors, and around them the violence subsided, as with the loss of their leader the Villa group melted away.

The BTP picked off a couple of stragglers and a lone BTP dog handler lengthened the lead on his dog slightly in order to allow him to encourage the remnants of the battered West Ham group back through the barriers and onto a train.

As they passed through the glass doors Francis said to Burrell, "Take them up to the BTP office and make sure that they are searched properly. I'll be up in a few minutes and then we'll get them off to the Lane."

He watched as Burrell led the small posse and their charges to the passageway leading down to the BTP police office. Just as they turned left Colin Murphy looked back at Francis. He had felt the comb in his pocket and knew that he was going to finish up with another charge of possessing an offensive weapon, "You fucking bastard," he shouted, before disappearing from view.

***

Francis stood quietly savouring a moment's peace, as he exhaled deeply and flicked ash onto the floor from his cigarette. Stood in the passageway adjacent to the goods lifts he was away from the tension that was still palpable on the concourse.

Colin Murphy was a good catch, and one that he had been after for a while. Whilst he knew that he would have to bail him later, if he could get him again he would be able to keep the wanker in custody.

He knew that Docker had history with Murphy and he was one of the top targets. Things were going well, and Docker had already implied that the next time he was away he would recommend that Francis was made Acting Detective Inspector.

Things were definitely on the up and he loved the freedom that Docker had bestowed on him – definitely his kind of boss.

Behind him, the concertina metal doors of one of the goods lifts opened.

As Francis turned out of idle curiosity to see who was getting out he was suddenly grabbed from the front and propelled inside the lift by several pairs of hands. The lift doors closed, and as they did so one of a group of five West Ham fans punched him hard in the stomach, knocking the wind from him. As he doubled up in pain he was taken to the grime-stained floor of the lift and several well-aimed Doc Martin boots did their work.

Francis was left in a heap on the floor as the lift slowly descended to the floor used by the postal workers. Few people knew that there were tunnels linking the railway station to the nearby Postal Sorting Office, and apart from the movement of parcels they were cold empty places, devoid of any sign of humanity.

Francis was bundled out of the lift and dragged half-upright to one of the walls.

The leader within the group gripped Francis by the jaw and spoke briefly to the half-conscious man, "Mr. Francis, we've got a message from some old friends in the smoke, south of the water – the message is - disappear matey or next time we meet they'll be putting what's left of you in a coffin."

The man indicated for the others to hold him firmly as with one movement he removed a Stanley knife from his pocket and slashed Francis once across his face, right to left, from ear to chin. As blood spurted from the razor-thin wound Francis was subjected to a further beating before unconsciousness allowed the pain to go away briefly.

He was found an hour later by a postal working driving a small electric tractor-towing Brute (British Rail Universal Trolley Equipment) which were trolleys linked together like a small train and loaded with GPO mailbags and parcels.

Seeing the state of Francis he dragged him onto an empty Brute and headed for one of the platforms.

***

Birmingham Observer – 23 August 1976:

'Hooligans in court: Several people appeared in court today after more than one hundred football fans fought in New Street after the Villa v West Ham match on Saturday. Those appearing included three West Ham fans accused of damaging a train on the way from

Aston to New Street Station.

In a separate incident a teenager from London appeared in connection with stealing a car and knocking down a pedestrian after the match. The eighteen year old mounted the pavement in Aston Hall Road and hit several pedestrians, slightly injuring one man. He was sent to a detention centre for three months and disqualified from driving for two years.

A seventeen-year-old Coventry youth was fined for throwing two toilet seats out of a train window at Witton and another five fans from Birmingham were each fined £15 for disorderly conduct. A seventeen-year-old youth from Birmingham was fined the maximum £100 for using threatening words and behavior at the match.

Police are also investigating a serious assault on an officer in plain clothes at New Street Station after the match. It has not yet been established whether this is football related. Detective Inspector Rob Docker was quoted as saying 'This was a serious assault and we will leave no stone unturned to find the perpetrators'. The officer remains in hospital in a serious but stable condition.'

***

The phone rang at 10pm and Mike Carter was first to it. After giving the police in Manchester the run around for most of the day it had been largely uneventful up North.

***

Birmingham Observer – *23 August 1976*:

*'Great start for Blues - Despite a draw at Old Trafford on
the opening day that would delight most managers, Willie Bell wants
more. He wants perfection. Even so, Blues could have had both
points after goalkeeper Dave Latchford appeared to be impeded for
United's second goal. To be fair, Pearson did nearly snatch it for
United with a header that hit the underside of the crossbar and had
their players claiming a winner. Blues held on in the heat for a very
good opening day point. Their goals came from Styles and Burns,
with Coppell and Pearson scoring for United. Final score 2-2, even
though the last couple of minutes were in doubt due to a bomb alert.'*

***

The entire firm had got back to Birmingham safely but Carter had
resisted the option of a pint and gone straight home. He had other
things on his mind.

Mike had been waiting for the call, and as the speaker at the
other end practiced his best London accent Mike allowed himself a
smile. There was no need for pleasantries as two men who were
normally rivals finalised their business transaction.

One up for 'JC', languishing in prison for something he
hadn't done, and no- one could possibly point the finger at Mike or
his firm. After all, a hundred police officers in Manchester could
verify that they were nowhere near New Street Station.

***

Pete's diary entry for the day told the rest of the story,

'The local police had another set of hard men. Same as the

ones in Brum. Same gloves. Same chin straps down. Same attitude. Different cap badge. They kept us hemmed in inside the ground and there had already been one announcement to say that the Blues fans would be kept in at the end. Thought they'd got it all sorted until Mike decided to go outside. He winked at me and Sam and worked his way through the police cordons doing his best to be respectful. Just an ordinary fan needing to get some medicine from his car for a heart condition. Bollocks of course. Just one minute before the end of the game there was a tannoy again. This time it was a bomb scare and we were asked to make our way out of the ground in an orderly fashion. Mike was outside with a big grin on his face. The police were running around like headless chickens. Mike always said he could do a cracking Irish accent. Walked back to the station and a quiet trip back. Mike seemed pre-occupied.'

Pete got the other diary out. It was full of musings about Joy which he knew were out of control but his obsession was complete.

He added another, *'She seems to have settled something in her mind, made a decision. If it's what I think it is, then I'm going to have to try and stop it, but at the moment I can't think how. What a mess!'*

***

Detective Inspector Docker sat next to Francis in a private room in the Accident Hospital, forty-eight hours later, and surveyed the damage.

Docker didn't do well in hospitals and wasn't planning on staying that long.

Francis was dosed up to the hilt with morphine, having suffered several fractures, and the left hand side of his face was heavily bandaged, covering the scar that would remain with him for the rest of his life.

Attacking one of their own was a cardinal sin – a line had been passed and someone would pay. If anything it strengthened Docker's arm and he knew that the issue of football hooliganism had now been moved up the pecking-order by the powers that be that spent their days looking out of windows and dreaming of advancement. He would have no problem in future getting what he wanted.

Docker knew however, that this attack had been personal, and that whilst the Force and the media were painting it as some mindless attack by hooligans it was much more than that,

"Time for you to think about a career change I think son. I know someone who can help you out with a bit of work in Spain but she's family and one tough cookie so don't think you can piss her about." Docker finally concluded the conversation.

Francis looked at Docker with a mixture of sudden dislike and fear. He knew full-well what the man was capable of. He knew that he was being cast-off but was also shit-scared.

He had stared death in the face and didn't like it.

Perhaps the man was right - perhaps it was time to put his ticket in and get some winter sun into his broken body.

***

If it was warmth Francis was after he could have stayed in Birmingham, as the tinderbox Midlands was alight over the weekend, and scores of acres of grassland went up in flames in the worst weekend for blazes on record.

There was a huge fire that threatened neighbouring houses at Sutton Park, which fire crews spent days damping down, and there were calls to close the park completely until the drought was over in an effort to prevent more conflagrations.

West Midlands Safari Park in Bewdley was also engulfed in flames where three thousand visitors had to be evacuated and animals rounded up. Even troops were called in to battle the fire.

There were scores of other smaller outbreaks of fire across the area.

***

Birmingham Sunday Observer - *29 August 1976*:

'Blues 2 – 1 Liverpool - Yesterday, after only eight days of the new season, Blues can feel very proud of four points out of six from games against three of the top teams, Leeds, Manchester United, and now Liverpool. An uninspiring first-half was forgotten as Blues inflicted Liverpool's first defeat of the season. A Trevor Francis strike on fifty-two minutes beat Clemence and provoked Liverpool onto all-out attack.

The goal came from a Dave Latchford clearance, two headers on by Burns and Withe and a right foot volley from Francis which kept low and smashed into the net close to the left-hand post.

In much welcome heavy rain, the game came alive and the visitor's efforts were rewarded in the 75th minute. A superb lob from Ray Kennedy found new boy David Johnson, who headed in at the far post. A draw looked on the cards for only a minute though. Kendall took a free kick from midfield and Joe Gallagher strode through the Liverpool defence to head past Clemence.'

***

Pete, as usual, had recorded events in his diary,

'Hundreds walked down Sarah's Road after the game, down Gray Street and into Garrison Lane. Mike leading the way. Me and Sam on the flanks. Police horses at the island got bricked again. Fuck knows why they keep putting them there. Easy targets as long as you can throw a brick from a distance. Lawley Street and Curzon Street and into town. A police cordon near Albert Street so the firm had to detour into Park Street and towards Digbeth High Street. All the time the police were trying to cut us off so as not to get into the city but Mike just kept moving us on quickly. He knows they can't match our speed. Too busy jumping in and out of vans. We're off again before they can get their helmets on. Eventually made it into Union Passage and Corporation Street trying to head down towards the ramp. Finally Mike managed to get us into New Street Station, only about fifty of us by then but enough to put the shits up some of the scousers who were hanging around on the concourse. Just 'bobble hats' really. They soon fucked off the other side of the barrier when Mike squared up to them. This is our town he bellowed so fuck off. They did.'

***

317

The media recounted the other headlines, as Colin Murphy decided to keep his head, and the firm's, down temporarily following his arrest.

Birmingham Sunday Observer – *29 August 1976*:

'Everton 0 – 2 Villa: Villa finally managed, and deserved, their first away-win since their return to the First Division. It was a fine display, topped with a spectacular goal by Brian Little in the twentieth minute. Up until then, Villa had to defend and show character, but the goal sparked them into life.

A mistake by Jones let in Graydon and his shot cannoned off for a corner to Villa. The corner was cleared to Gidman who picked out Little on the left-hand edge of the penalty area. He volleyed a perfect strike into the net. Villa went further ahead in the thirty-fourth minute. Leighton Phillips, who had a superb game in defence, picked out Graydon on the right with an inch perfect pass that split the Toffee's defence. Graydon ran in and his shot deflected past Davies into the net.

Everton pressed in the second half but found Phillips and Burridge in fine form. Bob Latchford, the ex-Blues striker, came close, and Dobson hit the Villa bar, but the claret and blues fully deserved the win.

Off the field it was a different story, as Manchester United fans ran riot again, in another weekend of football hooliganism in the Midlands. It is almost certain that Derby County's Baseball Ground will have fences put up to keep fans off the pitch after hundreds rioted at the end of Derby's goalless game with

Manchester United.

Elsewhere, at Wolverhampton's game away at Nottingham Forest the game hadn't ended when a mob of fighting fans came onto the pitch, stopping play for four minutes. Derby's game was all-ticket with a crowd of 34,000, and the policeman in charge said later, 'the only way to stop them is a fence. I have said this before. You couldn't stop them with a thousand police.'

The Derby chairman said, 'they are hooligans and animals. They spit and swear at you. Wherever Manchester United goes, trouble occurs. We don't have problems with any other clubs. It's not stressed enough that it's Manchester United fans who cause the trouble. I dare not tell you what I would do to them.'

The club secretary said that fences had been considered previously after a Chelsea game three seasons ago, but had not been progressed, but it 'now seems to be the only way to stop the fans.'

Both managers, Tommy Doherty and Dave Mackay, condemned the fan's actions which left many injured. Doherty said, 'What can football do? We try to play clean, entertaining stuff but you will always get some people who come to cause trouble.'

First-aiders treated sixty-five people at the ground, three policemen were slightly injured and at least thirty people were treated at Derbyshire Royal Infirmary. There were two arrests before the game and fourteen during and afterwards. Sixty-four fans were ejected.

At the Wolves' game, which they won 3-1, fighting spilled onto the pitch from the terraces and ordinary spectators had to run from bricks and flying fists. Brian Clough and Wolves' striker Bobby Gould asked fans to 'cool it', a tactic that enabled the game to be restarted. There were seven arrests.

Another eight arrests were made at Birmingham's match with Liverpool at St Andrews, 5 Liverpudlians and three Brummies.'

Hooliganism was most definitely still alive and well.

***

In the last week of August, days after Denis Howell was appointed 'Minister for Drought', severe thunderstorms brought rain to some places for the first time in many weeks. To Joy, the rain seemed to mark the end of an era, summer was ending and her life was about to change forever.

She had made an irrevocable decision.

Chapter Ten

'The Liquidator'

September 1976

Naomi had been telling Mel for weeks that Joy was over Ryan and never wanted to see him again. Mel now thought that might be a good thing. At the start he had misgivings over the relationship, and those reservations had certainly played out in Weston, but now he was hoping that Joy could influence Ryan to do two things, give himself up, and renounce violence.

It was a pretty forlorn hope, like Rob Docker, Mel believed in his heart that Ryan had nothing to lose now he had killed, and that Gary would be next, but it offered a way of saving Gary without betraying Ryan.

Mel was the only person in Birmingham, apart from Colin Murphy, who knew where Ryan was. There was a need for communication, and Mel was the most trusted person, by father and son. They spoke at prearranged times via a rotation of public phone boxes so there was no chance of the police doing any sneaky stuff like wire taps, although Mel privately thought that was the stuff of films.

Mel could sense, even down the telephone line, that Ryan had taken the news of Joy's rejection very badly. He sounded listless and without purpose, didn't seem concerned about his own future.

During the last call he had raised Mel's hopes by talking about giving himself up. He thought that he stood a chance of getting off for a couple of years for manslaughter and it didn't sound as if he were bothered either way. Then there had seemed to be a distinct mood change, a plunge into deeper despair and he had dashed those hopes by mentioning that he had nothing left to live for and needed to 'sort everything out', by which Mel thought he meant Gary.

In fact Ryan was contemplating confessing about Charlie, in order to free JC, the framed Blues fan, but Mel was by now fixated upon the threat to Gary and knew nothing of Ryan's other killings. The misunderstanding was to have serious consequences.

Then Naomi had announced Joy Carter's sudden change of heart. Mel had delayed doing anything at first whilst he thought things through, assessing the likely impact of the news upon Ryan, and the possible consequences for Gary and Roseanne.

Mel finally decided in favour of telling him. A Ryan with something to lose had to be less dangerous than the alternative. He mentally crossed his fingers.

Naomi's message got through. Despite everything, Joy wanted to see Ryan, to be with him. She knew now that it had all been a terrible accident, a mistake. To Ryan that meant hope, and that's all he needed to know for the moment. It also gave him a new sense of purpose as he started to make plans for a way out of the mess he was in. All thoughts of giving up evaporated. Ryan started planning a way out, for himself and Joy.

Mel kept his own counsel on the subject and kept the chain of communication, limited as it was, in place, looking for clues as to Ryan's intentions. He kept the change of heart to himself too of course, if Colin Murphy found out about Joy, Mel knew that the consequences would be dire and it wouldn't just be a slap around the ear. As he waited, Mel considered the options to protect Gary, and finally reached the conclusion that he also needed to turn his back on violence.

For her part, Joy's pain was lifted temporarily, and she would be eternally grateful to Naomi, who had proved herself a true friend. Naomi was uncertain whether she was doing the right thing, but she was young and falling into the clutches of love herself. Why shouldn't her best friend get a chance at it?

***

Elsewhere, other lines of communication were being kept open as Rob Docker manipulated the pieces he had left on the chessboard. The endgame was approaching.

Revenge and victory, victory and revenge, he turned the words over in his mind. He layered the moves and sat back, satisfied - the spider at the centre of the web.

***

The weeks passed and the 'beautiful game' continued unabated.

Birmingham Sunday Observer – *5 September 1976*:

'Villa 5 v 2 Ipswich - Andy Gray was absolutely brilliant as Villa demolished Ipswich. They have now headed the First Division

for two games running and the future looks bright if Gray and Villa carry on like this. Six points from eight and 14 goals is a statement of intent. Gray scored a stunning hat-trick that reduced Ipswich to stumbling uncertainty and Brian Little and Ray Graydon added two more.

Villa scored the first via Brian Little in the fifth minute, but when John Wark equalized in the sixteenth there was no indication of what was to come. Gray put in a breathtaking display of pace, power and work-rate that changed the game.

His first goal, in the 57th minute, was a flying header from a Little cross. The second came from Gray's thirst for the ball. He charged at Hunter 40 yards out, robbed him of the ball, crashed into the area and planted an angled shot past ex Blues keeper, Paul Cooper.

The hat-trick came in the 77th minute, just 40 seconds after Keith Bertschin had snatched a second by nodding in a Mick Mills free kick to make it 3-2. Gray strode onto a Gordon Smith long ball and struck it on the volley. Villa's fifth was a spectacular overhead scissor kick from Graydon. This Villa team looks good.'

Birmingham Sunday Observer – 5 September 1976:

'Norwich 1 v 0 Blues - The bad old Blues were back in their first defeat of the season. Apart from a combative Kenny Burns, Blues seemed off the pace. Trouble beckoned in the third minute when a Boyer header beat Latchford but was ruled offside. The let off lasted until the eleventh minute. Want fouled Suggett. The free kick was smashed against the Blues' wall by Ryan, it rebounded to

him and his shot was parried by Latchford to Boyer who scored.

Blues were much better in the second half as captain Kendall found his touch. Francis began making his trademark runs and Burns was everywhere, chasing and harrying. He nearly got a reward and Blues a point after a one-two with Kendall but Peters took the ball off Burns' toe before he could finish.

There was a bizarre ending to the match when the referee blew for full time then realised he was mistaken and there were three minutes left. Gallagher nearly equalized in that extra period but shot wide from a Kendall cross.'

***

Birmingham Sunday Observer – *12 September 1976*:

'Bham City 0 v 1 WBA - Albion were better than Blues with or without player – manager Johnny Giles. He was substitute at half time but Albion were in charge from the start. The winner came from a 30 yard Tony Brown rocket on the hour. Blues defence thought they had everything covered but Brown's strike dipped and swerved past Dave Latchford and hurtled into the top corner of the net.

Blues' usual performers were below par with Francis missing his usual magic. Blues had no answer to the wonder strike and never looked like getting back into the game. Off the pitch the local derby match between Blues & WBA was marred by hooliganism yesterday. West Midlands Police Special Patrol Group made more than twenty arrests in and around the ground and those arrested will appear at court tomorrow for disorderly conduct. One other was arrested for theft inside St Andrews.'

***

Birmingham Sunday Observer – *12 September 1976:*

QPR 2 Villa 1. *'Fine run ends - Villa's fine start to the season ended as they were put to the sword by a QPR side that finished as runners-up last season. QPR's stars sparkled as they completely outplayed Villa, despite the shock of a 30th minute goal by Andy Gray against the run of play. Stan Bowles in particular was mesmerizing.*

Gray's trademark goal came from a Mortimer cross that he bravely headed in, but the lead only lasted five minutes. Givens was left with too much room, and Burridge could only parry his shot to an unmarked Mason who struck the rebound into an unguarded net. Villa should have learnt from that, but they continued to back away as Ranger's charged at them and the second came in the 56th minute. Clement ran from the hallway line unchallenged, executed a neat one-two with Given and smashed the ball past Burridge. Villa showed character after going behind and came close to an equalizer twice through Andy Gray.

In the end though, QPR looked in a different class for much of the match.'

***

Football, football, and more football....it was what people lived for – and died.

Once, it had been all that mattered to Ryan.

***

On the Saturday morning, September 18th, the day of the big match, Ryan travelled south by train to Birmingham New Street, and got a taxi to the car-lot at Hockley. It was empty bar a hire car, and he had expected that. He had a key for the portakabin and knew that he could survive there unnoticed for the length of time that his plan required.

Business had not been good for a few months and his father had temporarily moved the cars and staff to the Summer Row location and the breakers yard in order to cut overheads. Ryan would be left alone and that's what he wanted and needed.

The location was ideal. No houses at all close to it, the nearest factory half a mile away, just a lot of dead people in the nearby Warstone Cemetery to keep him company.

The message had gone out via Mel and Naomi, to Joy, that he would wait for her there, and that he had a plan to get away. All she had to do was get there, and that was his reason for choosing this particular day.

Fortunately, the Benidorm holiday had gifted a new passport to Joy, and Ryan already had one, a legacy of football trips to Europe. They would journey to a New World, and start new lives together.

He had emptied his and Roseanne's savings. Australia was welcoming immigrants. They would be fine. Once inside, they would lose themselves in the giant continent and perhaps even change their names. It was the land of opportunity, everyone said so.

327

Floods of British people were going there, who would ever find them, or bother to do so?

He hadn't told Mel where they were going. Ryan *had* told Mel though that he was going to 'send a message' to Roseanne and Gary before he left. Mel's stomach had lurched as he assumed the worst and barely heard Ryan tell him to forget, be free, love Naomi if that was what he wanted, and to live his life.

Mel's only task now was to hire a car for the weekend, leave it parked on the lot, and push the keys through the cabin letterbox.

Ryan had suspected that Mel might find it hard to keep away, but he didn't want his old friend connected in any way to the elopement by his father. He had told Mel one little lie, that he and Joy would be meeting at half past midnight, but if the plan worked, they would be long gone by then. If Mel did turn up, he would find an empty cabin.

Satisfied that he had thought of everything, Ryan had wished Mel luck and put the phone down, another piece of his life closed.

He and Joy just wanted to be together. He would leave the phantoms of the past behind, Titch and his scream, Charlie and the flight of steps, Carter and the pool of blood on his shirt. He would even leave a note for Gary and Roseanne, wishing them well and stressing no retributions. They could come home. A line would be drawn under the past and the good Ryan would be able to forget. He and Joy could have a normal life.

Mel had listened to the buzz of the dead line for a full thirty seconds. It was Mel's moment of truth and he made his decision.

Ryan must have discovered where Gary and Roseanne were. No-one else was going to die.

Naomi passed Joy a phone number and told her when to phone it.

The date of Ryan and Joy's elopement had been carefully selected. It was local derby time. Blues were playing Villa and there was to be a showdown, a settling of accounts. Mel had told Ryan that Murphy and Carter, and the two firms, would all be preoccupied at Villa Park, and in the city centre afterwards. No one would be thinking about Ryan Murphy or Joy Carter for a few vital hours.

***

Birmingham Sunday Observer – *19 September 1976*:

'*Villa 1 v Blues 2 - Kings of the City! Blues end Villa run: The Blues army on the Witton terraces celebrated a famous victory that made them Kings of the City.*

The Villa fans had been in confident mood due to their team's great start to the season and when Andy Gray put Villa in front in the 13th minute everyone in the ground thought the goals would keep flowing, but it never happened. Instead Willie Bell's team hit back with a two-goal backlash before half time that rocked the home team, a shock from which they never recovered.

In fact, Villa had only themselves to blame as their defensive errors helped their arch rivals. Blues gambled on playing four talented men up front and it paid off. All the goals came from mistakes.

The Villa goal came from a mistake by Terry Hibbitt who failed to control a ball from Little in the goalmouth and Andy Gray was there to pounce and score. Blues' first came from a mistake by Nicholl from a left wing pass from Francis and Kenny Burns was there to equalize in the 29th minute.

Villa seemed to lose their way after that, apart from Ray Graydon forcing Dave Latchford into two saves. Blues' new £70,000 signing from Everton, John Connolly made the difference, beating Nicholl, Phillips and Carrodus before drilling the ball to John Burridge's left to shock and silence the Holte End hordes. The second half was a tale of Villa failing to penetrate a composed and confident Blues defence with the towering Joe Gallagher in commanding form.

In the end Connolly's goal was enough to bring misery to the Villa faithful and unconfined joy to the Bluenoses.'

***

In a second newspaper headline the score-line was heralded as *'Aston Villa 1 Birmingham 2 Police 36'.*

There were thirty-six arrests for disorder at the game, all for disorderly conduct. The trouble was confined to the hooligan elements of both clubs.

In Birmingham City Centre, around thirty pubs stayed closed until 8.30pm, fearing that intoxication before the match would lead to violence and vandalism. The police were clearly wising up to the tactics of Carter's and Murphy's firms and it had not been a good day for the boys, some of whom had been picked off by some pretty heavy-handed black leather-gloved coppers who just steamed in and dragged people away. Nothing serious in the way of charges, but both leaders knew their firms would not be able to soak up this rate of attrition for long.

Mike Carter was in a thoughtful mood, having narrowly avoided the men in gloves a couple of times himself. He needed to think this one through and decided on a war cabinet meeting.

Ryan and Joy's reliance on everyone being in town suddenly began to evaporate.

Mike took Sam, Pete and Spike home with him, and they sat in the kitchen trying to work out what was going on, who had been nicked, and where. Carol plied them with tea and coffee but kept her own counsel in the living room. Joy was upstairs agonizing about how she was going to perform a miracle, a small bag hidden away under her bed. She had made the phone call, but the plan was going badly wrong. She should have left by now.

The tea and coffee gave way to some cans of lager and they were still putting the world to rights, when Mike Carter heard Carol answering the front door. Voices were raised.

Next thing the kitchen door flew open and in walked Detective Constable John Burrell, closely followed by several heavyweight uniform officers.

"What the fuck", Carter stood up to protest and was immediately grabbed by two of them and handcuffed roughly. Sam and Spike got the same treatment.

As Carter was straightened up Burrell said to the three of them, "Shut up and listen. The three of you are being arrested on suspicion of a Section 18 wounding with intent on Detective Sergeant Nigel Francis at New Street Station. I could tell you what the caution is but you silly fuckers should know what it is by now."

Carol came into the kitchen screaming, "You can't do this. This is my house. They haven't done anything, they were all in Manchester. It was in the paper, same day Birmingham was away at United."

Joy sat at the top of the stairs – the world was going mad. Suddenly though, the door to freedom was opening. Excitement and hope quickened in her.

Carol Carter wasn't in the mood for civility and insisted, "You listening to me? This is bang out of order. You bunch of fuckers need a warrant. I'm going to phone our brief." She poked Burrell in the chest for good measure and instantly regretted it.

The policewoman with them had been redundant thus far, but Burrell soon put paid to that, "Lock her up, obstruction and assault police."

The kitchen exploded into a melee as a mass of handcuffed bodies were pulled and pushed through to the front door and out into the cold air to waiting vans. A screaming Carol brought up the rear, shouting "Joy stop here love. Just stay by the phone. Pete look after her don't leave her."

Even in the middle of wrestling in the doorway of the van a sudden, disquieting thought entered Mike's mind, *'Why have they left him behind?'*

The doors of the vans were slammed shut and they were gone.

Burrell sat in the front seat of one of the vans; following Docker's orders to the letter as usual, including finding a reason to lock up the wife. He knew that they didn't have a shred of evidence against any of them and that they would be released in the morning. He wasn't bothered; if they weren't guilty of this they were guilty of something, and anyway this was Docker's show and he could answer the difficult questions tomorrow.

No fool, Burrell had a sense that events were coming to a head and that change was in the air. *'Time to start looking at the books ready for the promotion exams,'* he thought.

***

In just a few moments, Joy found herself alone in the house with Pete.

She paused at the door, watching the van tail-lights disappearing along with her parents and felt the cold air of freedom beckoning, as Pete joined her.

She touched his hand lightly and headed for the stairs, "Pete I'll be back down in a minute. I need to speak to you."

In her bedroom she left a folded piece of paper on the side table – written on it the simple message *'Mum/Dad I'm sorry, I love you both with all my heart. But I have to be with him. We have to be together. There is no other way.'*

Joy went downstairs, left her bag in the hallway, and went to work on Pete, whose brain was going into overdrive.

Joy knew that Pete had feelings for her and played unashamedly on them. She had already taken him into her confidence about Ryan, and the fact that he had returned to Birmingham to run away with her. Despite his resistance to the relationship she felt safe with him and begged him to take her to the car-lot in his car.

"I need to go soon Pete. I'll never get the chance again. Tomorrow will be too late," she pleaded.

Pete was on edge, his mind in turmoil. "I need to make a phone call, it's important," he said finally, "And it needs to be private, I'll nip up to the phone-box on the corner, make sure you're here when I get back, I'll just be five minutes."

Joy didn't argue, she knew when she was winning.

It was nearer to ten minutes by the time Pete returned, but now his mind seemed made up, "I'll take you, but first I need a drink and the chance to talk things through. If I can't persuade you otherwise I'll take you to where you need to go and we will be there for midnight."

Joy went to interrupt, but Pete cut her off, "If I can't persuade you not to ruin your life with a murderer whose days are numbered, then I'll take you, but the deal is midnight and that's it. You must have Murphy's phone number, call and tell him the arrangement and that if we aren't there by ten past midnight you're not coming."

Joy made her phone call, warning Ryan that she would not be alone, but omitted voicing any doubt that she would be there at midnight. Nothing that Pete could say to her in the next few hours was going to change her mind.

***

Pete took Joy to a pub on the Bristol Road and then persuaded her to get a Chinese up by Holloway Head. This was the first time he had spent any real time alone with her and it felt good, but he knew he was fantasizing. Joy wouldn't bend an inch, although before leaving the Chinese she kissed him lightly on the cheek, and thanked him. He couldn't delay her any longer, but ten minutes early wouldn't make any difference.

At twenty-five minutes to midnight they were on their way to Hockley.

***

Outside the portakabin, the *'Second City Car Sales'* banner flapped in the wind against the metal structure, making Ryan uncharacteristically nervous. He just wanted Joy to get there so they could leave. He had hoped that they would have been long gone but it sounded as if Joy had run into some problems and he thanked his luck and the police for clearing the way by removing the Carters. Anyway, midnight would be fine. Nice and quiet. He had a sudden thought, *'That's nearly the time I told Mel......'*

Every minute that passed by was torture. Every minute he expected his father to storm through the door and to smash him against the back wall with a flurry of fists. Colin Murphy would soon know from his Celtic friends that Ryan was nowhere to be found and then he would start looking, and he would start with Mel. *'Shit, really hope Mel doesn't come.......'*

He calmed himself. Mel wasn't going to come, he wanted out too, Ryan could tell, and the note he had left in the cabin would hopefully put his friend in the clear, *'Dad, I can't take the violence anymore. I've done bad things and I need to be out of your life, for good. I want to be with her more than anything else. It's my decision and no-one else is involved or knows about this. Sorry I let you down, Ryan.'*

Another note lay by its side. *'Roseanne. I know now that I was wrong. You deserve a chance of love. You are free now, I am going where I won't be able harm you. I forgive you, please forgive me. Ryan.'*

***

Two pairs of eyes watched the car-lot from the rear of a Transit Van parked along the road. The only sound was the guitar thrash and vocal snarl of a Punk Band called the Sex Pistols, playing low on the radio,

"This crap will never catch on," mused Pat to Frank.Frank laughed, "It could be worse, it could be Dancing Fuckin Queen."

Patrick Quinn and Frank Fulford had forsaken their bikes for the van, and the leathers had been replaced by black donkey jackets.

Quinn played with the ignition keys – he was keen for this to be over with.

Frank was one of Quinn's inner-circle in the Black Souls Motorcycle Club and Quinn trusted him with his life. He was also ex-services and ex SAS, which came in handy, although as he had shown during their outing to deal with the fat-man, 'Roly', he was feeling his age.

They were waiting for the roads and streets to clear. Eleven had been the allotted time but Quinn was a professional. It had been too busy then, with some stragglers about from the pubs in Hockley, plus a couple who decided to stop and have a heavy snog just fifty yards away from where they were parked. To make things worse a police car had driven down Warstone Lane and parked up by the cemetery.

Quinn had nerves of steel but it had nearly spooked him. He always expected betrayal by Docker, but he held fast and breathed a sigh of relief as he watched two police officers produce bags of fish and chips and proceed to polish them off in quick time. It was twenty minutes before they left. Quarter to midnight, coast clear, five minutes and the job would be done. He nudged Frank and nodded.

***

Ryan heard the noise of an approaching car, and peered out through the nicotine stained venetian blinds.One car containing two people - it was no surprise to Ryan, as Joy had mentioned on her last call that one of the Blues firm was bringing her. He would have preferred her to take a taxi, as arranged, but she had assured him that the driver was a friend. In any event Ryan remained supremely confident in his abilities to deal with any challengers.

He looked at his watch, they were ten minutes early.

As Joy and Pete entered, Ryan clutched her to him, showing a tenderness that was reserved for her only. Pete looked on, ignored by Ryan, desolate but not done yet. Ryan noticed that the man had suddenly gone white, as if he had seen a ghost from the graveyard nearby.

"We need to go bab. We've got a plane to catch." Ryan was eager to leave. Pete blocked the way.

"Hold your horses Murphy. You're not going anywhere. I'm a police officer and I am arresting you for the murder of Tony Carter. There will be other officers here soon so don't try anything."

Joy's jaw dropped, "Pete stop kidding. I'm going and that's it."

Ryan weighed the man up, "I can't see any cavalry around mate and you're not gonna stop us, so shift it out of the way or you'll regret it."

Joy shouted, "No more violence Ryan. There's been enough. Please Pete, don't try to stop us."

Pete stood his ground and barred their way to the door, he had a sick feeling in his stomach and he knew he was alone, facing a man skilled in combat.

Docker had promised when Pete had called from the phone-box earlier that he would be sending police officers to arrest Ryan by 11.00 pm at the latest. Something must have gone wrong. Docker had told Pete to keep Joy under his control and away from the meeting place, but Pete's love for Joy was one thing that Docker had not budgeted for and it had clouded Pete's judgment.

Pete had expected it to be safe, to find an empty portakabin, and a chance to be next to Joy when she needed a shoulder to cry on as the arrest of her lover shattered her illusions.

As Ryan advanced, the door opened, *'thank fuck for that',* thought a relieved Pete.

***

The door swung open, but instead of blue serge and Rob Docker, a stranger to Pete appeared, with a gun in his hand. Pete was amazed, but it was the worst sight Ryan could have imagined.

Gary Docker was sweating and visibly shaking as the other three backed off. He had expected to find Murphy alone and now he didn't know what to do. Lloyd had passed on the warning from Mel together with Ryan's plan. Mel had been close to the blacks from the club for years. They were 'his people' and Gary was his best mate – he had to come first.

Lloyd had also told Gary, but not Mel, that Murphy was almost certainly the real killer of his father, and that Docker had pretty well confirmed it when they had met. Lloyd had also provided the gun and six bullets, for Gary's protection.

Despite Lloyds offer of help, Gary had finally decided to

travel up to Birmingham to face his enemy himself and to exact revenge.

Mel had told Lloyd that Murphy was planning to meet his new love at half past midnight so Gary had arrived early, but had been hanging around, hidden in the cemetery, waiting for the cops to finish their chips.

He was out of sight of the car-lot whilst hiding and had not seen Pete and Joy arrive. Gary was not a professional killer, and, as the police car left, he had pulled his weakening resolve together and made a mad dash towards his target, not even registering Pete's car parked on the road, engine ticking as it cooled.

He pointed the gun directly at Ryan and said, "I'm going to do you Ryan, you fucker. I know you murdered me Dad, you murdered one of the Carters, and God knows who else. The world'll be a better place without you in it. Me and Roseanne have had enough of hiding away from you, you fucker!"

Ryan took a step backward and raised his hands, "Listen Gary, it was an accident, I never meant to kill him, I didn't see the steps behind him, that's all."

Gary's voice trembled, 'That's all is it you bastard? You killed an old bloke who wouldn't have harmed anyone, you beat your wife, you knifed a bloke to death."

The gun wavered in Gary's hands but he gripped it and tried to focus.

In that moment Joy's teenage love was shattered by reality. If

Pete really was a cop, and suddenly she believed him, and if what this raving stranger was saying was true then....what if she had made an awful mistake?

Ryan tried one last plea, "You don't need to do this Gary, I'm leaving for good, I don't give a fuck about you and Roseanne anymore, I love Joy and we're gonna disappear forever. Just let it go, for fucks sake," he indicated Pete, "He says he's a copper - you're gonna need to do him too."

Gary wavered, he had been building up to this for months but he wasn't a killer and faltered - the hesitation was fatal.

Gary's attention skittered around the other three people in the cabin, Lloyd had told him there would just be Ryan, waiting for a girl who wouldn't arrive until later.

Pete saw his opportunity and made a grab for the gun.

***

Quinn had watched the new arrivals from the van. He and Frank had been about to open the back doors and unload the jerry cans when Pete's car had pulled up. Then Gary Docker had careered down the road and through the cabin door.

Frank commented nonchalantly to Quinn, "Fuck me it's like New Street Station in there. Do you think we should join the party?"

Quinn said quietly, "Not yet, let's see what happens," as he turned the ignition on and edged forward then stilled the engine again.

***

The gun clattered to the floor, under the office table, and as Pete struggled with Gary, the man who had already killed three times seized his opportunity.

The cold Ryan, the survivor, took over, and he slipped effortlessly back into his violent persona. Ryan picked the gun up, deliberately aimed it at Gary's head from close range and fired.

As Gary's brains blew from the back of his skull and spattered on the wall Joy screamed uncontrollably. It was a horror movie instead of a love story.

Pete knew that he was on his own, fighting for his life, and desperately launched himself at Ryan. As they grappled he somehow found an inner-strength and managed to get a firm grip on the hand holding the pistol but he couldn't match Murphy who delivered a jab and kick that sent Pete sprawling backwards.

Pete leapt back up and stared death in the face as Ryan levelled the gun at him.

"Ryan, no!" screamed Joy. She lunged forward to put herself between Pete and the gun, hoping to shield this decent man who had been her friend. Ryan couldn't stop the pressure on the trigger in time and the bullet struck Joy in the chest. She collapsed between them.

Pete sank to his knees and tried to feel for a pulse, ignoring the man towering over them with the gun still in his hand.

Pete looked up, saw the horrified look on Ryan's face and shouted, "We've got to get her to Dudley Road Hospital - now!"

Ryan's anger fled and he was consumed with despair,

"Get her in the car outside-quick." He kept the gun trained on Pete as the lawman dragged Joy outside and into the rear of the car, "You fucking drive!" he screamed.

At that moment Quinn started the engine of the Transit van, "Looks like we've got to earn our corn after all." He had heard the shots and was waiting to see who would come out of the cabin door.

***

As Pete edged into the roadway and started to drive in the direction of the Hospital, the Transit van hit the car broadside on as Quinn focused on disabling the driver's side. The impact was sudden and decisive, as Pete's head smashed into the windscreen and his body contorted. The van impacted upon the cemetery wall. Pete was stunned and trapped.

In the back seat which was already covered in thick red blood, there was no sound from Joy.

Ryan jumped from the front seat of the car, still clutching the gun, and desperately scrambled towards the cemetery. He had no idea who was in the Transit, but he recognised that they meant business. *'It's either the police, or Carter after his daughter and me. Most likely Carter.'*

One way or the other he had to get away.

Frank shot out of the van leaving Quinn, who was struggling to free the driver's door after the impact, behind. The old biker tracked the shadowy figure of Ryan as it melted into the shadows of Warstone Lane cemetery.

Quinn watched Frank disappear into the darkness, freed the door and went to the driver's side of the car. Pete was badly injured and semi-conscious, a trickle of blood dribbling from his mouth.

Quinn looked into the back seat. It was clear that Joy was dead, her eyes and mouth frozen open in a silent scream.

Pete roused and looked into ice-blue eyes but saw no compassion. He gasped, "I'm a police officer - help me. Please."

Quinn spoke softly, "Sorry mate, but you should have done as you were told. You're not supposed to be here. The problem is I hate cops and you've seen my face."

In one movement, learnt from his training in Northern Ireland, Quinn snapped Pete's neck and left him. He had a friend to find.

At that moment another shot rang out. Quinn scaled the cemetery railing and disappeared into the shadows. He crept silently through the tombs and gravestones, all his training kicking in. As his night vision grew he saw a dark shape on the ground. It was Frank, lying on his back between a row of gravestones. He was holding his stomach, and Quinn could smell an iron tang, blood. Despite being in extreme pain Frank put his finger to his lips and pointed towards the raised catacombs.

Quinn whispered reassuringly, "Leave it to me now. I'll be back." He didn't think Frank would be going anywhere under his own steam.

Quinn knew it would not be long before the sound of sirens was heard so moving with caution was no longer an option. There was a job to do, and a mess to be cleared up. Quinn was clever, and he had already mapped out a plan, just needed to finish the job.

He made his way tentatively up to one of the upper levels. Quinn was not a man to know fear but this was a creepy place and he didn't like it. He had also fucked up. The plan had been to kill Murphy and then to burn the cabin with Murphy inside it. Docker would cover his tracks. Quinn hadn't bought a gun with him, hadn't expected to need one.

Whereas Ryan had killed by accident, Quinn had done it for rewards and survival. He was ruthless, professional and had been trained by an expert.

He edged forward around the semi-circle of catacombs, peering into the darkness, when the snap of a twig behind him sent him diving behind a nearby tomb. A shot rang out and a piece of marble flew from a carved angel. Ryan scanned the shadows, but Quinn was gone.

Ryan rounded the tomb but there was no sign of the man. Ryan was in turmoil and in a hurry. He passed another mausoleum at a half-run, gun held out before him, and too late sensed a presence. A leg shot out and the gun disappeared over the edge to the lower level of the cemetery.

Ryan spun round to face Quinn. He could make out that his tormentor was older, almost middle-aged, but he instinctively recognised the stance, the balance of another fighter, *'Who the fuck is this bloke?'*

They circled each other on the walkway in front of the row of tombs; a drop of fifteen feet lay to one side, where marble gravestones stood like pale teeth, awaiting food.

"What do you want? I got no quarrel with you, just fuck off and let me get the girl to hospital," said Ryan.

Quinn as always was ice-cool, "Too late for that pal, she's dead. Prepare to pay for your sins!"

Ryan didn't want to believe that Joy was gone, and attacked. He aimed a flurry of kicks and jabs that would have dropped any of his football rivals, but every single one was blocked. He leapt backwards, panting.

"Not good enough," said the stranger, "Now it's my turn."

Ryan suddenly found himself fighting for his life. Blows began to land on him. This had never happened before. He backed away, and then launched a desperate assault, using everything he had ever learnt. He landed a couple of blows, and then he was flying through the air, over the edge of the walkway. He hit the ground and landed square onto a gravestone.

Ryan lay on his back. He could see the shadow of the man looking down at him, silhouetted against a backdrop of stars. He tried to move but he couldn't feel his legs. He was pretty sure that his back wasn't broken, but he needed time to recover, and time was running out. He cursed the heavens, cursed Tony Carter, Colin Murphy and his Villa firm, Gary Docker and Roseanne. *'How had it come to this?'*

As he watched the stranger make towards the steps to the lower level, Ryan struggled to comprehend how it felt to be a loser – he had never lost before.

The man loomed over him. Ryan could see the gun in his hand.

Quinn didn't have time for speeches but couldn't resist the moment, "I was pretty sure I'd find it, watched where it fell, going to need it for a nice touch."

He pocketed the gun and dragged the feebly struggling Ryan to one of the tombs, dumping him unceremoniously outside the rusting gate.

Quinn kicked out and the old lock gave, the gates swung open. He deposited Ryan inside, on the dusty floor between the stone caskets.

Quinn whispered into Ryan's ear in the darkness, the man was still conscious and knew what was coming, "This one's from Detective Inspector Rob Docker, Charlie Docker was his uncle." Quinn appeared to think for a moment, and then added, "But you hurt one of mine bad, and you would have paid this price anyway, Docker or no fucking Docker".

Quinn knelt on Ryan's chest and arms, pinning him down,

pressed the gun into Ryan's mouth and fired, his ears ringing in the confined space. He had assessed that the solid walls would muffle some of the sound and grant him the few minutes he needed to complete his tasks.

Moving swiftly, Quinn half-carried, half dragged Frank back to the van and deposited him in the back. Frank never once complained, but Quinn could see he was in a bad way, *'You slowed down a bit too much Frankie, should have waited for me.'*

Quinn then carried Joy's lifeless body to the tomb where Ryan lay. He placed her on the floor and then dragged Ryan's body across hers. Finally he placed the gun into Ryan's right hand after wiping it. As he left he scoured the ground by torchlight for drag marks, but the path was tarmac and there were none. He reasoned that any marks would show that Murphy had reached the path by the tomb under his own steam, so no one would suspect that he had been dragged those last few yards.

Quinn was always thorough, and he trusted Rob Docker not one jot. He set fire to the car containing Pete's body. It wasn't uncommon for cars involved in accidents to ignite and he needed to do his best to camouflage the blood on the back seat. He had done all he could, it was time to move, and quickly.

On the way back to the Black Souls' Clubhouse, with Frank groaning softly in the back, Quinn stopped at a telephone kiosk and made a call.

He had done his part – it was up to Docker to tidy up. It hadn't been the simple job he had been tasked with, but the result was the same.

***

Rob Docker changed the usual venue for the meeting – he needed some fresh air, not the stench of a van sat next to a man in black leather who he detested. They met in Cannon Hill Park. As they sat on a bench and surveyed the Canada Geese that seemed to shit everywhere, and on everyone, they made the perfect 'odd couple'.

Patrick Quinn spoke first, "I think you must be getting soft Mr. Docker, sitting out here in the dark. Not getting too much for you is it?"

Rob Docker gave him a tired look that belied his stone-cold interior, "Well let's just have a look at what we've got and make sure that we're done for the moment. Feeding the ducks with you is not my idea of fun."

Docker paused, "Gary is dead, pity about that but the bullet in his body will match the ones found in the gun in Murphy's hand. I hadn't expected that Gary would find his balls."

He went on, "One thing I always say for you Quinn, you're a fucking cold bastard, and there's a market for that. Anyway, it all came out OK. Scores settled, backs covered and not good for Colin Murphy's business, losing his son and heir and having a body in one of his car-lots. I'm not done yet with that bastard though. He still has a bit more to come."

Docker discussed this detail with Quinn and went on, "Ryan and Joy – a suicide pact. Very Romeo and Juliet, but with the notes that should seal it, plus the second note nicely provided the motive for Gary, and I've got a tame reporter who will make a good story from it after I've given her a good seeing too - a sad story with a very sad end. Tragic, brings a tear to the eye. Joy Carter won't be the last bird to get burnt through falling in love with a complete waster."

Quinn looked at the man he was bound to in blood. Quinn led a Hells Angels group, had been part of all sorts of violence and debauchery, but none of it matched the evil he saw in this supposed upholder of the law. "You really don't care do you?"

Dockers eyes never blinked, "No I don't, and don't try and kid me, neither do you." He continued. "Then there's the small matter of one off-duty police officer killed. The report will read that he was a hero who tried to arrest Murphy on his own initiative; which after all, is sort of true. No-one knows what really happened, so it will be assumed that Murphy made him drive, and then they struggled, leading to the crash.

Great shame that. I told him not to go, and that I would sort it. All he had to do was keep her under his control and away from there.

God only knows what he was doing there. I don't suppose he said anything to you did he?"

Quinn found it easy to lie to Docker. In fact their relationship was built on lies and half-truths, "Not a word, he was well gone from this world when I had a look at him. Pity you didn't tell me you'd got a copper undercover, I might have been able to cover his back."

Docker knew Quinn was lying but it didn't matter. Quinn

was a trained killer and never left any loose ends, "We are done. You just sort out that last issue and then we're done and you get what you asked for."

Quinn sighed, "The last time I heard that I'd ..."

Rob stopped him, "You've said enough Quinn. I can still bury you any time I want, so listen up."

Before they parted Quinn said, "I notice you didn't even ask me about my boy Frank, he's dying, and doesn't he count? He was someone's son once you know."

Docker stood up to leave, "I couldn't care less about a dead Black Soul. You're the leader; you took him there, if he wasn't up to it that's your fault."

Quinn wanted so much to smash those lying, cheating teeth in, but he wanted something else more, and quelled the urge. Docker continued, oblivious, "I'm sure the piss-up after the burial will go well. Are you going to bury him with that stupid fucking Black Souls ring on?"

Without waiting for an answer Docker walked off.

Quinn watched him depart. One day he would see Docker dead, he vowed, and stick that 'stupid' ring in his grave.

***

Docker was satisfied, everyone was where they needed to be – for the time being anyway.

It was perhaps time to treat himself to one of those new Ford Cortina Mark IV's. He had plenty of 'unregistered' cash to dispose of, but one place he wouldn't be buying one would be from Colin fuckin Murphy's car lot.

Leastways he could then go out for a decent drive with some bird and get away from Lilian.

***

That weekend, just miles away, the police prevented a race hate battle, as more than one thousand policemen were deployed in Walsall. The police message was clear: There will be no race war on the streets of the Midlands. Four months after the 'battle of Winson Green', police kept apart about 1,500 National Front supporters and 1,000 International Socialists as rallies were held in the run-up to the election campaign in the contest for Mr. John Stonehouse's seat.

Twenty demonstrators were arrested by police and charged with obstructing the police or disorderly conduct. Most were arrested when a one-hundred strong left- wing splinter group tried to reach the National Front rally point. There were at least two skirmishes before the National Front supporters reached the T.P Riley Comprehensive School in Lichfield Rd, Bloxwich, where the meeting was held.

The Chief Constable of the West Midlands took personal charge of the police on the ground. His deputy commanded a special Control Room on the top floor of Walsall Divisional Headquarters in Green Lane and said afterwards 'It was the biggest operation the force has carried out since the Birmingham bombings.'

To carry out the operation, policemen were ferried in busloads along the respective routes 'shadowing' the demonstrators as reserves to be deployed only in the event of trouble.

Soon after the children of the T.P Riley Comprehensive had left their desks on Friday afternoon, a squad of twenty policemen moved in. They stayed through the night and were relieved next day by colleagues who maintained a round- the-clock watch on the buildings. With the policemen inside and dog patrols outside, the police had ensured that no-one could hide in or around the buildings.

Special Branch officers' informants had passed on advance information to the force that a group was intent on making trouble. As a result the police were able to anticipate the troublemakers' moves and prepare counter-moves.

Tony Carter was long gone, but the philosophy that had turned his head lived on.

Chapter Eleven

'Keep Right On'

Frank Fulford lay on top of the bed in one of the clubhouse rooms, still dressed in his leathers, and suffered in silence. He had never been one for giving up but he was in agony and just wanted the pain to go away. He wasn't scared of the inevitable and death was the natural solution to this problem, and many others that still lurked in the back of his troubled mind. He had expected to die in the war, and had been on the way to drinking himself to death afterwards, until saved by the unlikely combination of a vicar and a Hells Angel President, so the life he had led in the Black Souls was all a bonus as far as he was concerned.

The man who had rescued him all those years ago, and given him a purpose in life again, sat on the bed, sharing a bottle of the best whisky that the Black Souls had behind the clubhouse bar. The harshness of the spirit on his throat made Frank cough, but it dimmed the pain as he and Quinn spent time sharing tales from the past and remembering good times - two brothers spending final moments together.

Quinn was not one to show tenderness, and was beyond showing tears, but Frank had been a big part of his life and he felt genuine regret for putting the man in the situation that had led to his death, although he accepted that it had been Frank's decision to make that fatal lone attempt on Ryan.

As Frank slipped slowly away Quinn took one more swig

from the bottle before closing Frank's eyes – a moment of respect for the life of a man who had stood four-square next to him and shown total loyalty.

Frank had one more journey to make.

Quinn could not afford to have the unnecessary attention of the local law and whilst the beat bobby was as thick as a plank he still needed to make sure that Frank's passing went under the radar. Every death had a cause attached to it and in Frank's case it needed to be one that would be plausible

Frank's body, together with his favourite bike, was taken to one of the minor roads near the village of Defford and laid out in the road. Quinn had managed to get a good part of the contents of the whisky bottle into Frank's stomach and the remainder was sprinkled over his body and leathers, before the bottle itself was smashed in the roadway.

For good measure Quinn rode one of their spare vehicles over Frank and the bike adding to the injuries to the man's body. Always a stickler for detail, Quinn had paid a friendly, but corrupt, doctor to extract the bullet and camouflage the entry wound. He inserted a wing mirror snapped from Frank's bike. It would do, no-one would be looking for a bullet wound and any post-mortem would be routine and cursory.

Lots of questions would have been asked about a murder, but a 'hit and run' accident involving a man who had already fallen drunk from his bike into the road would attract less.

The vehicle was torched afterwards and an anonymous call

went into the emergency services from a distraught driver who had hit someone lying in the road.

Only Black Souls council members knew the truth, and they would never betray the group.

Quinn reflected that this was starting to become a bit of a habit. Frank would however have approved of the manner of his going.

***

The funeral procession was huge by any standards, as Quinn let it be known that anyone who followed the biker's code should attend to show their respects.

This was not a day for rivalries as they lined up in ranks of four to follow the hearse, whilst Quinn and five of the leading Black Souls provided the escort at the front.

Frank's crash helmet sat proudly on top of his coffin, together with his leather jacket, and heads turned as several hundred bikes revved their engines constantly during the slow progress towards the church.

Upon arrival, four bikers saluted their comrade by performing a number of 'wheelies' backwards and forwards in front of the stationary hearse.

The local beat bobby was the only official police presence - Quinn had personally assured his safety. From several vantage points however, unseen eyes secretly made copious notes and took hundreds of photographs.

The choice of church had been easy. Frank went back to the one that had given him a home all those years ago, after the war, when he had been drifting and rootless, before Quinn met him and drew him into the Black Souls.

Inside, those who could get a seat listened to *'Black Sabbath'* through the tinny church speakers, one of Frank's favourites, as the coffin was borne inside.

Outside others gathered, as loudspeakers relayed a service given by the 'biker- friendly' vicar who had done a bit of riding himself in the past, encouraged by Frank. There was a surprise as the clergyman revealed that Frank had secretly continued the upkeep of the graveyard at the church that had succoured him in the 1950s.

There was no eulogy, but Quinn stood before the assembly after the vicar's speech and said simply, *'Life's too short for prayers. Frank wouldn't have wanted us to waste valuable drinking time, so let's get this done.'*

At the end of the service, *'Born to be Wild',* by Steppenwolf was belted out over the sound system as more than four hundred voices burst into song.

Six Black Souls lifted the coffin from its resting place during the service and bore it out into the graveyard that Frank had tended. It was a fitting resting place. Frank's body was committed to the ground and the 'Black Souls' buried their own man, taking it in turns shovel by shovel. Once it was done, they stood around the mound of earth and shouted, *'Angels Forever, Forever Angels'*, right arms raised in salute. Frank did indeed wear his Black Souls signet ring into whatever afterlife awaited him.

The send-off afterwards was anything but quiet as the 'Black Souls' opened up their headquarters to visitors for the first time. It was a calculated move on Quinn's part and certain areas remained firmly off-limits. He had however judged that this occasion would provide him with a fertile recruiting opportunity.

The next twelve hours descended into alcohol-fuelled debauchery, sex and wanton violence.

It was Frank's day, and it was just how he would have liked it.

***

Pete Stevens' wife could barely stand as she was supported by two of his colleagues behind the coffin. No shortage of black Crombie coats, black ties, and white shirts. The mourners were grim faced, one of their own had lost his life doing his job, and they were there to pay respects to a brave man.

Docker's report had described how Pete had phoned him to report the suicide pact intention and Murphy's location. Rob had ordered him to wait for back-up, but Pete had clearly decided to heroically attempt to arrest Ryan Murphy, and had been slain in the line of duty. A few privately wondered why, but no-one but Docker would ever know that Pete's infatuation had fatally clouded his judgment.

Of course, no-one knew the exact timings of Pete's call to

Rob, and any delay in Rob's own request for back-up to the car-lot was lost in the confusion. Nobody but Rob had any idea of the sequence of events and how Gary Docker had been involved. There had been some questions regarding Rob's relationship with his cousin, but Rob denied having seen him since Charlie's death, and the bodies, bullets and gun had tied up.

A sense of disquiet amongst Rob's colleagues and bosses remained, but inquests returned verdicts of murder and suicide, the world moved on, and memories faded.

Over in the Hole In The Wall club there was sadness at Gary's death, but justice of a kind had been done. Lloyd knew it didn't add up, but had no desire to tangle with Rob Docker for no good purpose.

A lone police piper played *'Lament For The Slain'* at the doorway of the chapel as the coffin passed through, Pete's helmet proudly placed on top of the coffin, the casket draped with the Force flag.

The tune was also known as *'Lament For The Dead'* and was said to have originated from the loss of life following the Battle of Culloden Moor in 1746.

The mourners filed inside, Rob Docker amongst them, passing between two lines of uniformed officers wearing white gloves.

The sense of grief was overwhelming as Pete's two young children looked on, hand-in-hand with their grandparents; they looked totally bewildered by the spectacle.

The service felt as if it was over before it started.

Rob Docker delivered the eulogy and spoke eloquently of the man's raw courage, and professionalism. He spoke of losing a friend, a colleague, a fellow police officer, a defender of the people, a man with a bright future in front of him – his life cut off in his prime. Docker spoke of Pete's love for his family and his hopes for the future.

It was all false, spoken by a man for whom words and values meant nothing.

Docker, if nothing else, was a man who knew how to raise the emotions of an audience as he applied pauses in just the right places for effect. He even seemed at one point to be close to tears himself. He pulled the strings of everyone sat before him in the congregation. Pulled their strings as a 'puppet-master' does, and got away with it, as he always did.

After thirty minutes, Pete was consigned to the flames and the congregation left as the recently released hit tune, *'Heaven Must Be Missing An Angel'* by Tavares played over the tinny church speakers. Docker went straight back to work. He wasn't interested in spending time with a load of 'has-beens' or 'wannabees' at the wake. Many of them had never taken a risk like he had; never put themselves in harm's way, never gambled. He had done all those things, and more, and preferred to be on his own. He felt no guilt or remorse; he doubted he would ever feel those emotions again after the events of last year.

No-one would ever know that Pete had come to love another

before he died, and that's the way it would remain. Docker had made sure that he was the first police officer to attend the flat Pete used for his cover, Rob's instinct for survival proving correct yet again. He had pocketed both diaries, destroying the one that related to Joy. The other one was evidence, and evidence meant power.

***

Colin Murphy and Mike Carter stood next to each other at the head of the single hearse containing two coffins side-by-side – Ryan and Joy joined together in death. Behind the hearse, two black limousines contained immediate members of both families.

Carol Carter played 'mother-hen' and did her best to keep both families together. Joined in grief, they sat dressed in black, sobbing silently, or not so silently, as the growing throng gathered around them.

Inside the hearse, claret and blue flowers for Ryan, and blue and white for Joy, covered the coffins, a club scarf in pride of place on the top of each coffin.

As the hearse moved off, with the two main-men, from each of the firms walking slowly in front, Blues fans and Villa fans mixed freely as they followed the cortege. Others lined the pavements and broke into applause as the procession passed. Flowers were thrown at the hearse and flags waved.

Spontaneously, some of the Blues fans broke into *'Keep Right On'* and sang in earnest for the club that they loved and the young life that had been snuffed out before her time.

The Villa fans seemed unable, or unwilling to respond.

Joy had been an innocent victim whereas Ryan was known to be a man of violence. The distinction between the two could not have been more defined. The 'bad' Ryan was buried, only Joy had seen the potential of the 'good' side, and that was buried too, with no-one to mourn for it.

At the end of the church service Murphy and Carter spoke briefly together before parting company.

There was to be no joint wake – that would have been a step too far. There would be something of a remembrance though.

***

Vivian, with the full support of Roseanne, refused to have anything to do with the beautiful game at Gary's funeral - not even a scarf.Football had taken her husband, and now it had taken her son.

It was by anyone's standards a normal affair – no processions, no regalia, no scarves, no singing, and no signs of any tribe, just those close to him- or at least the remnants.

Colin Murphy was told to stay away, and he obeyed.

Gary's mother stood straight and proud in the church – she shed no public tears. She was a Docker by marriage and as a family they had grown used to hardship and tragedy over the years. As she stood listening to the vicar's empty words about her son, her mind drifted back to Mary Docker – a loving woman with a hard exterior who had fought tooth and nail for her children.

They had both failed – at least in part.

Roseanne sat with Lloyd. He had a secret that she could never know – it was he that had taken the gun to Gary.

The new coupling drew some interested glances, but most shrugged, life had to go on. Docker filed it away for future use. He was at the service sat next to his wife Lilian. He still couldn't stand the stupid cow but she was sometimes useful for the sake of appearances

As they left the church the haunting tune sung by Michael Holm, *'When A Child Is Born,'* rang out.

After the service they went back to Charlie's house where the kitchen table was laid out with sandwiches, sherry, a few bottles of beer and wine. Lloyd and Docker studiously avoided any eye contact and made no effort to speak to each other.

Rob Docker stayed just long enough to show his respects, and not long enough for Lilian to get pissed. The attraction of anything in a bottle that dulled her senses was just too great an attraction for her.

He dropped her back home and went looking for better company.

Gary Docker's life had been wasted – this was not how it should have ended.

***

Roseanne had come home. The house was sold. She couldn't have set foot in it again and neither could she stay in Weymouth. It was full of good memories of Gary. He had hidden it all from her, the gun, his daily frets on the pier, his knowledge of who had killed his father, his final resolve to seek redress and make her safe.

Vivian had taken her in and the arrangement worked. Lloyd had kept an eye out for them both, and in time had asked her out. Colin Murphy had called one day, but Lloyd had been there and she didn't think he would call again - it was over.

***

Docker sat in his office with the door firmly shut.

Burrell stood behind him, arms folded. Having been made an 'acting sergeant' to replace Francis, he had also assumed responsibilities for informant handling.Spike shifted uncomfortably in his chair waiting.

He had not been in the presence of the detective inspector before and he was both frightened and curious, in equal measures.

Burrell had gone through the charade of 'arresting' Spike at his home and took his mother's claims of harassment and verbal abuse in good stead. He had seen it all before, and after all it was only a game.

Docker had ordered the meeting to tidy up some loose ends, and Burrell was also curious.

"You've had a good run Spike. You've done well, and now I'm gonna let you go if that's what you want."

A brown envelope sat on the desk between them.

Spike looked at him and felt a sense of panic rising as his face flushed, "What about me protection. You promised."

Docker paused for effect, "We nicked you with the others on the night of the deaths to cover your back, and we were looking after you. Pete Stevens was an undercover police officer. Depending on the outcome of this conversation it'll become common knowledge that he was responsible for most of the bodies that got nicked and you will be well in the clear."

Docker continued, "From today you're free if that's what you want, but that means no more protection and no more cash. If you get nicked you stay nicked. No cavalry to come to the rescue. Comprendez?"

Spike's mind turned over the implications, "What choice do I have?"

Docker replied, "There's always a choice son. You can stay in if you want, but if you do then your mission in life is to bring Mike Carter down completely. He's been wounded but I wanna see him smashed. It might take a year, it might take two, but you're well placed now to become his number two. Your job is to undermine him – who knows you might become the main-man yourself in years to come, with a spot of help from me. You scratch my back, and I'll scratch yours."

Spike was in fact shitting himself at the prospects of what the future might hold once he was cut adrift from his new friends in blue. He had been a reluctant player after Francis had first signed him up with threats of prison, and then, even worse, threats of exposure. The truth now however, was that he had actually come to like the feel of having the futures of other people in his hands. He liked the power – he was somebody, a secret agent, and Burrell had treated him better than that shit Francis.

Docker watched the cogs turning in Spike's head and grew impatient – he had another urgent meeting to get to, "Make your fucking mind up Spike or I'll ask Mr. Burrell here to march you round the Lock-Up a couple of times to help your concentration."

Spike made his mind up, "I'm in."

Docker smiled thinly as he leant forward and slid the envelope across the table towards Spike, "Good lad. You'll do fine. I pay well and look after my snouts. Just remember one thing though Spike. There's no going back and now you're as good as signed up in blood. I promise if you ever let me down that blood is what I will drown you in."

Docker stood up and smiled again, "Go and spend your money Spike," – the meeting was over.

***

Two hours later Docker arrived on foot at the car park in the Markets area, the usual meeting place. Quinn sat waiting in his car.For two men with so much history between them they still retained a sharp sense of animosity and personal loathing of each other.

As Docker slid into the front passenger seat Quinn tried to seize control of the conversation, "I want all this done and finished with. I want you to deliver on your fucking promise."

Docker was a tired man these days, but his mind was always looking for the next angle. "A promise is a promise Quinn – just that one little job to do and you'll get what you want – but I've been having a little think."

***

Violence had divided them in life and still divided them in death, but this was to be different.

With the funerals over, Colin Murphy and Mike Carter arranged to meet as agreed.

The two of them sat together in a back-street pub in neutral territory in Wolverhampton, with Benny and Sam Wild swapping war stories like old pals at a separate table nearby.

The double act had been broken - Mel had gone

The conversation was surprisingly cordial and professional. Without doubt the two leaders disliked each other intensely, and the preservation of reputations would mandate a resumption of hostilities in the future, but this was about a 'testimonial' for the 'fallen', and for this they would co-operate. They would honour their losses by doing what they did best. The effects of their bereavements still weighed heavily on them and they both knew that in their own ways they shared some responsibility for the outcome.

It was however, unthinkable that Blues and Villa could fight side-by-side on the Holte End, so a simple plan was devised. Carter would take the city-centre and Murphy would take the Villa Ground and the streets around it.

Deal done, they parted – the two men shook hands – no nonsense of trying to outdo each other as to who could squeeze the hardest, just a simple handshake and a nod.

***

By Friday lunchtime, New Street Station was littered with groups of Scottish fans who had come down early for the match. The concourse echoed to the sound of drunken Scots determined to drink Birmingham dry.

As many of them drank direct from whisky bottles, the BTP officers on duty had clear instructions just to try and keep the lid on. There were just too many to take prisoners and tie up officers desperately needed on the streets.

***

On Saturday 9 October 1976, Villa Park and Birmingham city-centre suffered some of the worst scenes of football hooliganism ever witnessed in the West Midlands. Ironically, the match was classed as a 'friendly' game.

In the morning scores of Rangers fans arrived on the night sleeper train from Glasgow which itself was delayed because of trouble en route with some fans being thrown off at Wigan Railway Station.

Reggie McNab was looking forward to settling a score and

whilst he had no expectations that he would come across Ryan again, anyone sporting a Villa scarf would do.

As the Scots made their way out of New Street Station, bagpipes and kilts swirling, Mike Carter was waiting with his boys. Unspent violence in his heart, he felt driven to purge his mind of the sadness that had enveloped him. He had a blood-lust and the Rangers fans would provide a vehicle for that thirst to be quenched.

Ninety extra officers had been drafted into the city to cope with the trouble, and Carter's boys kept them busy as they played 'cat and mouse' with them. Today Carter was determined to be the cat.

Some well-behaved Rangers fans went ahead of the mobs and pleaded with city centre shopkeepers to close their shops. They knew that a tornado was coming.

One shop, Peter Dominic in Priory Ringway, reported a roaring trade in drinks sales, whilst other angry Birmingham shopkeepers fumed, and cursed Aston Villa for arranging the game which was designed to fill a gap in the First Division schedule for Villa.

Eight buses were vandalised with windows smashed, and in one case a roof damaged as Carter's firm engaged in running battles in Corporation Street. This was not a day for tactics. It was about sheer brute force.

West Midlands Passenger Transport stopped buses running on nine routes that ran towards the ground, leaving lots of Saturday shoppers stranded in the city centre.

A mob of Scottish fans pelted shoppers with bread after snatching a basket of rolls in a subway. The laughter drained from their faces as the Blues firm came at them from both ends of the subway. With no room to take 'flight' they were left with no option but to 'fight' and it was a bloody battle that Carter made sure was short- lived.

One woman and her seventeen-year-old daughter had their hair pulled and milk showered over them by another mob in the Bull Ring.

Most of the public houses and bars in the city-centre closed their doors.

Teddy's, the city-centre pub, was cleared by police after one hundred and fifty fans started hurling glasses in a bar brawl, as Sam and Mike Carter combined forces to launch an attack. As some fans cowered behind the bar, every window outside was smashed before they surged through the premises.

***

Coaches began arriving at Villa Park as early as 3am with some Rangers fans taking advantage of a £1.50 fare 'Daybreak Special' for the seven hundred mile round trip. Police complained to road traffic commissioners over the coach company's deadline-breaking, but it was all too little, too late.

Coaches had been ordered not to arrive at Villa Park until sixty minutes before kick-off. However most of the fifty coaches that made the trip were in Birmingham up to nine hours before that deadline - nine hours of drinking time. As soon as the off-licences opened, the Rangers fans bought whisky, champagne, wine and beer, and began to drink themselves into a state of oblivion. Some fans were so drunk they could hardly stand.

One fifteen-year old boy who had been drinking bottles of red wine collapsed unconscious. Four hours before the kick-off, two teenage Rangers fans had already appeared in Birmingham Magistrates Court and been fined £135 for using threatening words and behaviour.

Chief Superintendent Colin Hutton, head of Aston Division later said, *'Drink was the major factor.'*

The front door of the Red Lion pub in Lichfield Road, Aston, was ripped off its hinges, while other pubs were also vandalised.

The landlord of the Golden Cross at Aston Cross, Aston, said, *"I have never been more terrified in my life. They went berserk. The language they used was vile; they grabbed bottles from the shelves, wouldn't pay for drinks and ripped down the curtains."*

There were sporadic incidents during the first half of the match as police confiscated cans and bottles. Villa led 1-0 through a Dennis Mortimer goal in the twenty-ninth minute, but it was at half-time that trouble flared, with hundreds of Rangers fans on the Holte End.

During the interval, supporters at the back of the Holte End surged towards the front forcing frightened supporters to spill onto the pitch.

By that stage some injured fans were being carried clear on stretchers and the second-half had kicked off by the time the field was cleared and all fans had been returned to the terraces.

In the Holte End, bricks, stones and bottles were thrown by opposing sets of supporters who by now were completely oblivious to what was happening with the game.

As Frank Carrodus put Villa 2-0 up on fifty two minutes at that end of the ground, the violence erupted again.

The goal sparked another surge as further missiles were launched.

This was the moment that Colin Murphy had been waiting for and he launched himself at the Rangers fans, many of them too drunk to respond effectively. A phalanx of Villa boys drove a wedge into the crowd as the casualties mounted, and once again fans were forced onto the pitch as they tried desperately to escape.

As Colin Murphy led the charge he found himself at one point surrounded by Rangers fans. As he punched his way out of the situation Reggie McNab found his mark with a wild slash from a Stanley knife that cut him on the back.

Not enough to slow Murphy down it would certainly leave a permanent mark. Ironically Reggie had reaped his revenge in a very personal manner but would never know it.

More than two hundred Rangers fans invaded the pitch and running battles broke out on the field as they were pursued by the Villa firm, whose ranks were swelled by some of the 'Saturday

Brigade'. Even some of the 'bobble hats' started joining in the fighting in an effort to repel the Scottish invaders.

Two supporters were stabbed during the mayhem, as Benny Doherty extolled the Villa 'up and comers' to *do the Scots bastards'*. He briefly wondered what Mel was doing now, then returned to the mayhem.

***

Mel and Naomi had in fact done what Ryan and Joy had failed to do - escape.

Lloyd had helped. He felt obligated towards Mel, who was wracked with guilt over what had happened and wanted to escape the world of violence. Mel was also the only person who knew that Lloyd had been in contact with Gary Docker and he suspected that was where the gun had come from, but never asked. He preferred not to know for sure.

Whilst Mel was too implicated himself to say anything, Lloyd, mindful of that and his new relationship with Roseanne, thought it better on the whole if Mel started a new life somewhere else. Naomi, heartbroken over Joy, and full of guilt at helping to set up the fatal liaison herself, had taken no persuasion. Lloyd had contacts all over the world so they picked a destination and were gone for good.

Their love, a true love, survived and prospered in a place of sun and tolerance for mixed marriages.

***

In order to escape the pitch invasion, Villa boss Ron Saunders, and Rangers counterpart Jock Wallace, waved their players back to the dressing rooms and both teams ran towards the tunnel.

Great Barr referee Derek Civil abandoned the game in the interests of safety.

In one sickening attack, a young Rangers fan was knocked to the ground and kicked unconscious on the Villa Park pitch by up to ten attackers, led by Benny.

They felt the absence of Ryan keenly, and today the Villa boys were fighting for him. Every Rangers fan smashed to the ground was one up to Ryan's memory.

Police lined up in front of the Holte End to try to stop further fans joining the fray.

At the height of the battle, one hundred and thirty police officers were deployed at the Ground.

As the violence continued inside, police with crash helmets were involved in five solid minutes of hand-to-hand fighting.

Dog handlers emerged from the Witton End to force fans back, and when some semblance of order had been restored at Villa Park, police lined the track.

Police were given emergency powers to open the gates and turnstiles, to allow frightened fans to flee the ground, and a loudspeaker announcement was made to clear Villa Park and the vicinity of the stadium.

One elderly woman living near the ground screamed from her doorstep at the protagonists to stop behaving like wild animals. With fighting erupting everywhere and people running riot all over the place she was petrified. Two hours later she suffered a massive stroke, was admitted to hospital and put on a life-support machine – another hidden casualty of the 'beautiful game'.

Away from the ground, mounted police chased troublemakers through the streets, and with long staffs drawn, dealt instant justice to anyone stupid enough to try to stand their ground.

The so-called 'friendly' match between Aston Villa and Rangers, the first time they had played each other for ninety years, had to be abandoned on fifty-three minutes. They called it *'Sick Saturday'*.

***

Colin Murphy sat in a cell at Queens Road Police Station nursing a sore head, and a sore back. He had been on the other end of a good pegging from an old copper who had simply had enough and dished his own form of punishment out vigorously from behind, before dragging the half-conscious man to a police van.

Outside his cell door, Murphy could hear pandemonium as more prisoners were dragged along the passageways, shouting and screaming abuse. A police surgeon had already declared Murphy fit to be detained – he was going nowhere for the moment.

Police made fifty arrests during the day.

Over seventy people were injured at the match, eighteen of

them seriously.

Several fans, including girls, were treated for severe cuts and head injuries from missiles. More had suspected broken bones.

Thirty St John's Ambulance men treated the injured as First Aid rooms overflowed. Eighteen people were ferried by ambulance to Birmingham General and Dudley Road hospitals.

The streets around the ground looked like the aftermath of a pitched battle with bodies lying in the road, on the pavements and littered about nearby car parks.

Divisional Superintendent Alfred Eddington, in charge of the St John's Ambulance first-aid unit commented to the media, *"I have never seen anything like it in over thirty years of nursing. I was on duty for the Bay City Rollers concert and it was nothing compared to this. Complete madness."*

Thirty police officers were injured and four were taken to hospital - one with a suspected fractured skull.

Murphy was satisfied with the day's work. He had lost his son and there was nothing that the courts could do to him that would take away the pain. It had been a fitting memorial though.

Mike Carter had made it home but a lot of the boys had been nicked, including Sam, and one or two had finished up in hospital.

Carter was not done yet, and he fully intended on taking the firm out again on Sunday to look for stragglers. As he stood at the kitchen sink, running cold water over his bloodied knuckles, Carol looked at him in contempt.

They had lost their beautiful daughter and this was his way of dealing with it. Her life of loyalty had shattered whilst walking behind the cortège.

She felt alone and trapped – this would be their last autumn together. She couldn't face the rest of the season.

***

After the events at Weston, and the deaths in Hockley, Rob Docker had accelerated his plans. As he sat on the front table in the main hall at Tally Ho Police Training Centre, facing two hundred weary-looking officers, at 5am in the morning; he knew that the risks had all been worth it.

He listened to the Assistant Chief Constable stressing the fact that football hooligans were criminals pure and simple, and that today was about smashing two of the most violent gangs in the city. His detective superintendent bored the assembly to death by laboriously dealing with methodology, legislation, and complaints procedures – then it was Rob's turn.

Docker took centre-stage and milked every minute of it. He knew that a good result would help to secure promotion, and the arrest of fifty good targets from both the Blues and Villa firms would do him no harm at all. Better still, Mike Carter and Colin Murphy would be getting their front doors smashed in and would finish up getting charged with conspiracy to commit violent disorder by the end of the day. Pete had been a diligent note taker, and his diary was a valuable tool in the fight against them.

Whilst a dead man couldn't testify, Docker was sure that they had plenty to pin on the two men who had challenged his authority.

Docker didn't give a fuck that both families were still grieving for their loved ones – they had wanted to play dirty and he had responded in kind.

In truth Titch's death would always remain an accident, as would Frank Fulford's.

Whilst 'JC' had been convicted of Charlie's manslaughter, Vivian and Lloyd knew the truth, but neither would speak, Vivian to protect her nephew, and Lloyd to protect himself.

JC would do his time.

As Rob had told Vivien, "He's guilty of plenty, just got away with it. It's justice, let him stew."

Ryan was the villain of the piece, graphically portrayed as such by reporter Jane White in a double-page special containing hitherto unknown facts from an 'inside' source – a true scoop!

History would know him as a violent man, a triple-killer, responsible for the murders of Tony Carter, Joy Carter, and Gary Docker.

It was a shame that Gary and the girl had died, but overall things had been packaged up nicely.

At the end of the day it had been a good operation and Docker was almost done.

Colin Murphy's car pitches were his pride and joy, his power-base, and his symbols of influence and strength. As he stood surveying the charred remnants of twenty cars on the main car-lot, he knew that he had lost, and he knew how, and worse, who to. As the anger rose inside him he felt powerless and beaten.

Benny Doherty picked through the charred remains. The Scenes of Crime officers had long since gone although the police tape remained flapping in the wind. It didn't take a degree in forensic science to know that these were arson attacks – the air stank of petrol. Murphy did not for one minute think that any suspects would be identified.

The graffiti slogans, *'Shit on the Villa'* and *'KRO'*, sprayed across the steel containers, converted into offices, provided an obvious clue. Murphy spat, *'much too obvious.'*

No-one had noticed the motorbike tracks through the edge of the ash, and the rain soon washed them away.

***

Six years later, and Mike Carter stood on the terraces at Maine Road, watching Birmingham City play Manchester City.

At forty-seven years of age he had put a bit of weight on but he was still a formidable figure, and together with Sam Wild, no-one was about to start bothering them, not the opposition, not the new Blues firm on the block 'Apex', and not even the local coppers who still insisted on giving them plenty of 'eyeball' but left it at that. He got the occasional nod of acknowledgement from some of the old sweats but in the main, younger eyes were averted.

Carol had long since gone after Joy's death – it was simply too much for her. She blamed Mike, his business and the football firms. She could not exist beside them.

Likewise Brian Carter had led his side of the family away from Mike, the death of his son Tony rendering their relationship as brothers 'null and void'

Sam and Spike had stood by him, but the knowledge that a copper had infiltrated the heart of the firm and gained Mike Carter's complete trust had led many to question his judgment.

He had been dogged by bad luck since Joy's death. The careful tactics seemed to fail repeatedly. He was no longer the leader, and whilst he had kept things together for a few months after the shootings, any 'new arrangements' were to be short-lived and there were plenty of people waiting in the wings vying for the position of 'top dog'.

Even to this day Sam was unaware that the Liverpudlian that Pete Stevens had saved him from all those years ago in the pub was in fact a Regional Crime Squad officer - all part of Rob Docker's elaborate plan to introduce Pete into the firm.

These days Spike was doing very well as one of the main boys, but only he knew the dangerous double-game that he played following that fateful arrest for shoplifting in Birmingham City-Centre, years before.

Rob Docker had reminded him many times about their first meeting at Steelhouse Lane just to keep him on his toes.

Mike Carter pulled the collar of his bomber jacket up against the cold wind that swept across the terraces – ice-cold and biting – leaving a chill in his bones that reminded him of better times.

To his left he was suddenly aware of a crowd movement at the front, as Blues fans moved towards the fence dividing them from the Manchester City firm.

From his position towards the back he could swear that he heard the chant *'Zulu – Zulu'* from the Blues ranks.

What the fuck ever happened to *'Keep Right On'* he reflected bitterly – this lot would never make a decent firm – not in a million years – bloody bits of kids!

***

Dramatis Personae

(With a very big nod to William Shakespeare)

The star-cross'd lovers:

Ryan Murphy: Son of Lord Murphy.

Joy Carter: Daughter of Lord Carter.

The Prince and his retinue:

Rob Docker: Prince of Birmingham.

Pete Collins: City watchman and suitor of Joy.

Nigel Francis and John Burrell: Watchmen and loyal retainers of the Prince.

Lilian Docker: Wife of Prince Robert.

Charlie Docker: Uncle of Prince Robert.

Vivian Docker: Wife of Charlie Docker and Aunt of Prince Robert.

Jane Smith: Reporter, mistress of Prince Robert.

Diverse Watchmen and retainers.

House Villa:

Colin Murphy: Lord of House Villa.

Mel Price: retainer of Lord Murphy.

Benny Doherty: retainer of Lord Murphy.

Gary Docker: Cousin of Prince Robert and retainer of Lord Murphy.

Lady Murphy, (deceased): Wife of Lord Murphy.

Roseanne Murphy: Ryan's Murphy's first love and wife.

Diverse hooligans and 'hangers-on'.

House 'Blues':

Mike Carter: Lord of House Blues.

Tony Carter: Nephew to Lord Carter.

Brian Carter: Brother to Mike Carter.

Sam Wild: Retainer of Lord Carter.

Greg 'Roly' Lyall: Retainer of Lord Carter.

'Spike': Retainer of Lord Carter.

Lady Carol Carter: Wife to Mike Carter.

Naomi Green, Joy Carter's best friend.

'Titch': Young retainer of Lord Carter.

'JC': Young retainer of Lord Carter.

Diverse hooligans and 'hangers-on'.

Others:

'Lloyd': Proprietor of the 'Hole in The Wall' club'.

Patrick Quinn: President of the 'Black Souls' Motorcycle Club.

Frank Fulford: Member of the 'Black Souls' Motorcycle Club.

Diverse Glasgow Celtic and Glasgow Rangers hooligans.

***

Acknowledgments

Paul Dickinson. Cover.

Carol Dickinson, Jason Pavlovs and Sue Burrows. Critical Readers

Birmingham Library Archives Department.

Birmingham Mail and Sunday Mercury.

Author Biographies

Stephen Burrows joined West Midlands Police in 1983, working in Birmingham, Wolverhampton and Walsall. He performed a wide variety of roles in ranks up to and including Detective Superintendent. These included uniform command, complaints and discipline, (including internal and cross force enquiries) and CID command, (including Serious Crime Investigation, Child Protection and Head of Intelligence).

In 2002 he transferred to Warwickshire Police as Chief Superintendent (Area Commander), then became Detective Chief Superintendent, (Head of Crime) for the force, a post held for 5 years. He was trained as Senior Investigating Officer, in Kidnap command, and all levels of Firearms Command amongst other skills.

He retired in 2013 following thirty years' service, eleven of which were spent at Chief Superintendent rank. He currently works for The Home Office in the field of Communications Data.

The author's first joint venture with Michael Layton was the first book in this series, a historical crime fiction novel also available on Amazon, called **'Black Over Bill's Mother's'**, (June 2016). A joint non - fiction book recounting policing experiences in Birmingham and Walsall, **'The Noble Cause'**, is available on Amazon, (November 2016). A further non-fiction book, **'Walsall's Front Line'**, will be published in Spring 2017.

Michael Layton QPM joined the British Transport Police as a Cadet on the 1st September 1968 and, after three years, was appointed as a Police Constable, serving at Birmingham New Street Station. In 1972 he transferred to Birmingham City Police, which amalgamated in 1974 to become the West Midlands Police, where he eventually reached the rank of Chief Superintendent in 1997.

On retirement from that Force in 2003 he went on to see service with the Sovereign Bases Police in Cyprus, and then returned to the British Transport Police in 2004, initially as a Detective Superintendent (Director of Intelligence), and then in his last two years as the Operations Superintendent at Birmingham, where he continued with his passion for combating football violence, until finally retiring again in 2011.

In the January 2003 New Year's Honours List he was awarded the Queens Police Medal for distinguished police service.

He is the co-author of a book entitled *'Hunting the Hooligans – the true story of Operation Red Card'* which was published in July 2015 by Milo Books, and the author of *'Violence in the Sun – a History of Football Violence in Cyprus'* which was published as an EBook also by Milo in May 2015. More recently he has also co authored/authored *'Tracking the Hooligans – A history of football violence on the UK rail network'* by Amberley Publishers, *'Police Dog Heroes' – a history of the British Transport Police Dog Section'*, and *'Birmingham's Front Line – True Police Stories'* also by Amberley.

Michael has since started working with Stephen Burrows and they have co-authored *'Black over Bill's Mothers'*, a historical crime fiction book, and a non fiction book, *'The Noble Cause' – policing in the West Midlands in the 80s/90s*. A further non – fiction book,

'Walsall's Front Line', will be published in Spring 2017.

Michael is now a self-employed consultant engaged predominantly with crime and community safety issues.

PLEA FROM THE AUTHORS

Hello dear reader. Thank you for reading to the end of the book, we hope that means that you enjoyed it. Whether or not you did, we would just like to thank you for buying it, and giving us your valuable time to try and entertain you.

If you would like to find out more about our other fiction and non-fiction books then please search on our names on Amazon. We also have a Facebook Page, 'Bostin Books', and Linkedin and Twitter accounts.

If you enjoyed this book we would be extremely grateful if you would consider leaving a review on Amazon.co uk, (or the Amazon site for your country). To do this, find the book page online, scroll down, and use the 'write review' button.

The most important part of a book's success is how many positive reviews it has, so if you leave one then you are directly helping and encouraging us to continue on our journey as authors. Thank you in advance to anyone who does.

Printed in Great Britain
by Amazon